SWEET ANARCHY

Also by Nathaniel Benchley:

Novels
SIDE STREET
ONE TO GROW ON
SAIL A CROOKED SHIP
THE OFF-ISLANDERS
CATCH A FALLING SPY
A WINTER'S TALE
THE VISITORS
A FIRM WORD OR TWO
THE MONUMENT
WELCOME TO XANADU
THE WAKE OF THE ICARUS
LASSITER'S FOLLY
THE HUNTER'S MOON
PORTRAIT OF A SCOUNDREL

Biographies
ROBERT BENCHLEY
HUMPHREY BOGART

Play
THE FROGS OF SPRING

Editor
THE BENCHLEY ROUNDUP

Junior Books
GONE AND BACK
ONLY EARTH AND SKY LAST FOREVER
FELDMAN FIELDMOUSE
BRIGHT CANDLES
BEYOND THE MISTS
A NECESSARY END
KILROY AND THE GULL

Motion Picture
THE GREAT AMERICAN PASTIME

Nathaniel Benchley, 1915 –

SWEET ANARCHY

DOUBLEDAY & CO., INC., GARDEN CITY, NEW YORK
1979

Library of Congress Cataloging in Publication Data

Benchley, Nathaniel, 1915–
Sweet anarchy.

I. Title.
PZ3.B4258Sw [PS3503.E487]   813'.5'4
ISBN: 0-385-14867-4
Library of Congress Catalog Card Number 79-7039

FOR ROBERTA PRYOR

for good and sufficient reason

Ile Sauvage
Autumn 1978

SWEET ANARCHY

1

The offshore islands, formed at the end of the last glacial period, are a mixture of terminal moraine and sandy outwash, and on the smaller ones the sense of the sea is always present. Even on calm nights the surf makes a soft, breathing noise, and in the daytime, though the sea may be invisible beyond the hummocks and dunes, there is a feeling of distance in the sky that comes only over the ocean. The result is a mood of isolation, and total removal from the problems of the rest of the world.

On an evening in spring, when a light fog had moved in from the sea and spilled into the hollows on the moors, a man walked along the winding road that led to the island's principal town. He was tall, and over one shoulder he carried a musette bag, which flapped against his hip as he walked. He wore a Navy watch cap and a quilted goose-down vest, warm enough for the daytime but hardly adequate against the cold that would come later. From behind him came the sound of an automobile, its tires squealing on the sharp curves, and he turned and looked back, but the car shot past him without slowing, and he had to jump to avoid being hit. He resumed his walk.

After a few minutes he heard a second car, this one going more slowly, and as soon as it came in sight it began to slow down. It was a pickup truck, new and in good condition, and in the back were two large dogs, one black Labrador and one of uncertain breed, who eyed him with interest as the driver came to a halt and opened the door. The walker looked at the dogs, and hesitated.

"Don't mind them," the driver said. "They're just for show. Get in."

"Thank you." The walker glanced once more at the dogs, who seemed to be mentally dismembering him, then got in the front seat and closed the door.

"All the way into town?" the driver asked, starting up with a lurch. The car was clearly unfamiliar to him, and the paint smelled new.

"Yes, please."

The driver looked sideways at his passenger, who was young, with the beginnings of a blond beard. The hair that protruded from beneath his watch cap was tousled but not overly long, and the driver estimated that a couple of months ago he could have passed inspection in the armed forces. "You new around here?" he asked.

"Yes, sir."

"English?" He knew the accent wasn't local, but couldn't quite place it.

"No, sir. American."

"Is it all right to ask what you're doing here?"

The youth hesitated, then said, "This and that. I came for the solitude."

The driver considered this. "Well, if that's what you want, you come to the right place."

The youth nodded but said nothing, and for a while there was silence. Then the driver, unable to curb his curiosity, said, "What takes you into town?"

"I come in to buy groceries."

"You mean you do your own cooking?"

"That's right."

Another silence. Then: "If you'd made it tomorrow night, you coulda come to town meeting."

The youth glanced at him. "Can anyone come?"

"As an observer. But this is going to be something special —you shouldn't miss it."

"What's happening?"

"We're going to vote on secession."

"From what?"

"From the State. Or from the United States, if they care to make an issue of it."

"Why?"

"So many reasons I couldn't list 'em all. We're being screwed by the State, screwed by the United States, and screwed by everybody except Tillie Lester's cat. We've had enough, and we intend to put a stop to it."

"I see." The youth looked out ahead at the lighted church steeple, which shone like a polished needle in the gathering dusk. The town appeared as calm and serene as a Christmas card, and it was hard to imagine it a nest of discontent and rebellion. Then he remembered what he carried in his musette bag, and said, "Could you tell me where the police station is?"

The driver's eyes flicked toward him. "That's some funny place to buy your groceries," he said.

"I know. I want to stop there before I do my shopping."

"Any trouble?"

"No, no. Just—" He left the sentence unfinished.

The driver waited for something more, and when it didn't come he said, "I'll drop you there. It's on my way."

The police station had once been a clam bar and hamburger stand, and the two detention cells occupied what had been the refrigerator area in the rear. With the counter removed, there was room for the duty officer's desk, the telephone switchboard, and the file cabinets in the front, while

the single sanitary facility was out back, where the clamshells had once been dumped. As a nod to the putative prisoners' civil rights it had been enclosed against the elements,
but as security against escape it might as well have remained out of doors. The one bright note was that few
prisoners had ever been detained long enough to need to use
it.

The Police Chief, whose name was Luther Maddox, was
sweeping out the cells when the youth came into the station.
Maddox was tall, and had thin bones, and looked as fragile
as a praying mantis. The only heavy thing about him was his
eyebrows, which formed an unbroken thicket from one side
of his head to the other, without even a notch to acknowl-
edge the bridge of his nose. Without pausing in his sweeping, he said, "What can I do for you?"

"I have something here I found," the youth replied,
reaching into his bag. "I think it might interest you."

Maddox slowed the pace of his broom. "Stolen property?"
he asked, as though afraid to know.

"No." The youth produced an item wrapped in newspaper, and opened it to reveal a dry, brownish object that
looked at first like a piece of driftwood. "A human foot."

Maddox dropped his broom, and came forward slowly.
"Where'd you get it?" he asked.

"I found it in the road, out near Cossett Point."

Maddox examined the object in silence for what seemed
like several minutes. "That's a bear's foot," he said at last.
"That ain't no human."

The youth stared at him. "I beg your pardon," he said.
"I've seen a bear's foot, and I know what it looks like. This
is no bear."

Maddox returned the stare, and his eyes turned hostile.
"How do you know so much about it?" he asked. "What's
your name?"

"Jensen," the youth replied. "Sam Jensen."

"Where do you live?"

"You mean where is my home, or where—"

"Where do you come from?"

"Before I came here, I was in Wisconsin."

"What are you doing here?"

"I've rented a small house, on Cossett Point."

"I said what are you doing?"

Sam took a deep breath. "I intend to write a play."

"About what?"

Sam felt his temper stretching like a rubber band. "I have a number of ideas," he replied. "But they are all subject to change."

The drama was slippery ground for Maddox, and he backed off. Glancing at the shriveled foot, he said, "Well, all I know is that *looks* like a bear's foot. And until someone tells me—"

"Have you ever had bears here?" Sam asked.

"How would I know?" Maddox replied. "All I know is a bear ain't illegal, so long as he don't harm nobody. And that thing there ain't going to harm a living soul."

"And certainly not without claws."

"What do you mean by that?"

"Those are toenails, not claws," Sam said, pointing.

Maddox inspected the foot for a moment, then snatched it up, bundled the newspaper around it, and dropped it in a desk drawer. "I'll send it up to Harvard," he said. "They'll know what it is."

"*Har*vard?" said Sam, incredulous.

"The lab, at the Med School. They got all sorts of tests they can run. If they say it's a bear, it's a bear."

"And if they say it's a hunan?"

Maddox retrieved his broom, and continued sweeping. "We'll worry about that when it happens."

Sam paused. "Well, I just thought you might be interested," he said, and turned toward the door.

"You're new here, so I'll give you a piece of advice," Maddox replied, without looking at him.

Sam stopped. "What's that?"

"Don't make no more trouble than is absolutely necessary. Try not to rock the boat, and you'll enjoy your visit a lot more."

"Thank you." Sam started out, but again was stopped.

"One more thing," Maddox said. "How come you come all the way here from Wisconsin to write a play? They got some law against it out there?"

"It's a long story. How much do you want to know?"

"Just what I asked."

"I came here because I understood it was quiet. Is that all right?"

Maddox nodded and said nothing, and after waiting a few seconds Sam went out into the night. As he headed toward the supermarket he tried to reconcile the people's desire for secession with their apparent urge to retain the status quo—or not to rock the boat, as Maddox had put it—and the best he could do was conclude that they were so dedicated to the status quo that they would destroy it in order to maintain it. With this unsettling thought he selected a shopping cart, and wheeled his way through brightly lighted corridors of canned and packaged foods, pet needs, detergents, light bulbs, pre-cut and plastic-sealed meats, and frozen TV dinners, while signs for bargain specials dangled in the air, and a phantom orchestra played "When I Grow Too Old to Dream."

He was hungry when he finished shopping, and he decided that rather than cook at home he would splurge and buy a hamburger at a place he had passed several times but had never been into. It was called the Sink Hole, and while neither the name nor the exterior was appealing, he reasoned that whatever they served would probably be within his price range. Also, in spite of the fact that he knew it would make him lonesome, he wanted company. When he was alone in his shack, with nothing but the yellow copy paper in front of him, he felt no need of anyone or anything else, but when he came into town, and saw other youths with slim-hipped and satin-haired girls, he began to ache with loneliness. He knew himself well enough to know that once he relaxed his self-imposed discipline he could forget about his play, and his thin margin of cash would soon evaporate. Secretly he hoped that what he was writing would be a screenplay, but superstition forbade him to mention this to anyone, including himself.

When he opened the door of the Sink Hole, he was met by a blast of noise. The only light came from candles in hurricane lamps, and somewhere in the gloom a singer was flailing away at an electronically amplified guitar. Smoke hung heavy in the air, and reeked with the burnt, musty smell of marijuana. Sam made his way to a long table in the rear of the room, found a seat, and after hanging his jacket and musette bag on a peg he sat down. The other people at the table glanced at him, then looked away, and if they said anything it was lost in the crashing din from the guitarist. He noticed that a girl across and down the table from him looked at him longer than the others, pretending to study something on the wall behind him, and for a moment he was tempted to return the look, and see what happened. He was accustomed to having girls look at him—some of them would even stop talking when he entered a room—but he never attributed this to any quality in himself; he thought all girls did that whenever they saw an unfamiliar face.

A waitress appeared in front of him and said something, but her words were inaudible and he leaned forward and cupped one hand to his ear. "I beg your pardon?" he said.

"I said, would you care for a cocktail?" she repeated, more loudly. Her face was the shape of an apple, and its roundness was accentuated by her small mouth and large eyes, and the fact that her hair, parted in the middle, framed it on both sides.

"No cocktail, thank you. Just a beer."

She had to lean forward to hear him, and he caught a faint whiff of lilies of the valley. "That's what I meant," she said. "Nobody orders cocktails around here."

Sam smiled. "Then why did you ask me?"

"Don't look at me. That's what they tell us to say." She was still leaning toward him, and her face took on a slight glow.

"Just a beer, then. And a hamburger."

"What kind of hamburger?"

"A regular one."

"We don't have regular ones. We have the Manhattan, which is with melted cheese and bacon; we have the Texas, with chili and raw onions; the Boston, with baked beans; the Dory Fisherman, with codfish cheeks; and we have a couple of others that I forget. I've only been working here a week."

Sam pretended to think, keeping his eyes on hers, and the glow on her face began to shine. "I'll have the Manhattan," he said at last. She nodded, and vanished, and he sat back in his seat. Stop that, he told himself. That is exactly what you said you wouldn't do. He glanced down the table, and saw that the girl who had been looking at him was now regarding him with a frankly speculative stare, and he held her eyes for a moment before looking away. This is terrible, he thought; just when I'm full of good intentions it seems to be coming at me from all sides. He knew from experience there was no such thing in his life as a casual relationship, and he promised himself that when the waitress came back he wouldn't talk with her; he'd just take the dish and start eating before she could open a conversation.

Then she appeared, and placed a large stein of beer in front of him, and he smiled and said, "Thank you."

"My pleasure," she replied. "What do you think about secession?"

He had the beer halfway to his lips, and paused. "I just heard about it tonight," he said. "I don't know what to think."

"A lot of people I know are for it." The guitarist had stopped playing, and it was possible for her to talk in a normal tone. "They say if we split from the country we can make our own laws, and have legalized pot and all things like that. Some of them even want the hard stuff legalized, but I'm not so sure that's a good idea. I mean, if everybody is zonked all the time, who'll wash the dishes?"

He looked at her to see if she was serious, but her expression remained unchanged and it was hard to tell. "That's one way to look at it," he said. "I must admit I never thought of it that way before."

"Can you imagine a world of dirty dishes, and all that grease? It would be revolting."

He laughed, and took a sip of his beer, and was relieved when she laughed too. "You paint a grisly picture," he said.

"And I should know. You ought to come back in the kitchen here sometime." Then, as though changing gears, she said, "I hope you don't mind my asking, but are you Australian?"

"No. Why?"

"Your accent doesn't sound American."

"Well, I was in Australia recently. I guess I pick up the local accent wherever I am."

"God forbid you should pick up—" Before she could continue someone said, "Miss!" in a loud voice, and she said, "Excuse me," and disappeared. Sam sipped his beer and tried to sort out his reactions, which were confused.

When she returned with his hamburger, she put the ketchup and mustard dispensers in front of him and said, "I'm sorry I got carried away like that. I don't usually talk that much."

"Please don't apologize," he replied. "I enjoyed it."

"No, but you of all people. You must think I'm a pushy type to be gabbing away like that, and I don't even know your name."

"It's Sam."

"Mine is Lennie. But there I go again."

"What do you mean?"

"You didn't ask. I seem to be saying a lot of unnecessary things all of a sudden. Maybe it's the barometric pressure or something."

"What does that have to do with it?"

"Didn't you ever notice how some days you feel like you could take on the world, then other days it's almost more than you can do to drag yourself out of bed? I mean literally?"

"Yes, but—"

"I read somewhere it's the barometric pressure that does it. High pressure you feel great, low pressure you want to cut your wrists. Same as at the full moon. When the moon is full, people do all sorts of weird things—get in fights, break crockery, get married—even the animals feel it. Sometimes at the full of the moon a lot of rabbits will gather in a circle and see who can jump the highest—and that's an absolute fact. A friend of mine saw it. He tried to join them, but they wouldn't play. Apparently this was a rabbits-only operation —segregated, so to speak."

He looked at her in fascination. "What is your real name?"

"Lenore." She dragged out the last syllable as though it were a yawn. "Of all the names to lay on a little girl—you might as well call her Marie Antoinette."

"There's nothing the matter with Lenore."

"I'm glad you think so. My uncle once had a female donkey named Lenore. What a bitch."

Sam began to laugh, and choked on a piece of meat; his breathing stopped, and he felt his face grow tight. He tried to stand up, but the table prevented him, and all he could do was raise his hands.

"Bend forward," Lennie commanded, and when he did she reached over and hit him a crack between the shoulder blades that not only jarred the meat loose but also came close to driving his face into his plate. He straightened up slowly, wiping the tears from his eyes. "Thank you," he said weakly.

"It was my fault to begin with," she replied. "I shouldn't have told you about Lenore. I'm talking altogether too much tonight."

Another customer called her, and she went away and left him to finish his meal alone.

He went out into the night air, and as he headed away from town he began to wonder if he had come to the right place for solitude. Unless I'm careful, he thought, I'll have no more solitude than a subway guard. Then he thought of the foot, and wondered if solitude might even be dangerous.

2

Town meeting was usually held in the American Legion hall, on the theory that the assorted battle flags and trophies would be a fitting reminder to the citizens of their patriotic duty, but on this occasion it was decided to move to larger quarters, the better to handle the anticipated crowd. The high school gymnasium was selected as the largest indoor space available, and row upon row of folding chairs were set up on the basketball court. These were for the qualified voters; observers either stood at the rear or found what seats they could in the bleachers that lined both sides. Chief Maddox stood at the door, and under his watchful eye the incoming townspeople gave their names to be checked against the voting sheet. When Sam arrived, the Chief hesitated for a fraction of an instant, then waved him toward the back of the room.

The moderator was Dennis Fenwick, who had conducted

every town meeting in recent memory. Although technically an attorney he had spent most of his time in real-estate and land-court matters, and there were few areas on the island that he had not, at one point or another, either surveyed or examined in the books, with an eye toward possible purchase. He was large, with a florid complexion, and when he walked he wheezed as though he had air brakes. Town meetings were mercifully short, because he could stand on his feet for only so long before his arches began to give way. There had been a time, before his tenure, when the meetings ran on into the night, and those with the strongest bladders were those who cast the deciding votes, but now it was an unusual one that lasted past ten o'clock, and if there was still work on the agenda it was put over until the following evening. Since this was a special meeting there was only one item, but nobody could guess how long it would take.

Sam watched the people as they filed in and took their seats, and although he tried to classify them by type they resisted any overall description. There were the obvious workmen and fishermen, with large, heavy hands and leathery necks; there were youths of his own age group, some with beards and some with long hair and some with neither; there were white-collar types, with pale faces and soft, pudgy hands; and among the women there were some lean and leathery and some young and attractive, but on the average they were of medium height and tended toward heaviness in the hips. The clothes ranged from padded vests, like Sam's, to business suits to sweaters to horse-blanket sports jackets, and among the women there was a preponderance of tweeds and housedresses. Experienced meeting-goers wore clothing that could with decency be removed as the place grew hotter, because by ten o'clock it had usually taken on the characteristics of a Senegalese locker room.

Lennie was among the last to arrive. She looked around the crowded room, saw Sam, and had started toward him when Chief Maddox steered her toward one of the bleacher

seats along the side. She turned obediently and picked her
way through the other spectators until she found a seat on
the top row, where she sat down and again looked over toward Sam. He saw her, and tried to pantomime that he
would see her afterward, but he was sure she didn't get the
message because she just looked puzzled. Then he reminded
himself of his oath of celibacy, and decided it was probably
just as well.

On the podium, Dennis Fenwick rapped his gavel for
order, then blew into the microphone. No sound came from
the speakers, and he blew again with the same result. He
turned to a man behind him and said something, and all
other conversation ceased. From across the room someone
called an unintelligible remark, and someone else laughed,
and then there was silence.

"It'll be just a minute," Fenwick said, his voice sounding
strangely small. "Soon as Buster finds out WHAT THE
TROUBLE IS." The speakers blared the last words, and everyone laughed. "All right," Fenwick continued, in a lower
voice. "The meeting will come to order." He cleared his
throat. "You all know why we're here, but in order for everything to be legal I'll read the notice anyway." He read
the call for a special meeting, for the purpose of drawing up
a list of grievances against the State and making the case for
secession, such document as finally agreed upon to be submitted to the voters not later than the second Tuesday after
the first Monday in the month following the adoption of the
declaration. "Is that all clear?" he asked when he had
finished reading. There were murmured sounds of assent,
and Fenwick went on, "Now, following the usual procedure,
I'm going to ask each speaker to wait until a microphone is
brought to him, and identify himself loud and clear so
everyone'll know who's talking. Just raise your hand if you
want to speak, and Buster or Albert will bring you a mike."

A man raised his hand; Fenwick nodded at him, and the
man rose and began to talk. Sam recognized the owner of

the pickup truck who'd given him a lift the night before, but he couldn't hear a word the man was saying.

"Just a minute, Edgar," Fenwick cut in. "Wait till you get a mike, then give your name, and *then* talk. What have I just been saying?"

A microphone on a long cord was passed in to where the man was standing, and he took it and said, "Edgar Morris. I just want to make sure that at the top of the list you make a note to abolish the excise tax. I just bought a new pickup truck, with steel-belted heavy-duty radials, overhead cam-shaft—"

"Edgar—" Fenwick tried to break in, but Morris wouldn't be stopped.

"—torsion-bar suspension, synchronized maxi-flex gear-box—"

"Edgar—"

"—and you know what it cost me? Sixty-eight hundred and fifty bucks, and that was *before* the excise tax. The excise tax added—now get this—the excise tax added three hundred and fifty bucks, so in all I'm looking at a tab for seventy-two hundred bucks, and that's a goddam outrage. That's all I've got to say."

"We should be so lucky," a man near Sam observed as Morris handed back the microphone and sat down.

"We'll make a note of your observation," Fenwick said. "For the moment, I think we should confine ourselves to—ah—broader matters."

A heavyset man in a madras sports jacket stood up. His complexion suggested that he had spent the winter in Flor-ida, and the contrast between that and his shock of bushy white hair made him look almost like a photo negative. He produced a paper from his inside pocket, and cleared his throat. "I've made a few notes here," he began.

"The mike, George, wait for the mike," Fenwick said.

The microphone was passed to him, and he said, "I've made a few—"

"Your name first," Fenwick prompted.

In obvious irritation, the man said, "George Markey. M-a-r-k-e-y. I've made a few notes for what I think should be the preamble to our declaration, and with the chair's permission I'd like to read them."

"Go right ahead," Fenwick said.

Holding the paper at arm's length, Markey read: "When in the course of human events it becomes necessary for the people of an island to separate themselves from the mainland, and to assume the responsibility for governing themselves that God granted to them or should have, a decent respect for the opinions of others requires that they say why. We hold—"

"Why what?" Fenwick interrupted.

Markey looked up, and glared at the moderator. "What do you mean?"

"Does it mean why are we separating, or why did God grant us the responsibility? Or should have?"

"Look, Mr. Moderator, this is patterned on—"

"I know what it's patterned on, but if you ask me you should either have stuck to the original or made up a whole new preamble. Preferably in English."

Markey's face turned from a light tan to dark mahogany. "Am I going to be allowed to read this, or not?"

"Read it, but let's confine ourselves to the grievances." Fenwick paused, and puffed for air. "We've got enough business ahead of us here, without wasting time on preambles."

"The hell with it." Markey crammed the paper in his pocket, and sat down. He handed the microphone back as though he were making a sword thrust.

Sam leaned toward the man next to him. "Who's he?" he asked.

"Who ain't he?" the man replied. "Chairman of the Selectmen, president of the bank—Christ, you name it, he's probably it."

"Has quite a temper, hasn't he?"

"That's his Sicilian blood."

"Markey? Sicilian?"

"Try spelling it M-a-r-c-h-i."

Fenwick rapped once with his gavel, and looked around. "Does anyone care to list any specific grievances?" he asked. Several hands went up, and he nodded to a woman in a print dress wearing a hat trimmed with cherries. "Madam Selectwoman," he said. "Or should I say Selectperson?"

"Selectwoman will do." She stood up, and when the microphone reached her she said, "Agnes Tuttle. If you ask me, our most valid complaint is our lack of representation in the Statehouse. They're passing laws that concern us—that have a direct effect on us—but they're not letting us have a say in the making of those laws. That's taxation without representation, which, you will remember, our forefathers classed a tyranny."

"Amen to that," someone said, and there was scattered applause.

"So be it," Fenwick said, making a note. "Grievance Number One is so recorded. Any others?" He pointed to one of the upraised hands, and said, "All right, Norris."

A small man, wearing a gray cardigan and plaid shirt buttoned at the neck, stood up. "Norris Webster. What bugs me is the amount of money we pay in taxes as against what the State does for us. Every bottle of liquor I sell I've not only had to pay a Federal tax on, but also a walloping big State tax, *and* the cost of getting it here, so I'm having to sell liquor at two, three times what it cost on the mainland. Now—"

"The mainland people pay those taxes, too," Fenwick reminded him.

"I know, but the cost of getting it here makes it that much worse. My point is, here we're pouring all this money into the State, and what do they do for us? They patch up a stretch of road every now and then, and they pick up some of the tab for the school, but what else? Nothing! I figured

out that for every five dollars we give them we get one in return, and that just don't make sense. I don't mind paying
taxes, just so's I get something out of it, but this way it's
utter damn foolishness. We're being suckered, is what we
are."

Again there was applause, and Fenwick wrote on his pad.
"Next?" he said.

This time the speaker was a man who looked superficially
like Primo Carnera, with a bulbous jaw and prominent
gums. He gave his name as Emil Corning, and went on,
"What gripes my ass—"

Fenwick interrupted him with a rap of the gavel. "Let's
mind our language, Emil," he said. "This isn't the Waterfront
Club."

"What gives me a pain," Corning said, amidst scattered
laughter, "is the damn-fool government regulations and the
inspectors they send down here to enforce them. Out at the
boatyard we got inspectors crawling around like termites,
and every time I sell an outboard I almost got to strip it
down to the piston rings to prove it don't violate some ordi-
nance dreamed up by a guy sitting on his—uh—butt up in
State Street. The government got their noses into everything, to the point where a decent American don't have a
chance to make a living. I say live and let live, and screw all
government inspectors."

He sat down to loud applause, and a number of hands
went up. Fenwick recognized a tall, lanky man wearing a
tweed suit and holding an unlighted pipe in his teeth. "Dr.
Amberson," he said.

Dr. Amberson removed his pipe, took the microphone,
and for a moment seemed undecided as to which he should
talk into. Then he said, "One thing we haven't mentioned
yet is the matter of land. We all know there's only so much
land on an island, and that land can support just so many
people. Once the developers take over we're lost, because
they care only for the fast dollar and disregard the future.

And the State has the power to mandate a development any place they see fit, no matter what the feelings of the affected community may be. There has already been talk of a State-mandated housing program here, and if it goes through we might as well kiss the island goodbye. As I see it, our only hope is to declare ourselves outside the jurisdiction of the State—in other words, to secede, and secede now, while there's still time."

When the applause had died down Corning was on his feet, speaking without the microphone. "I don't think we should go on record against builders," he said loudly. "Building's a big part of our economy, and—"

"You've already had your say, Emil," Fenwick broke in. "Lots of people want to talk, and we don't have all night." He nodded to a short man with large ears, whose features seemed to be compressed into the middle of his face, clustered around his nose like the petals of a flower. "Mr. Turpin," he said.

"Lester Turpin," the man said into the microphone. "I don't think we ought to be too hasty with this secession business. I mean, look where it got the Confederate States. Secession means trouble, and trouble won't attract people to the island. Whenever I sit down to write an editorial, I try to think what the island is all about, so's the paper will reflect what we really are. And nine times out of ten I'll write my lead editorial on the autumn colors on the moors, or the beauty of the surf, or the sight of a deer in the morning fog, and I think that's what people like to read. If we get all hot and bothered and secede, then we're going to be like any of those cockamamie countries over in Africa, and we all know nobody wants to go *there.* If you put a gun at my head you couldn't get me to write an editorial attacking the United States, and as I see it, that's what you'll be wanting me to do. I want everything to be peaceful because that's what most people want, and I think they want to read about the good things rather than the bad."

"Nobody's asking you to attack the United States," Fenwick said. "Seceding from one state don't mean we're attacking the country as a whole."

"As far as I'm concerned, we are," Corning put in. "If any more of them goddam government inspectors—"

Fenwick rapped his gavel smartly. "Save it for the general discussion, Emil," he said, and Corning subsided, muttering.

The next speaker was a lady in her mid-forties who still showed the traces of earlier good looks. Her eyes were clear and her figure was trim, but her facial muscles showed the effect of years of strain, and her hair was in slight disarray. She identified herself as Muriel Baxter, and said, "Before we cut ourselves off from the mainland completely I think we should look ahead, and see what we'll be losing. Without State aid of some sort, the school is going to be in really desperate straits. For just one thing, the matter of textbooks— we're able to get our books through various government programs, and the wear and tear on them is such that they're in need of replacement every year. If we don't have the books we'll be reduced to teaching from the blackboard, and we might as well go back to the one-room schoolhouse system."

"And not a bad idea, either," Corning remarked loudly. "My pa was taught in a one-room schoolhouse, and it didn't do *him* no harm." He said it fast, to get it all in before Fenwick cracked his gavel, and the result was an approximate dead heat.

"I say good riddance if we get rid of government textbooks," Morris added, from his seat. "Just because they give us books they think they can tax us for everything else, and I wind up paying seventy-two hundred bucks for a pickup—"

"Let's have some order here!" Fenwick shouted, pounding his gavel. "Miss Baxter still has the floor."

"That's all I have to say," Miss Baxter concluded quietly. "There are some things we can't do without and some things we can't supply ourselves, and I believe we should think twice before we throw them away." She sat down as three people stood up, all shouting to be heard. Fenwick motioned to one of them, and the others sat down.

The speaker was a short man wearing a windbreaker and clutching a Day-Glo orange hunter's cap in both hands. "I say that's a goddam insult to us as Americans—" he began, but Fenwick cut him off.

"Please identify yourself," Fenwick said, "and mind your language."

The man gave a name that sounded like "Glamis Tillik," and went on, "I still say that's a goddam insult to us as Americans. If we—"

"I said mind your language!" Fenwick cut in sharply.

"I am minding my language! I mean every goddam word of it, and no legal-minded son of a bitch is going to stop me! If we can't use a little good old American know-how, and—"

"Sergeant at Arms, eject this man!" Fenwick ordered, to Maddox, and Maddox came down the aisle eyeing the man warily, as though he were a sparking catherine wheel.

"You can eject me but you can't shut me up!" the man shouted. "I know my rights! What the hell ever became of free speech in this country? What ever became of a man's liberty? What ever became of free enterprise? The government's taken the whole goddam thing away from us, and is trying to brainwash our children with Communist books they deal out in the schools! Well, I ain't about to—" He stopped, and grappled with Maddox, who had slipped behind him and pinned his arms. Two other men came up to help Maddox, and as they carried him out of the room he shouted, "They're after us right now! The Communists got boats lying off shore, waiting to take over! You think I'm crazy, just go look! Look off Gander Rip, and you'll see! You'll see!" There was a brief silence, and then the sound of a slamming door.

"Sorry about that," Fenwick said. "Freedom of speech is one thing, but freedom to disrupt is quite another. This is a legal meeting, and I intend to keep it that way." He paused, breathing hard, and the overhead lights picked up a glisten of perspiration on his forehead. "Now," he said when his breathing returned to normal, "does anyone have any further grievances? Specific grievances against the State, that is." He looked around but saw no hands, so went on, "All right, then, let's consider those we have already noted. Are there any comments?" A forest of hands appeared, and he hesitated before selecting a speaker. "Mrs. Tuttle," he said at last, and the Selectwoman arose, brushed imaginary crumbs from her lap, and folded her hands in front of her. It was clear she was trying to establish an attitude of dignity and calm.

"We have heard several suggestions tonight," she said in measured tones, "some concerning the general good, and some stemming from more—ah—personal motives. I think we should separate these two, because personal grievances have no place in a decision that will affect the entire community. I mentioned taxation without representation, and this is, I believe, in the field of the general good. However, we have heard other complaints, from people who simply don't like the idea of taxes, and this I think is unrealistic." Both Webster and Morris started to their feet, but were stopped by two taps from Fenwick's gavel, and Mrs. Tuttle continued, "If we are to have a government at all we must have taxes, and those who want them abolished are putting their own selfish interests above those of the community. A community without taxes is a community without government, which is anarchy, and I don't believe that anyone here would knowingly vote for anarchy." She sat down, and Webster and Morris shot up as though impelled by springs. Fenwick recognized Webster.

"I resent the implication I'm against taxes," he said, looking at Mrs. Tuttle. "What I said was—"

"Nobody mentioned you by name," she replied. "If the shoe fits—"

"You might as well have. What I said was I was against paying all these taxes and getting nothing in return, but since you bring *up* the matter of taxes, how come the Assessor raised the rates on every property in town but yours? You got something going with—"

"Order!" Fenwick shouted, with a resounding crack of his gavel. "The speaker will limit himself to the subject at hand!"

"She was talking about taxes," Webster replied. "So was I."

"You will avoid personalities, or you will be denied the floor."

Webster shrugged. "I was only wondering," he said, and sat down.

Mrs. Tuttle rose, and looked at Fenwick. "May I be allowed to reply to this accusation?" she said.

"Nobody accused you of nothing," Webster replied from his seat. "If the shoe—"

"To this implication, then?"

Wearily, Fenwick said, "Madam Selectwoman, I am trying to confine this discussion to the question of secession, and if—"

"I feel that I have been publicly insulted, and should be allowed a public rebuttal."

"Then someone else will have something personal to add, and we'll be here all night. I understand your feeling, but your request is denied. Mr. Morris has the floor."

Red-faced, her eyes glazed with rage, Mrs. Tuttle sat down, and Morris said, "I'm not so sure that anarchy would be a bad idea. Anarchy is freedom, and the American Revolution was fought for just that. Anarchy allows a man to do as he damn well pleases, without the government looking over his shoulder and stealing his money and butting in on everything he does, and if you want my opinion I say that's a good thing. We got no more freedom now than they got in Russia, and to me that's a hell of a way to live. Now, I figure that without taxes my pickup truck would have cost about—if you figure no taxes anywhere along the line, and no government regulations—about two thousand—"

Fenwick tapped his gavel. "Can we leave the pickup truck out of it?" he asked. "I'd like to deal in broader terms."

"I was making a point," Morris replied tartly. "Some people don't seem to understand what you're talking about unless you spell it out for them."

"Why don't we take that chance?" said Fenwick. "I think most of us get your drift."

"It sure as hell don't sound that way."

"If you have nothing further to add, I'll recognize Mr. Corning." A tap of the gavel and Webster sat down slowly, as though trying to think of something more to say, but Corning was already talking.

"I think we should settle this matter of land development," he said. "Conservation is one thing, but restricting all building is another, and I don't think we should make laws that are going to keep people from building. If you stop building you stop business, and that's going to be worse than what we got now."

Dr. Amberson was on his feet in an instant. "I didn't say I was against *all* building," he said. "I said I was against State-mandated housing programs which order building without regard to local conditions."

Fenwick rapped his gavel, but Corning ignored him. "It comes to the same thing," he said. "You're against one kind of building, you're against 'em all, just like if you're pregnant, you're pregnant, and no halfway in between."

"That's the most idiotic statement I ever heard!" Dr. Amberson began to gesticulate with his pipe, disregarding the now steady rapping of Fenwick's gavel. "You can no more lump all building together than you can lump all diseases—you can't say if a patient has gout he also has pneumonia, just—"

"How would *you* know the difference?" Corning replied loudly. "Think back a little, and you may—"

"Gentlemen!" Fenwick bellowed, but by now others had joined the fray, and the tattered remnants of order had vanished into chaos. Markey stood up and added his bullhorn voice to the din.

"Mr. Chairman!" he shouted. "If I may have the floor!"

Fenwick rolled his eyes toward Markey like a heifer going to slaughter, and made a futile waving gesture with the broken shaft of his gavel. Markey took it as a signal to proceed and, invoking his office as Chairman of the Board of Selectmen, he gestured to Chief Maddox to blow his whistle. The piercing trill cut through the pandemonium and people stopped, frozen in mid-action. Corning and Dr. Amberson had been removing their jackets, Lester Turpin was halfway under his chair, Mrs. Tuttle had her umbrella raised over Webster's head, and Morris had made his way behind Miss Baxter and was crouched like a panther, ready to spring. With the blowing of the whistle they stopped, paused, and then resumed their seats.

Markey glared about the room, as imperious as Napoleon. "This meeting will come to order," he said. "And the first person to be out of order will be ejected. Is that clear?" Nobody spoke, and he went on, "At the beginning, I read the proposed preamble to our declaration, and I think that, in spite of some minor quibbles, it sets a tone that—"

"Hey, George," Morris said, raising his hand. "Look at—"

"If you don't mind, I have the floor!" Markey snarled. "Save what you have to say until I'm finished. This preamble is in the spirit of our—"

Other people were now murmuring, and Morris said, "I'm not kidding. Just look—"

"Are you trying to be ejected?" Markey replied.

"No, but look at Dennis. I think he's dead."

Markey looked behind him, and there, slumped across the podium, was Fenwick. His face was purple, and before anyone could reach him he slid quietly to the floor, as limp as wet seaweed.

"Jesus Christ, why didn't you say so?" Markey exclaimed, and then Dr. Amberson made his way up to the dais, kneeled down, and reached for Fenwick's wrist. Next he put his ear against Fenwick's chest, and after a moment he straightened up.

"He's alive," he said. "But only just. Get the ambulance."

The business of the meeting was forgotten; people stood quietly and waited. Sam went across to where Lennie was standing, and she took his hand and clutched it in silence. Then they heard the wheep-wheep-wheep of the ambulance siren, and saw the windows blink with its flashing light, and finally two orderlies appeared, wheeling a stretcher between them. With some difficulty they managed to clamp an oxygen mask to Fenwick's face, which was rapidly losing color, and bundle him onto the stretcher. Then, with Dr. Amberson acting as outrider, they hurried down the aisle. In a few moments there came the thump of the ambulance doors; the siren started up, then faded in the distance.

Markey mounted the dais, and took the speaker's microphone. "Ladies and gentlemen," he announced, "this meeting is adjourned."

"What about secession?" someone asked.

"The main points have already been made," Markey replied. "I—the Selectmen will draw them up in legal form, and they will be presented to the voters for final consideration. I think we should all go home now, and pray for the speedy recovery of our beloved Town Moderator. Good night."

As the somber crowd shuffled toward the exits, Sam remembered an incident earlier in the evening, and said to Lennie, "That man who was thrown out—what did he mean, there are Communist boats off the shore?"

"Search me," she said. "I think he's just out of his tree."

A man next to them overheard, and said, "There's been a

boat off Gander Rip the last week or so, but it ain't no Communist boat. Looks more like a yacht to me."

"What's it doing?" Sam asked.

The man shook his head. "I ain't about to explain people in yachts," he said.

3

Sam lay on his cot and listened to the surf. Somewhere nearby a pheasant croaked, and in the distant pine trees a crow cawed out a precise, insistent message, faintly echoed by another. Here, Sam thought, was all the solitude he could ever ask for, but his mind was churning like a washing machine, and any attempt to concentrate was doomed before it began. After almost a year of hitchhiking and working his way across a good portion of the earth's surface, his accrued military and mustering-out pay was almost gone, and the goal that had led him on, the candle in the darkness, was still as far away as it had ever been. His first idea had been to do a present-day Pilgrim's Progress; this gave way to a dramatization of the search for identity, and as time went by his plan changed form and direction until it was almost unrecognizable. Every time he thought he had a new approach he found it had been done before: Pilgrim's Progress became Launcelot's quest for the Grail, which in turn developed into a form of waiting for Godot, and he finally decided that what he needed was perspective, the kind that can come only through solitude. He felt he had something to say, but he couldn't identify it precisely enough to give it form, or even words. He had a gnawing feeling he might be wasting his time, but this was a thought so frightening that he wouldn't let himself dwell on it. At twenty-seven he felt he could see the gleaming tips of the icebergs, and feel the cold winds that swept down from the thirties, with hints of the blasts from the country of middle age beyond.

He rolled off his cot, put on a pair of shorts and running shoes, and jogged down through the dunes to the flat sand, where he ran for an hour along the shifting edges of the waves.

After a breakfast of bread, peanut butter, and coffee he sat down at the worktable and stared at his notes, but his eyes glazed over and the words meant nothing, and at the end of a half hour he gave up all attempts at work. He got dressed and, telling himself that the change of scenery would do him good, set out on the road toward town. As he walked he thought back on the town meeting, and saw it as a microcosm of democracy—the arguments, the personal interests, the recriminations, and the general bungling—and he knew that out of all this something would eventually happen, and that whatever happened would probably be for the best. He found it hard to believe, but it had worked so often in the past there was no reason to think it wouldn't work now. Get to the grass roots, he thought, and that is where you'll find the answers.

He heard a car behind him, and turning around saw an old, paint-spattered Wagoneer. A ladder was lashed to the roof, and the back was full of paint cans, and as it slowed down and stopped next to him he saw, painted on the side, "Arthur Gibbon—House & General Painting." He got in, said, "Thank you," and sat back as the car started up. The driver, who he assumed was Gibbon, said nothing. Glancing at him, Sam was reminded of those rubber balls with faces on them which change expression when squeezed. Gibbon's face in repose was faintly glum, but gave the impression it could change radically at an instant's notice. He stared out at the road ahead as though he were alone in the car. Usually, when being given a ride, Sam let the driver start the conversation, but in this instance there was too much he wanted to know to stay silent for long.

"What do you think about secession?" he asked, when it was clear Gibbon wasn't going to volunteer anything.

"Bunch of gah-damn foolishness," Gibbon replied.

There was a pause while Sam waited for Gibbon to elaborate, but he didn't, so Sam said, "Did you go to town meeting?"

"Never been to one yet," Gibbon said. "I see no reason to start now."

"How will you know how to vote? I mean, without hearing both sides of the—"

"I never vote."

"You mean never?"

"That's right."

"Not even for President?"

"Especially not for President."

"Why not?"

"The way I see it, there's enough trouble in the world without getting into arguments. If I was to vote for one guy for President, and someone else was to vote for the other guy, then we'd get in an argument as to who was right; we'd both most likely get sore, and wouldn't change each other's thinking for a minute. That's just a damn-fool waste of time, is all that is."

"But you don't *have* to say how you voted. That's what the secret ballot is for."

Gibbon shook his head. "If you vote you're going to talk about it, and if you talk about it, then someone's going to disagree with you. You save yourself a lot of grief if you don't vote in the first place."

Sam digested this for a moment, then said, "What makes you think secession is foolishness?"

"The people who want it ain't thinking of the island— they're thinking of themselves, and no good ever come of that."

"Still, there was a lot of—"

"Look," Gibbon cut in, "I just finished telling you I don't like to argue. You're free to think what you like, but don't go trying to convince me of nothing, O.K.?"

"I'm sorry," Sam said. "I wasn't trying to convince you of anything; I was just trying to straighten things out in my own mind."

"Don't try so hard, and you'll find everything straightens out by itself."

"I hope so."

Gibbon's face warped itself into a smile. "Relax," he said. "The graveyard's full of people who tried too hard."

They drove the rest of the way in silence, and when they reached the edge of town Gibbon said, "Which way you going?"

"I hadn't really thought," Sam replied. "I just thought I'd come to town."

Gibbon gave a little cackle of laughter. "You must have a lot of time on your hands," he said.

"Well—yes and no." Sam looked at his watch, which showed about ten minutes before eight. Workmen's trucks were darting in and out of side streets, some drivers steering with one hand while they drank coffee with the other, and on one corner a knot of children waited for the school bus, holding their books and lunch boxes with numb resignation. "I guess I'll just go down Main Street," Sam said. "Have a cup of coffee at the drugstore, and see what happens after that." In the back of his mind he realized that one probable reason for his coming to town had been to see Lennie, but there were still four hours until the Sink Hole opened, and he had no way of knowing where she'd be until then. Better if I don't find her, anyway, he thought. That's not in the plan of things, and I shouldn't let myself forget it. He reached for the door handle, and said, "Thank you for the ride." As an afterthought, he added, "And the advice."

"Anytime," Gibbon replied.

Sam got out, but before he could close the door Gibbon said, "Are you from a newspaper or something?"

"God, no," replied Sam. "Why?"

"You seemed interested in what's going on, so I thought you might be writing a story."

Sam laughed. "I am about as unemployed as it is possible to be. I was at town meeting, and there seemed to be a lot of things that needed answers, but I'll remember what you told me. I'll let them come to me."

"You plan to be in town this afternoon?"

"What time?"

"Four, or thereabouts."

"I might. Why?"

"You know where the Waterfront Club is?"

"No."

"You can't miss it. Go straight down Fletcher's Wharf, and it's between that and the one to the south."

"And?"

"I'll be there after four. You want answers, you'll find more answers there than you ever had questions."

"Thank you. I might do that."

Gibbon nodded and drove off, and Sam started walking down Main Street. He was in the residential area, where the houses all looked neat and freshly painted, with well-trimmed lawns and hedges. Bursts of yellow forsythia showed in the gardens behind, and the new leaves on the sycamore and elm and maple trees formed a light green lacework overhead. Across the street a woman was sweeping her front walk, and farther down a shirt-sleeved man appeared, pulled by a midget terrier on a leash. The atmosphere of peace and contentment was such that Sam was reluctant to go on; he wanted to stay where he was and let time come to a stop. After a few blocks he began to see signs of commerce: the bank, which wouldn't open for another hour, and then the stores, some still closed and others showing signs of imminent opening, with their owners sweeping

off the sidewalks and polishing the windows. He decided
that the town woke up by sections: first the laborers and artisans, who had to be on the job at eight; then the store-
keepers and other tradespeople, who didn't start until anywhere from eight-thirty to nine-thirty; and then the
unemployed—the retired, the pensioners, and, later on, the
vacationers—whose time was their own and who could sleep
as late as they pleased. He, who had been up since sunrise,
felt that the early part of the day brought with it a feeling of
promise that was more exciting than any other time, and he
would no more have slept late than he would have taken
chloroform. He wondered if Lennie was still asleep, and decided that, with the hours she probably kept, she could
afford an extra hour or so. Then he wondered where she
slept, and with whom, and he quickly decided he didn't
want to know. Anyway, he told himself, it was none of his
business.

He crossed the street and headed for the drugstore, and
passed a door on which was hung a large black bow, so
large it looked almost like a cluster of dead crows. The door,
he saw, was that of the Masonic Hall, and above the bow
was a small white card bearing Dennis Fenwick's name and
dates. Fenwick had, apparently, died the night before, either
on his way to or shortly after entering the hospital. Remembering Fenwick's pallor as he was carried out of town meeting, Sam guessed he probably didn't even make it to the
hospital. He pondered the effect it would have on the secession movement, then realized Fenwick hadn't been a
member of the town government; he was simply Town
Moderator, and George Markey was still in charge of matters. Nothing would change, except that a new Moderator
would have to be elected.

He soon found out that, although nothing would actually
change, the town reacted as though the Board of Selectmen,
the high school football team, and the choir of the Methodist
church had been wiped out by a bomb. All flags except

that at the post office were flown at half-staff, the American
Legion Memorial Horse Trough was decked in black crepe,
a black-bordered picture of Fenwick appeared in the window of the newspaper store, and a movement was started to
rename the Veterans of the Spanish-American War Flagpole
in Fenwick's honor. Manny's Curiosity & Sperm Goods
Shoppe closed for the day, as did Cora Metternick's Bundles
for Babies Yarn Store, and only by threat of heavy fines was
Police Chief Maddox able to prevent the entire force from
taking the day off. Father O'Malley, of St. Brendan's Church
of the Mists, sent his vestments on a rush order to the
cleaner's, anticipating a larger turnout than at any funeral in
recent years, and a crypt in the basement of the church was
made ready as a temporary resting place for Fenwick's casket, pending the construction of a mausoleum at the cemetery. The only person who was not, in one way or another,
shocked by the event was Fenwick's physician, Dr. Lucius
Pardle, who had been warning him about his blood pressure
for the last ten years.

In the home of George Markey, the reaction to Fenwick's
death was muted. Markey lived in one of the more elegant
houses on upper Main Street. It was within easy walking
distance of the bank, but Markey felt that as president he
shouldn't arrive at work on foot, so every day he made an inspection tour of his other interests—the electric company, a
liquor store, a dry-goods shop—driving his royal blue Mercedes, which he eventually left in a "No Parking" space in
front of the bank. On Thursday nights, when the Selectmen
met, he had his wife, Ella, drive him and then pick him up,
since to park a Mercedes, no matter whose, on the street at
night was to invite vandalism. The radiator ornament was
the first to go (Markey had already had to buy three), and
then came the slashing of the tires, the dousing with paint,
and the breaking of windows. The vandals' identities were
known with reasonable certainty, but none was ever appre-

hended or even questioned. The police had enough trouble with their own cars as it was, without inviting retaliation.

On this particular morning Ella Markey had come downstairs early, having been awakened by a premonition, which she could not shake, that it was going to be a long day. Some five years younger than her husband, she was now in her early fifties, and both her looks and her accent were testimony to an off-island upbringing. She spoke with the easy assurance and the soft "r" of a native of suburban Boston, and she had managed to keep her face and her figure free from the effects of, respectively, sun and starchy foods. Where other local matrons would have a bit of fudge or layer cake as a midmorning snack, Ella Markey would never eat anything more substantial than celery or carrots between meals, and she had the ability to look trim and well tailored in the roughest tweeds. Her father, a professor of history at Harvard, had drilled into her the fact that one could be tweedy and still civilized, and that only the uneducated and the immigrants let themselves get fat. When she dressed for some special occasion, Ella Markey could cause any number of husbands' minds to wander and their wives to chafe.

She went into the kitchen, where the cook had not yet arrived, and was heating the water for some instant coffee when the telephone rang. As she answered it she glanced at the clock, which showed 7:45, and as always when a call came at an odd hour she mentally ran through the whereabouts of the three Markey children. George, Jr., was in San Francisco, where the time was 4:45, Mary was at college, where—

"Hello?" she said.

"Ella, is George up?" It was the familiar voice of Agnes Tuttle, and Ella relaxed.

"Not yet," she replied. "Is it important?"

"Dennis died last night."

"No! George called the hospital before we went to bed, and they said he was resting comfortably."

"Well, I suppose you could say he's resting comfortably now. He just isn't breathing." Agnes was known for her direct approach, which was one of the reasons she was elected to the Board of Selectmen.

"Do you want me to wake George?"

"Not if he's still asleep." There was the faintest hint, not of reproof, but of condescension, or magnanimity, that Ella caught and fielded like a hot rivet.

"If he isn't up he should be," she said. "I'll have him call you back."

"It's not that pressing; let him have breakfast first. I just thought he might want to call a special meeting of the Selectmen, to see where we go from here."

"I'll tell him." She heard the sound of water running upstairs, and said, "He's up now. He'll call you shortly."

She hung up and went upstairs, where Markey, his bushy white hair standing out in all directions, was gazing glumly at himself in his bathroom mirror. The Markeys had separate bedrooms and baths, and she had the momentary feeling she was entering a strange house. "George," she began, and he jumped.

"God damn it, how many times do I have to tell you to knock?" he snarled. "Is there no place in this house where a man can have privacy?"

Her jaw tightened, and all expression left her face. "Forgive me," she said. "Agnes Tuttle just called to say that Dennis died last night. She thought you might want to hold a special meeting." She turned and left the room and went downstairs, where the kettle with her coffee water was shooting clouds of steam into the kitchen. She snatched it off the stove and poured it into a cup, but her hand was shaking so that she spilled a good deal, and a puddle of steamy water spread over the counter. She mopped it up, spooned the coffee into the cup, and then, holding the cup in both hands,

sat down and sipped the scalding drink. By the time Markey
came down her rage had abated, and she was once again
calm.

"Where the hell does Agnes Tuttle get off, telling me to
have a special meeting?" Markey asked, looking around the
kitchen. "And where the hell is Daisy? Is this her birthday,
or something?"

"Agnes wasn't *telling* you to do anything," Ella replied.
"She just thought you'd like to know. And Daisy is only
about ten minutes late. That's nothing to fret about."

"So long as that's all. Last time she was late she was a
whole day late, and said she took it off because it was her
birthday. To my knowledge she's had three birthdays this
year, and if you were to count by her birthdays she'd be a
hundred and ten. I don't pay her for having birthdays, I pay
her for an honest day's work."

"Relax. She'll be here."

"I'm damned if I'm going to relax until she gets here. I'm
hungry."

Quietly, Ella put down her coffee cup and rose. "What
would you like?"

"You know what I feel like?" Markey rubbed his hands
together. "I feel like a good, old-fashioned *pan bagna*. That
gets a man in shape for the day like nothing else."

Ella's expression, as she went to the bread box, was that of
someone about to muck out a stable. "I told Agnes you'd
call her back," she said.

"I'll call her back when I'm good and damned ready. Give
me a cup of coffee before you start the *bagna*."

She poured him a cup of coffee, which he took into the
dining room. Then she put two thick slices of bread on a
plate, poured olive oil on one, and followed that with a layer
of sliced tomatoes. Next she peeled a large clove of garlic,
crushed that over the tomatoes, and covered it with flat
fillets of anchovies. Finally she put the second piece of
bread on top and poured olive oil over the whole sandwich,

letting it soak down through the bread. She had just finished the operation when the back door opened and Daisy came in, breathless and apologetic.

"Sorry to be late, Mrs. Markey," Daisy said, hanging her coat in the broom closet. "My condenser coil has bought the farm." Daisy was living with a garage mechanic, who was determined to teach her the intricacies of the internal-combustion engine. "I finally had to borrow one from Anton."

"That's perfectly all right, Daisy," Ella replied. "Would you mind taking this in to Mr. Markey?" She held out the plate, and Daisy regarded it as she would a snake.

"Yes'm," said Daisy, taking it from her.

"And don't mind if he seems a little upset," Ella went on. "Mr. Fenwick died last night, and right now things are at sixes and sevens."

"I don't know what that means, but I get your drift," Daisy replied, and vanished into the dining room.

Ella listened for any eruption from her husband but none occurred, so after a moment she made herself another cup of coffee and took it up the back stairs to her bedroom. In what seemed like a short time she heard his footsteps on the front stairs, and then he was in her doorway.

"I'm off," he said.

"Did you call Agnes?"

"I'll call her later."

"I told her you'd call her right back."

"Tough tit. You told her without asking me."

Ella took a deep breath and folded her hands in her lap. "If anyone calls, you'll be at the bank?" she said.

"Later on. I want to go down to the Land Office first."

She looked at him with an unspoken question. "I see," she said.

"No, you don't."

"All right, I don't. I assume it has something to do with Dennis."

"Assume anything you want."

"Will you be home for lunch?"

"I'll let you know."

She nodded and turned back to her dressing table, and looked at herself in the mirror as he went down the stairs and out the front door, and she continued to look in the mirror until she heard the sound of his Mercedes driving down the street. What she saw in the mirror was faintly depressing, since in the bright morning light the small scars of age and strain and general attrition were as clearly marked as road maps, but she took a certain comfort from the fact that in the fairly recent past at least one man had found her attractive. And that George knew about it. He may have thought he'd won, but it was a Pyrrhic victory because the memory would be with him forever.

The building that housed the town offices had once been an icehouse. Situated on the main commercial wharf, it was handy to the fishing boats that needed ice to refrigerate their catch, and in its time it had also dispensed coal, grain, and other bulk commodities. Then the fishing fleet moved to more lucrative waters and the building fell into disuse, and was saved from total collapse only by the inspiration of one of the Selectmen, a builder by trade, who saw its renovation into an office building as a chance to do the town a favor and at the same time work out an agreeable arrangement for himself. This being in the days before conflict of interest was even heard of, nobody had the slightest question about the deal. In fact, if it was thought about at all, it was considered an example of good business sense.

The clerk in charge of the Land Office was Charlie Ketchum, who claimed he had deeds in his records showing the original purchase of land from the Indians. There were wags who maintained that Charlie had drawn them up himself, but cold statistics made that impossible: the first land transfer was in the seventeenth century, and Charlie was still a few years shy of a hundred. Nobody questioned that he would make it into his second century, but to give him three was a pleasant fiction.

When Markey arrived Charlie was opening the windows, to air out the smell of dust and crumbling paper. Dr. Pardle had told him that unless he got some fresh air in the room he was likely to expire of emphysema or some arcane form of silicosis, so every morning at the start of work he went around opening the windows, then went around a second time closing them. When he had finished this ritual he dusted off his hands, sat in his horsehair-padded chair, and said, "Yes, George, what can I do for you?"

"I suppose you heard about Dennis," Markey said, in the tone used only for the recently departed.

"Heard about it last night," Charlie replied briskly. "Dennis was a goddam fool. If I told him once I told him fifty times, he should get rid of some of that weight or else the whole machine would quit. But no, he said he liked it fat, so I said go ahead, but when you drop dead don't come whining to me. Any doctor coulda told him the same, and probably did. I know Doc Pardle wanted him to lose weight; he told me so."

"Still, it's a great loss to the town," Markey said.

"I guess that all depends. Is that what you come to tell me?"

"No." Markey dropped his funereal air. "I wondered if you had any list of Dennis's holdings."

"You mean real estate? Christ, I wouldn't know where to begin."

"But don't you have a file on him? I mean, under his name?"

"Why? What do you want to find out?"

"I just wondered." Markey laughed. "You know—call it curiosity."

"It ain't filed that way, George. Now, if you want to know about a certain piece of property I can get out the papers on that, and give you every owner back to the Indians. But if you want to know what property So-and-so has, it'll take a year. Is this something the Selectmen are interested in?"

"No, no." Markey laughed again, this time more loudly. "That would be the last thing the Selectmen'd want to get into. I told you, it's just curiosity."

Charlie shook his head. "I wish I could help you, George, but things ain't rigged that way."

"Well, forget about it," Markey said jovially. "I just happened to be going by, and the thought popped into my head. I'm sorry I wasted your time."

"You didn't waste none of my time—I got all day. I just ain't got all year."

Markey laughed, slapped Charlie on the shoulder, and went out. Charlie picked up a paper clip, put one end in his mouth, and chewed on it as he stood by the window and watched Markey get into his car and drive off. He stood by the window for several minutes, chewing on the paper clip, then he looked at his watch and went slowly up to the second floor, where he joined the other town officials in their nine o'clock coffee break.

4

It was exactly twelve o'clock when Sam went into the Sink Hole, and until his eyes became accustomed to the gloom he was unable to see if Lennie was there or not. He had the brief sensation of being in a shadowy pool, with waitresses darting past him like trout, and it wasn't until he sat down at a table that one finally noticed him. She dropped a menu in front of him and said, "Would you care for a cocktail?"

"A beer, please," he replied, and when she returned he thanked her and said, "By the way, is Lennie here yet?"

"Lennie's off today," the girl replied. She started away, then stopped and came back. "Is there anything I can do for you?"

"Uh—no, thank you," said Sam. "Nothing important."

The girl smiled, said, "I see," and disappeared. She was back in a couple of minutes. "Would you like me to give her a message?" she asked.

"No, thanks." He wished he'd never brought the matter up, and to change the subject he said, "It looks like the whole town's gone into mourning. Do they do that often?"

"You know how it is," the girl replied. "Anything to break the monotony. Fenwick just gave them the excuse."

"I don't see so much monotony, with this secession business coming up. That could get downright lively." He found he'd unconsciously slipped into the local speech pattern, but did nothing to correct it.

"That, if you'll pardon my saying so, is a big load of bullshit," the girl said primly. "These people will no more secede than they'll chop off their right hands."

"A lot of them seemed quite worked up about it last night."

"Again, anything to break the monotony. If the United States Government had suggested we secede, you'd be able to hear the screams in Kiska."

"I take it you're not born here."

"Me? I was born in Terre Haute, Indiana. I used to teach in the school here, but I couldn't take the flak."

"Flak?"

She made a gesture of dismissal. "It's too long to go into. If we're going to swap life stories, we should do it after hours—which, I might add, would be all right with me."

He started to say, "Anytime," but checked himself and emended it to "Thank you. I'll remember that."

"Now," she said, dropping her conversational tone, "are you here for lunch or just for beer?"

"I guess I'd better eat something." He glanced at the

menu and said, "I think I'll try a Dory Fisherman. And another beer, please."

When she'd left he remembered Gibbon's invitation, and wondered what he could do to pass the time until four o'clock. The day had been shot long ago as far as work was concerned, so he told himself his best move would be to do as much else as possible, in the hope of finding an inspiration or a clue that would get him started. But between now and four . . . He glanced around the rapidly filling room and saw that the customers were a cross section of the working element of the town, leaving out only those who ate out of lunch boxes and those whose meals were served by domestic help at home. He recognized several of the people he'd seen at town meeting: Edgar Morris, the man with the new pickup truck who'd given him a lift; Lester Turpin, the editor of the weekly newspaper; Emil Corning, who ran the boatyard and sold outboard motors; and finally, coming in with someone he didn't recognize, was Agnes Tuttle, the only female member of the Board of Selectmen. The noise level was such that Sam couldn't hear what the various people were saying, but from their actions he guessed they were discussing secession rather than Fenwick; their voices were loud and their faces animated, and every now and then someone would pound the table with his glass. If this was a ploy to break the monotony, Sam thought, it was certainly a successful one.

He looked again at Agnes Tuttle and the man with her, who were the only two not actively involved in a discussion. As they took a table, the man, clearly a stranger to the premises, looked around as though he'd suddenly found himself in the primate house at the zoo, and said something to Agnes in a low voice, and she smiled and replied with something equally inaudible. He was of medium height, with artificial blond hair and a tropical tan. His expression suggested a smile even when he wasn't smiling; his lips covered his too-white teeth only at rare intervals, and seemed always in a state of flux, ready to fly apart in what he clearly considered a radiant gesture of goodwill. His clothes hinted at the tropics, or at least a southern resort; they were of hues suggestive more of golf clubs and summer cocktail parties than of day-to-day living, and he was as out of place in the Sink Hole as he would have been in a nunnery.

Which was precisely the reason Agnes had chosen the Sink Hole for lunch. He had called her at her home, shortly after nine o'clock, and at first his name had meant nothing to her.

"Williams," he said, enunciating clearly, when she asked him to repeat it. "Dustin Williams. I own the land at Cratchett's Farm."

"Oh, yes," she said, mentally picturing the Norman château that had been erected, a few years previously, on what was once a working dairy farm.

"You're a hard person to get hold of," he went on. "I've been trying since eight, but your line is always busy."

"Today's a bit hectic," she replied. "Dennis Fenwick died last night."

"Who?"

"Dennis Fenwick. He was Town Moderator."

"Oh. For a minute you gave me a start—I thought you meant my old friend Lawrence Hennick, chairman of the board of International Wabash, president of Amalgamated Tin, director of—"

"What can I do for you, Mr. Williams? I assume you had some reason for calling."

"What? Oh, yes. Would it be possible for us to have—uh—say, lunch today?"

"In reference to what?"

"I'd rather wait until we can talk."

"Yes, I suppose so."

"Good. Then should we say twelve-thirty, at the Whaler Arms?"

"Ah—better not there. Their kitchen is being renovated, and the food is full of paint."

"Where would you suggest?"

She gave him directions for getting to the Sink Hole, and as she hung up, her husband, Omar, looked at her with interest.

"Why'd you tell him that?" he asked, pouring himself a cup of coffee. "They're not doing anything at the Whaler."

"No, but the food is inedible, and besides, this is apparently something confidential."

"Then why the Sink Hole? With that crowd—"

"If we were at the Whaler there might be one other couple, and the waiters would hear everything we said. With a nice noisy crowd around us, nobody'll be able to hear a word."

Omar Tuttle spooned sugar into his coffee and shook his head. "It's as well we don't live on the mainland," he said. "If we did, you'd have one leg up now on being President of the United States."

"Tush," she said, secretly pleased. Then she looked at her watch and added, "I wonder when our peerless leader is going to condescend to call me back."

"You mean Markey?"

"Who else?" She made a sudden decision, and reached for her coat and purse. "I'm going shopping," she said. "If he calls, tell him I'm away on important business, and you don't know when I'll be back."

"And if he asks what the business is?"

"Tell him you don't know. Which will be the truth."

She went out, leaving Tuttle alone with his coffee, and he sat and stared out the window while pensively scratching his crotch. His job, which was repairing radios and television sets, had no fixed hours and was based in his own workshop, so he was self-employed in the fullest sense of the word. Luckily he had no need for personal prestige, because Agnes would have overshadowed him no matter what he did, and he was content to be able to do his job and do it well. But a transistor or a wiring diagram or a cathode-ray tube offered very little in the way of conversation, and his one release in that area was the Waterfront Club, where he would go at the end of the day and say all the things that had piled up in his mind during working hours. When he got home he had what Agnes called his Waterfront Club smile, which implied he knew more than he was telling, and he would go to sleep in front of the television set immediately after supper.

Agnes met Dustin Williams in front of the Sink Hole, and the minute he got out of his car she recognized him. He was one of the summer people, who were passionately proprietary about the island from about July 4 until Labor Day, and then hit out for warmer climes with the onset of autumn. Some of them, to be fair, had businesses that took them away, but others simply followed the crowd, playing golf and bridge and going to cocktail parties and seeing the same faces year in and year out. If I had their money, Agnes thought, I'd buy a farm in Wisconsin and meet some new people, or even talk to the cows, which would at least add a touch of novelty to the conversation.

He came toward her, baring his teeth in his most winning smile, and when they'd shaken hands she said, "You may find this a bit noisy, but I can promise you nobody will overhear anything. In fact, you may have to shout even to have *me* hear you."

He laughed. "Good," he said. "That will give me an excuse to sit close to you."

She looked at him to see if it was a joke, but she couldn't tell; his face wore a fixed expression of joviality, which was no more revealing than a mask.

They took a table in one corner, next to one occupied by Emil Corning, and Agnes maneuvered it so that Williams's back was to Corning, thus making it impossible for Corning to hear what Williams said. She was quietly congratulating

herself when Corning was joined by Norris Webster, her
bête noire from town meeting, who she was sure would go
out of his way to eavesdrop. Well, the hell with him, she
thought; until I know what's on Williams's mind I don't
know how much difference it will make. But he's not going
to hear *me* saying anything; that I know for sure.

They ordered drinks—Williams a bloody mary and Agnes
a white wine—and then, in his most unctuous tone, Williams
said, "I must say, when I planned to meet the lady Selectman I didn't plan on her being as handsome as you."

All right, Agnes thought, I'm going to make him work for
it. "Why not?" she said.

"Well—I mean—"

"Is there some rule a Selectwoman should be ugly?"

"Not in the least. It was just a passing remark. As my
good friend Johnny Mitchell used to say—"

"May I ask you a question, Mr. Williams?"

"Of course." He was obviously relieved to be, for the moment, off that particular hook.

"Why did you come to me, instead of to George Markey?
After all, he's Chairman of the Selectmen."

Williams smiled, his teeth gleaming in the dim light. At
close range, Agnes could see the line where his toupee met
his real hair. "That's easy," he said. "That's what you might
call psychology. I know many chairmen of the board; as a
matter of fact, I'm a chairman myself—of the Lock-Joint
Pipe Company, the Amalgamated Blown Glass and Copper
Company, and the Pari-Mutual Fidelity Insurance Company
—and I know that if you want something done you don't go
to the chairman, because the chairman is just in charge of
broad policy decisions and doesn't do any of the work.
When I was adviser to Governor Tibbett, he used—"

"Who?" said Agnes, not believing she'd heard right.

"Charlie Tibbett. T–i–double b–e–double t. He was Governor of this state before—"

"Governor Tippett spelled it with a 'p.'"

Without missing a beat, Williams said, "That's what I said. He was an old friend of mine— Ah, here are our drinks now." He took his bloody mary from the waitress, raised it in salute, and said, "Cheers." Agnes raised her wineglass in reply, and as she sipped it she was aware of pressure from his knee under the table. She moved her leg away and set down her glass.

"I guess it's time we got down to business," she said. "Just what is it that you want?"

"I'll have to answer you in a roundabout way, because it's an extremely sensitive matter. If the wrong people—"

"If you expect any cooperation from me, you'll have to tell me what it's about. Otherwise, we're just wasting our time."

"Would you like to order first?" The waitress was hovering nearby, and he gestured her to the table.

Agnes started to balk, then decided it would be easier to go along. She ordered a Manhattan hamburg and an iced coffee, while Williams studied the menu.

"That Texan," he said at last. "Is that real Texas chili? My old friend Clint Murchinson told me never to—"

"The meat comes from the A & P," the girl replied. "The chili comes in a package. Where the package comes from is anybody's guess."

"I'll have the Manhattan," Williams said, and handed her the menu. "And another bloody mary, and a wine for Mrs.— ah—Tuttle."

"I'm fine," Agnes said, putting a hand over her glass.

There was silence after the girl left, and Agnes felt she could see Norris Webster's ear enlarge and turn, like a radar antenna, to monitor her conversation. Williams cleared his throat.

"As I was saying," he said, "this is an extremely sensitive matter, and should be known by as few people as possible." Agnes simply stared at him and said nothing, and he went on, "Therefore I'll have to ask that you repeat our conversation to nobody. It is to be treated as top secret. Is that agreed?"

"I have told you before," Agnes replied, "that until I know what you're talking about I will agree to nothing." To herself she thought, it'll be a cold day in hell before I agree to anything this turkey says.

"Put it this way," said Williams. "Who owns the offshore waters?"

"The *waters?*" said Agnes. "You mean the fishing rights?"

"Specifically, I mean the land beneath the waters."

"Well, the government just extended the boundaries to two hundred miles offshore, so I suppose they do."

"You mean the United States Government."

"That's right."

"But supposing you were to secede. Who would own it then?"

Oh-ho, thought Agnes. *Now* we have it. "It still would be United States property," she said. "We plan to secede from the State, not from the Union."

"Don't the states own their offshore lands? And wouldn't you own yours if you were to secede?"

"I tell you, Mr. Williams, you'd better take that question to the Attorney General's office. That's a matter of legal argle-bargle that I'm in no position to decide."

He thought for a few moments. "There could be a great deal of money for someone who—ah—became affiliated with this," he said.

"With what?"

He stared at her. "What do you think?"

She put down her napkin and stood up. "I didn't come here to play guessing games," she said. "Thank you for the wine."

He half rose in his chair. "Don't you want your lunch?" he said. "I mean, there's no point—"

"There's no point continuing the conversation," said Agnes. And with that she retrieved her coat and purse, and left. Williams hung halfway between sitting and standing, then sank back in his chair. He took out his wallet, threw some bills on the table, and followed her outside, but by the time he reached the street she was nowhere to be seen.

At their table, Webster and Corning looked at each other for several moments without speaking.

"I wonder what that was all about," Webster said at last. "Who was the guy with her?"

"Dustin Williams," Corning replied. "A big pain in the ass who comes to the boatyard in the summer, trying to impress me with his yachting experience. If you ask me, the only yacht he ever had was the kind you play with in the tub."

The waitress arrived with her loaded tray and looked at the empty table.

"You can forget about that couple, honey," Corning said. "They suddenly remembered an important engagement."

The waitress's lips tightened, then she saw the money Williams had left, and gathered it up and put it in her apron pocket. "Easiest ten bucks I ever made," she said, and took the sandwiches to another table.

"What would Agnes Tuttle be doing with Williams?" Webster asked. "Could you hear anything they said?"

"I couldn't hear him. I get the picture she was kind of chewing him out."

"Yeah, but why?"

"Don't look at me. I know no more than you do."

"I think I'll ask around. I might come up with something interesting."

"You got to do more than ask, if you think you're going to get anything on Agnes."

"You never know till you try, do you?" Webster grinned, showing a line of ragged teeth, and bit into his sandwich.

Sam had observed all that went on without being able to hear the dialogue, but he found he could invent his own script just by watching the people. He realized this was of little help as far as his own project was concerned, but his own project seemed for the moment to have faded into the background. He wasn't abandoning it, he assured himself; he was just waiting to gather more material before starting the actual work. Looking around the room, he saw Lester Turpin, the editor of the paper, eating alone, and he was struck by a thought so sudden and so beautiful that it could only have been divine inspiration. He got up and made his way to Turpin's table, and said, "Excuse me, sir, may I speak to you for a minute?"

"Glad to have company," Turpin replied, forming his tightly clustered features into a smile. "Sit down."

"Thank you, sir." Sam took a chair, unsure of how to begin.

"What can I do for you?" Turpin wiped his plate with a pickle and popped it into his mouth.

"I wondered if you had a job open on your paper," Sam said. "Not a permanent one, but say for a couple of months or so."

Turpin regarded him with interest. "Doing what?" he asked.

"Anything. Anything or everything. I can write, I can—"

"Can you write an obit?"

"I can try."

Turpin thought a moment, then shook his head. "I'd like to give you the Fenwick obit, but that wouldn't be fair. I've been sitting here going crazy trying to sort it out."

"What's so hard about it?"

Turpin looked at the overhead rafters a moment before answering. "When a well-known town figure dies," he said finally, "it can't be just your run-of-the-mill obituary. It must praise without being fulsome, it must speak of the town's loss without being ridiculous, and it must be emotional without being maudlin. It should try to tell the truth, but only the kind of truth the bereaved like to remember, and it should be written with dignity and grace. Try to mix all those elements together and you'll see what I mean."

"I do," said Sam.

"Have you ever done any reporting?" Sam had his mouth open to reply when Turpin went on, "Never mind. It doesn't matter. I'll find out soon enough."

"I've done a number of different things," Sam said. "I'm presently trying to write a play."

Turpin smiled, as though he already knew it. "Yes, of course," he said. "How well I remember. . . . I know what you can do. How would you like to do some interviews, and find out how the people stand on secession?"

"Fine," said Sam. "Any special people?"

"Anybody. Everybody. Get a cross section."

Sam paused, trying to phrase his next question. "I got the picture at town meeting you were—uh—rather strongly against secession," he said. "What do I do if—"

"You write down just what the people tell you," Turpin broke in. "If they come out eighty-three to one in favor, so be it. I don't try to make opinion; I try to reflect it, and that's why I said what I did. If I'm wrong, then we'll print it the way it comes out."

"Fine," said Sam. "I just thought I should ask." He saw that the waitress had come to his table and was looking for him, and he put up his hand and beckoned to her. She brought him his check.

"I thought you'd skun out on me," she said, handing it to him.

"Do I look like the kind who'd do that?" Sam produced some money and began to count it out on the table.

"That's one of those things you never can tell," the girl replied. "They say it takes all kinds to make a world."

There was a hint of irritation in her voice, which Sam disregarded. He'd found that to query a minor complaint would often release a flood of major woe, and he'd developed the habit of closing his ears to the early signals. Turpin, however, had his senses tuned up to full gain, and when the girl left the table he smiled.

"I'm afraid I broke up a tryst," he said. "She expected to meet you later."

"Not me, she didn't," Sam replied. "We had no date."

"She thought you did."

"Mr. Turpin, you may say you reflect opinion, but in this case I'd say you're dead wrong."

"I wouldn't," replied Turpin cheerfully. "And you might remember this when you do your interviews: it isn't what the people say that's important, half as much as it is how they say it. Look in their eyes, and you often won't need their words."

5

Sam spent the afternoon interviewing people, with results that were only mildly rewarding. The first person he approached was a grizzled character sitting on a bench in front of the paper store; his eyes were bloodshot, and he wore a lumpy peaked cap that looked as though he'd retrieved it from the bilges.

"Excuse me, sir," Sam said. "May I speak with you a moment?"

"About what?" the character replied, scarcely moving his lips.

"About secession. I'm taking a poll for the paper, and—"

"Don't know nothing about secession. Grampa was with the 20th Maine at Gettysburg and to hear him tell it the Rebels was a seedy lot, but I warn't there, so I don't know. Grampa said we whupped 'em good, though, if you want to put that in yer paper."

"I didn't mean that—" Sam began, then changed his mind. "Thank you," he said, and moved on.

He next encountered a bland-faced man, with small eyes and a small mouth, who when he talked moved to within six inches of his listener's face and spoke in a low and almost confidential voice. "I'm glad you asked me," the man said when Sam posed the question. "Do you have a minute?"

"Yes, sir," Sam replied, trying to back away, but the man followed as though trying to bite Sam's nose. His breath smelled of cigars and old muscatel.

"I'm not a native here," he said, "but I've been here long enough so's I almost count as one. Of course, you're not a native unless you're born here, and I was born in Teaneck, New Jersey, and came here for the first time in 1926. I was only a little shaver then, but I can tell you I never wanted to be anywhere else. Why, just once I went to the Ramapo Mountains, and do you know what they looked like to me? Can you guess?"

"Well, sir, what I—" Sam started, but the man wasn't listening.

"They looked like nothing more than a line of molehills. 'You call *them* mountains?' I said to my wife. 'If those are mountains you can give me the seashore any day in the week.' My wife comes from the state of Washington, where they tell me they do have mountains, but for me seeing is believing and I'll take nothing on hearsay. My—"

"About secession—" Sam said.

"I'm getting to that. My wife and I met on a streetcar in Boston; I'd gone up there to have a tooth pulled—broke it on a splinter of bone in a lamb chop; just split it up the middle neat as you please, and lost a fifty-dollar inlay in the process —and I stood up to give her my seat because the car was full, and she noticed my mouth looked funny because I'd just had the tooth pulled and was chomping on a wad of gauze, and she said—"

"Sir, do you think we could—"

"Don't be so impatient. How can you understand what I'm saying unless I give you the background?"

"What I'd like to know is how you feel about secession."

"Exactly. I heard you the first time. It doesn't take a brick wall to fall on *my* head, you know; I'm not like some of these people, and I won't mention any names, you have to tell them three times it's raining out before they'll come in the house. I remember one time—"

Sam recalled Turpin's advice to look into people's eyes, but this man's eyes were no more revealing than buttons. He had become so hypnotized by his own voice that he had ceased to think—which, come to think of it, was as good a clue as any—and Sam had the feeling that if he were simply to walk away without saying anything, the man would probably continue to talk as though he were still there. He thought briefly of opening his fly and peeing on the man's leg to see if *that* would produce a reaction, and the picture so pleased him that in spite of himself he began to smile, then to laugh.

"You think that's funny," the man said. "Let me tell you something that happened last year. No, I guess it was two years ago—three at the outside. Now that I think of it, it didn't happen; it was something I was going to do and then never got around to. At any rate, there was the three of us— George, Goosy Pellick—he was called Goosy because one time—"

"Was that the fire whistle?" Sam said suddenly, and the man stopped.

"Was what the fire whistle?" he asked.

"That! Can't you hear it?" The man cocked his head to one side, and before he could say anything more Sam said, "I'll get back to you later—I've got to go see where the fire is!" He ducked around a corner, leaving the man staring into space.

It occurred to him he might have better luck with someone who worked in an office; those who drifted around the streets had too much time on their hands and no real focal point for their thoughts. A man who sits on a bench all day, he reasoned, has time to hear all sides of a question and no real necessity for making up his own mind. He can argue one way one day and another way the next, and nobody will notice the difference, because they are all thinking what they want to say when he's through. Sam looked around and saw the office of the electric company, so he crossed the street and went inside. A thin woman in her early fifties was behind the counter, leafing through a stack of payment slips. A rubber tip on her index finger darted like a snake's tongue as she counted.

"May I speak to you a moment?" Sam asked.

The eyes behind the steel-rimmed glasses regarded him coldly. "About what?" she said. "If it's a bill, you'll have to take it up with—"

"It's not a bill," said Sam. "It about secession."

"Who wants to know?" The eyes didn't change expression.

"I'm doing this for the paper."

"Are you using names?"

"Not if you don't want me to. I'm just trying to get a cross section of opinion."

She thought for a moment. "All right. No names. What do you want to know?"

"Are you for it, or against it?"

"For it."

"Why?"

"To get away from the government. We need more freedom, and less government."

"I see." He made a note. "And what is your complaint against the government?"

"First, there's too much of it. Second, it's a dupe of the international Communist conspiracy."

"You mean the United States Government is?"

"I do. They've been taken in by the international Communist conspiracy. When they gave up prayers in the schools, they gave in to the Communists."

Sam was now scribbling frantically. "Anything else?" he asked.

"A great deal else. Are you familiar with the thoughts of Robert Welch?"

"I'm afraid not."

She reached under the counter and produced a pamphlet, which she passed to him. "Take this," she said. "If you have any further questions, let me know."

Sam heard the door open behind him, and said, "One more thing—" but the woman was looking at the incoming customer. As Sam left, he heard the man say, "This bill is a goddam outrage—on a twenty-five-dollar meter reading I get a twenty-dollar surcharge; what the hell kind of sense does that make?" and the woman reply, "I'm sorry, sir, but we don't set the rates; they are established off-island. You can look them up in the—" and then the door closed behind him and he was outside. He scanned the pamphlet the woman had given him and dropped it in the nearest trash can.

Looking at his notes, he saw that his score was not impressive: one non compos mentis, one victim of total recall of trivia, and one John Birchite. He wondered where the people were he'd seen at town meeting, those who had ideas of their own and were able to express them, and he concluded that they were by no means in the majority. It wasn't fair to base his conclusion on three examples, but it was going to make it harder to come up with a coherent news story. Maybe it's always this way, he thought; maybe it's the coherent minority who do the moving, and the incoherent majority who bumble along and do as they're told. It doesn't say much for human initiative, but maybe initiative is like albinism: found only in a select few.

In this glum frame of mind he went to the supermarket, thinking that perhaps at the check-out counter he might get

his cross section of opinion, and as he watched the customers come cattle-like through the chutes, putting their
purchases on conveyor belts to the cashiers, who punched out
figures on computerized machines, he realized that to ask
for any rational thought was to ask for the impossible. The
people were so programmed into the routine that they went
through it numbly and without thinking: with glazed eyes
they reached into their purses and wallets and peeled out
sheafs of bills, then picked up their packages and wheeled
them out, having thought no more deeply than to wonder
how many mouths a smoked butt of pork might feed. As an
experiment, Sam took a strip of cardboard from an empty
carton and, borrowing a felt pen from a clerk, wrote on it:
"Secession—For or Against?" Then he drew a line down the
center, put "For" at the top of one half and "Against" at the
top of the other, and stationed himself next to the exit door.
As people came past he asked them their choice—he didn't
ask them to mark the card, because mostly their arms were
full—and he put a check mark in the appropriate column as
they replied. This way he amassed a respectable number of
answers in fairly short order—some people walked past him
in silence, and others said they hadn't made up their minds
—and the result was something like three to one in favor of
secession. Although Sam didn't ask for reasons, some people
lingered to explain, and they were usually secessionists
whose grievances were loud and not always rational. Taxes
and food prices were high on the list, followed closely by government interference in business and paternalism in general.
"Big Brother" was mentioned often, and every now and then
the clear waters of reason were muddied by obscenity. Sam
thanked each one, made the check mark, and tried to remember some of the more telling arguments. At one point
he happened to glance at the clock over the frozen-foods
section and saw it was ten minutes to four, so he added up
his answers, returned the pen to the clerk, and headed for the
waterfront.

The Waterfront Club was in what was once a ship chandlery. Originally intended as a refuge from the weather for men who worked on the docks, it had grown to where it was a full-fledged social and civic organization, with enough attention devoted to ecological and educational projects to warrant a tax-free status. Its members covered a broad spectrum, both socially and financially, from the locals who virtually lived in the clubroom to summer residents who occasionally brought houseguests for cocktails, with the idea of showing them what island living was really like. Membership requirements were simply that a person be "of good character" and be vouched for by two members, but so many people qualified under these rules that a limit had to be established, and the Waterfront Club moved into a class with the Racquet and Union League clubs, where admission depended on the death or resignation or expulsion of a member. Nobody had ever been expelled from the Waterfront Club, although one man had his bar privileges suspended for telling the Chief of Police to go fuck a tin goose.

Gibbon was already there when Sam arrived. He was standing at the bar, holding a bottle of beer and talking to Morris and Webster, and when he saw Sam he beckoned to him, and introduced him to them. Sam already knew Morris as the man with the pickup who'd given him a lift, and he recognized Webster from town meeting and from the Sink Hole—he was still wearing the gray cardigan and plaid shirt he'd worn the day before. There was a mumbled exchange of names and then Gibbon said, "What'll you have?"

"A beer, please," Sam replied, groping in his pocket for money.

"You can't pay; you're a guest," Gibbon said, and put a bill on the bar.

Webster, whose head was no higher than Sam's chin, took on the faintly truculent air of a small man talking to a larger one. "Did I see you with Lester Turpin at the Sink Hole?" he asked.

"You could have," Sam replied. "I stopped at his table."

"I thought so. You know Agnes Tuttle?"

"By sight."

"You know the guy she was with today?"

"Easy, here comes Omar," Gibbon said quietly, as Omar Tuttle sidled up to the bar.

"I know very few people here," Sam said to Webster. "I haven't been here long, and mostly I stay out of town."

"What do you do?"

"Chrissakes, Norris, lay offa him," Gibbon put in. "You heard him say he's new here."

"Just asking," Webster replied. "No offense."

Omar Tuttle slid his beer bottle along the bar toward them. "Evening, gents," he said, and they all greeted him and Gibbon introduced Sam. "Been quite a day, hasn't it?" Tuttle said.

"So far," Gibbon replied, sliding his empty beer bottle to the bartender.

"I got thinking about Dennis this afternoon," Tuttle went on, "and I got wondering who was going to do his funeral oration."

"What's the matter with Father O'Malley?" Gibbon asked. "It's his candy store."

"I should think Dennis would rate something a little extra," Tuttle replied. "Some town official, or something."

"Christ, you don't mean George Markey, do you?" Edgar Morris put in. "Did you hear him at town meeting? Get him to do it, and we'd have the whole Declaration of Independence, *plus* the Constitution."

"What about the judge?" Tuttle said. "I mean—"

"You mean Cyrus Pepper?" Webster said. "He don't have the guts to do it. If someone was to fart, he couldn't quiet the laughter."

"There's one thing you gotta say for Judge Pepper," said

Morris. "With him, we got as close to anarchy as you can have and still be legal."

"You and your anarchy," said Webster. "If we was to have anarchy, you'd be the first one screaming for police protection."

"If we had anarchy we wouldn't need police," Morris replied. "Everybody would be brothers."

"And you know how you spell 'brothers'? B-u-l-l-s-h-i-t."

"I wouldn't be so sure about that. Once you get rid of taxes, everything will iron itself out."

"Let's be serious here," Webster said. "What'll happen when we secede? The—"

"If we secede," Gibbon emended.

"We will—don't worry. The State will call out the National Guard, and send them down here to police us. We should have a plan, so's we'll be ready when they come."

Emil Corning, who was standing nearby, spoke up. "You don't need to worry about the National Guard," he said. "They don't let them have bullets these days. I think our problem may be with the Coast Guard."

"Easy," said Morris. "Don't let 'em ashore."

"The Coast Guard are Federal," Webster said. "We got no quarrel with them."

"So are your taxes Federal. Or at least some of them." Corning took a deep pull on his beer and went on, "As I see it, we've got to go for the whole ball of wax. If we secede from the State we'll have to let the Federals know we'll stay in the Union only on our own terms, and I somehow don't see them liking that. I think we got to be prepared to defend ourselves against all comers, up to and including the Army, Navy, and Marines."

"Hot damn," said Morris. "That'll be anarchy for sure."

"You got any ideas how we're going to do this?" Webster asked. "You're talking about biting off a pretty big mouthful there."

"Not so big," Corning replied. "If we take on the whole

mob, we'll have the rest of the country on our side. We'll be the underdogs, and that'll make the troops look like bullies. The public would rather lose a war than have it thought they was bullying anyone, so we'll be home free. We can even put in for reparations when it's all over."

"You mean we just sit here and let 'em walk over us?" Webster said.

"Hell, no. We put up a fight—or what looks like a fight. We can take some boats from the yard—I can think of three offhand I haven't been paid for—and sink 'em in the channel, so nobody can come in the harbor. Then we set up a patrol of other boats around the island, and if we see an LST or something trying to land, we just gang up on 'em and make 'em look silly. No Navy man is going to risk a collision with a small boat, because it'll go on his record and work against his promotion, so all we have to do it threaten to collide and they'll turn away. Those boys all got their fingers on their numbers, and don't you forget it."

"It seems too easy somehow," Webster said. "I think you must be overlooking something. Suppose they come in by plane?"

"Put obstacles on the landing strip. Old cars—sawhorses—whatever. Then if—"

"I think I can foul up the radio beacon," Omar Tuttle put in. "Warp the beam by ninety degrees, and if they're making an instrument approach they'll go straight the hell out to sea."

"Good thought," said Corning. "If there's fog, that'll take care of it nicely."

"If there's no fog we can make some," Tuttle went on. "Get a lot of old tires and burn them to windward of the strip, and it'll be as good a smoke screen as you could ask for."

"Keep thinking," said Corning. "We're going to need every idea we can get."

"I think someone should be in overall charge," Morris

suggested. "It's all right to have ideas, but there should be someone who could see they're put into practice. Now, I could set up a—"

"You silly asshole, you're the one who wants anarchy," Corning cut in. "Who are you to be talking about setting up a system?"

"Anarchy is a system—of sorts," Morris replied, then lapsed into silence.

"I think maybe Omar should be in charge," Corning said. "He's got all the radio gear in his shop, and he could set up a sort of command post, with everyone reporting in to him. Also, with his connections with the Selectmen"—he paused and winked at Tuttle—"he can give us the hot poop as to what's on *their* minds."

To Tuttle, who was on his second beer, the idea seemed almost too good to be real. To think that he should be put in charge of such an operation was a prospect of such stunning proportions that it took him a few moments to realize the possibilities. "I'd be happy to," he said at last. "Unless there's someone feels he might be better at it."

Nobody offered a counter-suggestion, and Corning ordered a round of beer to seal the bargain. Then he looked at the door, where a man in oilskins had just entered, lugging a monstrous striped bass. A couple of people cheered, someone said, "Is that a member or a guest?" and the man in oilskins heaved the bass onto a hanging scale. There was a clatter, and the hand on the dial whipped back and forth and finally settled on forty-three pounds six ounces. There were whistles, and some laughter, and the man tottered to the bar and ordered a beer.

"There's more goddam bass out there'n you can shake a stick at," he said. "I had to fight to keep 'em outa the boat."

"Where'd you get him?" someone asked.

The man took a long swallow, wiped his mouth with the back of his hand, and said, "Gander Rip. Right in close.

There's birds working all along the rip, but the big fish are in close."

Suddenly Corning's face lighted up. "Anybody want to go out?" he asked.

"It'll be an hour before we can get there," Gibbon said. "You think they'll still be biting?"

"We got two more hours of tide. If they're biting like this now, think what they'll be like at sunset."

"I'm game," Gibbon said, and turned to Sam. "You want to come?"

"Sure," replied Sam. "I've never done it, but I'd like to try."

"There's nothing to it," Corning said. "You let the fish do the work. Omar, you want to come along?"

Tuttle had finished his second beer and was starting his third, which was usually his limit, but the euphoria of his new position made him feel adventurous. "Hell, yes," he said. "Count me in." Then, as an afterthought, he added, "I better call Agnes first, so's she won't worry."

He went to the phone booth, and Webster watched him go. Webster was still stinging from his clash with Agnes the night before, and was determined to get something concrete against her, but he didn't know if he stood a better chance by going fishing with her husband or staying behind to see what he could find out about her and Dustin Williams. He decided to stay behind, on the theory that Omar Tuttle probably didn't know what she was doing and wouldn't say if he did, whereas any number of people might be able to cue him in on Williams. When Corning asked if he'd like to come along he said, "I got work to do," and let it go at that.

Morris, on the other hand, was eager to go fishing. His only project beyond secession was a long-range and nebulous one, and involved having carnal knowledge of Muriel Baxter, the schoolteacher. This was such an intricate proposition, in view of Miss Baxter's reputed ironclad hymen and the fact that he knew her only slightly, that an evening of fishing wasn't going to change matters one way or the other. His campaign, if such it could be called, made Hannibal's shepherding of elephants over the Alps look like a stroll in the park, and he knew that if he were to stand even the slightest chance of success the groundwork had to be laid with infinite care. Either that or wait for anarchy and rape her as she emerged from the supermarket.

"All right," Corning said when Tuttle returned from the phone booth. "I'll go over to the yard and get my boat, and you guys get beer and sandwiches and whatever you want. I'll gas up and be back here in fifteen minutes."

As they were leaving the club, they passed Chief Maddox on his way in, and Sam, who was feeling cheered by his beer and the prospect of fishing, smiled broadly. "Any word on that foot yet?" he asked.

Maddox looked startled, then glared at him. "It's still up at Harvard," he replied, and went to the bar.

"What foot is that?" Morris asked.

"Just something I found," Sam replied.

Morris thought for a moment, then said, "Was that why you wanted the police station?"

"That's right." Sam was sorry he'd brought the subject up.

"What kind of foot was it?"

"I don't know. The Chief thinks it's a bear."

Morris considered this in silence, then said, "I'll be a son of a bitch."

They went to Webster's liquor store, where they stocked up on beer, cocktail salami sticks, cheese, crackers, and, as Gibbon put it, "in case it gets cold," a bottle of whiskey. Just to see what would happen, Gibbon told the clerk to charge the order to Webster, but the clerk shook his head. "No way," he said. "He don't buy liquor for *no*body."

"Even if he's going fishing with us?" Gibbon asked, lying by implication if not by words.

"Even if he was going fishing by himself," the clerk said. "He's got a flat rule not to take a drink unless someone else has bought the bottle first. If I was to charge this to him, he'd have my balls nailed up on that Budweiser sign by sundown."

For some reason this struck Tuttle as hilarious, and he laughed so hard he tottered into a pile of tinned hors d'oeuvres and bottled olives, which rolled and bumped and scattered across the floor. He started to pick them up but the clerk told him to forget it, and as the others helped Tuttle, still laughing, out of the store, Sam wondered if he was going to be a problem. Essentially that would be Corning's lookout, but still Sam didn't relish the idea of having to go after Tuttle if he fell overboard. He remembered one time on a troop transport when a man had fallen over the side, and he knew how fast a head could vanish in a rough and darkening sea.

But the sea was calm this evening, and as they left the harbor Sam stopped thinking about Tuttle. Corning's boat was something over thirty feet long; it had a small cabin forward, and a pulpit on the bow from which a person could either cast with a surf rod or, in appropriate circumstances, wield a harpoon. The after section was a large cockpit, in which were chairs, a fish box, and holders for the trolling rods. The sun was behind a bank of clouds in the west, and its rays fanned upward and out, coloring the sky and the tops of the clouds on both sides. As Corning opened the throttle the boat surged forward, and Sam had a feeling of peace and contentment that was both relaxing and exhilarating; he wanted to shout with the sheer pleasure of it. Instead, he accepted the beer that Gibbon passed him, and raised it in salute to all hands. Corning, at the wheel, was the only man without a beer; he said that someone had to stay sober in case of emergency.

"What kind of emergency do you expect?" Tuttle asked, laughing. "A submarine attack?"

"You never can tell," Corning replied, and reached into the cabin door and turned on the radio. He tried a couple of channels, hoping to pick up talk from other boats, but there was no traffic, so he switched to the main Coast Guard frequency, where all distress calls and other important messages were broadcast. Tuttle watched him with professional interest.

"You on 2182?" Tuttle asked, and when Corning nodded he said, "It should be coming in better than that. Mind if I take a look?"

"Be my guest," Corning replied, and Tuttle went into the cabin, turned off the radio, and began to take the back off the set. "Just don't lose anything," Corning warned him. "I may need it later."

"Don't worry about me," Tuttle replied, and popped a screw from the set into his mouth.

Gibbon looked back at the wake, which spread out in a widening V astern. "Christ, if this ain't peaceful," he said. "It'd take an awful lot of this to kill a man."

"Once we secede you can have all of it you want," Morris replied. "And you won't have the goddam government sitting on your shoulder telling you what to do."

"I can have all of it I want right now," said Gibbon. "The government don't give me no grief."

"Little do you know," Morris said darkly. "They're everywhere, and into everything."

"So are mice. I don't get my tits in a flurry over mice, so why should I about the government? Have another beer."

Morris started to say something more, then reached in the cooler chest and brought out a beer. He twisted the cap off and threw it over the side.

Gibbon's face broke into a grin. "That's more like it," he said. "Ain't that better'n arguing?"

"Yes and no," Morris replied. "You can argue all night, and never have to take a leak."

They had been going for about a half hour when Tuttle put his head out of the cabin and scanned the horizon. "Seen any boats around?" he asked.

"No," said Corning. "Why?"

"I'm getting something on a weird frequency."

"Can you tell what they're saying?"

"No. It's in voice code. He seems to be giving positions, but they're all coded."

"Have a beer," Gibbon suggested. "Maybe that'll make it clearer."

"Don't mind if I do." Tuttle took the beer Gibbon handed him, and disappeared back into the cabin.

Morris had been silently staring at the sea, and he now rose and said, "I have an idea." Bracing himself against the slight motion of the boat, he went to the cooler chest, took out the whiskey, and poured a little in his beer bottle. "Too much beer is bad for the liver," he said as he resumed his chair. "You have to dilute it with something every now and then." He took a swallow of the mixture, then said, "Anybody here know that Muriel Baxter?"

"If you mean the teacher, no," said Gibbon. "I know of her."

"I wonder how come she never got married." Morris was looking at the wake as he spoke.

"The story I heard," Corning put in, "was she was engaged to a guy who was killed in the war. You can take that for what it may be worth."

"Which war?" Morris asked.

"What difference? You're just as dead in one war as in any other."

"Yeah, but it's a way to guess her age."

"What's all this about?" Gibbon asked. "You got the hots for her or something?"

"Could be," said Morris.

"Edgar Morris, champion of lost causes," Corning said. "First it's anarchy, then it's Muriel Baxter. Did you ever think of trying something possible for a change?"

"Go ahead and laugh," Morris said, and took another pull on his bottle.

There was about an hour and a half of daylight left when they reached the rip. Gibbon rigged four lines, using both white and yellow feather lures, gave a rod to Morris and one to Sam, then called to Tuttle, who was still in the cabin. "Omar, your office hours are over!" he said. "Come out and fish!"

"I'll be right there," came Tuttle's voice, and Gibbon shrugged, put the fourth rod in a holder, and sat down and tested the drag on his own line.

The rip was caused by the tide flowing across a sandbar; on the upstream side the water was smooth, but when it reached the bar it began to swirl and boil and broke up into short, choppy waves. The idea was to keep the boat on the upstream side, and let the tide carry the lures back into the rip, where the fish were waiting for the smaller baitfish to be swept across the bar. When Corning started across the rip the boat began to buck and roll; the chairs skidded back and forth, and the men sitting in them had to brace themselves with one hand while they fished with the other. In short order Tuttle appeared from the cabin, his face the color of putty, and groped for his chair, which had tumbled into a corner of the cockpit. He didn't take the rod that Gibbon had rigged for him; he just hung on with both hands to whatever he could reach, and waited, wide-eyed and perspiring, for the motion to stop.

"The rip's just making up now," Corning observed. "She ought to be a real bitch later on."

"Hear any more of that code?" Gibbon asked, and Tuttle swallowed, started to speak, then nodded instead. "Try a shot of whiskey," Gibbon suggested. "That'll settle you down." Tuttle clenched his jaws and shook his head, and Gibbon turned back to his fishing.

They started near shore, where the bass had been caught earlier, but the fish had apparently moved. There were no birds diving and, more important, no fish even touched their lures. Corning scanned the water for any signs but saw nothing, so he maneuvered the boat slowly out along the rip to seaward, hoping at least to pick up a loner that had strayed from the school.

Sam had never done this kind of fishing, and he found himself waiting, almost holding his breath, for a fish to hit. It seemed to him that the water must be teeming with bass, all following his lure, and his muscles were tense as he waited for the strike that must come at any second. At Corning's suggestion they reeled in and checked their lures for weed, but the lures were clean, and as Sam let his run out he wondered what he'd do if a fish should take it before he'd had time to set the brake. But nothing happened; he might as well have been dragging his lure through the bathtub, and he slowly began to decide that the ocean was barren of fish, and that no more would ever be caught. He had a beer, to see if that would change his luck, but still nothing happened. The sun sank lower, the sky turned pink, and the horizon became dark and smoky. A light breeze sprang up, which riffled the surface of the water and put flecks of white in the rip.

It was Corning who broke the silence. "I wonder who that is," he said, and when they looked where he pointed they saw a ship, just visible in the darkening horizon haze. It was hard to tell how big or what kind it was; it was simply a hull, and at that distance it seemed not to be moving. "Could that be the guy who was sending the code?" he asked.

Tuttle, who had revived slightly in the fresh air, shrugged. "I can't tell by looking," he said. "I'd have to try to raise him, and get him to give his location. And if he was using code, he doesn't want his location known."

"I think I'll give him a try anyway," Corning said, reaching in for the microphone. "What frequency was he on?"

Tuttle hesitated. "The set isn't quite fixed yet," he said. "The sea got to me before I could get it back together. I'll fix it in a couple of minutes."

"The sooner, the better," Corning said quietly. "I don't like being out here—"

He didn't finish the sentence, because at that moment Sam felt a gigantic tug on his line; the tip of his rod snapped down in an arc, and he shouted, "Hey! Jesus!" as his line began to run out in short, shrieking jerks. "He's taking the line!" he cried. "What do I do?"

"Let him take it," Corning said. "Just keep your tip up, and don't give him any slack. Make him work a little before you try to bring him in."

"Fish!" Gibbon said as his rod bowed over, and then Morris said, "I'm on," and three lines were fast.

"Get your line out, Omar," Corning said to Tuttle, as he eased back on the throttle to lessen the strain on the others. Tuttle paid his line out slowly and hesitantly, as though afraid he might anger a fish by hooking it.

It seemed to Sam that he had hooked a wild horse. It tugged and bucked and veered from side to side, taking out more line than he was able to reel in, and his left hand, which was grasping the rod, ached all the way up to the elbow. With his right hand he would take a couple of turns on the reel whenever the pressure lessened, and by watching Gibbon he learned to ease the job by raising the tip of the rod as far as he could, then cranking in furiously as he lowered it. Gradually, by what seemed like half-inch steps, he began to work the fish toward the boat, then there would be a long shriek on his line, and it would all go out again. He was aware of Corning reaching over the side with a gaff and bringing a gleaming, flopping bass into the cockpit, but it was Morris's fish and not his, and his was still somewhere out of sight. With the speed cut and the wheel unattended, the boat drifted back into the rip and began to rock violently; Sam's chair almost overturned, and he was flung against Morris, who had somehow managed to foul his reel and was becoming enmeshed in long loops of line. All around them shrieking, squealing terns filled the air and dove into the water, harrying the baitfish that the bass were attacking from below, and all about them was noise and confusion. Finally, after what seemed like an hour, Corning brought Sam's fish aboard; Sam's arms were like lead, and when Corning threw the lure back in the water Sam let it run out slowly, glad for a small period of rest. A fish hit it before it had gone five yards, and the fight began again.

Suddenly Morris yelled, "Son of a *bitch!*" and Sam looked around to see Morris, his rod, and the snarls of tangled line go over the side. Corning, who had just taken a fish off Gibbon's line, jumped for the wheel, skidded in the fish slime on deck, and went down heavily. Cursing, he pulled himself up and opened the throttle as he swung the boat around. It was getting dark, and for a moment they lost sight of Morris's head in the rip, then Sam spotted a waving arm and pointed it out, and Corning headed for it at full speed, slamming the bow of the boat into the waves. Then he slowed down, so as not to hit the struggling man, and threw a line over the side. But one of Morris's hands was bleeding so badly he couldn't hang on, and they had to haul him into the boat like a giant tuna, with Sam lifting his arms while Gibbon got a boathook through his belt. When finally Morris lay, gasping and bleeding, on the deck, Corning looked down at him in quiet disgust.

"Well, I'll be dipped in shit and rolled in bread crumbs," Corning said. "How did you ever manage a stupid-ass trick like that?"

Morris tried to wrap a handkerchief around his bleeding hand, but it did no good. "I was trying to unsnarl my line," he said. "I threw the feather over the side to get it out of the way, and a goddam fish took it. My hand got caught in the line."

Corning looked around and saw they were much closer to the other boat, which showed simply as a shape in the gathering darkness. It carried no lights and was moving at about five knots. "A hell of a time to be without a radio," Corning said. "I'll just go over and see if I can borrow some first-aid gear."

"I'm all right," Morris said. "If you got a rag, it'll stop the bleeding."

"I don't have a rag, and I don't want you bleeding all over my deck. The rest of you, reel in your lines. The fishing's over for the evening."

But reeling in was not all that simple; two of the lines still had fish on them, and it was another ten minutes before they could be boated. Then Corning turned on his running lights and headed for the larger boat. As they approached, the other boat turned on its lights, and Corning headed for its stern so as to close without danger of collision. When they got near they saw something in the water ahead which looked like a tapered cylinder wrapped in life jackets. It was being towed, and when they had almost reached it a voice came out of the dark, loud and electronic and faintly frantic.

"Get the hell away from there!" it commanded.

Corning cupped his hands and shouted, "I need first aid! I have a casualty aboard!"

"Oh, cut it out," Morris said. "I'm not that bad. Give me a drink, and I'll be all right."

"I said get the hell away from there!" the voice repeated. "If you come any closer, we'll shoot!" Corning paused, trying to think what to say, and there was a pinpoint flash of light, a crack, and the hollow smack of a bullet hitting the water.

"He don't sound too friendly," Gibbon said. "Sounds like he don't want to see us."

Corning stepped back to the wheel, and veered his boat away. "I wonder what put the bug up *his* ass," he said.

"Do you know what that was he was towing?" Tuttle asked, as Corning opened the throttle and headed back toward land.

"Couldn't tell," Corning replied.

"Did you ever see a proton magnetometer?"

Corning glanced at him. "No, and I never saw a purple cow, either. What the hell are you talking about?"

Tuttle thought for a moment, then said, "That's the trouble. I'm not sure."

"Well, thanks for the tip anyway. If I should see one, I'll tell it you were asking."

Tuttle drifted back aft and looked at the dark loom of the other boat, which had turned off its lights. "You still got some of that whiskey?" he asked.

Gibbon, who was helping Sam bandage Morris's hand, said, "Right in the cooler chest, there. Just save some for the wounded."

Tuttle took a big swallow and gasped as it went down, then made his way forward and into the cabin, where he turned on the light and went to work completing his assembly of the radio.

6

Fenwick's funeral was described by lay observers as "the full treatment." Father O'Malley, resplendent in his newly cleaned vestments, conducted the service with an air of benevolent contentment, like a mother hen with a brood of prize chicks, and the honorary pallbearers included representatives from every branch of the town government. At first it was thought that the Selectmen should be the actual pallbearers, but a complication arose when it was pointed out that there were only five of them and one was a woman, and while no woman had ever been known to be a pallbearer, it might be taken amiss if Agnes were to be omitted. The matter was settled by having George Markey, Police Chief Maddox, Fire Chief Homer Benbow, Judge Cyrus

Pepper, Dr. Lucius Pardle, and Sergeant Ed Mancusi, of the State Police, carry the coffin. As Father O'Malley met them with their flower-covered burden and preceded them up the aisle to the altar, there were those in the congregation who reflected that it was the first time since the previous Easter that Fenwick had been in the church.

"And it took six men to get him here," Omar Tuttle whispered to Agnes.

"Shhh," said Agnes.

The choir, which had been in almost constant rehearsal since Fenwick's death, sang their "Ave Maria" and "Te Deum" with an expertise born of long practice, but Father O'Malley had decided, as a gesture to the non-Catholics among the mourners, to throw in "Now the Day Is Over," and "Lead, Kindly Light," which gave them some trouble. The contralto and the first tenor, who had been having an affair all winter and were no longer speaking, seemed determined to nudge one another off key, and the rest of the choir lacked the confidence to come in over and drown them out. The result was spotty to say the best, and everyone was relieved when the reading of the Gospel began.

Lester Turpin and his wife had invited Sam to sit with them, so they could identify the celebrities for Sam's newspaper coverage of the funeral, and Sam listened with fascination as Father O'Malley intoned:

"The reading today is from the Seventh Chapter of the Book of Matthew. 'Judge not, that ye be not judged. For with what judgment ye judge, ye shall be judged: and with what measure ye mete, it shall be measured to you again. And why beholdest thou the mote that is in thy brother's eye, but considerest not the beam that is in thine own eye? Or how wilt thou say to thy brother, Let me pull out the mote out of thine eye; and, behold, a beam *is* in thine own eye? Thou hypocrite, first cast out the beam out of thine own eye; and then shalt thou see clearly to cast out the mote out of thy brother's eye. Give not that which is holy unto the dogs, neither cast ye your pearls before swine, lest they trample them under their feet, and turn again and rend you.'"

Father O'Malley then went on to enlarge on this theme in his sermon, not mentioning Fenwick directly but managing to imply that Fenwick was beyond the criticism of mere mortals, and that everyone else should be so lucky. He concluded: "And when he comes before the Greatest Moderator of them all he will be lifted up in triumph and in glory, to life ever after. And if God in His infinite wisdom should grant to this island the blessing of independence from the crushing burdens that now oppress us, we may be sure that the spirit of Dennis Fenwick will sing the loudest hosanna of all the angel choir. Let us pray."

An almost visible shudder passed through the congregation as George Markey rose from his seat among the pallbearers and made his way to the lectern to deliver the eulogy. He cleared his throat, glanced at the blanket of flowers over the casket as though trying to memorize the design, then, pitching his voice to reach the people in the farthest pews, he said, "Friends, neighbors, islanders: I am here to bury Dennis, not to praise him. He needs no praise from me, because he was an honorable man. It has been said that the evil men do lives after them, while the good is often buried with them, but in Dennis's case it will be the good that lives on, while whatever bad there may have been will be buried with him, and soon forgotten."

The Turpins and Sam looked at one another with incredulity while Markey went on, and when he had finished, and people were lining up to take the wafers and wine of Holy Communion, Turpin said, "How in God's name did he ever get hold of *that*?"

"Ella must have given it to him," Turpin's wife replied. "He'd never have thought of it himself."

"She really must hate him. That was as good a job of sandbagging as I've ever seen."

"Don't be so sure. I'll bet nine out of ten poeple didn't spot it."

"Still. What a thing to do to a man."

"Why should she hate him?" Sam asked.

Turpin shook his head. "It's a long story."

"Considering what he had to work with, I don't think he did too badly," Turpin's wife said. "Mark Antony's speech was all sarcasm, and George made it sound sincere."

"Look at her," Turpin said, nodding toward the altar. "Don't tell me she didn't sandbag him."

They looked, and saw Ella Markey returning to her pew. She radiated more health and well-being than could be expected from the simple act of taking Communion, and Sam almost expected her to break into a song or a soft-shoe dance step.

"Something she's been doing agrees with her," he said.

"They say it always does," said Mrs. Turpin.

"Grace!" said Turpin, and she smiled and was quiet.

"I get an odd feeling about this service," Sam said. "I get the feeling people are trying to apologize for Fenwick without actually saying so."

"Nonsense," Turpin replied. "It's just their way of talking."

"But that reading from Matthew—why bring all that up? And why did he go into the pearls-before-swine business? That's a whole new train of thought."

"You're looking at it too closely. You're trying to find things that aren't there."

"I'm just taking my cue from what I heard."

Turpin smiled. "You're new here. Some words have different meanings from what you're used to."

Following Communion there was a final rendition by the choir, then a prayer for Fenwick's soul, and then the Benediction. In all, the service had taken forty-five minutes, which was short by some standards. But Father O'Malley hadn't wanted to antagonize the Protestants and agnostics present, so he kept it under an hour, which he found was the limit of the attention span of non-believers. If they went in dreading an hour-and-a-half service and came out in half that time, he found they were pleased and grateful, and this was always a good thing. Father O'Malley liked to keep as many people happy as possible.

Outside, George Markey received congratulations on his eulogy while his wife Ella stood quietly by, listening for anyone who might have spotted the source. But if anyone had they didn't mention it, and Ella was able to divide her attention between her husband and those of her friends and acquaintances who greeted her. Out of the crowd emerged a short man with a Florida tan and bright resort clothes, and as he approached her husband she made a mental note to find out what kind of man wore white loafers and no socks to a funeral. The man shook Markey's hand effusively and said something she was unable to hear, and after a while he moved away, his face still set in a rictus-like parody of a smile.

"Who was that creep?" she asked in a low voice.

"Never saw him before," Markey replied. "I think he said his name is Williams."

"What did he want?"

"He just congratulated me on the speech."

She shook her head. "He wants something," she said. "Nobody could be that oily without a reason."

"All right, then, you tell me," Markey said testily. "All I know is what he said. He apparently has a lot of influential friends."

Ella knew when she'd run into a stone wall, so was quiet.

Norris Webster also spotted Williams, and decided to see what would happen if he took the direct approach. "Excuse me," he said as Williams started away. "May I ask you a question?"

Williams stopped, and looked him over. "What do you want?" he said.

"I believe you know Agnes Tuttle," Webster said. "I was just—"

"Agnes who?" said Williams.

"Agnes Tuttle, the Selectwoman. You and she—"

"Never heard of her." Williams turned and walked off, leaving Webster staring after him.

Oh-ho, Webster thought. I guess there's more to this than meets the eye. He looked at his watch and, observing that it was almost noon, headed for his liquor store to see if the funeral had significantly changed the day's take. He was aware that business was usually slow the morning of a funeral, but in this case he thought the pattern might have changed. His habit was to check the cash register twice daily, in order to spot any irregularities of a suspicious nature. He knew to the penny how much money he had and where it was, and he decided to bring this same attention to detail to the matter of Agnes Tuttle's private life. Normally he could analyze a person's liquor account and get a rough outline of their activities, but not knowing Williams's name he was unable to go into his books for any hint in that direction. The first move, obviously, would be to identify Williams.

When he got to the store, his clerk was sitting behind the cash register, reading a copy of *Oui*. He jumped up as Webster entered, and dropped the magazine to the floor. "Short funeral?" he said, trying to cover his confusion.

"Long enough," Webster replied. "Do you know a guy, maybe in his early sixties, wears flashy clothes and has light-blond hair? Looks like a horse when he smiles."

The clerk thought. "Is he summer or winter?" he asked.

"Summer, from the way he dresses. I never saw him around, but that don't prove much."

"It's hard to say," the clerk replied. "A lot of them summer people look alike, what with the clothes and all. Can't tell 'em apart any more'n you can a Chinee."

"If this guy'd been in here, I think you'd know him."

"Maybe he phones in his orders, or has the butler do it. Maybe he even brings his own—some of them summer people bring all their likker up on the company plane."

"All them company planes should crash," Webster muttered. "They're breaking the law."

"Well, without seeing this guy I can't tell you who he is," the clerk said. "Is it all that important?"

"You never can tell." Webster moved behind the cash register and opened the cover to remove the tape, then spotted the copy of *Oui* the clerk had dropped. He picked it up and leafed through it slowly. "Christamighty, Ferris, why don't you go get laid?" he said, handing it back. "It'd be a lot better for you than looking at all that garbage."

"I can't get laid," the clerk replied. "I'm broke."

"I didn't say you had to spend any money on it. Don't you know someone who'll put out for nothing?"

"Yeah, but she's an awful dog. And even she wants a Coke, or something. If maybe I could have an advance on—"

"Then you'll just have to wait till payday. Think about Columbus—he didn't get laid for forty days and forty nights, so compared to him you're in clover."

"Thinking about Columbus don't do nothing for what ails me. Anybody who can get his jollies thinking about Columbus has gotta be some weird duck."

"It's nothing more'n mind over matter." Webster tore off the tape, closed the cover, picked up the charge slips, and headed for his office. "It's a lousy two weeks to payday, and anyone can hold still that long."

"Speak for yourself," the clerk muttered, half under his breath, and opened up the copy of *Oui*.

In front of the church, Sam and the Turpins watched the crowd as it dispersed, some people going to their homes and some to the Sink Hole and some to the Waterfront Club; although it was Friday and technically a working day, there was no thought of anything's being accomplished between now and five o'clock. The day was shot, and different people took their own different ways of making use of what remained of it.

"When do you want me to do this story?" Sam asked as the Turpins started for their car.

"Monday will be plenty of time," Turpin replied. "I've got the obit and the editorial in this week's issue, so anytime before next Wednesday will be all right. But if you have it done by Monday we can go over it, and make sure it's what the people want to read."

"Which is what?" said Sam.

"Their own names," said Turpin with a smile, and he took his wife's elbow as he helped her into the car.

Emil Corning and Dr. Carl Amberson were both on the Conservation Board, and neither one had spoken to the other since their near-fisticuffs at town meeting. Now Dr. Amberson, who was secretary of the Board, spotted Corning and his wife in the thinning crowd, and decided it was time to mend the breach. He greeted them as though nothing had happened, and said, "Emil, I suppose we ought to have a Board meeting soon. When would be good for you?"

"What's come up?" Corning asked.

"Nothing in particular, but I think we ought to see what our stand will be in the event of secession. We'll have a lot more power, and I think we should decide how to use it."

Corning shrugged. "Any time is good for me," he said. It appeared he was still nursing the remains of his grudge.

"It seems to me we ought to be ready to take some positive action," Dr. Amberson went on, in as friendly a tone as he could manage. "The big danger, if we secede, will be that people will just drift along and take everything for granted."

"All right," Corning said. "You name the time, and I'll be there."

"I'll talk with the others, and let you know." Dr. Amberson tipped his hat to Mrs. Corning, then rejoined his wife.

"So you're still speaking?" Jeanette Amberson said.

"Barely," her husband replied. "I think the son of a bitch has something up his sleeve."

When the Markeys got home, George Markey said to Ella, "How do you think it went?"

"I think it went just fine," she replied. "Everyone seemed to like it."

Markey sat on the sofa, undid his tie, and stretched out his legs. "That calls for a drink," he said. "Vodka and Campari. Lots of ice." Ella began to make the drink, found the ice bucket was empty, and took it to the kitchen. "And a twist of orange," Markey called after her.

When she returned he was thumbing through a battered copy of the plays of Shakespeare. He stopped at a bookmark and began to read. "I wish he was a little easier to figure out," he said. "That highfalutin language gets me down."

"Like what?" said Ella, dropping ice into his glass.

"Like"—he ran his finger over a page—"like 'What cause withholds you then to mourn for him?' Just what the hell is that supposed to mean?"

"Just what it says. It means you loved Caesar once; why don't you mourn for him now?"

Markey studied the page. "It seems to me he took a goddam roundabout way of saying it."

Ella handed him his drink. "That was the way they spoke then."

"When I thought of using this I wondered if people would be thrown by the language, but then I thought, what the hell, I can fix it up so anyone can understand it. I guess I was right, because nobody seemed to complain."

"Everyone I talked to thought it was fine," Ella said, making a drink for herself.

"I think it was a good idea, if I do say so myself." He riffled the pages to the front of the book, and looked at the handwritten name. "Ella Blodgett. Your maiden name looks funny now." He closed the book and tossed it aside.

"I'll take it," Ella said, holding out her hand.

He passed it to her. "Keep it around, in case I should ever need it again. You never can tell."

"No," she said, holding the book close to her. "You never can."

"What about young Sam?" Grace Turpin said, taking off her hat. "Does he plan to stay here long?"

"I don't think so," her husband replied. "He's just kind of groping his way at the moment."

"He seems awfully nice, but shouldn't you know a little more about a person before you hire him?"

"I haven't hired him, exactly. I've just retained him to do a couple of jobs until he gets himself straightened out."

"Straightened out of what? Is he in trouble?"

"I told you, I don't know. I think he just doesn't know what he wants to do. He says he's writing a play, and you know what *that* means."

"Oh, the poor dear."

He looked out the window. "You know," he said slowly, "I sometimes wonder if—"

"Lester Turpin, we've been married thirty-five years, and if you ever write another play I will walk out of this house so fast it'll make your head spin. I wasn't strong enough for it when I was younger, and I'm certainly not strong enough for it now. If you want to go back to the jungle you can, but I'm telling you now it's not for me."

"It's not for me either; you know that. I was just going to say I sometimes wonder if I'd done things differently, and hadn't listened to everybody's advice, it might have worked. I'm not planning on going anywhere."

She was quiet for a moment, then said, "I'm sorry. You know what they say about a burned child."

"You're not alone in that."

"Let's have a drink," she said. "This day has made me jittery."

"How come?"

"I don't know how come. I just want a drink."

He went to the kitchen, took a half-gallon jug of white wine from the refrigerator, and poured two glasses. As he handed Grace's glass to her, he said, "How are your vibes?"

"Terrible," she replied. "My nerve ends are twanging like harp strings."

"About anything in particular?"

"I don't know. I get the feeling we're all on the edge of a precipice, looking down into a bottomless pit."

He lifted his glass. "Well, cheers anyway," he said.

"Cheers," she replied.

When Judge Cyrus Pepper and his wife got home, Matilda Pepper went to the kitchen without removing her hat and put a kettle on the stove. Her husband followed and observed her with mild interest.

"What's that for?" he asked.

"You go lie down," she replied. "I'm fixing you some broth."

"I'd rather have a drink."

"Do as I tell you. You're too old to be carrying a heavy thing like that coffin—if you're not careful your back will go out again, and you know how impossible you are when you're sick."

"There were five other men with me, and it wasn't all that heavy anyway. I'd much rather have a drink."

"You'll have a drink when I say you can. You're going to have this broth first, and then you're going to lie down. Now, go on. Get out of the kitchen."

He turned and drifted into the living room, where he sat on the sofa and began to thumb through an old copy of *House & Garden*. After a while he tossed the magazine aside and said, "I wonder if we're really going to secede."

"What did you say?" came Matilda's voice from the kitchen. "You'll have to speak up!"

"I said I wonder if we're really going to secede!" the judge repeated, more loudly than he'd intended.

"You don't have to scream," Matilda replied, appearing with a mug of beef broth. "I'm not deaf, you know. Now, lie down and take this." She handed him the mug.

"It's easier if I take it sitting up," he said. "Is it all right if I do that, and then lie down later?"

"Do whatever you feel like," Matilda said. "I'm just thinking of what's good for you."

He blew on the broth, took a tentative sip, and set the mug down. "What I meant about seceding," he said, as though she'd asked him, "was that if we do, it's going to put me in a funny position."

"Oh?" She removed her hat and set it on the newel post.

"Yes. I'm appointed by the State, and if we break away from the State that will mean I legally have no power."

"Well, don't point it out to anyone, and I'm sure they won't think of it. You can go on just as you are."

He took another sip of the broth. "And that brings up the next thing. I hate being in charge of people's lives."

"In what way?"

"In changing their whole life style. It's up to me to say that a human being, who has been free as a bird, must now go and be penned up like some animal in a cage. I hate it. If I had my way everybody would be free, and could do as they please."

"You'd be very popular with rapists and murderers."

"Oh, I don't know that it makes any difference. I used to be tough—you know as well as I do, they called me Castrating Cy—but then the same people would appear before me over and over again, and I began to wonder what was the point of my being there. Now I think maybe the realistic thing to do is just arrest them for appearance's sake, and turn them loose. It comes to the same thing in the end."

She looked at him for a moment, then said, "I think that funeral has made you depressed. Funerals do that to you—you get a whither-whither feeling, and begin to cry."

"I'm not crying! I'm just thoughtful."

"There's very little difference. You cried after Dormer Lindblad's funeral, and asked me to join you in a suicide pact."

"That was different. Besides, I wasn't serious."

"You looked awfully serious to me. It was a good thing I'd taken the blade out of my razor."

"Pish. That was just a gesture."

"Well, you can make another gesture now, and go upstairs till I have lunch ready. Take off your shoes and lie down, and in a half hour or so you'll feel more cheerful."

"But I—"

"Don't argue. Take your broth and go upstairs. And see if you can go to the bathroom. That always makes you feel better."

She left him and went back into the kitchen, and after a few moments he rose, picked up the mug of broth, and went quietly up the stairs.

When the Turpins had driven away, Sam pocketed his notes and headed for the Sink Hole. He didn't dare hope that Lennie would be there; it seemed like weeks since he'd seen her, when in actual fact it had been only three days. He told himself that if he'd seen her every day he wouldn't be this anxious, and that furthermore he didn't have anything to be anxious about, but he couldn't help looking around the room when he arrived, observing the waitresses rather than the vacant chairs. As he'd expected, she wasn't there, so he took the first place he saw and sat down, wondering what to do with the rest of the afternoon. He decided to interview a few more people on the secession question, then go to the paper and write the story. That would leave him the weekend to do the piece on Fenwick's funeral, which would require some care—among other things, to make sure all the names were spelled correctly.

The same waitress he'd had before appeared at the table, and made a big production of wiping the already clean surface, bending over to give him a full view of her breasts, of which she was clearly and justifiably proud. "Hi, there," she said, looking at him. "The same old beer?"

"Please," Sam replied, changing his position slightly.

She vanished, and returned in short order with a foaming stein, which she put in front of him. "In case you were wondering," she said, "Lennie's not on today."

"Is she sick?" Sam asked.

"No, she's having domestic problems." The girl resumed her polishing of the table.

"Oh," said Sam. "Is she married?" Jiggly-joggly went the breasts.

"Well, yes and no." Jiggly-joggly-jiggly-joggly. "It's kind of hard to tell." Jiggly.

"What's so hard about it?" Jiggly-joggly. "A person is either married or they're not."

The girl straightened up. "In this case they are, but they probably won't be for long."

"I see." It had never occurred to Sam that Lennie might be married, and he felt oddly let down. "Well, I guess that's the way it goes."

"Yeah. The minute you plan a picnic, you know something's bound to go wrong."

"What picnic?"

"Lennie and I were going to have a picnic today—I'm off from three till seven—but now she's all snarled up in her personal life, and I'm stuck with the makings."

"Where would you picnic today? That wind still has fangs in it."

"I know a place. It's a hollow in the dunes, and if that gets too cold there's a shack nearby. We picnic there all the time."

"Well, well." Sam could sense the question coming up, but did nothing to avoid it.

"Would you like to take Lennie's place?" the girl asked.

He started to think of all the reasons against it, then said, "Yes, that sounds fine. How do I get there?"

"I'll get a couple of bikes. Come by here at three, and I'll have everything ready."

Well, what the hell, Sam thought, as the girl went to another table. It beats staring at a piece of paper in a typewriter.

The girl, it developed, had studied yoga and was as supple as an eel. She had muscles in several bizarre places and could use them with the dexterity of a juggler or the power of a milkmaid. She was not quite a contortionist, but it seemed to Sam that odd parts of her showed up in the most unlikely attitudes, and he was hard put to it to keep pace with her gyrations. The blanket, which she had originally spread in the hollow in the dunes, became too sandy for either comfort or common sense, and they repaired to the shack for the duration of the afternoon. The prandial part of the picnic consisted of a bottle of white wine, slices of salami, cheese, ham, and red onion, and a loaf of Italian bread. When they had finished eating they put the shack in order and buried their debris, then they dressed and went out, closing the door behind them. The girl mounted her bicycle, said, "Ouch," and started down the road. Sam pedaled after her, and when he got abreast he said, "Who owns that shack?"

"No idea," she replied. "I've never seen anyone near it. It probably belongs to some native."

They pedaled in silence for a while, and then he said, "One more question."

"What?"

"What's your name?"

She laughed. "I was wondering when you'd get around to that. You promise not to jeer?"

"Of course."

"It's Felicity."

"Oh," said Sam. "Well—"

"I'll say it for you," she said. "It takes all kinds to make a world."

7

The Conservation Board consisted, aside from Dr. Amberson and Emil Corning, of Dr. Lucius Pardle, George Markey, and Norris Webster. Their primary function was to stake out, or purchase, certain land areas that would be immune to development, on the sensible theory that over-development would in the long run turn the island into a seaside slum and destroy the attraction that brought people there in the first place. The hitch, of course, came in where to draw the line between a healthy building program and suburban sprawl, and no two people seemed to agree as to exactly where this line should be. In the entire history of the Board, no meeting had ever come up with a unanimous decision except that to adjourn. The vote was always split, and often bitter.

Dr. Amberson had managed to get the others to agree to meet on Tuesday evening, with the promise that the meeting would be a short one. He wanted, as he'd told Corning, to think about the future, and all he intended to do was give the members a few possible ideas to consider, so they could have come to some conclusions when they met, at a later date, to establish a definite policy. He knew better than to hope for anything conclusive in a single meeting.

They met at seven o'clock, in the Selectmen's room of the town office building. When Dr. Amberson arrived Sam was waiting in the hall, and Dr. Amberson looked at him without recognition.

"Anything I can do for you?" he asked.

"Yes, sir. My name is Sam Jensen. Mr. Turpin sent me over to cover the meeting."

"You mean for the newspaper?"

"Yes, sir."

Dr. Amberson thought briefly while he unlocked the room and turned on the lights. "I guess there's no harm in that," he said finally. "But I don't think you'll get much of a story."

"Well, he thought that what with the possibility of secession and all, it might be a good idea to know what the different groups are doing."

"It would be a splendid idea," Dr. Amberson said, "if only the groups themselves knew." He set his briefcase on the table and unsnapped the clasp. "Just sit in the back of the room, there, and I don't think anyone will object."

Sam took a seat as indicated and watched the others as they came in. They were all familiar to him except Dr. Pardle, who reminded him of a Yorkshire terrier in a high wind. Hair seemed to sprout out in all directions, and his eyes were squinted as though peering into a gale. When Corning came in he recognized Sam, and turned to Dr. Amberson.

"A new member of the Board?" he asked.

"No," said Dr. Amberson. "He's from the paper."

"The *paper?*" Corning stared at Sam. "Did Lester Turpin send you here?"

"Yes, sir," Sam replied.

"I don't think we want that," Corning said to Dr. Amberson. "These meetings aren't supposed to be publicized."

"There's no rule one way or the other," Dr. Amberson replied. "They're open to the public unless there's a specific reason for an executive session."

"Well, I move for an executive session right now."

"Why? Do you have something confidential to discuss?"

"No, but I don't think everything we say should be blatted about in public."

"Sorry. That's not good enough."

"What the hell," Markey put in. "We can let him sit in for a while, then throw him out if anything—uh—delicate comes up. We don't want to antagonize the press if we don't have to. Isn't that right, Doc?" He turned to Dr. Pardle.

"I knew his brother," Dr. Pardle replied. "Died of the whooping cough, back in '08."

Markey laughed and slapped him on the back, jarring his dentures loose. "That's telling 'em, Doc!" he said.

"All right, gentlemen," Dr. Amberson said quietly. "The sooner we begin, the sooner we'll be done. My main reason for calling the meeting was to start us thinking on what our approach will be in the event of secession. To give you one example, if we secede from the State, then all State building codes and laws will be void, and we'll be left with a vacuum in which anybody can do as they please."

"That's not up to Conservation, that's up to the Building Inspector," Corning put in. "Who builds what is none of our business."

"In the strictest sense, you're right. But Conservation deals with the preservation of property as well as of land, and—"

"I say keep our noses out of it," Corning said. "It doesn't concern us, so we should stay clear."

"That was just one example," Dr. Amberson said, with forced calm. "There are many others. I simply don't want us to be caught without a plan, in the event that all rules are suddenly suspended. I believe we should think ahead a little, and—"

"I hope you don't mind me butting in," said Markey, "but you're getting into Selectmen's country there. We're the ones who make the rules for the community, and we're the ones who'll take over if we secede. Or I should say when we secede. Conservation doesn't make any rules; it follows them."

Dr. Amberson looked at Webster. "Norris, do you have any comments?" he asked.

"The way I see it, we ought to pull in our horns," Webster replied. "Every time we accept a piece of land for Conservation we're doing the town out of tax money, so the town raises the taxes to make up for it. Until we get rid of *all* taxes, I say we shouldn't accept no more land, because we're just throwing good money after bad. That's all *I* got to say."

"We're going to go into that shortly," said Dr. Amberson. Then, to Dr. Pardle: "Lucius? Any comments?"

"Any day but Thursday," Dr. Pardle said, and Markey laughed and slapped him on the back again.

"All right, then." Dr. Amberson pulled some papers from his briefcase, scanned them quickly, and said, "Here we have something of a mystery."

"I move we go into executive session," Corning said, glancing at Sam.

"There's no need for that right now," Dr. Amberson said. "Here are the facts: Conservation has just been notified that Dennis Fenwick left us, in his will, a hundred and forty-five acres of land in the center of the island, in a triangular piece centered roughly on Flack's Pond and running north to Blueberry Hill, west to Claman's sheep pasture, and south to what is known as the Flat Rock. We—"

"God damn it, now I insist we go into executive session!" Corning said.

Dr. Amberson looked at him with mild curiosity. "Oh?" he said. "Why?"

"I'll tell you when the reporter has left the room."

Nobody spoke, and after a moment Dr. Amberson turned to Sam. "Would you mind leaving us for a few minutes?" he said.

Sam rose, and Corning glanced at him and said, "Nothing personal, you understand."

"I understand," said Sam, and then, to Dr. Amberson: "Should I wait outside?"

"I should think so," Dr. Amberson replied. "This probably won't take long."

"I wouldn't bet on it," Corning said.

When Sam had left, Dr. Amberson said to Corning, "All right. You have the floor."

"Dennis couldn't have left that land to Conservation," Corning said, his face beginning to turn red. "It is a goddamned, flat-ass, out-and-out impossibility!"

"Why?" Dr. Amberson was becoming calmer as Corning grew more angry.

"Because I own it, that's why!"

"Are you sure?"

"Of course I'm sure! What the hell do you think I am—some goddam ninny who doesn't know his own property? That land is mine, and I can prove it!"

"How?"

"I have the deeds! Do you want me to go get them?"

"Well"—Dr. Amberson cleared his throat—"when I learned of this bequest I called Charlie Ketchum, in the Land Office, and asked him to verify the boundaries—purely as a matter of form, you understand. He called back in a while and said there seemed to be someting odd about the whole thing, and when I asked him what, he said he'd rather not go into it on the phone. He said he'd bring the papers here tonight, and let us see for ourselves."

"But I've *got* the papers!" Corning protested. "All he can have are duplicates of mine!"

"We'll just have to see." Dr. Amberson looked at his watch. "I told him to be here at seven, but I guess in his business time doesn't mean much. He deals in decades rather than hours."

"Very funny," Corning said. "Remind me to laugh."

"Brings to mind a case I had in the big flu epidemic," Dr. Pardle said. "The one in '19. Had a patient quit breathing and go cyanotic on me—blue as a Yale sweater. I figured it was the mucus and all had clogged his breath pipe, so I did a tracheotomy right there on the spot. Come to find out, it had nothing to do with the flu; he'd swallowed the cork on a pill bottle, and it got lodged down there tight as a bung. That was before we had these plastic tops."

"So you saved his life?" said Markey.

"Well, not exactly. He died later on that day. Never knew for sure what got him."

There was a rattle at the door, then it opened and Charlie Ketchum appeared, his arms full of file folders and rolled-up maps. The Board members watched in silence as he spread his documents on the table, and then he pawed around among the papers until he found the one he wanted. He looked at Corning and said, "I understand you bought this land?"

"I sure as hell did," Corning replied. "I can show you the papers."

"I have the copies here. And when you bought it, was it mortgaged or was it unencumbered?"

"It was free and clear. No strings."

Ketchum found another paper. "Well, here's the interesting thing," he said. "Apparently it *was* mortgaged, and for the next ten years Dennis Fenwick paid the mortgage installments, so the title reverted to him."

"That's impossible!" Corning shouted, and when Ketchum passed him the paper he held it as though it were an asp. "I was told—" His voice became strangulated with rage, and he stopped.

"Who was your lawyer?" Ketchum asked.

"What? Oh—come to think of it, Dennis was."

Ketchum nodded, then unrolled a map. "Now, here's the property line the last time it was surveyed, which shows . . ." He went into the details of the land but nobody was listening, and he finally rolled up the map and concluded, "So according to the terms of the will, that is all Conservation land as of now, and the Fenwick estate takes the tax deduction."

"I'll contest the goddam will, is what I'll do," Corning said.

Ketchum shrugged. "Do you have it anywhere in writing that the land was unencumbered?"

"Not in writing, no. But I was given to understand—"

"Then you'll be wasting your time to take it to court. They don't go by hearsay, especially when the other party to the hearsay is dead." Ketchum rolled up the map and looked around. "Are there any other questions I could help you with?"

Dr. Amberson glanced at the Board members: Corning was in shock, Markey looked bemused, Webster was glancing at his watch, and Dr. Pardle was quietly chortling at some memory. "No, I guess not," Dr. Amberson said. "I think we might as well adjourn. And thank you all for coming."

"No trouble," Ketchum said, and headed for the door.

Sam was in the hall as they all trooped out, and Dr. Amberson looked at him and said, "Sorry, but it turned out to be a short meeting."

"Can you tell me what went on?" Sam asked.

Dr. Amberson shook his head. "I wish I could, but I can't."

Markey followed Ketchum into the Land Office, where Ketchum was returning the various documents to the files. "Just out of curiosity, Charlie," Markey said, "was there any other name than Dennis's on those deeds?"

"The deeds?" said Ketchum. "No. Why?"

"Or on the reversion of title?"

"No. Should there have been?"

"Not necessarily. I just wondered."

"All it said was in view of Dennis Fenwick having paid the mortgage for ten years, the title now was his."

"Who drew it up?"

"I guess he did. Can you think of anyone else who might?"

"Now that you mention it, no . . . Well, that's the way it goes, I guess."

"Sure is. Win a few, lose a few."

"All right, then, Charlie, good night."

"Good night, George."

Markey went outside, where the sky was crimson in the sunset and the windows of the waterfront buildings seemed to glow with fire. A herring gull, perched on the roof of a shed, stretched out its neck and brayed a maniacal laugh, then took off and swooped low over the water in search of garbage. Markey's face, as he headed for his car, was set and expressionless, and his lips barely moved as he muttered, "That bastard—that dirty, double-crossing son of a bitch."

Sam was of two minds as to what to do about the newspaper story. One thing would be simply to run a paragraph saying there had been a short meeting, at which general subjects were discussed before the Board went into executive session, and the other would be to dig around a little and try to find out what had happened. Corning, he knew, wouldn't tell him, nor would Dr. Amberson, although he might get something from Charlie Ketchum or Norris Webster, or conceivably even from George Markey. And if he *could* get something in the paper, so much the better; Turpin was paying him space rates rather than a flat salary.

He saw Markey's blue Mercedes zoom away from the office building and head uptown, and he mentally crossed Markey off his list for the evening. Everything considered, he figured that Webster would be the most likely prospect; Webster would undoubtedly be at his liquor store until the nine o'clock closing time. The store, which was called the Fo'c'sle Grog Shop, was strategically located on that part of the waterfront where anyone going to or from the wharves had to pass it, and Webster did a brisk business not only with tourists but also with boat crews, fishermen, and other traditionally thirsty types. Sam now headed for the red and green running lights that flanked the store's front entrance, trying to think of a ploy that would get Webster to talk.

As Sam went in, the clerk was coming out, and Webster was calling after him, "Remember, a half hour don't mean forty minutes and it don't mean thirty-five; a half hour means thirty minutes, no more and no less."

"Christ, don't I know it," the clerk muttered as he hurried past Sam. "I barely got time to piss, much less eat."

Webster looked at Sam. "Yes, sir," he said. "What can I do for you?"

"I'm not quite sure," Sam replied. "I'd like to look around."

"It's all here," said Webster, gesturing to the shelves. "Anything a man could ask for. Our motto is 'Your Thirst Is Our Living.'"

"Do you have Aalborg akvavit?" Sam asked.

"No call for that sort of stuff," Webster replied quickly. "Try again, in English."

On the pretext of studying the labels, Sam said, "You missed quite a fishing trip last week."

"When was that?" Webster's cheerful manner was beginning to fade.

"When we went out on Corning's boat. From the Waterfront Club."

"Oh, yes. I was busy."

"That's right." Still studying the shelves, Sam said, "Was there anything important at that meeting just now?"

"You mean Conservation?" Webster said. "Not much. They're all about the same."

"I gather there was some ruckus about the land Fenwick left."

"You might say that."

"But nothing out of the ordinary?"

"Hard to tell. Probably not."

There was a pause, and Sam said, "Do you have Irish Leprechaun beer?"

"Not after St. Pat's Day. That's the only time we get a call for it. You go to the Sink Hole now and then, don't you?"

"Now and then," Sam agreed.

"Did I see you there the day Agnes Tuttle was having lunch with some weird guy looked like a window dummy?"

"Yes, I think so."

"You don't happen to know his name, do you?"

"I don't recall. What was it that got Corning so upset about the Fenwick land?"

"This and that."

"It sounded as though he thought *he* owned it."

"That guy with Agnes—you know what he does for a living?"

"No. But I know someone who knows his name."

"Who?"

"Did Corning think he owned the land?"

"You might put it that way."

"George Markey knows his name. He introduced himself to Markey after the funeral."

Webster nodded.

"What's Corning going to do about it?" Sam said.

"Not much he can do. Now—are you going to buy something, or can I start doing the accounts?"

"I guess there's nothing more I need. It was nice talking to you."

"Same to you," said Webster, putting his key in the cash register. "Have a good day."

Well, Sam thought, when he got outside, I'm just about where I was before—several hints, but no story. He decided to walk along the wharves and breathe in the air of the waterfront while he tried to sort matters out in his mind. It was too early in the season for the large boats to be in, but he could dimly see the small fishing and scalloping boats moored in their slips, and hear the slap of the waves against their hulls. The wind was from the east, bringing with it the smell and the chill of the open ocean, and mingled with it were the smells of seaweed, tidal flats, and creosote. A blinking red light marked the harbor entrance, and farther away a pinpoint of green light winked on and off, identifying the seaward end of the jetty. There was silence except for the small sounds of the waves, and the occasional tapping of a loose halyard against a mast. Sam breathed deeply, and all at once it seemed that nothing mattered except his being there; the land hassles and the Conservation Board and the idea of secession were no more important than the barnacles on the pilings, and he wondered why people became so worked up over relatively trivial matters.

He remembered the night he'd gone AWOL from the Army: they were on night maneuvers and he'd been creeping across a field, under instructions to get as close to the Blue Army as he could, and report their disposition back to the Green Army command post. He'd crawled for what seemed like a mile, festooned with all sorts of communication equipment, and then he'd heard a noise ahead and had dropped flat, waiting. After a while he rolled on his back and looked up at the sky, where the stars were bright and hypnotic and in some areas so close togther they looked like luminous smoke, and as he identified the Big Dipper and Polaris and Orion and the Sisters of the Pleiades a feeling of the lunacy of what he was doing came over him, and he shrugged off his equipment, stood up, and walked off at right angles to his previous track. At one point, and at one point only, he was stopped by a sentry demanding the password; he replied sourly, "I'll give you three fucking guesses," to which the sentry said, "Don't blame *me*, man," and let him pass. He walked the rest of the night unchallenged.

Now, as he neared the end of the wharf, he heard the sound of someone blowing their nose, and saw that what he'd at first taken for a small barrel was in fact a person—a female—sitting hunched up with her feet hanging over the water. She blew her nose again, and Sam guessed she'd been crying.

"Excuse me," he said, and started away.

She said, "Oh!" and turned around, and even from her silhouette he could tell it was Lennie. "It's you!" she said in a clogged voice. "What are *you* doing here?"

"Just taking the air. I didn't mean to disturb you."

"You didn't. I'm glad to see you." She patted the planking beside her. "Sit down."

He squatted beside her, and caught the same lilies-of-the-valley scent he'd noticed before. "I've been wondering where you were," he said.

"Yes. So Phil told me." Her voice sounded flat.

"Who's Phil?" he asked.

"Felicity. The waitress. Surely you remember *her*."

"Oh. Uh—yes." There was an odd note to her voice, which suggested that Felicity might not be the totally closed-mouth type. "I just learned her name the other day."

"So she said. It takes all kinds to make a world."

God damn it, he thought. I might as well have laid the Associated Press wire service. "Some things happen by surprise," he said.

"Don't apologize. It's nothing to me." She laughed, but the effect was dimmed by the fact that her voice was still clogged.

"Well"—he tried to think of a way to change the subject—"what's that other expression? Water under the dam?"

"You mean water *over* the dam. Over the dam, or under the bridge."

"That's right. Anyway, forget it. I'm kind of rattled. Let's talk about something else. I went to—"

"Why are you rattled?"

He stopped, and thought a moment. "I guess because I never thought I'd go to bed with anyone named Phil."

She lay back on the planks and laughed until she was almost crying again. Then she sat up slowly, and once more used her handkerchief. "My, it's a long time since I laughed like that," she said.

"Whatsername said you were having some trouble," Sam said. "I'm sorry."

"Well, it'll pass. I guess it already has; now it's just the matter of getting used to it."

"Is there anything I can do?"

"Nothing I can think of. But thanks anyway."

He started to say something more, but sensed she wanted to close the subject, so he said only, "If you need anything, feel free to call."

"Thank you."

They sat for a while in silence, looking out over the water, and then Lennie shivered. "I guess I'd better go home," she said. Before he could offer to take her, she added, "And I'm such lousy rotten company I wouldn't ask a dog to come with me. You trot along to the Hole, and if anyone asks you, tell them I'll be back to work tomorrow. That'll be the only way I can keep from going crazy."

"Can't I—"

"No, thank you. Good night." She turned away, and he heard her walk down the dock, then crunch across a footpath to the street. He saw her pass quickly through the yellow glow of a streetlight, and then she was gone.

When he arrived at the Sink Hole the music was in full blast, and he took the one empty seat he could find, in a darkened corner at the far end of the room. He didn't think any of the waitresses had seen him, but in a few minutes Felicity arrived with a stein of beer, and set it in front of him. She said something he couldn't understand, and he shrugged and they both waited for the number of be over. Then they both started to talk, and both stopped.

"Go ahead," she said.

"I just saw Lennie," Sam said. "She said to tell you she'd be back to work tomorrow." Felicity nodded, and with a slight edge to his voice he went on, "She also had a fairly clear picture of our picnic at the shack."

"She must have a good imagination," Felicity said quickly. "Which reminds me—how deep did you bury the garbage?"

"I don't know," Sam replied. "You saw me—I'd say a foot or so. Why?"

"Some dog must have been messing around. I was out there today, and it was all dug up."

"Well, he can't have got much. All I buried was a wine bottle and some scraps."

Felicity started to say something more, then a customer called her and the music started up, and Sam settled back with his beer.

Next day, when he went to the newspaper office, he told Turpin about the Conservation meeting and added, "Apparently Fenwick did Corning out of some land, but I don't know any more than that. I think I could probably find out more if I dug around, but I wanted to ask you first if I should."

"I'm glad you did," Turpin replied. "Forget the whole thing."

"You mean don't even mention the meeting?" Sam saw his pay for one night's work slipping away.

"No point mentioning it if you can't say what happened. And whatever they did in executive session is none of our business. This is a reporting newspaper and not an investigating one, and that's the end of it." Turpin saw the expression on Sam's face, and added, "But as far as pay is concerned, we'll consider you wrote about a half a column. Does that seem fair?"

"It does indeed," said Sam. "I couldn't ask for better."

8

The newspaper was officially called *The Clarion Press*, but local usage had changed this to *The Bugle Squeeze*, and finally just *The Squeeze*. It had been founded, back in the late 1890's, by a group of merchants who wanted a vehicle to advertise their wares, and from the first its editorial policy had been geared to the likes and dislikes of the community, rather than anything to do with the news. It fell on thin times during World War II, when tourism dropped off to nothing and the stores had little to sell, and it was then that Lester Turpin bought it. He and Grace managed to turn out the copy necessary to fill the pages, and Grace gradually took on the duties of the special writers as they succumbed to old age, failing memory, or general apathy. Grace knew which were the paper's most popular features, and she kept them going long after the original writer had faded from the scene. Thus in one column she would do the waterfront news, under the by-line Old Salt; in another she would become Kitchen Katie and relay hints on seven different ways to cook tuna fish; and on occasion she did the "Who Caught What" column, a list of the significant fish caught during the previous week. Once a pixie in the composing room put the "Who Caught What" logo over the list of patients in the hospital, and as a result Turpin had to go to the expense of hiring a proofreader, to check each page before the press run started. It ran up the budget, but it helped the tone and general credibility of the paper.

Grace Turpin was the last person one would associate with newspaper work. Small and sparrow-like, she had an eye for the absurdities of everyday existence, and she would chirrup with pleasure whenever she ran across something that would liven up one or the other of her columns. The news, to her, was whatever might be worth reading, and if it was faintly rowdy or suggestive, so much the better. She could be serious, and could deliver thundering diatribes on anything that concerned her deeply, but the trivial aspects of human folly were what delighted her most and were the mortar that held her columns together.

As Sam passed her desk, folding the money Turpin had just given him, she looked up at him and said, "You weren't by any chance in the Navy, were you?"

"No'm," Sam replied. "For what it may be worth, I was in the Army. Why?"

"There's a technical pronunciation I'm looking for. I know you pronounce 'forward' 'forrad,' and 'windward' 'windard,' but how do you pronounce 'leeward'? 'Leed'?"

"My guess would be 'loord,'" Sam replied.

She pecked it out on the typewriter, and examined it. "It looks funny," she said.

"Why do you need the pronunciation?" Sam asked. "Why not just spell it the way it is?"

"Old Salt has to talk in dialect," she replied. "Otherwise, people won't think he knows what he's saying. And I'm here to tell you it's a royal pain." She lifted the top of the copy paper, and read: "'The schooner *Effie W.*, on a nor'east tack from Mystic, come about and put into port Thursday to duck the 80-knot breeze out Argentia way, then sloped off to loord and was hull-down by five bells.'" She looked up at him. "Makes your blood tingle, don't it?"

"Is that all the column is?" Sam asked.

"Oh, no," she replied cheerfully. "Come winter, we get a lot of wrecks. Drownings. Lost with all hands. I can tell you, it keeps a girl young." An idea struck her, and she pecked furiously, using only her two forefingers, then said, "See how this sounds: 'Will whoever lost his/her wallet under Greasy Pennock's overturned dory on Scup Beach please identify same and reclaim it. Greasy says it's undamaged save for some caulking compound dripped on it. He adds identification will be made a mite easier by some of the snapshots inside. Nuff said.'" She looked at Sam, waiting to see his reaction.

"I think it's—" he began.

"You're absolutely right." The telephone rang beside her, and she picked it up and said, "*The Clarion Press*. May I help you? . . . The editor is busy right now, but I'm the assistant editor. Who is this calling? . . . Yes, and I'm Marie Antoinette. Let's stop . . . Oh, my God." She put her hand over the mouthpiece, and called, "Lester! Pick up the phone! It's Walter Cronkite!" She listened until Turpin took the phone in his office, and then she hung up. "What in the world could *he* want?" she said.

"You'd know better than I," Sam replied.

"Sit down," said Grace, and when Sam took a chair she said, "I don't feel I know anything about you."

He shrugged, and smiled. "There really isn't much to know."

"My husband tells me you're writing a play."

"Oh, that." Suddenly, his play seemed very far away. "That was an idea, at one time."

"Where do you come— Excuse me. Do you mind my asking you all this?"

"Go right ahead. I have no secrets I can think of."

"Do you have a home?"

"In a sense. My mother lives in Michigan."

"Your father?"

"He died. He was in the Resistance, and the Germans caught him. He was never very healthy after that."

"Which Resistance?"

"Danish. He escaped to England, and met my mother. She was a WAC. They were married, and came to Michigan after the war."

"This is really none of my business, but it just occurred to

me—I mean, you seemed sort of lost, and . . ." She let the
sentence trail off.

"I don't feel lost." He smiled broadly. "In fact, I feel more
at home than I have in a long time."

"I'm glad. Were you in Vietnam?"

He shook his head. "I enlisted afterward."

"Why?"

Before Sam could answer, Turpin came out of his office,
looking as stunned as though he'd just been notified of the
Pulitzer Prize. "Well, what do you ever-loving know about
that?" he said. "CBS wants to send a crew up to cover the
secession story."

"But we haven't seceded," Grace replied. "What is there
to cover?"

"The day we vote, and the pros and cons, and all the rest
of it. They want a camera here when the final decision is
made."

"Suppose we decide not to secede? Where's their story
then?"

"A lot of wasted film, I guess. That's their worry."

Grace looked at the calendar on the wall beside her
desk. "When is it we vote?" she said. "The second Monday—"

"The second Tuesday," her husband corrected her. "Not
later than the second Tuesday after the first Monday of the
month following this. That will make it"—he lifted the calendar page—"Tuesday the eleventh, or two weeks from yesterday."

"I wonder how they found out," Grace said.

"I suppose one of our off-island subscribers told them. We
do have a certain circulation in America, you know."

"Yes, but I never realized we were all that important. I
thought this was just a matter between ourselves—us and
the State."

"Remember, my dear, 'No man is an island, entire of itself . . .' "

" 'Therefore never send to know for whom the bell tolls; it

tolls for thee.' I know, but I somehow got the picture things were different out here."

"Never. We just have to pretend they are." He paused, and looked at Sam. "I suppose, if we're going to be on national television, we ought to make some kind of preparations."

"Like what?" said Sam.

"That's just the problem. I don't know."

"I say, forget the preparations," Grace said. "They want to see us as we are, so let's just go about our business as though nothing were happening. What I'd really love would be to have the TV people ask, say, Lucius Pardle what he thought about secession, and have him say, 'Secession from what?' That would make the whole thing worthwhile."

"I ran into someone just like that when I was interviewing," Sam said. "He thought I was talking about the Civil War."

"That would be Gummy Trask," Turpin said.

"What's his real name?"

"No idea. He had all his teeth pulled when he was twenty-one, and later gummed a girl half to death. That's the only name he's known by."

"This is all very enlightening," Grace said, "but it isn't getting my Old Salt column done. Anybody heard anything hot on the waterfront?"

Turpin looked out the window. "It'll be low tide in about an hour," he said.

"I'll use it," said Grace, "but only as a last resort." She pecked briefly at the machine, then read: "'Low water last Wednesday come just about on schedule—a mite after four bells.'"

"I know something you can use," Turpin said. "Did you know you can cook fish in the dishwasher?"

"Oh, sure," said Grace. "And broil a steak in the toilet. I need something useful."

"I mean it. You get a fillet of fish, spread mayonnaise

on it and wrap it tightly in aluminum foil, then put it in the dishwasher for one cycle. It comes out steamed."

Grace stared at him for several seconds. "I'll save it for next year's April Fool column," she said.

Turpin shrugged. "It's your column. I'm only trying to help."

"Editors should edit," said Grace. "They shouldn't try to be creative."

Turpin looked at Sam. "Did you ever fly an airplane?" he asked.

"I've held the controls," Sam replied. "Why?"

"I keep thinking we ought to have an aviation column, but Grace won't do it. She hates to fly."

"I've told you, I'll do your column," Grace said. "But it'll be only one word—CRASH!"

"You see what I mean," said Turpin.

"I could give it a try," Sam said. "Is there anyone out at the airport I might talk to?"

"There must be several. There's Crazy Looie Gonzales, otherwise known as the Flying Squirrel. There's Gimpy Dalton, and the man they call the One-Eyed Mouse. Any one of them would be glad to talk to you."

"Would I have to fly with them?"

"That would be up to you. I just want odds and ends about flying, like the waterfront column."

"Nothing is like Old Salt," Grace announced firmly, as she began to peck out an item. "Old Salt is unique, and you should beware of imitations. How do you pronounce 'gunwale'?"

"'Gunnel,'" her husband replied.

Grace tapped out a few more words, then said, "How do you like this? 'Charlie Tooker come up with a cracked rib or two t'other night when he got bent over the gunnel tryin' to hoist anchor. Come to find out, he'd fouled his anchor on a scope of chain from the *Nettie L.*, which fair bowed Charlie in two when she took off to loord.'"

"I like it," Turpin said. "If it were about anyone but Charlie Tooker, you could say it had human interest."

The door opened, and Arthur Gibbon came in. He had taken off his coveralls, but there was white paint on his shoes, his hat, and his nose, and he reached for his wallet with two fingers, as though afraid to get paint on it. He recognized Sam, and grinned at him. "I thought you said you wasn't a reporter," he said.

"I wasn't, when you asked me," Sam replied.

Gibbon opened his wallet and took out a folded piece of paper, which he handed to Turpin. "Got an ad for you," he said. "The boys down at the Club would like it if you'd run it this week and the next."

"No reason not to, if they're willing to pay for it," Turpin replied. He unfolded the paper, and read: "'Giant First Annual Secession Clambake, Wednesday, May 12.'" He stopped, and looked at Gibbon. "You're having a bake this early in the season?"

"Seems that way," Gibbon replied. "That's what the boys want."

Turpin read on: "'Waterfront Club members & guests $3 a head, all other $12.50 . . .' Isn't that a little steep? That's twenty-five bucks a couple."

"We want to keep out the riffraff," Gibbon said. "The boys figure there'll be enough going on, without asking for trouble from the bad drunks and such."

"'The bake will begin at noon,'" Turpin read, "'on the beach at Gordon's Neck. In case of rain, at the Waterfront Club, all those who can fit in. In case of no secession, the bake will be held anyway.'" He put the paper in his pocket. "How big an ad do you want?"

"Nobody mentioned that," Gibbon said. "Just enough to catch the eye, I guess. Use your own judgment." Then he looked at Sam, and said, "You want to come as my guest? It'll save you a few bucks."

"That would be great," Sam replied. "I'd like—I mean, can I—"

"Sure, if you know one."

"I don't know if she'll come, but I'll ask."

"Well, if she won't, you got time to scare up another. It's still two weeks away."

"Now, about paying for this ad—" Turpin said.

"Just bill the Club," Gibbon said. "By the time the bake's over, they should have plenty in the till."

When Gibbon had left, Grace looked at the door and said, "There go my vibes again."

"In what way?" Turpin asked.

"Bad. I don't know." She shivered and rubbed one forearm briskly, as though to restore circulation. "Having a party to celebrate—it's sort of like the ball before Waterloo." She stared at the copy in the typewriter, then pulled it out and set it aside. "Maybe a couple of recipes will make me feel better," she said. "Give me again that thing about fish in the dishwasher."

On Turpin's advice, Sam went to the lunchroom at the airport early next morning, to see what he could gather for an aviation column. It turned out that a fair proportion of the town's officials, artisans, and personalities breakfasted at the lunchroom, which was known officially as the Prop Wash Restaurant and Lounge. Police Chief Maddox was there, at a table with Fire Chief Homer Benbow; Edgar Morris shared a table with Lena Femble, a toothsome blonde from Monsieur Arthur's Hairdressing Salon who gave every appearance of having been with Morris since the previous afternoon; Dr. Stanton Wiesel, the town's oldest dentist, shared a plate of fried clams and crullers with his mother, Letitia (more generally known as either Aunt or Uncle Lettie, depending on one's point of view); and the other tables were occupied by assorted lawyers, delivery drivers, carpenters, plumbers, and a few would-be airline passengers. The passengers could be distinguished by their hats; they wore city hats with narrow brims and small, brightly colored feathers, in some cases shrouded by plastic covers, while everyone else wore caps of one sort or another.

Sam took a stool at the counter, next to Sergeant Ed Mancusi of the State Police, and ordered a coffee and English muffin. Mancusi looked at him and nodded absently, and Sam smiled. "They do a good business here, don't they?" he said.

"They do that." Mancusi was lean-jawed and handsome, and looked something like the State Trooper in a highway safety poster. His puttees and Sam Browne belt glowed like black satin, and the butt of his pistol, protruding from its holster, seemed as big as a howitzer. His blue uniform clung to him without a crease. If it were not for the fact that the State Police were discouraged from being over-friendly with the locals, Ed Mancusi could have had any girl on the island, singly or in groups.

Sam let his gaze wander around the room, looking for anyone who might be an airplane pilot, but with the exception of the officers and the putative passengers everyone was dressed more or less alike. You could no more tell a pilot by looking at him than you could an embalmer (as it turned out, Hosmer Curtin, the local undertaker, was among those present, trying with only moderate success to keep his thumb out of his mouth while he ate a tuna-fish-salad roll), and Sam finally turned to Sergeant Mancusi for help. "Do you know a man named Gonzales?" he said. "Or Dalton, or—"

"You mean the Flying Squirrel?" Mancusi replied. "Sure. He and Gimpy Dalton are at that table over in the corner, there."

Sam looked where Mancusi indicated, and saw two men sitting at a table for four, sipping coffee and sharing a large order of buttered toast. They seemed in no hurry to leave—in fact, they appeared to be waiting for someone—so Sam had a second cup of coffee while he finished his muffin. Then he paid the countergirl, thanked Mancusi, and made his way to the table in the corner. The two men looked at him as he approached, and Sam said, "Mr. Gonzales?"

The one on the left, who bore a fleeting resemblance to Jerry Lewis, nodded, but said nothing. Dalton, who was so fat it was hard to imagine his fitting into an airplane, reached for another piece of toast and began to lather it with strawberry jam.

"I'm from the newspaper," Sam said to Gonzales, whose expression didn't change. "Mr. Turpin would like to start an aviation column, and he suggested I talk to you gentlemen."

Gonzales's face brightened, and he turned to Dalton. "Hey, Gimpy, we're going to be famous!" he said. "He finally got around to it!" Dalton, his mouth full, nodded, and Gonzales said, "Sit down. What can we tell you?"

"Well—anything that would make news," Sam replied. "What's been going on—any plans you have for the future— what you feel about secession—you tell me. I'm here to listen."

Gonzales looked at the ceiling, trying not to smile. "Should we tell him what we feel about secession, Gimpy?" he said.

"Why not?" Dalton replied, after swallowing. "It's no secret."

"In a way it is. We don't want the Air Force to hear about it."

"Screw the Air Force. What can they do?"

"They might think of something."

"Not unless they've changed since *I* was with them. Nobody in the Air Force has had a new thought since the Bomb."

"You want them to drop the Bomb?"

"Screw the Bomb. They wouldn't dare."

"Well, then, in a nutshell, here it is," Gonzales said. "So we secede. Then what?"

"I don't know," said Sam after a pause. "What?"

"So the State tries to get us back, but they can't. They can't get enough Troopers or Guardsmen out here to take over the Boys' Club, much less the island. So they call on the Federal Government. Now, the only way the Federal Government can get troops out here—and this is always supposing they want to—is to drop 'em in by parachute, and this is where we come in." He paused, waiting for Sam to ask the inevitable question.

"How?" said Sam. "What do you do?"

"About six or eight of us—Gimpy, the Mouse, myself, and a few others—we fly a crisscross pattern beneath the troop carriers, and we scare the shit outa them paratroopers. No paratrooper, no matter how psyched up he is, is gonna jump if he's got a lot of air traffic below him. And just to make sure"—he paused, savoring the next bit— "just to make sure, we're gonna string long strands of nylon line between two, three of our planes, so we'll be cutting through the air like a scythe. There ain't a paratrooper alive who'll jump into that."

"Supposing something hits the line," Sam said. "Wouldn't that damage your planes—or make them crash?"

"The line'll have a breakaway element where it joins the wing tip," Gonzales said. "It'll look a lot more dangerous than it really is." He glanced around as the door opened. "Here's the Mouse," he said. "What kept you, Mouse? We been waiting for you."

A thin man, with a pointed nose and a squint that appeared to shut one eye completely, came over to the table and sat down. "My horizontal stabilizer come loose," he said. "She was flappin' like a beaver's tail."

"You get her fixed?"

"Yeah. Come to find out, the trim rod corroded through. Must be the salt air."

"Mouse, this young man here"—Gonzales indicated Sam— "is from *The Squeeze*. They're gonna start an aviation col-

umn, and he wants some hot poop. I been telling him about
our plans."

The Mouse examined Sam with the one eye that appeared
to be partially open. "What do you think?" he said.

"It sounds—ah—interesting," said Sam. "Very interesting."

"You taken him up yet?" the Mouse said to Gonzales.

"I was getting to that," Gonzales replied. "I just met him
a couple minutes ago." To Sam, he said, "How about it? You
want to come up while we do a dry run?"

"Actually, I get the picture pretty well," Sam replied. "I
don't think it'll be necessary to—"

"You don't know the half of it," Gonzales said. "I just
gave you a quick outline. There's a lot more I didn't mention."

"Some other time, maybe"—Sam glanced at his watch—
"right now I have to get back to the paper and start a—"

"You know what I think, Squirrel?" the Mouse cut in. "I
think this young feller's chicken."

"Not in the least," Sam replied. "I'd be delighted to, but
right now I'm just—"

"You talk like you was chicken," the Mouse said. "That's
chicken talk if ever I heard it."

"Well, if that's what you think"—Sam swallowed—"then
I'll come up with you. I mean—you leave me no choice."

"Finest kind." Gonzales looked around and caught the
waitress's eye. "Can we have the check here, honey?" he
said. "We gotta go play zoomie in the sky."

He paid the check, and as they filed out they passed the
table at which the Police Chief and the Fire Chief were sitting. It occurred to Sam, in a flash of mad inspiration, that
if he could get Maddox to arrest him it would get him out of
flying with Gonzales, and no matter how long he spent in
jail it would be preferable to the alternative. As he passed
the table he heard the Fire Chief saying, ". . . so I slapped
the son of a bitch with a dozen violations, and that shut him

up. Anyone thinks he can play wise-ass with me has got another—" He stopped as Sam leaned over his shoulder.

"Hey there, Old Soak," Sam said to Maddox. "I don't suppose you found out about that foot yet, did you?"

Maddox glared at him. "Get out of here," he said.

"In my own good time," Sam replied. "This is a public place. So you're still sitting on the evidence, hey?" He raised his voice enough so that people at the nearby tables looked around.

"It was a bear's foot," Maddox said through clenched teeth. "Now, bugger off."

"Hey!" Gonzales called from the door. "Are you coming, or not?"

Sam paused, then said, "I'm coming," and followed the others through the door. He walked in a daze, like a condemned man going down the long corridor to the execution room.

Outside, they went around the side of the building to the area where the private aircraft were parked. They reached Dalton's plane first, and helped him untie the wing lashings that held it to the ground. It was a well-worn Beechcraft Bonanza, with a V tail, and they watched in fascination as Dalton mounted the wing, then squeezed himself into the pilot's seat.

"Gimpy don't really sit in that airplane," Gonzales observed. "He wears it."

The Mouse's plane was next, an old high-wing Piper with tricycle landing gear, and when Sam and Gonzales had helped him unlash it they moved on to where an ancient Luscombe was parked behind a hangar. It had the old-fashioned landing gear, with a small tail wheel at the rear, and it bore an emblem certifying it as a classic antique. When Sam climbed into the right-hand seat he saw it had stick controls, instead of the usual wheels. The seats were covered with cracked black leather, and when Gonzales started the engine the instrument panel vibrated like a tun-

ing fork. Gonzales unhooked his radio microphone, blew
into it, and said something to the control tower, then
switched frequencies and talked first to Dalton, then to the
Mouse. Their replies came through, loud but garbled, from a
speaker behind his head. Then he opened the throttle, and
the plane began to trundle heavily across the grass. The
other two formed in behind him, and they headed toward
the end of the runway with all the grace of three camels
walking on their knees. Gonzales glanced at Sam's seat belt,
said, "Make sure it's good and tight," and Sam tugged at the
end of the belt until he felt his thighs were in a vise. In
front of him, the instrument panel jiggled and shuddered.

When they reached the end of the runway Gonzales
stopped, set the brakes, and opened the throttle. The plane
shook as though in a hurricane; the instrument needles
danced, and noise filled the cabin and pounded on Sam's
ears. Then Gonzales cut back the throttle and spoke again to
the control tower; there was a squeal as he eased up on the
brakes, and the plane began to roll forward. Then they were
on the runway proper, and he once again opened the throttle, said, "Here we go," and leaned forward slightly as the
plane gathered speed. The wheels rattled and bumped and
clattered, and then Sam felt the tail come up, and in a moment the sound of the wheels stopped and he felt pressure
on his seat as the plane rose sharply into the air. Gonzales
made a wide, climbing turn as the other two took off, and
Sam could see them below him like gulls, gradually coming
closer. Finally the three planes formed in a line abreast and
headed for the eastern end of the island. The day was clear
but the horizon was smoky with haze, and Sam had the feeling he was floating in a separate, noisy world, totally removed from the problems of others.

His memory of the next half hour was jumbled and
punctuated by periods when he must have blacked out.
Gonzales would say something to him, apparently explain-
ing the next move, then would speak into the microphone,

and when the other two had acknowledged he'd begin to hurl the plane about the sky. Sam would see the horizon rise, and feel the catch in his breath as the plane gathered speed in a dive, then the horizon would drop suddenly out of sight and he'd be staring at blue sky, while his insides went hollow and the horizon reappeared from above his head; then the sickening plunge straight at the earth, and the pullout that turned everything in him to lead and made darkness appear at the edges of his vision. Sometimes the horizon, instead of dropping away, would roll slowly around the plane, while Sam's insides tried vainly to keep up with the motion, and every now and then he'd spot one of the other planes out the side window, flicking past with the speed of a bullet. At first he tried to brace himself, but then he found it was easier if he relaxed, preferably with his eyes closed, and tried to minimize the churning sensations in his head and stomach. It was, he decided, a little bit like the state of drunkenness known as "whirly bed," a particularly unpleasant condition he'd known only twice, and when he'd accepted that, he was able to open his eyes and, if not actually enjoy himself, at least not be paralyzed with terror.

Finally, when he'd begun to resign himself to living forever in an astral washing machine, Gonzales leveled off, eased back slightly on the throttle, and looked at him, grinning. "How'd you like it?" Gonzales asked.

Sam tried to affect nonchalance. "Not bad," he said. "You do this often?"

"As often as we can. We still got a few bugs to work out of it yet."

"So I noticed. You think it'll be effective against paratroops?"

"It surer'n hell oughta be. I know *I* wouldn't want to jump with all that going on."

"You have a point there."

They were headed back toward the airport, and as they

came in over the sea Gonzales said, "Ever do a nose-high slip?"

"I honestly don't remember," Sam replied.

"If you'd done it, you'd remember. It's a quick way to land. Watch."

Instead of coming in at a normal glide angle, Gonzales advanced the throttle a bit, pulled the nose up, and dropped one wing. The plane settled sideways, and Sam saw the runway markers coming up at him through his window. At the last instant Gonzales brought the plane level, cut the throttle, and landed. "Nothing to it," he said. "You can land on a dime." He taxied off the runway onto the grass as Dalton's plane came in the same way. The Mouse, who was last to land, misjudged by a fraction and blew the tire on his left wheel; his plane spun around and came to a stop facing in the opposite direction. The radio erupted in a burst of profanity, and Gonzales laughed. "The old One-Eyed Mouse," he said. "If it ain't one thing with him, it's surer'n hell gonna be another."

When Sam got back to the newspaper office the strength had returned to his legs, which had been so rubbery he'd almost fallen on alighting from the plane. Grace Turpin looked up at him, and after a moment said, "You look as though you'd been flying."

"How can you tell?" Sam asked.

"You have that surprised-to-be-alive look. Did you get enough for a column?"

"I don't know till I try to write it. I don't think so." Then an idea came to him. "I think I'll just say we have a secret weapon," he said. "So secret we can't give any of the details."

"And what, precisely is it?" Grace asked.

"It's very simple," Sam replied. "They're all crazy. Stark, raving lunatics."

9

"A man named Williams called," Ella Markey said when her husband came home for lunch. "Dustin Williams. Did he get you?"

"No," George Markey replied. "What number'd you give him?"

"I told him to call the bank."

"Well, he didn't." He thought a moment, then added, "Norris Webster was asking about him, just this morning."

"What did he want to know?"

"He wanted to know anything *I* knew, which isn't much."

"Is Williams the man who came up to you after the funeral?"

"Uh-huh." Markey apparently felt he'd said enough, so changed the subject. "Did Daisy ever get her goddam car fixed?" he asked.

"I assume so. I didn't ask."

"Well, she was late again this morning. If she's going to shack up with a mechanic, you'd think at least she could make it pay off."

"The reason she was late this morning was she had to go to the hospital for a blood test."

"Oh, God. Don't tell me she's pregnant."

"I said blood test. For all I know, she's planning to get married."

"You shouldn't have to guess. If you're going to hire someone, you ought to know everything there is to know about them. That way, they can't pull any fast ones on you."

"Next time I hire someone, I'll let you make out the questionnaire."

He gave her a level stare. "Was that supposed to be a smart crack?"

"Not in the least. You know what kind of information you want, so why don't you ask the questions?"

"That's up to you. I can't worry myself about the goddam household in addition to everything else. I got enough on my mind as it is." He looked at his watch. "How long to lunch?"

"About fifteen minutes. She didn't start the soufflé till you called."

He headed for the stairs. "Come on."

"You mean right now? There's barely time to—"

"I said come on." He started upstairs, and after a moment she took a deep breath, clenched her jaw, and followed him, fumbling for the side zipper on her dress.

At the liquor store, Norris Webster said to his clerk, "Does the name Williams mean anything to you? Dustin Williams?"

"Oh, sure," the clerk replied. "Come July and August, we make two deliveries a week out his way. Sometimes three."

Webster went into his office and pulled out a thick ledger, in which were the accounts for the last half of the previous year. He ran his finger down the left-hand column, and whenever he came to Williams's name he ran his finger across, to see what the order had been. He found the usual amount of scotch, gin, and vodka, and an unusual amount of liqueurs such as crême de menthe, B&B, Bénédictine, Drambuie, apricot brandy, and Kahlúa, which to him indicated (a) that Williams was married and (b) that he and his wife did a good deal of entertaining. There was also imported cognac and both domestic and imported wines, and here Webster ran into a problem: he, personally, knew nothing about wines, but he had studied the orders of customers who were experts in the field, and he knew their patterns reasonably well. Mr. and Mrs. Dustin Williams, it appeared, felt they should serve imported wines to their guests, but the wines they ordered were similar to American wines of the same category, and all of them tended toward the sweet side. Thus there were imported sparkling Burgundy, Château Olivier Graves, and Château d'Yquem, balanced on the domestic side by Blue Nun, Cold Duck, and Almadén Rhine wine. (The Château d'Yquem, Webster guessed, must have been for a special occasion; there were two bottles of that for every two dozen bottles of the others.) Also, for what occasions he couldn't guess (picnics? boating?), there were premixed manhattans and whiskey sours, and every now and then some grenadine syrup and maraschino cherries. He closed the ledger, wondering where Agnes Tuttle fitted into the picture.

The next book he opened was smaller, but no less revealing. It was Webster's rule not to grant charge accounts to transient summer visitors until he had run a complete check of their credit rating, with bank references, other charge accounts, and so on. The only way a customer could avoid this scrutiny was to buy a house on the island; once that was done, Webster knew he could slap a lien on the property for any unpaid bills. He knew that Williams now owned a house, but he guessed that he had rented for at least one season before buying, and that his references would therefore be on file. Webster went back five years in the book before he found the name Dustin Williams, and when he found it he sat back and looked out the window. The listing was in the name of Mrs. Dustin Williams, née Margaret Wambley of Brookline and Pride's Crossing, and her credit was impeccable: the Old Colony Trust Company, the State Street Bank & Trust Company, Shreve, Crump & Low, the Ritz-Carlton Hotel Company, Tiffany's, Nieman Marcus, and Mark Cross. With money like that, Webster thought, what in the name of God is she doing buying Cold Duck? He closed the book, returned it to the shelf, and locked the office door as he went out.

"Find what you wanted?" the clerk asked.

"Yes and no," Webster replied. "I'm going out for lunch."

"Yesterday was payday, you know," the clerk said.

"You'll get your money," said Webster. "Just don't be in such an all-fired rush."

It was Saturday, and the lunch-hour crowd at the Sink Hole was heavier than usual. Webster found he had to sit at a long table with a number of people he didn't know, although he recognized one or two as having occasionally bought beer at his store. He always identified people by their orders; until he knew them on a first-name basis he thought of them in terms of what they bought, and even with those he knew the best he could recite how much and what kind of liquor they'd bought during the last month. Thus the Turpins were Mr. and Mrs. Soave Folonari, Corning was Emil Vodka and Cranberry Juice, the Ambersons were Dr. and Mrs. King William Scotch, and so on. He was, at the moment, sitting amidst a lot of Schlitzes, Ballantines, and Budweisers, and nothing they said or did could possibly be of interest to him.

As he munched glumly on his hamburg and baked beans, Webster reviewed his campaign against Agnes, and found that he had become rather badly sidetracked. In looking for something to pin on her he had wound up investigating a man with whom she had sat briefly at lunch, and his only hope of nailing something on her would be to prove (a) that Williams was either a thief, or corrupt, or immoral, and (b) that Agnes was involved with him to an extent that was detrimental to the best interests of the town. Finding such proof might be extremely difficult, but Webster was not a man to give up easily once he'd developed a grudge. And when someone maligned him and his motives in front of the town meeting, as Agnes had, they could expect the grudge to last for a lifetime.

At a nearby table for two the customers paid their check

and left, and after a few moments Dustin Williams made his way through the crowd and took a seat. He was unaware of Webster's staring at him as he scanned the menu; he was preoccupied with his thoughts, and Lennie had to ask him twice if he would care for a cocktail. Then he started, and looked up. "Oh—" he said. "Yes. A—a daiquiri. Very dry, with a twist of lime." Then, for the first time seeing Lennie's face, he gave her his toothiest smile and said, "And you'll remember that the next time I come in, won't you, dear?"

"Remember what?" Lennie asked.

Williams's smile remained, frozen on his face. "How I like my daiquiri."

"I'll try," said Lennie. "But I won't promise anything."

She went to the bar, and Williams resumed his brooding study of the menu. He had just called the Markey home, and been told by the maid that Mr. and Mrs. Markey were "resting," which was such an odd phrase to use in the middle of the day that Williams could only conclude Markey didn't want to talk to him. But he couldn't understand it; Markey had seemed agreeable enough when first approached, and there was no apparent reason for him to change his mind. Unless Agnes Tuttle had got to him, and . . . but why would she do that? And if she *had* got to him, what could she have said? She hadn't listened to enough of Williams's proposition to know any details, so she could only have relayed a warning in the broadest possible terms, and that should not have been enough to turn Markey off. If anything it should have made him curious, so what could explain this obvious lie that he was "resting" before lunch? The more he thought about it, the stranger it became, until he finally concluded that the only thing to do was proceed as planned and pretend it had never happened. Markey was too important to him to be derailed by a minor misunderstanding.

Lennie appeared, set a folded paper napkin in front of

him, and on it put a daiquiri. She started away, but Williams stopped her. "Wait a minute," he said.

She looked back. "Isn't that right?"

"I'll tell you when I've tasted it." He put it to his lips, took a sip, then put the glass down and pushed it toward her. "Too sweet," he said. "I specifically said very dry."

She took the glass away and Williams looked around the room, to see if there was anyone he recognized. He thought he might have seen Webster before but he wasn't sure, and for the rest they were all strangers. Considering the average social level this was understandable—and, as far as he was concerned, preferable—but he wondered if it might not be a good idea for him to know *some* of the people in the community, just on general principles. Not to become friends with them, or anything like that, but to let them know who he was, so they'd know what to expect and could behave accordingly. The trouble was, he didn't know how to begin.

Lennie returned with his drink, and stood by while he put it to his lips. He took a sip, ran it around in his mouth, and said, "Much better. It's not perfect, but it'll do. I don't imagine you knew Jimmy, the barman at the Paris Ritz."

"He was never in here," Lennie replied. "If he was, I'm sure I would have spotted him."

"Oh? Do you know what he looked like?"

"No, but I can tell a phony at twenty paces." Her tone was gentle, almost loving, and she smiled as she spoke.

"Jimmy was no phony, I can promise you," Williams said. "I've seen him make a puce café in a coffee cup that you couldn't tell from a café expresso."

"What did he use, a blender?" Lennie asked.

"No, he stirred it. Chilled, and stirred. My old friend Andy Gide said he'd never tasted better."

"Well, I guess that's what happens when you travel. Just one surprise after another." For her, this game held no more challenges.

"What do you do when you're through here?" Williams asked, with what he intended to be a meaningful look.

"You mean at this table, or at the restaurant?" Lennie decided to make it as hard for him as she could.

"I mean at the restaurant. Do you go straight home, or do you—perhaps—tarry along the way?"

"Well, first I go to the delousing station, then I get a—"

"To the *what*?"

"Delousing station. After a day of working with the customers here, you've no idea what you may have picked up."

He relaxed, and laughed. "Yes, of course. Well, now, I was wondering if you—"

"Then I get an onion-and-bologna sandwich, and go down to the docks and eat it. It helps me unwind. If I didn't have my onion-and-bologna sandwich I'd never get to sleep."

Williams thought for a moment, then said, "I think you're putting me on."

"Would you like to order lunch, or will you have another cocktail?"

"You know why I think you're putting me on?"

"Why?"

"Greta Garbo was the only person I ever knew who liked onion-and-bologna sandwiches. She'd eat them at all hours of the day or night."

"So why can't I like them, too?"

"It's just too much of a coincidence. I remember one night I'd picked her up to take her to the opera, and she said that before she went anywhere she'd have to have—"

Suddenly, Lennie spotted Sam making his way toward the back of the room, and she cried, "Darling!" and rushed up to him, threw her arms around his neck, and kissed him. As she did, she whispered, "I'll explain later," then put her arm through his and led him back to Williams's table. "This is my husband," she said to the startled Williams. "He just got back from Paris."

Williams nodded, said, "Pleased to meet you," and finished his drink.

"Would you care for another cocktail?" Lennie asked, still clutching Sam by the arm.

"Just give me the check," Williams replied. "I didn't realize how late it is."

Lennie tore the check off her pad and put it on the table, and when Williams put down five dollars and told her to keep the change, she said, "Thank you, sir. Have a nice day." Then she mopped off the table and motioned for Sam to sit down.

"Is there a telephone around?" Williams asked. "I have to call my broker."

"There's a pay phone right by the rest rooms," Lennie replied. "You can't miss it."

Williams moved off, and for a moment Sam and Lennie looked at each other without speaking. Then she said, "I'm sorry about that. It was the only way I could turn him off."

"I'm not sorry about it at all," Sam replied. "It was the best greeting I've had in a long time."

"You want your usual beer?"

"What I want, and what I came in here for, is to see if you'll come to the clambake with me."

"What clambake?"

"The secession clambake, on the twelfth. The day after the vote."

"That'll be what—a Wednesday? Tuesdays and Wednesdays are my days off."

"Then will you come?"

"I've told you, I'm not very good company."

"You'll be no better company if you just sit around and mope. It'll do you good to let down your hair and shout a little."

She smiled. "Is that what you do at a clambake?"

"I have no idea, but I wouldn't be surprised. There certainly can be no rule against it."

"All right, then, I'd love to come. Now would you like your beer? I can't spend all day gabbing with the customers."

"Remember me? I'm not a customer—I'm your husband."

She turned away without replying, and went to the bar. Then another customer called her, and it was several minutes before she returned with Sam's beer. "I'm sorry," she said. "I seem to have been neglecting my duties."

Sam was going to apologize for the lame joke about being her husband, then decided it would be better to let the whole matter drop; rehashing it would probably do more harm than good. So he said, "My needs are simple," and took a sip of his beer. Felicity went past and gave him a long sidewise look, which he ignored.

The pay telephone was affixed to the wall outside the men's room, surrounded by a thicket of phone numbers, graffiti, and cigarette burns. Williams put in his dime and dialed Markey's number, and was relieved when a voice other than the maid's answered. "Mrs. Markey?" he said, and when the voice replied, "Yes," he went on, "This is Dustin Williams. Is Mr. Markey there?" He wished he could have called from an office, where there was less background noise and he could sound more commanding; there was something about shouting into a public telephone that was undignified and put the caller at a disadvantage. In a few moments Markey came on, and Williams repeated his identification and said, "I wondered if I might be able to have a word with you."

"You're having a word with me right now," Markey replied. "What do you want?"

"It's nothing I can talk about over the phone. May I come to your house?"

"I'm going back to the bank in a few minutes. Come to my office there."

"I'd rather see you at your home, if you don't mind."

Williams knew it sounded odd, but there was nothing he could do about it. "Bernard Baruch once told me the best place to do business is—"

"I don't know any Baruch. Is he an islander?"

Suddenly, Williams realized he had the upper hand. "I can't explain him to you now," he said. "You might call him the grand mogul of American finance. He said important business should always be done in the home."

There was a pause, then Markey said, "All right. You know where it is?"

"I know," said Williams. "I'll be there in five minutes."

When he got to Markey's house Williams raised the silver door knocker and tapped twice, then brushed at the creases in his jacket while he waited. The door opened, and Daisy ushered him into a parlor off the front hall, where Markey was waiting. Then she retired, clearly under instructions to close the door behind her. Markey, who was standing by the fireplace, acknowledged Williams's greeting.

"What can I do for you?" he asked when they had shaken hands.

"I hope you understand this is all confidential," Williams said, glancing around the room. "That's why I preferred not to talk in your office."

"I guessed as much," Markey replied. "Sit down." His pre-lunch coitus had left him feeling lethargic but unsatisfied, and the wine he'd had with lunch had added a faintly acid heartburn to his lethargy. He wished Williams would say what he had to say, and say it fast. "Let's start with this Baruch," he said. "Who is he, and what's he got to do with me?"

"He was a banker," Williams replied. "A financier. A good friend of mine. He used to hold court on a park bench, and people would come to ask him for advice on—"

"I thought you said he did business in his home," Markey interrupted.

"He did, he did. But he was in such demand that even

when he went out, to sit in the park and relax, people would come up to him and ask for words of wisdom. He was truly the guru of the financial world."

"First you called him a mogul, and now a guru—was he some sort of Hindu or something? His name sounds like he was a Jew."

"He was. Those were just figures of speech. He—"

"What's all this got to do with me? You didn't come all the way here to tell me about some New York Jew."

"No, of course not. I was just—"

"Then what's on your mind? I'm due back at the bank right now."

Williams took a deep breath. "Mr. Markey," he said, "what I want is very simple. I want the rights to any minerals or oil that may be found in the waters surrounding the island. Nothing more, nothing less."

Markey pursed his lips. "Nice idea, but we can't give it to you," he said.

"Why not?"

"The offshore land belongs to the State, or the Federal Government. They don't seem to have made up their minds which."

"But supposing you secede."

There was a long pause, and then Markey said, "I never thought of that."

"It would seem to me that an island is not only the land itself but also the water immediately surrounding it. I mean, you *have* to have control for a certain distance. And if you control the water, it follows that you must control the land beneath it. That's only common sense."

"You may have a point there. I'll have someone look into it."

"Well, that brings up the next item. The fewer people who know about this, the better it will be for all concerned. Take John Sutter, for instance. Look what happened to him."

"Never heard of him. What happened?"

Williams spoke as though from a prepared script. "Gold was discovered on his property in California, back in 1849," he said. "The word got around, and instead of making money Sutter lost everything he had. People came from all over the world, and tore his property to pieces looking for gold. He lost his workmen, his sheep, his cattle—everything. Instead of being a millionaire he went bankrupt, and all because he didn't keep the news of the gold strike to himself."

"So what do you suggest?"

"I suggest that only one person need know. One local person, that is."

"Who's that?"

"Who is head of the local government?"

"It's a kind of loose setup, really. The Selectmen are elected for terms—"

"But you are Chairman of the Selectmen, are you not?"

"Yes."

"And is there anyone with power over you?"

"Not really."

"Then there's your answer."

Markey had picked up a silver letter opener from the desk beside him, and was toying with it as though it were a dagger. He tossed it back and forth between his hands, then made a short stab at the air in front of him. "I guess you're right," he said.

"Now, in return for these rights," Williams said, "we are prepared to be more than generous."

"Who is 'we'?" Markey asked.

"Call us a syndicate. It doesn't matter."

Markey held the letter opener up as though balancing something on the tip. "And what do you mean by 'generous'?"

"That would have to be agreed upon. Basically, it would be a percentage of anything we might find."

"Suppose you don't find anything."

Williams shrugged. "You win a few, you lose a few."

Still looking at the tip of the letter opener, Markey shook his head. "Not good enough," he said.

"What do you mean?"

"I'd need something up front. I'm the one who's sticking his neck out."

"What would you want?"

The tip made circles in the air. "Fifty."

"Impossible. That's our operating expenses for a week."

"Then forty."

"I'll have to talk to them. I may be able to get you twenty, but not a nickel more."

"Twenty is chicken feed these days."

"Twenty thousands bucks is twenty thousand bucks. The whole thing is being done on speculation. We don't even know there's anything out there."

"Then why are you so anxious to get the rights?"

"In case we *should* find something, we want to be prepared. We want to be able to move fast, before the word gets around."

Markey studied the tip of the letter opener. "Then you should be willing to pay for it."

"We are, but there are limits to everything."

Markey lowered the tip, and pointed it at Williams. "Right," he said. "And I have my limits, just like you have yours. My bottom limit—the very least I'll go for—is thirty-five, and you can tell your buddies that unless I get it, they won't even able to pick up clamshells on the beach. Is that clear?" The tip remained pointing at the bridge of Williams's nose.

Williams was quiet for a moment, then said, "I think you're making a big mistake."

"That's my business. You want something from me, you're going to pay for it."

"My old friend Art Burns told me that where money is concerned, there's only one—"

"I don't know Art Burns, and I don't give a rat's ass what he told you. You just remember what *I* told you, and that'll be good enough."

Williams rose. "I'll pass the word along," he said. "I can't promise anything."

"You pass the word, and I'm sure everything will work out finest kind."

Williams started for the door, then stopped. "There's no need to be unfriendly about this, you know," he said.

"No need at all," Markey agreed. "Just don't think you're dealing with some hick-town sucker."

"It never crossed my mind. I've dealt with the top men in American business—Tom Watson, Joe Kennedy, Bernie Baruch, you name it—and I can tell a good businessman when I see one. You rank right up there with the best."

Markey held out his hand. "Just so long as we understand each other."

"We do," said Williams as they shook. "Indeed we do."

Daisy ushered him out, and as the door closed behind him he wondered if she'd been waiting in the hall during the entire conversation, and, if so, how much she'd heard. Then he reasoned that secrecy was more important to Markey than it was to him, so he really had nothing to worry about. As he got into his car he saw Norris Webster across the street, and recognized him as the man he'd seen at the Sink Hole earlier. It didn't strike him as unusual that Webster should be loitering about Markey's house; he knew nothing about the man, except that—suddenly, he remembered that Webster was the one who'd asked him about Agnes Tuttle after the funeral. He tried to fit this into some sort of pattern but couldn't, and as he put his car in gear he concluded that the inner workings of a small town were no concern of his. There was only one thing that concerned him, and it looked as though that was, as the saying went, in the bag. By spending a lousy thirty-five thousand dollars now, he stood a good chance to make millions in the near future. And this, for someone who twenty years ago had been in a Broadway chorus line, was not bad at all.

10

As it turned out, all three networks were interested in the secession story, but they didn't all send their own crews to the island. It seemed simpler to rely on their various local affiliates, who would be covering the story anyway and from whom they could take whatever footage they needed. And of that there was more than enough: beginning on Wednesday of the week before the vote, reporters and photographers began coming to the island in a trickle that turned into a stream that turned into a flood. One crew could consist of a field producer, a cameraman, an assistant cameraman, a sound man, an assistant sound man, two electricians, a script girl, a makeup man, and a special-effects man, all with specific, if not always necessary, jobs to perform. The island's rooming houses, which were just beginning to emerge from their winter mothballs, were suddenly flung onto a full summer footing: the rooms were aired out, the bedding was laundered, and the rates were tripled as though it were already August. The closest anyone could remember to a similar invasion was during a total eclipse of the sun, when the island's population was doubled overnight by people swarming in to witness the event, invisible elsewhere on the mainland.

In addition to the television crews there were reporters from the wire services, feature writers, political analysts, human-interest specialists, and a number of characters in dark suits and sharp-toed shoes, who were reputed to be Mafiosi looking for a place to set up a gambling casino. It got so that a local inhabitant could barely walk down the street without being interviewed by someone, and there was an alleged case of two reporters interviewing one another, each under the impression that he was talking to a remarkably intelligent native. The rumors, as usual, outstripped the facts by about ten to one: Not only was Walter Cronkite rumored to be on island, he was supposedly being duped by John Chancellor, who had bribed the locals to tell Cronkite nothing but lies; President Carter was going to send Zbigniew Brzezinski (known locally as "What's-his-face") to the island if secession was voted, in order to negotiate conditions for its return; President Carter was going to send Amy to the island, to reason with the mothers among the secessionists; Frank Sinatra was going to use the island as location for a motion picture about secession, with Spiro Agnew playing the President; and, finally, Irving Berlin was going to compose a National Anthem for the island if its independence became total, and Barbra Streisand would record it with the Boston Pops orchestra, Arthur Fiedler conducting. Most rumors are based on at least a grain of truth, or possibility, but these had none; they were spawned solely by the excitement of being the center of national attention and the wild surmise that is loosed by an apparent miracle.

On the day following the arrival of the first camera crew Omar Tuttle had been in his repair shop, trying to decode a radio broadcast. He had managed to find the frequency on which he'd heard the strange messages the day he went fishing with Corning and the others, and for the last few days had been periodically monitoring it, trying to find some pattern to the broadcasts. There would be long periods of silence, followed by an occasional terse message, and Tuttle logged the time of each one to see if they were sent at a prearranged hour. The pattern that emerged was inconclusive, and all he could determine was that it was a two-way channel; messages were being sent and received at both ends. It could be two ships, or it could be the one ship talking to a shore station, and until he could make something out of the code he had no way of knowing what was going on. He knew only that someone was reporting something, and someone else was replying with either instructions or information. Along with the times of the broadcasts, Tuttle logged what words he could make out, in the hope that they might accumulate into a discernible pattern.

On this particular morning the reception was clearer than usual, and Tuttle stopped his work and picked up a pencil as he heard the sender say, "Big John—Big John. Over." There was a tone of excitement in the voice that hadn't been there before, and it communicated itself to Tuttle. He wet the tip of his pencil, and wished he had a tape recorder handy.

"Fat Boy, this is Big John," came another voice. "Over."

"John, I have a positive. I repeat, a positive. Over."

"Positive what? Positive turtle? Positive canary? Specify. Over."

"Positive aardvark. Request instructions. Over."

"What is your bedstead? Over."

"My bedstead is—uh—wait a minute . . ." There was a long pause, then the voice came in again: "Big John, this is Fat Boy. My bedstead is lamprey plus six wigwams, moray plus eight wigwams. Over."

Tuttle scribbled furiously to record the words, although they would mean nothing without a cue sheet. It seemed evident that Fat Boy had found something, and was giving Big John the location on a prearranged chart, or grid, but beyond that the message was gibberish.

"Fat Boy," came the voice of Big John, "continue as before. Over."

"*Continue?*" There was incredulity in Fat Boy's voice. "I've already found it! Continue what? Over."

"Continue as before. Repeat, continue as before. Over."

There was a pause, then Fat Boy said, "Roger. Do you want further reports? Over."

"Affirmative. Proceed as though nothing repeat nothing has happened. Is that clear? Over."

"Roger, Big John. As though nothing has happened. Over."

"That is correct. Big John out."

"Fat Boy out."

There were two clicks, and then the quiet rustle of static. Tuttle turned off his receiver and looked at the words he'd written. He remembered the boat they'd seen, and the long tail strung out behind it, and the more he thought about it, the surer he was that the object wrapped in life jackets was a proton magnetometer. This was an electronic device that could scan and analyze the ocean floor, and register the presence of whatever substance it was set for. Thus it could detect manganese, iron, lead, oil, or any number of other elements, and record with a stylus the areas of greatest concentration. The message he'd just heard announced a find of some sort, which for reasons of their own the people in charge of the operation did not want made public. If Tuttle knew what "aardvark" stood for he'd know what had been found, but lacking that . . . He decided to take the message to Agnes and see if it meant anything to her. One advantage to having a wife on the Board of Selectmen was that she often knew things the rest of the citizens didn't.

His repair shop was behind the house, so he didn't see the cars parked out front as he went in the kitchen door. He heard voices, and saw the white glare of floodlights in the living room, and his first thought was that Agnes had been murdered and the police were taking pictures of the scene. He hurried into the living room and was almost felled by the heat, and for a moment all he could see were men standing around. Some were adjusting lights, others were moving reflectors, and still others were setting a camera on a tripod, while someone called for quiet and someone else called loudly that he was out of gaffer's tape. Sitting on the couch, with the lights blazing on her, was Agnes, while a makeup man dabbed powder on her forehead and a sound assistant tried to conceal the wire that ran from the pencil-sized microphone that hung around her neck.

"Agnes!" Tuttle cried, and someone shouted, "Quiet!"

"It's all right, dear," Agnes said, shading her eyes against the glare and looking for him. "We're just having a little interview." She seemed totally at ease, even enjoying herself.

"All right, Mrs. Tuttle, let's do it once again," a man said. "And this time please try to look at the reporter, not the camera."

"I'm sorry," Agnes said. "I can't help seeing that little red light."

"Why not put a tape over it?" someone suggested.

"Ralph!" the producer shouted. "Where's Ralph?"

"He went for coffee," another man said. "He'll be back in a minute."

"Save the lights," the producer said wearily. "We'll have to wait till he gets back." The lights went out, and the room turned dark.

"I've got a Band-Aid in the kitchen," Agnes said. "I could put that over it."

"Sorry," the producer said. "It's Ralph's job. No one else can do it."

"Then I just won't look at it," Agnes said. "We needn't wait for Ralph."

"No, we might as well get it right," the producer replied. "Take ten!" he said loudly, and everyone began to move about.

"May I stand up?" Agnes asked. "I feel I've been sitting on that couch all day."

"Yes, but don't go far, if you don't mind. We have five more interviews to do today."

Agnes came over to where Tuttle was standing. She looked faintly unreal in her makeup, and he had the feeling he was talking to a stranger.

"Did you want me for something?" she asked.

"Ah—" It took him a few moments to remember why he'd come into the house. "Yes, as a matter of fact, but it can wait. How long have you been doing this?"

"They came just after nine."

He looked at his watch. "That's over two hours. Aren't you almost done?"

"I don't know. We've only tried a couple of takes."

"What are they asking you?"

"We haven't got around to that yet."

"Here's Ralph now!" the producer said. "Ralph, will you put a piece of tape over the red light on that camera? It distracts Mrs. Tuttle."

"Sure thing." Ralph stripped off an inch of tape from a roll in his pocket and stuck it over the light.

"All right, places, everybody!" the producer called. "Let's go! Lights!"

"It's not ten minutes yet," someone said. "You said take ten."

"Well, we've got to get going, or we'll never be done here. Come on."

"George has gone for cigarettes. He said he'd be right back."

"Save the lights," the producer said.

Finally everyone returned, and Agnes went to her place on the couch. The lights went on. "Now, let's make this one—" the producer began.

"Hold it," the cameraman said. "I need to reload."

The producer turned to the reporter. "What are you going to ask her?" he said.

"I don't know," the reporter replied. "I thought we'd just wing it. It'll be more natural that way."

"Suppose she freezes up."

"We won't know till we try. I like these things to be natural."

"O.K.," the camerman said after a couple of minutes. "Ready to go."

"Quiet, everybody!" the producer called. "Roll 'em!"

"Speed," said the assistant cameraman.

"Action," said the director.

"We're in the home of Mrs. Omar Tuttle," the reporter said into his microphone. "Mrs. Tuttle is the first woman to be elected to the Board of Selectmen—or should I say Select-persons? Which do you prefer, Mrs. Tuttle?"

"It's nothing to me," Agnes replied. "Suit yourself."

"Well, then." The reporter cleared his throat. "Perhaps you—"

"Cut!" said the producer. "Charlie, don't clear your throat like that. Or at least say 'excuse me' if you do."

"That was supposed to be a chuckle," the reporter said.

"Chuckle, my foot. It sounded as though you were about to hawk one."

"Look, I should know when I'm chuckling and when I'm not. That was a humorous reaction to Mrs. Tuttle's 'suit yourself.'"

"All right, let's do it again," the producer said. "But if it's going to be a chuckle, let's hear a chuckle and not a TB ward."

"Tell me, Mrs. Tuttle," the reporter said after the preliminaries were over, "how does it feel to be the only—ah—female on the Board of Selectmen?"

"Like being the only woman in the men's room," Agnes replied. "Only not quite so—"

"Cut!" said the producer. "Mrs. Tuttle, I think we should try to be a little less earthy, if you don't mind. There'll be children watching."

"I'm sorry," Agnes said. "He asked, and it was the first thing that popped into my mind."

"Well, let's say something like 'the locker room,' then. And, Charlie, let's get to the point as quickly as we can, O.K.? This is about secession, not about Mrs. Tuttle."

"It was to establish her character," Charlie replied sourly.

"I think we've done that. Now let's get on with it."

On the next take, the reporter said, "Mrs. Tuttle, just what is this secession movement all about? Can you give us some background information?"

"Taxation without representation," Agnes replied. "It's as simple as that."

"In—ah—what way?"

"Don't you remember your history? 'Taxation without representation is tyranny.' James Otis is supposed to have said it, but what he actually said was: 'No parts of His Majesty's dominions can be taxed without their consent.' The same holds true today, as it did then. If we are to be taxed by the State, then we good and well ought to be represented in the Statehouse. There are some who want to do away with all taxes, but that is unrealistic. All I say is—"

"Thank you—" the reporter began, but Agnes was in full flight and wouldn't be stopped.

"I say taxes are a fact of life, just like constipation or hemorrhoids, and—"

"Cut!" the producer shouted. "I'm sorry, Mrs. Tuttle, but you can't say that on the air."

"Why not?" said Anges coldly. "You advertise them."

"We have nothing to do with the commercials. What they say is their own business."

"It comes over the same channel. You mean you can say 'shit' in the commercials and not in the news programs?"

There was silence, then someone in the back of the room laughed. Agnes was visibly angry, and the producer chose his words carefully. "We go by certain rules," he said. "We don't make these rules, but we have to obey them. It is up to—"

"It's the same with us," Agnes cut in. "That's why we're seceding. We won't obey rules we didn't have a hand in making."

The producer turned to the cameraman. "I don't suppose, by any miracle, you're still rolling," he said.

"I cut when you said to," the cameraman replied.

The producer nodded. "That film would have been worth a cool million, just by itself," he said. Then he turned to the reporter. "Let's wrap this up," he said. "Do a sign-off, and we can splice it in later. Quiet, everybody! Roll 'em!"

The camera panned from Agnes to the reporter, who said, "Thank you, Mrs. Tuttle," then faced the lens. "That was Mrs. Omar Tuttle, the only—ah—distaff member of the Board of Selectmen, who has been giving us her view on secession. Thank you again, Mrs. Tuttle, and good night. This is Charles Musgrave, your Charlie-on-the-spot reporter."

"Cut!" said the producer. "That's it!" The lights went out, and people began to dismantle the equipment and take it away. In a half hour the Tuttles' living room looked as it had at eight-thirty that morning, except that the ashtrays were piled high with cigarette butts, cardboard coffee containers stood about on the floor, and the wastebaskets were full of plastic cups, crumpled brown-paper bags, and doughnut fragments. Agnes started upstairs to change her dress, then stopped.

"You said you wanted to see me about something," she said. "What was it?"

Her husband thought a moment. "I'm damned if I can remember," he said. "It's gone clean out of my mind."

The portable television cameras required fewer personnel, and they were used for the sidewalk interviews and general shots around the town. One crew was stationed near the post office, and questioned those citizens who were willing to stop and talk, while another crew went after long shots, trying to establish the physical appearance and atmosphere of the island. The thinking behind these latter was that if the island should indeed become an entity of its own, it would be a good idea to have some stock footage on hand for future reference.

One enterprising crew got into Judge Cyrus Pepper's chambers, having tried unsuccessfully to photograph him while court was in session. He agreed to answer a few questions provided he could remove his robe; he didn't want anything he said to carry the slightest hint that it was an official pronouncement. He sat behind his desk, his fingertips forming a tent beneath his chin, and his white hair, backlighted by the window behind him, looking like a luminous milkweed puff. "What would you like to know?" he asked.

"How does it feel to be the law?" the reporter asked. "Does it give you a feeling of power?"

"In the first place, I am not the law," the judge replied. "The law is already written in the books."

"But if you secede there'll be nobody over you, will there?"

"We have not yet seceded. That decision will be made in good time."

"Still, you'll have to do something about crime. Won't that all be in your hands?"

"No more than it is now."

"What I'm getting at is that you'll be a dictator. You can punish whom you want for what you want. How does that appeal to you?"

"You overstate the case," the judge said mildly. "In the first place, there is no crime here, so there's nothing to punish."

There was a pause, and the reporter said, "Would you say that again?"

"I said there is no crime here, as such. A few broken windows, some high-spirited pranks, a driver having one too many cocktails—that sort of thing. But no crime."

"No theft? No larceny? No breaking and entering?"

"Oh"—the judge waved his hand in dismissal—"every now and then someone'll borrow something and forget to return it. Or take someone else's car for a joyride, and have an accident. Or perhaps, if the weather is bad, they may get into a house in order to have a dry place to sleep. But by and large

this is a peaceful community, and I see no reason for it ever
to change."

"It must make life pretty easy for you."

The judge smiled. "I am not without my dilemmas."

"Such as?"

"I'm not at liberty to discuss them."

"What's the stiffest sentence you ever handed down?"

"You mean in my entire career, or just here?"

"In your career."

"Oh, well, let's see . . . I used to be known for my sever-
ity, so that's a hard one. There are several life sentences I
remember—I'd rather not talk about them."

"And here?"

"Irrelevant. I've told you, there is no crime here."

The reporter looked at the photographer. "You got everything you want?" he asked.

"I don't suppose there's any rope lying around," the cameraman replied.

"Why?"

"I'd like to make it into a hangman's noose, and get a shot
of the judge holding it up. With a smile like, you know?"

The judge's voice hardened. "That is not funny," he said.

"No offense," the photographer said. "Only asking."

When they reached the street, the reporter said, "I just
don't buy that no-crime business. There ought to be some
place where we could check."

"What about the police station?"

"If the judge says there's no crime, the fuzz is likely to say
the same. No cop with a brain in his head is going to make a
liar out of the judge."

"So where do we check?"

"Let's try the newspaper. They may have some stuff in
the morgue."

Grace Turpin had just finished her cooking column, and
had taken it in to her husband's office, when the two men

came in. Sam was at his desk in a corner, trying to hammer out an aviation column, and he welcomed the chance to break it off.

"May I help you?" he asked.

"Yeah," said the reporter. "Where would we find the statistics on crime in the community?"

Sam thought about this. "I'm new here," he said. "I think Mrs. Turpin will be the one to help you." Grace came out of Turpin's office, and Sam said, "These gentlemen are looking for statistics on crime. Do we have any such?"

Grace looked blank, and called over her shoulder, "Lester, we don't have a file on crime, do we?"

Turpin appeared. "Why?" he said. "Who wants to know?"

"We've just been talking to the judge," the reporter said. "He said flatly there's no crime here, and I can't believe that. I'd like to see some figures, if you have them."

"Well," Turpin said, "that's kind of hard. We print the court calendar each week, but since most of the cases are either dismissed or have suspended sentences they don't really count as crime. You need a conviction or a sentencing to make a crime, don't you?"

"Beats me," the reporter said. "But are you telling me nobody's ever gone to jail?"

"Oh, no," Turpin replied, looking at Grace. "There was that fellow back about five years ago who—"

"Six," Grace said. "The year of the rabbit plague."

"That's right. Six years ago. He knocked his wife down with a secondhand Bronco, and drove back and forth across her till someone called the cops. He did time in the House of Correction."

"Did he kill her?"

"No. It being an old car the wheels were sprung, and he could never catch her square. She was some black and blue, though."

"That wasn't why he did time," Grace put in. "He was a cashier at the Safeway, and they found the week's take in the back of the Bronco."

"Come to think of it, you're right. But they'd never have found it if he hadn't been using his wife as a drag strip. Mostly, people around here are slow to suspect anyone." As an afterthought, he added, "Of their own."

Suddenly, Sam had an idea. "I know what you can do," he said. "Go down to the police station and ask for the Chief, and tell him you understand a human foot was found in the street. See what he says."

The reporter stared at him. "What is he likely to say?"

"He's likely to say it's a bear, but don't believe him. I happen to know it's a human."

"How do you know?"

"I was the one who found it. I turned it in, and it's just about driving him crazy."

The reporter looked at the photographer, who shrugged and said, "What can we lose? It might make a good picture. Does he still have it?"

"Ask him," Sam replied. "I'd be the last to know."

They left, and Sam went back to staring at his aviation column. The Turpins were quiet for a few moments.

"That was probably not a very smart thing to do," Turpin said.

Sam looked up, surprised. "Why?"

"If the Chief wants to call it a bear, he probably has a very good reason."

"Sure. If it's a human he may have a crime on his hands, and the last thing he wants is to have to solve a crime. I haven't been here long, but even I can tell that."

"There's also a thing called rocking the boat. More than anything else, he hates to have someone do that."

Sam gave Turpin a long look. "Do you know what this foot is about?" he asked.

"No, and I don't intend to. I've told you, this is not an investigative newspaper."

"Well . . . It'll still be interesting to see how he reacts."

"Possibly. But if I were you I wouldn't go near him for the next little while."

"Why? What can he do to me?"

"You'll be happier if you don't find out."

Chief Maddox was at his desk, working on a model of the whaleship *Charles W. Morgan*, when the television men came in. He saw the portable camera, and the lights, and the microphone and battery pack, and his first thought was that there'd been an accident of some sort, and they were coming to tell him about it. He tried unsuccessfully to hide the *Charles W. Morgan* behind a pile of papers, then stood up and said, "What can I do for you?"

"We're from WFIX-TV," the reporter said. "We're here on the secession story."

"The vote's not till Tuesday. There's no story here now."

"Well, we'd like some background material about the island. If it's going to be a separate state, or country, we ought to know as much about it as we can."

The Chief considered this. "I suppose you have a point there," he said.

"And if you can spare us the time, we'd like to have a few words with you."

"About what?"

"Conditions in general. Maintaining the peace. You know."

"All right. Where do you want me to stand?"

"Just sit at your desk, there." The reporter nodded to the photographer, who switched on his lights and flooded the police station with a white glare. "If you want, you can be working on your model," the reporter said, in a carefully offhand way. "Just the way you were when we came in."

Maddox started to reach for the model, then pushed more papers in front of it. "Go ahead with your questions," he said.

"Tell me, Chief," the reporter said, into the microphone,

"do you foresee any problems maintaining order if the island should secede?" He pointed the microphone at Maddox.

"None I can think of," Maddox replied.

"What is the present crime rate?"

"There is none."

"No crime at all? That's very unusual, isn't it?"

The Chief shrugged. "We do things different out here."

"What problems *do* you have?"

"Oh—driving to endanger. Assault and battery. Public drunkenness. Pranks."

"What are pranks?"

"You know—broken windows—fences ripped up—tires slashed—that sort of thing."

"You mean vandalism, don't you?"

"I suppose you could call it that. We call it pranks."

"How many arrests do you make in, say, a week's time?"

"One or two."

"Is that all?"

"No point in doing more."

"Why not?"

"They never get convicted."

"Never?"

"Damn seldom. Uh—excuse me—not often."

"Do you have much trouble with dogs?"

The Chief looked puzzled. "Dogs? No. Why?"

"Or any other animals?"

"There are no other animals."

"None at all? No rabbits?"

The Chief grinned. "We got rabbits, all right. But I never yet had to run a rabbit in for disturbing the peace. The same goes for deer."

"But aside from dogs and rabbits and deer, there are no animals on the island?"

"Oh, and cats."

"But no moose? Or panther? Or lynx? Or bear? Or wolf? Or ocelot?"

The Chief, who had been jovially shaking his head, said, "Not a one. And never has been."

"I see. Now, Chief, perhaps you can help me. I have heard on good authority that a human foot was found in the road here not long ago. Do you know anything about that?"

The Chief's eyes blazed, and he half rose from his chair. "Who told you that?" he said.

"That doesn't matter. Is it true, or isn't it?"

"It's a goddam lie! That was a bear's foot, and I can prove it!"

"Do you have it here?"

"Hell, no, I threw it away. But any goddam fool could tell it was a goddam bear's foot, and whoever says it wasn't is a spotted-ass liar! Now, turn that goddam machine off and get the hell outa here!"

"But, Chief, you just told me there were no bears on the island, and never had been. How can—"

"I don't give a hoot in hell what I told you—I'm telling you now it was a bear's foot, and you can both get your asses the goddam hell outa here or I'll lock you up for disturbing the peace! Now, go on! Get out!"

As they walked away from the police station, the reporter said, "I knew that no-crime story was too good to be true."

11

The interview fever grew more intense as voting day drew near; it was almost as though the media wanted to register every voter's opinion before he or she cast the actual ballot, thereby making the vote a mere formality. Such data as were available were fed into computers, but the machines, lacking any established pattern to guide them, came up with a variety of answers that ranged from all-out civil war to the re-election of Dwight D. Eisenhower. One imaginative computer programmer, searching for a guideline to feed into his machine, went back to the history books and selected salient incidents leading to the fall of Fort Sumter, and was rewarded with a detailed forecast of the first battle of Bull Run. There was no way to foretell how the vote would go, because such a vote had never been taken before. In 1861 secession had been a cumulative affair, with the various state legislatures declaring their positions over a period of time, but here it would either stand or fall on one day's balloting.

One of the off-island reporters, scanning *The Clarion Press* for feature material, found himself perusing the waterfront column, and he stopped in amazement at an item that read:

> Full moon next Tuesday, voting day, will be the Flower Moon, our Almanac says. Old-timers may recall it was at the full of the Flower Moon the bark *Ettie W. Spofford* went down with all hands just off Gander Rip. Also in the Flower Moon Charlie Huskins dropped out of the mizzen shrouds of the *Cyrus P. Talford*, Noonan Manchez drove his goat cart into the surf and neither he nor the goat was ever heard from again, and Logan Warren became the oldest man ever to be keelhauled. Looks like the Flower Moon means the wrong kind of flowers for folk hereabouts, so let's keep our hatches battened tight and hope nobody opens the sea cocks on Tuesday.

The reporter reread the item, then folded the paper, put it in his pocket, and set out for the newspaper office. Grace Turpin, who had just taken over the gardening column, was thumbing through a pile of seed catalogues when he came in.

"I'm from the Concord *Observer*," he said, in answer to her look. "Could you tell me where I'd find Old Salt?"

"He has an office here," Grace replied.

"Is he in?"

"What do you want to ask him?"

"I'd like to talk with him about his column."

"He's authorized me to answer any readers' questions."

He looked at her closely. "Then he isn't here?"

"If you have any questions I'll try to answer them," Grace replied. "Otherwise, I'm really quite busy."

"All right." The reporter pulled the folded paper from his pocket and said, "This item about the Flower Moon. Do you know what he was getting at?"

"It should be obvious. He was saying the Flower Moon is unlucky for the islanders, and he hoped they wouldn't do anything under its influence they might regret."

"In other words, he's against secession."

"You could put it that way."

"Why? He's the first person I've heard of so far who isn't a hundred percent in favor."

"He's not the only one. There are others."

"What are their reasons?"

"You'll have to speak to them. I can speak only for Old Salt."

"What are his reasons?"

"I've told you."

"You mean he's basing them on superstition?"

"Not superstition. Call it the law of averages."

"How?"

Grace paused. "There are some things that just feel wrong," she said. "You can go in a house, and the minute you step inside it feels wrong. Unhappy. Uncomfortable. Another house will feel clean and pleasant. And it has nothing to do with the lighting. The most brightly lighted house can make your skin crawl if it feels wrong. That's the way Old Salt feels about secession. He feels it's like jumping into a black void." She rubbed one forearm.

"And do you believe this?" the reporter asked.

"Why shouldn't I? I've seen it prove out too many times not to believe it."

"I take it you and Old Salt have talked a lot about the subject."

"Every week at the very least, Old Salt and I have a real, old-fashioned heart-to-heart talk. I feel I know him as well as I know myself."

"And he's what you might call clairvoyant?"

"You might. He has good and bad vibes, and more often than not they're right."

The reporter gave her a long stare. "What might his vibes tell him about me?" he said.

Grace returned the stare. "They might tell him you drink too much, and are afraid of losing your job."

"How do you—" The reporter stopped, then said, "Very interesting."

"Anything else you'd like to know?"

"Ah—I guess not. Give him my best next time you see him."

"I'll do that." Grace went back to her seed catalogues, and the reporter drifted outside.

St. Brendan's Church of the Mists did a brisk business on Sunday. The attendance was nowhere near that for Dennis Fenwick's funeral, but that had been a civic rather than a religious affair and had drawn people of all persuasions, many of them simply because they felt they should be seen. Now, two days before the secession vote, there was the feeling that people were seeking spiritual guidance, or at least touching base with the Deity, before making a decision that could affect the rest of their lives. Father O'Malley was pleased to note that the collection plate was unusually full, and tried not to equate this with the ritual sacrifices of pagan mariners, who slaughtered a sheep or an ox or a goat before setting out on a perilous voyage. Then Agamemnon came to mind, preparing to sacrifice his daughter Iphigenia, and Father O'Malley became mired in pagan similes until he luckily thought of Abraham and Isaac, thus facilitating his return to the comfort and safety of the Christian church. He saw Norris Webster among the congregation, and reasoned that an extra dollar from Webster was the equivalent of offering a son to sacrifice, so the Abraham and Isaac comparison held true. Provided, of course, Webster *had* put in an extra dollar, which was by no means certain. Father O'Malley wished he could keep his mind from wandering like this while the collection was being taken, but no matter how hard he tried he found that the imminent appearance of money set him to speculating, and not always in a Christian way.

For the theme of his sermon he chose Exodus 5:1–3, and read:

"'And afterward Moses and Aaron went in, and told Pharaoh, Thus saith the Lord God of Israel, Let my people go, that they may hold a feast unto me in the wilderness.

"'And Pharaoh said, Who is the Lord, that I should obey his voice and let Israel go? I know not the Lord, neither will I let Israel go.

"'And they said, The God of the Hebrews hath met with us: let us go, we pray thee, three days' journey into the dessert, and sacrifice unto the Lord our God; lest he fall upon us with pestilence, or with the sword.'"

He expanded on this theme for a half hour, likening the Governor of the State to Pharaoh, and saying that pestilence had already begun to ravage the mainland in the form of greed, corruption, governmental meddling, and creeping Socialism, and that the sword was sure to follow. He didn't mention the Russian Backfire bomber by name, but he said that the Enemy was poised to strike, and that we, lulled by the lies of the lily-livered politicians, would be annihilated in one fell swoop. It was time, he said, for the islanders, the children of Israel, to pack up their goods and chattels and flee into the desert, where they could praise the Lord and escape the impending holocaust. He concluded with a prayer for divine guidance on Tuesday, but it was already abundantly clear which way he was going to vote. He really meant divine reassurance and used "guidance" only because of its stronger overtones of humility.

It was a breezy, sunny day, and as the congregation filed out the wind plucked at the ladies' hats and played lewd tricks with their skirts, in some cases revealing expanses of flesh like distant flashes of lightning. A television crew was waiting on the sidewalk, taking quick shots here and there and waiting for a likely subject to interview. They spotted Muriel Baxter, the high school teacher, coming down the steps with one hand on her hat and one on her skirt, and the reporter told the photographer to hold the camera on her. He cleared his microphone, and approached Miss Baxter as she reached the sidewalk.

"Excuse me, ma'am," he said. "May I talk to you for a minute?"

Miss Baxter hesitated. Normally she would have refused, but on Friday she had been publicly abused by the parent of a child she'd reprimanded, and she was still seriously thinking of quitting her job and moving somewhere else. She felt no need to be cautious in what she said; in fact, she was bursting with things she wanted to say, none of them tactful. "What would you like to know?" she asked.

"First, your name and occupation." He pointed the microphone at her.

"Muriel Baxter, schoolteacher."

"How do you feel about secession?"

"I'm against it. The school badly needs State aid, and without it there will be chaos . . . Even more than now."

"What do you mean by that?"

All right, she thought, I've opened the can of worms, so I might as well go on with it. "There is no discipline," she said. "The older students do exactly as they please, and with complete impunity tell the teachers to go to hell. And when

I say 'go to hell' I'm using a euphemism. Their parents back them up, and there's nothing we can do."

"Can't you expel them?"

"Yes, if we want to have the school burned down." Years of piled-up frustration had started a landslide in Miss Baxter's mind, and the words came pouring out with no thought on her part. "The little children are fine and wonderful and they want to learn, but they see what the older ones are getting away with, and pretty soon they start doing the same thing. As I see it, there's no end to it, because nobody will do anything."

"Supposing you could do anything you wanted—what would you suggest?"

"I would suggest a return to the whipping post—for the parents."

"The *parents?*"

"That is correct. Ten or more years ago they had what were called the teen-age riots on the Sunset Strip, in Hollywood. Every Saturday night these kids would fill the street, break windows, overturn cars, and all the rest of it, just for lack of anything else to do. Their parents had given them money to get lost for the weekend, and the parents were furious when every now and then they had to come down to the police station and take a child home. So Mayor Yorty put through an edict that any time a child was booked three times for disorderly conduct, that child's *parents* would receive a stiff fine and/or jail sentence. That was the end of the teen-age riots. That is what's needed here." She stopped, and found that she was trembling. "Now, if you'll forgive me, I think I've said enough." She turned, and hurried away.

"Wait a minute!" the reporter called. "Miss Baxter! You've got to sign a release!" He produced a piece of paper from his pocket and waved it after her, but she kept on walking.

"I'll take it to her," Edgar Morris said, stepping up and reaching for the paper. He had apparently been standing behind Miss Baxter, because neither the reporter nor the photographer had noticed him before.

"Who are you?" the reporter asked.

"A friend of hers. Give it to me, quick, before she gets away." The reporter gave Morris the paper and a pen, and Morris hurried after Miss Baxter. He could still smell her perfume, which he had been inhaling as he stood behind her, and he thought he could catch faint wisps of it as he made his way through the departing crowd. He caught up with her at the corner, and said, "Excuse me, Miss Baxter."

She stopped, and looked at him. "Yes?" she said. It was the first word she had ever spoken to him, and Morris felt he would remember it the rest of his life.

"They want you to sign a release," he said. "I don't know what it means, but they asked me to take it to you." He held out the paper and pen, and Miss Baxter took them and read what was on the paper.

"If I don't sign this, they can't use the interview?" she said.

"Beats me," Morris replied. "That's the way it sounds." He wanted to prolong the conversation, but couldn't think how.

For a moment Miss Baxter was tempted to withhold the signature, and to ask that the interview not be used, but then she remembered the parent on Friday, who had taken her by the front of the dress and shaken her before the whole class, telling her that she would goddamned well leave his son alone, and her rage returned. She signed the paper with a flourish, and handed it and the pen back to Morris. "There you go," she said.

Morris felt uncomfortably like a messenger boy, but in the circumstances there wasn't much else he could do. Then an idea came to him, and he said, "Would you like a copy of this?"

"I don't see why," she replied, then changed her mind.

"It might not be a bad idea—just in case. I don't know what it'll prove."

"You never know, and you can't be too careful," Morris said. "Don't you bother to wait; I'll get it for you and bring it to your house."

"Do you know where I live?"

"No, but I can find out." Suddenly, Morris's head was full of wild and wonderful thoughts.

"It's 15 Apple Lane, but—it's kind of hard to explain. Maybe I'd better wait right here."

"No, no—go on with what you were doing. This may take a while, because if he's interviewing someone else I can't interrupt him. I'll get it to you—don't you worry about that." Morris dashed off before she could think of anything else, and was relieved to see that the reporter was interviewing none other than George Markey. Markey was in a jovial and expansive mood, and was answering questions before they were asked.

"I foresee a great future for the island," he was saying. "I think that once we've shaken off the bonds of mainland bureaucracy there's nothing we won't be able to do. We have our own resources—make no mistake about that—and with a little island know-how we can put them all together and make a—and become totally self-sufficient."

"How do you propose to do that?" the reporter asked.

"There are some things I'm not at liberty to discuss," Markey replied. "But let me put it this way: if the gnomes in the Statehouse think they can starve us into submission, or bring us to our knees by withholding vital supplies, well, all I can say to them is they have another think coming. And, to anticipate your next question, our quarrel is with the State and not the Federal Government, but if the Feds think *they* can put the squeeze on us, they, too, will find out different. We can take care of ourselves and of our own, and we don't need any off-islanders to tell us how to do it."

"Those resources you spoke of," the reporter said. "Could you be a little more specific about them?"

"Everyone knows our traditional resources," Markey replied. "Our fish and our shellfish and our—and so on, but this is an age when new things are being discovered every day, and there is no limit to what may be found on and around our shores. Kelp—do you realize that one of the primary sources of iodine is kelp? And that our beaches are strewn with literally tons of kelp? There's a fortune in that one item alone, and countless other fortunes to be made just by knowing what to look for. The possibilities are endless."

"Has anything actually been found?" the reporter asked. "Anything that wasn't already known to be here?"

"Not at the moment, no. But that's only because nobody has taken the trouble to look."

"Well, thank you very much, George Markey, and good luck to you and the island."

"Thank *you*," Markey replied, starting to move away.

"Just a minute, sir. Would you sign this release?" The reporter held out a form which Markey read, signed, and returned as though it were a prized autograph.

Morris produced the release Miss Baxter had signed, and gave it to the reporter. "She wants a copy," he said.

"A *copy?*" the reporter said. "For what?"

"Don't ask me. All I know is what she said. She said she wanted a copy, just in case."

"Well, the hell with her. I don't have enough forms I can afford to go around giving out duplicates."

Morris started to argue, then realized it was pointless.

"That Markey character," the reporter said. "You know him?"

"Everybody knows him," Morris replied.

"Does he know what he's talking about, or is he full of shit?"

"A little bit of each. About half and half."

"That's what I figured. Still, he's a town official, so I guess we'll use him."

"If you don't," Morris said, "your life won't be worth a plugged nickel."

The reporter laughed. "How about you?" he said. "Would you like to be interviewed?"

Morris had been so preoccupied with Miss Baxter that he'd forgotten about the island's problems. "You wouldn't want to use me," he said. "I'm an anarchist."

"Are you serious?" the reporter motioned to the cameraman to start rolling, and held out the microphone. "What's your name?"

"Edgar Morris."

"And you say you're an anarchist?"

"That's right. As I see it, there's no difference between one government and the next—the only decent thing is to have no government at all, and let everyone do as he pleases. If we can have real anarchy here then it'll be worth seceding; otherwise it'll just be another form of government and we'll pay the same stupid taxes and obey the same stupid rules and be just as unhappy as before. I bought a brand-new pickup truck—"

"Just a minute. You're against all taxes and all government and all rules, is that right?"

"Yes. I just want to be happy."

"And you feel you'll be happy if there is no government."

"I'll be free, and that's the same thing as happy."

"Go ahead."

"That's all. Everyone should be able to do as he pleases, and thumb his nose at the government."

"What about things like the police and fire departments? They're government, aren't they?"

"Oh, someone would take care of them. I just don't want them on my back."

"By the way, what do you do for a living?"

Morris hesitated. "I carve things out of driftwood. Birds—dragons—fish—things like that."

"Are you going to vote for secession?"

"Hell, yes. At least it'll be a change. And if things fall apart like I think they will, then we may have anarchy. It's a long shot, but worth taking."

"Why do you think things will fall apart?"

"I don't know. It just figures."

"I hope you don't mind my saying, Mr. Morris, that for an anarchist you sound uncommonly depressed. I always thought that anarchists were full of rage and fire and noise."

"I guess you'll have to put me down as a depressed anarchist, then. You can keep your hair on fire for just so long, then your scalp begins to hurt. I just want—"

"I know. To be happy."

"That's right. And fat chance."

"Well—I wish I could say good luck, but I'd honestly hate to see anarchy—"

"I know. You're one of them. No hard feelings. You want me to sign that release now?"

"If you will."

Morris signed, and they shook hands, and then Morris walked away in the general direction of the Sink Hole. It being Sunday, the bar wouldn't be open for another half hour, so he veered off and walked along the waterfront, trying to frame in his mind how he would (a) begin and (b) maintain a conversation with Miss Baxter. For reasons impossible to explain he found her irresistible, and he knew that if he blew his one chance at conversation with her he would be lost. Lost in more ways than one, because he had the feeling that if she should turn him down, or laugh at him, he might very well attack her. Attack, rape, whatever—and that would be the end of him. In a society run by rules the transgressor was doomed, and motives and mitigating circumstances were seldom taken into account when the punishment was meted out. Of course, if he could come up before Judge Pepper he would be as good as home free, but that was a risky chance to take because the case might be heard off-island with another judge, and the results could be disastrous. The best move was not to get in trouble in the first place, but that was easier said than done.

At one o'clock he went to the Sink Hole, where he had three ryes with ginger ale and began to feel better. The world no longer looked as hopeless as it had, and it occurred to him that he could spend the rest of his life rehearsing his conversation with Miss Baxter; the only sensible approach was to see her face to face, right now, and let events shape themselves. Rehearsed conversations never worked out, because the other party always had a reply that hadn't been counted on, and the whole carefully laid structure collapsed. He remembered the first time he'd dated a girl (it had been called dating then) he had worked out an elaborate plan of attack, which had hinged on the girl's agreeing to go for a midnight swim. He moved cautiously through her outer line of defenses, skirting the obvious booby traps and minefields that could have led to an immediate rejection, and when he felt he had reached her—so to speak—Siegfried Line, he opened the car door and said, "What do you say? Should we do it?" The girl's reply was instantaneous. "I'd love to," she said. "I really would. But I've just had my hair done, and I'll ruin it if I go swimming without a cap." He suggested they buzz home and get her cap, and she replied it would wake her grandmother and besides she had a hard day tomorrow and really ought to get some sleep. He tried once to regroup his forces, but the setback turned into a retreat that turned into a rout, and he finally slammed the door shut, started the car, and took her home. He kept a bathing cap in the glove compartment thereafter, but was never able to set up that particular approach again.

With this in mind, and another rye and ginger under his belt, he went into the men's room, examined his hair and teeth, cleaned his fingernails, and set out for 15 Apple Lane.

The daylight had a queer quality to it—it was too bright in some spots, and too dark in others—and he had the feeling that there were more ridges in the sidewalks than before. He felt that perhaps he should take a shower, but that seemed like a long and complicated operation, so instead he detoured past the drugstore, bought a small bottle of after-shave cologne, and splashed it on his face and shirt. Then he put the bottle in his pocket and continued on his way.

He had no trouble finding Apple Lane, which made the crossbar of an "H" between two larger streets, but there seemed to be no number 15. The numbers on one side ran from 1 to 13, and on the other side from 2 to 10, and look as he might, he could find neither 12, 14, nor 15. Finally, wondering if she had intentionally given him a wrong number—and feeling rage rise within him at even that suspicion—he knocked on the door of number 13 and waited. It was opened by a woman who looked at him without expression and said, "Yes?"

"I'm looking for number 15," he said, as though accusing her of having hidden it.

"Fifteen?" She frowned. "Who do you want?"

"Miss Baxter. Miss Muriel Baxter." He tried to sound faintly haughty, but knew it didn't come off.

"Oh." The woman's face cleared. "You go across and down that path behind number 10. You can't see it from the street."

He thanked her and did as she directed, and found a small, snug house with bursts of yellow forsythia beneath the windows. He went to the door and knocked, feeling his heart begin to pound, and when there was no answer he knocked again, more loudly. Still there was no answer, and he hesitated, then reached for the doorknob and tried it. The door opened, and he put his head inside and called, "Miss Baxter?" No sound. "Miss Baxter?" he said again, and this time caught the smell of her perfume. As though pulled by an invisible rope, he went into the house and looked around. Her perfume was everywhere, and it put the stamp of her personality on everything he saw: the book-covered table in the center of the room, the small and battered portable typewriter, the stacks of magazines, and the card table on which were laid out students' examination papers, all said "Muriel Baxter" to him, and all seemed intensely personal. He knew he shouldn't be in the house, and he knew that if she came back and found him her first move would be to scream, but the hypnosis of her perfume was such that he couldn't pull himself away; he had to see the whole house, because he might never get to see it again. Her bedroom was small and neat, and the pictures on the dresser pleasant although in no way unusual. There were two, in gilt frames, that were obviously her father and mother: solid, clear-eyed, midwestern people, dressed in formal clothes and giving the impression they never wore anything else. Then there were baby pictures, of children too young to be identifiable, and one full-length snapshot of a young man in a Navy ensign's uniform, smiling self-consciously at the photographer. That was all; that was apparently the only part of her life she wanted to remember. The clothes in her closet were either for daytime or informal evening wear, and there was no sign of what could even remotely be called a ball gown, but the overall effect on Morris was such that he wanted to shut himself in the closet and never come out.

He heard voices outside, and in a flash of panic realized there was no way to explain what he'd been doing; he'd trapped himself by wallowing in the aura of Miss Baxter, and now was as good as in jail. He shot out of the bedroom and into the Pullman-sized kitchen, where he wrenched open the back door and almost literally fell outside. Then, gathering himself together as best he could, he rounded the corner of the house and headed for Apple Lane. The voices, he saw, had come from children playing behind number 10, and they gave him no more than a passing glance as he turned down the lane and out of sight.

When Miss Baxter got home from lunch, which she'd had at the house of a friend, she knew the minute she entered the living room that someone had been there. Nothing seemed disturbed—she checked the living room, bedroom, and bath, taking care to look behind the shower curtain—but there was something in the air, a hint of cheap cologne, that was foreign to anything she'd ever smelled and certainly foreign to anything she'd ever had in the house. Her bedroom smelled most strongly of it, particularly her clothes closet, but there were traces of it in the living room, and when she went in the kitchen she could barely catch it at all. Then she saw the kitchen door standing open, and she felt her scalp tighten. Quietly she went to the door, looked outside, then pulled it closed. All right, she thought. Now what do I do? Call the police? There's nothing to report. Someone came in the house, and left by the back door. Maybe it was that strange man who was going to bring the copy of the release—she looked again in the living room, but could find nothing either added or missing—but if he did, why didn't he just slip it under the door? He must have had a reason, whoever he was, but what was it? . . . Well . . . She stood in the middle of the room, and suddenly the house, which had been home-like and welcoming for many years, took on a faint air of menace. She picked up the telephone and dialed the police station, and as she waited for an answer she thought that if this were a suspense thriller the line would have been dead when she picked it up. Well, at least that hadn't happened.

"Hello," she said when a voice answered. "This is Muriel Baxter, at 15 Apple Lane, I just want to report that sometime during the last"—she looked at the clock—"three hours someone came into my house. He didn't take anything, or break anything. He just came in, and left by the back door. . . . No, I'm afraid it wasn't. I don't usually lock it in the daytime. . . . That's right. I just thought you ought to

know. If anyone reports any prowlers, or anything. . .
Thank you. Have a nice day yourself."

She hung up and took a deep breath. For all the good *that*
call did, she thought, I could have put the message in a bottle and thrown it out to sea.

12

The voting, when it came, was something of an anticlimax.
It seemed as though everyone had been polled, or interviewed, or questioned, to the point where there wasn't a
surprise left, and the consensus was that the island would
vote for secession by a margin of better than three to one.
Balloting took place in Town Hall, where the voters, after
being checked off on a master list, took their ballots to an
area resembling a racetrack starting gate, where each stall
contained a stubby yellow pencil on a string, and where
there was sufficient privacy to make the vote legal. Then
the ballot was handed to a man who cranked it into a
box; the voter was once again checked off on a second
master list, and then left the building, feeling somehow
cleansed by having performed a civic duty. The whole procedure was carried out under the baleful stare of Chief
Luther Maddox, who looked as though he expected armed
insurrection at any moment. Sam, who had gone down to
Town Hall more or less out of curiosity, saw the Chief
standing guard and decided to go elsewhere. He wasn't exactly afraid of Maddox, but he remembered Turpin's warning and felt it wiser not to press the matter.

Of the town's 1,873 registered voters, there were 1,720
who cast their ballots, an all-time record. Of those 153 who
did not vote, two were in the intensive-care unit at the hos-

pital, twelve were off-island and had neglected to arrange
for absentee ballots, three had such paralyzing hangovers
they were unable to walk, one had awakened in the wrong
house and had phoned his wife to say he'd been called off-
island for the day, one thought the voting was not until the
following day, and the remaining 134 felt that the result was
such a sure thing that their votes wouldn't mean anything
one way or the other. This latter group was right, but not
by as much as they'd thought: the final count was 1,047 for
secession and 673 against, a negative vote of surprising size,
since so few had been willing to speak out against it before-
hand. The polls closed at 7:00 and by 9:30 the tally was
complete; when the result was announced the church bells
began to peal, automobiles raced through the streets with
their horns blaring, shotguns and flare guns and saluting
cannon hammered at the night air, and people who hadn't
spoken to one another all winter embraced and danced and
cheered like demented geese.

The State Governor had been watching the television
news coverage on and off throughout the day, and when the
bulletin was read on the ten o'clock news he stared glumly
at the set, while his cigarette burned unnoticed toward his
fingers. "Wouldn't you know it," he said, at last, to his aide.
"Wouldn't you goddam know the bastards would choose an
election year to pull something like this."

"It's going to be tricky," the aide observed. "There's no
denying that."

The Governor gave him a sour look. "Thanks for clear-
ing that up," he said. "Thirty-five thousand dollars a year I
pay you for advice, and you tell me this is going to be tricky.
They could have told me that at the zoo, and at the zoo I
have a free pass."

"It was just an offhand remark," the aide said. "It wasn't
meant to be deep."

"Well, thank God for that." The Governor felt the heat of

his cigarette, and suddenly stabbed it out in an ashtray. There was a knock at the door, and his press secretary came in.

"The reporters are here," the press secretary said. "They want to know when you'll have a statement."

"When I'm good and goddam ready," the Governor replied, dusting his hand on his trousers. "I'll have a statement when I think of something to say."

"They want something now. They say they've got deadlines to make."

"Well . . . tell 'em I'm working on it. Tell 'em I've got it under advisement. Tell 'em anything you like, only don't bug me with it. I've got enough on my mind as it is."

"Suppose I say you're adopting a policy of watchful waiting. That should hold them for tonight."

"Fine. Tell 'em I speak softly and carry a big stick. That'll give 'em something else to chew on."

The press secretary left, and the aide said, "I think that watchful-waiting idea is the best."

"You don't think it'll make me look like a do-nothing? Even *Coolidge* got out the National Guard, for Chrissakes, and he did it two months before election—I can't let them say that Coolidge had more guts than I."

"Nobody's going to remember Coolidge unless you remind them, and anyone who does a flashback to Coolidge is cutting his own throat. If you ask me, you should do the watchful-waiting bit. Let the bastards secede, and see—"

"*Let* them? They already have!"

"O.K. Just see how far they can go without State aid. There's that other expression—let them turn slowly, slowly, in the wind."

"Yeah. That worked like a charm, didn't it?"

"This is different. Your choice here is to let them hang themselves, or to go in and punch them around and play goon boy, and these days anyone who does that is out of his tree. It might have been all right when Coolidge was Governor, and the police were on strike, but you'll never make it wash if you jump on a bunch of citizens. They've got everything going for them—the minute you put one Guardsman over there they'll be calling you George the Third. And Coolidge may have got re-elected in 1919, but I can sure as hell promise you George the Third won't get elected today. There's not a bookie in the world who'd even give you odds."

"All right, but if this backfires it's going to be your neck."

"I'm aware of that. But I'd rather lose one lousy island than look like Hitler."

"That one lousy island brings in a lot of tax money."

"So tax someone else. Tax a nunnery. But don't get military. The minute you do they'll start accusing you of using napalm."

There was a perfunctory knock, and the press secretary reappeared.

"The reporters won't buy that watchful-waiting business," he announced. "They say they want to see you in person."

The Governor sighed. "All right," he said. "Write out something for me to say."

"Excuse me," said the aide, "but in circumstances like these I think it's better if you wing it. If you go out with a prepared statement it'll look as though you're reading something Fred wrote for you—which will in fact be the case. Your image here should be loose, fielding each problem as it comes along, and not all uptight and saying someone else's words. You should look *in charge*, is the main thing."

"By God, if you're wrong," the Governor said as he headed for the door, "if this thing gets bitched up at the very start—"

"Just be yourself, and everything will work out fine," the aide said, rising and following him out of the room. "And Fred and I will be right behind you, in case any clarifications are needed."

When they reached the press room the lights were on and the cameras were set up, and the Governor strode to the podium with the air of a policeman about to make an arrest. He grasped both sides of the lectern and looked around the room. "I'd like to make one statement first," he said. "If there are any questions after that, I'll be glad to answer them." He paused, then went on, "This whole secession business is a tempest in a teapot. When the islanders have had time to reflect on what they've done, I feel sure they'll rescind the whole declaration of secession and rejoin the State as lawful, satisfied citizens. Any resident of this State knows that if he or she has a legitimate grievance, my door is always open and my time is his—hers—and there is no reason whatsoever for any precipitate action. Islanders, being removed from our shores, may feel a certain sense of isolation, but I can assure them that they and their problems are as much in my mind as those who—whose problems—people and their problems—as those across from the Statehouse."

The aide and the press secretary exchanged glances, and the press secretary ran his tongue across his lips.

The Governor dabbed his upper lip with a handkerchief, and said, "Are there any questions?" Several hands shot up, and he pointed at one reporter, who rose.

"Sir," the reporter said, "you've said you're going to wait until the islanders come to their senses and rejoin the State. Is that correct?"

The press secretary was about to intercede when the Governor said, "I did not say 'come to their senses.' I said when they 'have had time to reflect.'"

"That amounts to the same thing, doesn't it?"

"Except it's your phraseology. If you're going to quote me, quote me correctly."

"Well, supposing they don't come to their senses. What will you do then?"

"I'll cross that bridge when I get to it. Next question." He pointed to another reporter, a portly lady in tweeds and low-heeled shoes, whose notes spilled out of her lap as she stood up.

"You said you'll cross that bridge when you get to it," she said. "Does that mean you have no contingency plan for the future?"

"Mrs. Dorty, I have plans for everything," the Governor replied, and there was scattered laughter.

"Then could you tell us your plan in case the islanders don't return? Would you use the National Guard?"

"The very idea of force is repugnant to me," said the Governor. "But I wouldn't want to rule it out as a last resort. I have to keep my options open, and I don't—ah—believe this is the time to spell them all out in detail. Next question."

This reporter was a thin, elderly man with a hearing aid, who spoke in an unnaturally loud voice. "I have a question, Governor," he said. "It's a question I've been asking since May of 1976, when you said your first move would be to trim expenses on the—"

"This press conference is about secession," the Governor cut in. "If you have any other questions, make an appointment with my press secretary."

"I've tried that, too," the reporter said, sitting down. "No better luck one way than the other."

The next reporter to be recognized read from notes he had obviously prepared before the meeting. "Sir," he said, "could you give us an idea of (a) the amount of tax revenue that will be lost to the State if the island remains seceded and (b) how you intend to make up for that loss of revenue? In other words, what areas may expect to be more heavily taxed than at present?"

The Governor cleared his throat. "You bring up an interesting point," he said. "The revenue loss would obviously depend on the length of time the island remains seceded, so there is no accurate way to put a figure to it at this point in time. However, we know exactly the penalty the island will have to pay for every month its taxes are in arrears, so the longer they remain seceded, the more they will have to pay when they eventually return. Thus it seems safe to forecast that nobody else will have to pay a nickel more in taxes than they do now."

"That is always assuming the island returns," the reporter said.

"Correct. Looking at it realistically, they have no other option. Next."

This reporter held a sheet of yellow paper in his hand, which he consulted before saying, "Governor, it just came over the wire services that three states have offered the island citizenship. Do you have any comment on that?"

"*Three* states?" the Governor said, incredulous. "What are they?"

Reading from his sheet, the reporter said, "The governors of Maine, New Jersey, and North Carolina have all invited the island to join them. New Hampshire is working out the details before making a firm offer."

"They're crazy!" the Governor replied. "They can't do that!"

"It says here they did."

"What did the islanders say?"

"There's been no word on that yet. They may not even have heard about it."

After his momentary loss of aplomb the Governor regained control, and smiled. "Well, I don't think there's any worry there," he said. "Those states are in no position to offer the islanders anything we can't. If the islanders are in a mood to secede they'll secede from any state you care to name, and only time will bring them back. It may be a longer or a shorter time, but they'll be back, and, when they come, it will be to their parent state. Make no mistake about that."

"Would you care to estimate how long that will be?" a reporter in the back of the room asked.

"Certainly not. I just know it will happen. And now, la-

dies and gentlemen, I bid you all good night." He turned
and strode briskly from the room, followed by his aide. The
press secretary stayed behind, to try to gauge the tenor of
what the news stories would be like, and to fill in what
figurative cracks had been left in the dam. This was always
the trickiest part of a news conference for him, because the
Governor seemed to make good sense while he was talking,
and it was only in retrospect that little globs of double-talk
showed up. The press secretary liked to have the reporters
bring them up now, rather than when they got back to their
desks.

"How do you think it went?" the Governor asked his aide
when they were safely behind the doors of his office.

The aide reached in a cabinet and brought out a bottle of
Bourbon, from which he poured two drinks. Then he
reached in another cabinet, a simulated bookcase in which
was a small refrigerator, and dropped ice in the glasses. He
handed one to the Governor.

"Generally speaking, I think it went O.K.," he said. "I
could wish you hadn't been so surprised about the offers
from Maine and the rest. That was unfortunate."

"Well, God damn it, I *was* surprised. Who wouldn't have
been? Who do those bastards think—"

"The point is that you shouldn't ever *show* surprise. If
you're going to be in charge, you should know everything
everyone else does. If they tell you Idi Amin has just been
elected Pope, you should be able to say, 'Yes, I know,' and
go on to the next subject."

"That's easier said than done . . . Oh, that one guy
brought up a good question—just how much do we take in
from the island in taxes?"

"I don't have the figures in front of me," the aide replied.
"But I'd say about five mil, give or take."

"And how much do we shell out?"

"A million three, at the most."

"That's going to make a difference, isn't it? A total loss of three million seven."

The aide shrugged. "Peanuts. As you so wisely observed, it'll all be made up in fines."

The Governor took a swallow of his drink, and stared at the oily swirls of liquor in the glass. "I just wish I could get Coolidge out of my mind," he said. "He didn't sit around on his butt and theorize—he *acted*."

"Governor, that was before you were even born. If you're going to go back into ancient history I can cite you any number of people: John Wilkes Booth didn't theorize either, and look where it got him—burned to death in a barn. Benedict Arnold didn't theorize, and his name will go down in history as the prime traitor of all time. Guy Fawkes was a man of action, and they're *still* hanging him; for over three hundred and seventy years they've been hanging him every November. Lord Cardigan was one rootin'-tootin' action freak, and you remember what happened to the Light Brigade? Wiped out. I could go on all night. There is a great deal to be said for theorizing, and don't ever let anyone tell you there isn't."

"I suppose so. But they've never yet put up a statue to a theorist; it's only the admirals and generals you see in the parks."

"And poets—don't forget Emerson and Longfellow and Whitman. But if it's only a statue you want, I can have one commissioned tomorrow—tonight. Give me the phone."

"I wasn't serious."

"You were, but this isn't the time for it. Get this island screw-up settled, and then it'll be time to talk about a statue."

The Governor drained his drink and held the glass out for a refill. "Just incidentally," he said, "do you know the names of any good sculptors?"

13

The secession clambake was held on a spit of land that curved out from the main body of the island and formed the upper end of the harbor. It could be reached either by boat or by four-wheel-drive vehicle, and its main advantage lay in the fact that, being composed mostly of sand and pulpy vegetation, the fire hazard was virtually nil. During the past few days members of the Waterfront Club's entertainment committee had been bringing in stones the average size of bowling balls and arranging them in the pits that would eventually comprise the foundation of the bake. They also brought in loads of wood—driftwood, fence posts, strips of planking from dismantled houses, parts of old shacks, anything that would burn—and stacked it beside the stones as fuel for the fires. Then, at half tide on the morning of the bake, they went along the sides of the harbor inlets with burlap bags, filling them with rockweed, the kind of seaweed that has small bubbles of water in the leaves, which makes the best kind of steam when heated. These bags, of which there were more than a dozen, were left soaking in the water at the edge of the beach, staked in place to keep the tide from rolling them away.

It was decided that, since the bake would take two hours from the lighting of the fires to the unveiling of the first course, it would be the part of wisdom to have the process half completed before the first celebrants arrived. This would allow an hour for so-called cocktails, which would provide the right festival atmosphere and still leave the people able to manage their food when they got it. Experience had shown that a two-hour cocktail period resulted in more food being dropped in the sand than eaten, whereas a half hour was too short, and the food got cold and soggy while people had the one more warm-up drink they felt they needed. What happened after the meal was up to whatever minor god Dionysus had put in charge of the event, and was no concern of the entertainment committee's. They were responsible for getting the food to the people, and nothing further. (They had been forced to take a firm stand on this once, when they were sued by the mother of a young lady who had crashed the party with an off-island spinning-reel salesman, and had subsequently discovered herself to be pregnant. The case was thrown out when, first, the young lady could produce no ticket stub to prove she had legally been at the party, and second, the actual site of the impregnation became clouded. Club members, when questioned, swore they had seen nothing unusual about her behavior, which was the literal truth.)

In order to keep to the schedule, therefore, the stones were formed into three separate piles, each pile like an igloo in that there was space inside. Kindling was put in this space, and the planks and boards and driftwood and the rest were stacked in pyramid form around and over the stones; kerosene was poured over the lot, and one by one the bonfires were ignited. Each one burned for an hour, the flames being continually fed to make sure an even heat was maintained, and then the ashes were knocked away, and the stones, white and cracked and smoking with the heat, were raked out flat and covered with a layer of rockweed, which hissed and spat and steamed as it hit. The food was arranged by courses, the first being soft-shelled clams, hot dogs, and sausages, wrapped in separate cheesecloth bags, and these were put on the bake and covered with another layer of weed. Then seawater was poured on, to make more steam, and the entire mound was covered with a tarpaulin, onto which a crew began to shovel sand until it looked like one large sand hill. The sand was continually tested to see if any heat was escaping, in which case more sand was added for extra insulation.

The second and third fires were tended the same way, to cook the subsequent courses. Normally corn would have formed a large part of the menu, but it was too early for corn, so extra sausages were substituted instead. For the rest there were lobsters, chicken, bass, both sweet and white potatoes, mussels, eels, and, in short, anything that could be cooked by steaming. The mixture of the various flavors, plus the salty tang of the rockweed, was what gave the bake its unique character.

People began to arrive at noon, just as the first mound was being covered with sand, and it was clear that some of them had been celebrating secession since the night before. Edgar Morris was red-eyed and owlish, greeting everyone with a smile and laying one finger along the side of his nose as though he knew something nobody else did; Emil Corning laughed unnecessarily loudly and often, punctuating his merriment by digging his elbow into his wife's ribs; and Omar Tuttle, while not showing the usual signs of drunkenness, looked as though he were about to be sick, which only Agnes knew was proof he'd been into the sherry before breakfast. The Turpins, who were the only known anti-secessionists in the crowd, did their best to maintain expressions of neutrality, and even to pretend they were enjoying themselves. Lester Turpin had argued Grace into coming on the ground that, if they were to reflect the feelings of the community, they had damned well better find out what those feelings were. He had guessed wrong about the island's desire to secede, and it now behooved him to read the local mood a little more accurately.

As often happened at Club functions, members showed up who were seldom seen around the clubhouse, and among these was George Markey, who appeared bringing Dustin Williams as his guest. Ella Markey was conspicuous by her absence. Markey played the jovial host, introducing Williams to anyone within range, and Williams, who was dressed as though for a Palm Beach wedding, flashed his toothy smile about like a rotating aero beacon. As a bow to the sporting nature of the occasion he wore a mesh golf cap, with an arcane club emblem on the front.

Two people were particularly interested in Williams's presence with Markey: one was Agnes Tuttle, who deduced that Williams had gone to Markey when she refused to have anything to do with him, and the other was Norris Webster, who had been doing his best to pin something on Agnes and Williams, and now found his theory apparently shot to hell. He was left with a lot of background information on Williams and very little else, and it irritated him to have missed the mark so completely on Agnes. He stood by the free-beer tub, glowering at Agnes and wondering what else he might be able to charge her with.

When Sam and Lennie and Gibbon arrived, having come overland in Gibbon's Jeep, the party was just moving from the first, awkward stage, when people stood around and drank their drinks faster than necessary, to the second, more relaxed stage, where conversation came easily and with fewer generalities and platitudes. Secession, as a subject of conversation, had burned itself out in the previous two weeks; now that it was an accomplished fact there seemed very little to say about it, and whatever the consequences were would become evident in the near future. In a sense it was like talking about the weather: everyone has his own theories about the wind and clouds and barometric action, but when the hailstorm hits there's nothing left to say, and all hands take cover and make small jokes while they wait for it to pass. Except that in this case it wouldn't pass; it was here to stay, and it was up to each individual to make the most of it.

From her job at the Sink Hole, Lennie knew a good many of the celebrants by face if not by name, and Sam found himself having to wait his turn in order to have a word with

her. She wasn't forgetting him; she was simply having a
good time, and in the back of his mind he hoped it might
help her forget whatever ghost it was that still seemed to be
following her. Gibbon went off to help the men with the
bake, and Sam sought out the Turpins, who were standing
slightly apart.

"Welcome!" Turpin greeted him. "So far, you haven't
missed a thing. The beer is in that big tub, over there."

"Thank you," Sam replied. "Do you want me to take
notes, or should I write it all from memory?"

"Let's see what happens," Turpin replied. "Enjoy yourself, and if anything special comes up we'll make a story out
of it. Otherwise we'll just give it a paragraph."

"I was hoping you'd say that," said Sam. "I don't seem to
have brought a pencil."

At that moment Lennie appeared, and Sam introduced
her to the Turpins. She pointed at Edgar Morris, who was
heading off into the crowd. "Who's he?" she asked. "I know
his face, but that's all."

"His name is Morris," Turpin told her. "Edgar Morris. He
carves things out of driftwood which, for reasons I cannot
explain, sell for a good deal of money."

"Is he single, or is his wife off-island?"

Turpin seemed amused by the question. "He is single," he
said. "Do I gather he's been—"

"Not at me," said Lennie. "Not yet. But he's wearing
enough cologne to stun a horse. Usually only single men do
that, or married men if their wives are off-island."

Turpin laughed, and looked at Grace. "I'll remember that,
next time you leave the island," he said.

"You do that," she replied. "It'll warn the girls, so they
can hide."

At that moment George Markey came up and joined
them, bringing with him Dustin Williams. "I'd like you to
meet an old friend of mine," he said in his bullhorn voice.

"Dusty Williams. He has connections that'll come in right handy, now we're a country on our own."

"How interesting," Grace Turpin said. "What are they?"

Williams, who recognized Lennie's face but couldn't remember from where, glanced quickly at her before reciting his list of credentials. Then he spun off a half dozen names and said, "That's just a partial list, of course, but I think I can safely say that if there's anything the island needs I can find the person to supply it."

"How absolutely fascinating," Grace said. "And what's there in it for you?"

Turpin, who had never heard Grace ask a rude question of a stranger, looked at her in astonishment, but Williams remained unruffled.

"Call it patriotism," he replied. "I'm a property owner here, and I want to see the island make out the very best it can. Johnny Dulles once told me that—"

"Who Dulles?" said Grace.

"You knew him as John Foster Dulles," Williams said with a smile. "To me, he was always—"

"Of course!" Grace said. "The one whose friends called him Foster!"

"That's right. At any rate—"

"Dear, would you like me to get you a drink?" Turpin broke in, moving between Grace and Williams. "You know you don't want to catch another chill."

"Come on, Dusty, there are some people I'd like you to meet," Markey said, taking Williams by the arm and steering him away. When they had moved off he said, in a low voice, "Don't mind Grace Turpin. She gets a little bitchy at times."

"Nonsense," said Williams. "I found her amusing."

"What in God's name were you thinking of?" Turpin said to Grace when Markey and Williams had left. "If you want to challenge him to a duel, you just hit him in the face with your glove."

"He gave me bad vibes," Grace replied, smiling. "He's a phony."

Turpin looked over to where Markey was introducing Williams to another group. He was quiet for a while, then shrugged.

"Remember," Grace said, "this is not an investigative newspaper."

Agnes and Omar Tuttle had watched from a slight distance, and observed the scene without comment. Then Tuttle said, "Did I ever tell you about those radio broadcasts?"

"What radio broadcasts?" Agnes replied, only half listening. She was still watching Markey and Williams, and wondering how close an association they'd worked out.

"The day you were interviewed," Tuttle said, and belched slightly. His second beer had neutralized the sweetness of the sherry, but his digestion still wasn't all it should have been. "I came in to tell you, but then the interview got everything sidetracked, and I forgot."

"I guess you didn't, then," said Agnes. "What was it?"

"These messages were in a sort of code. It sounded as though someone had discovered something offshore and was reporting it to someone else, and that person said to pretend nothing had happened. It sounded kind of fishy, and I wondered if you knew what it might be. All I can tell is, someone is looking for something—we saw their boat the day we went fishing—and they've found it but are pretending they haven't. Do you know who it could be?"

Agnes didn't take her eyes off Markey and Williams. "Yes," she said at last. "I think I have a very good idea."

Gradually the party entered its third stage, where people no longer stayed with those with whom they'd come, and instead circulated through the crowd exchanging quips and banter and, in some cases, keeping an eye out for possible action. There were, as always, the more settled married couples, who brought cooler chests and canvas chairs and installed themselves on a patch of sand from which they didn't move for the duration of the party, but there were also those for whom the clambake was a chance to open new horizons, and they made the most of it. There were also, inevitably, children of assorted ages, who raced about like crazed minnows and prevented any one group from relaxing for too long.

Arthur Gibbon was not married, and it seemed unlikely that he ever would be, because at the end of a day's work his main pleasure was to go fishing or clamming or scalloping or hunting, and anything domestic was low on his list of priorities. But he didn't mind female company—in its place— and after a few beers he could even become faintly ardent, although he often spoiled things by bursting into laughter or making an overly direct remark. Now, finished helping with the bake, he got an icy beer from the tub, stripped off the top, and looked around. Sam and Lennie, his guests, seemed to be having a good time, so he had no responsibilities there and was free to operate on his own. He spotted Dora McCardle, a woman in her late thirties whose husband had recently run off with the baby-sitter, and since she was standing alone he reasoned no harm could come from having a word with her. He approached her and, indicating her empty glass, said, "May I get you another drink?"

"No, thank you." she replied primly.

Gibbon couldn't think of anything more to say, so he drifted off.

Lennie had momentarily vanished in the crowd, and Sam was surprised to see Felicity, the waitress from the Sink Hole, coming toward him. He didn't know with whom she'd come to the bake, but he guessed the possibilities were endless. She greeted him warmly, although with no implications of anything more, and said, "I found an interesting thing the other day."

"Oh?" said Sam. "What was that?"

"Remember I told you a dog seemed to have been digging at the garbage? Well, I decided to bury it a little farther from the shack, so if it did get dug up it wouldn't look like it was mine, and I came on this queer thing, all rusty like, with a chain at one end."

"What was it?" Sam asked.

"I don't know. It was about yea long"—she indicated almost two feet—"and there were these two long pieces of steel that were bent almost double, and then a sort of circular thing in the middle with jagged edges, like teeth. I couldn't make head nor tail of it."

Sam laughed. "It sounds like a bear trap, or—" he began, then stopped. "Where did you say you found it?"

"Out behind the shack. Maybe twenty yards away, in the dunes."

"What did you do with it?"

"Nothing. I couldn't figure out what it was."

"Is it still there?"

"So far as I know."

Lennie appeared out of the crowd, followed by a youth in a Day-Glo hunting cap. "I gather you two have met," she said to Sam.

"Uh—yes," Sam replied. "She was just telling me about a—"

"It's something I found behind the shack," Felicity said. "I thought it was just a rusty piece of metal, but Sam seems to think it's some sort of treasure."

"I didn't say that," said Sam. "I would like to see it, though."

"I'll bet you would," Lennie said, slipping her arm through his. "But not today. Remember me? I'm your date today."

"Well, some big deal," said the youth in the Day-Glo cap. "Where does that leave me?"

"Pretty much where it found you, I guess," Sam replied pleasantly.

The youth looked at Felicity. "I got a boat here," he said. "Want to go for a spin?"

"What kind of boat?" Felicity replied.

"Boston Whaler. Sixty-five-horsepower Evinrude. She'll do—"

"No, thanks. My kidneys aren't up to it."

The youth gaped like a bass, then turned away in search of a more likely prospect.

A table had been set up, on which were hors d'oeuvres—cheese and crackers and onions and pickles and salami—and Gibbon cut himself a large chunk of cheddar and popped it in his mouth. Then he cut another, smaller piece, and put it atop a thin slice of onion on a cracker. He took a swallow of beer to cleanse his mouth, then as daintily as possible he carried the cracker and cheese to Dora McCardle.

"Would you be interested in some cheese?" he asked.

"No, thank you," she replied.

"Freshen your drink?"

"Thank you, no."

Gibbon ate the cracker and cheese in one gulp, and went to get a cold beer.

"I can promise you one thing," Dustin Williams said to Emil Corning.

"Go ahead," Corning said with a grin. "You can't frighten me." He was having his usual vodka and cranberry juice, and had moved from a plastic on-the-rocks glass to a highball glass to the cranberry-juice jar, into which he periodically splashed more vodka. He stood as though the beach were the deck of a moving ship.

"I can promise you," Williams said, "that you will have the services of the top men in international law. I know them all—Foster Dulles, Dean Achinson, Dean Rusk, Hank Kissinger—and all I have to do is make one phone call, and they'll come running."

"Even the dead ones?" Corning asked. "That's some trick, if you can do that."

"Henry the K isn't dead, and make no mistake about that," Williams said. "He and I had dinner just last week, and he told me that any time I needed anything—anything at all—I had only to call. Of course, if Nixon were still President—but that's another story."

Agnes Tuttle saw that Markey was temporarily separated from Williams, and she went up to him. "May I speak to you a minute?" she said.

Markey put his arm around her. "Agnes, old girl, you can speak to me any time you want," he said. "What's on your mind?"

"Did Dustin Williams come to you about offshore rights?" Agnes said.

Markey's arm remained on her shoulders, but his smile faded. "Why?" he said.

"He came to me, and I'd have nothing to do with him. Now Omar tells me he's heard on the radio they've found something offshore."

"On the *radio*?" Markey withdrew his arm.

"On Omar's radio. It's in code, but he says he can tell they've found something, and are trying to pretend they haven't."

"Well, well, well," said Markey. "What do you know about that?"

"I just thought you'd like to know," Agnes said.

"You were absolutely correct," said Markey. "One hundred thousand percent."

Someone had made up an island flag, with a cluttered design of stars and waves on a blue field, a sunrise in one corner and a crescent moon in the other, and the "Don't Tread on Me" slogan across the bottom. It was nailed to an old mast, which had been brought along for the purpose, and three men were now trying to implant the mast firmly in the sand. Others gathered around and offered advice, and one man, who had brought a 10-gauge saluting cannon, stood by with his hand on the lanyard, waiting for the flag to be officially declared raised.

"Does it remind you at all of Iwo Jima?" Grace Turpin

asked her husband, who had just brought her a new drink.

"Don't ask me," Turpin replied. "I was only a correspondent."

"But you were there."

"I was so terrified I can't remember. When they raised the flag, I was looking for a place to throw up."

"Well, that's the way I feel."

"Drink your drink and be quiet. This is supposed to be a celebration."

The cannon went off with a boom and a flash of fire and white smoke; a few ladies squealed, and then there were cheers and applause. Finally Markey mounted unsteadily onto the hors d'oeuvre table while four men held the legs, and he raised his arms for silence. The speech that followed was largely incomprehensible, because of both the delivery, which was slurred, and the audience, which was in a mood for ribald repartee, and after a while Markey waved and clasped his hands over his head, and just managed to get down without falling. There were more cheers and applause, then someone bellowed, "Chow down!" and the bake was officially ready.

Gibbon helped the men as they carefully shoveled the sand off the first mound, then rolled back the tarpaulin and exposed the steaming food. Long trestle tables had been set up, with paper plates and pots of melted butter, and the people began to line up and wait their turns as the cheese-cloth bags were plucked open and the steamed clams shoveled out. Gibbon saw that Dora McCardle was still alone, and thought that one more try couldn't hurt. He filled a paper plate with steamers, put a small cup of melted butter on the side, and took it to her.

"Care for any clams?" he asked.

"No, thank you." Her tone by now was icy.

He counted to three, then said, "Well, you know what they say on the mainland."

"What's that?" said Dora.

"Piss on you," Gibbon replied, and gave the plate to a passing child.

One by one the mounds were opened, and the food, which had seemed like enough for a full combat division, began to disappear. Large garbage cans were set up for trash, and while some empty clamshells were left on the beach all lobster shells and chicken bones and cans and bottles and glasses were dropped into the garbage cans, the plastic liners for which were removed and replaced when they became full. The food brought a temporary lull in the other activity, but its long-range effect was an invigorating one, bringing renewed strength to some who had started to slow down. Sam was cheered to see that Lennie was still enjoying herself; her eyes sparkled and she laughed easily, and her whole attitude was that of a child suddenly let out of school. When he asked her, unnecessarily, if she was having a good time she laughed, gave him a sideways look, and said, "If this is secession, we ought to do it more often." An aura suggesting static electricity had built up around her, giving Sam the feeling she might glow in the dark.

Some of the children started a Frisbee game, which led to a softball game, and then a few of the boat owners began a form of aquatic rodeo, running obstacle courses around floating objects and in general roiling up the water off the beach. When this palled, someone produced a door that had been brought as firewood and not used, and this was tied by a long line to the stern of a bass boat, a powerful open-hulled craft with an inboard engine. The owner of the bass boat took the controls, and Gibbon tended the line as the boat was backed in to shore and the door held by two men, just touching the sand. Then amid a good deal of laughter a man stripped to his shorts, stood on the door, and grasped a steadying line that was attached like reins to the forward edge. At a signal the boatman gunned his engine, the towline grew taut, the two men holding the door gave it a push, and the door and its rider were launched. They headed straight out from shore, and when the boat finally turned, the door skidded sideways and the rider went off in a plume of spray. He was towed back to shore, where he dried himself in front of a fire and another man took a turn.

Dustin Williams had been watching the operation with faint amusement, and when the third man went off Williams turned to Markey and said, "There's nothing to that. I could do it blindfolded."

Markey looked at him. "You want to try?"

"Why not?" Williams kicked off his white loafers, put them on his beach towel, and walked toward the water.

"Hey," Markey said, following him. "Aren't you going to take off your clothes?"

"No need to," Williams replied. "I won't get wet."

"You're crazy," Markey said. "But if that's the way you want it—" He called to the boatman, who was edging in toward shore, "I've got a customer for you here! He wants to show us how it's done!"

Everybody stared at Williams, who waited quietly for the door to be brought to the beach. He straightened his golf cap, buttoned the middle button of his canary yellow blazer, flexed his legs to loosen the crotch of his purple slacks, then stood, relaxed and confident, at the water's edge. The door touched the sand and the two men grasped it; the steadying line was handed to Williams, and he stepped onto the door and said, "Let's go."

The boat engine roared, the men gave the door a mighty shove, and there was a surge of water as the boat and the door gained speed. They headed straight out as before, then the boat made a slow, easy turn, and Williams rode the door in a wide arc behind it, bumping slightly as he crossed through the wake. The boat straightened out and gained speed, then made a sharp reverse turn, and Williams, like the end man on a snap-the-whip, almost flew through the air. But he kept his balance, and on the next turn he rode the door out to the side so that it was almost on a level with the boat. Then he cut back and zigzagged through the wake, making as graceful a figure as was possible considering the generally unseaworthy condition of the door. Then something happened. From the shore nobody could tell exactly what it was, but the boat slowed down, the engine coughed once, and then stopped. Slowly, gently, the door began to sink, and at the same time Williams began to scream. The water reached his knees and then his hips while he struggled to remove his wristwatch, then he went all the way under and only his hand was seen, holding the watch in the air. Finally that vanished, and his golf cap was left floating on the surface. Gibbon, who had been helping the boatman with the engine, now hauled in quickly on the towrope, and in a few moments he had Williams over the gunwale and into the boat. He left him, a wet and twitching lump, in the stern, while he returned his attention to the engine, and in a few more minutes the watchers on shore saw a cloud of blue smoke and heard the cough and putter of the engine, and the boat turned toward the beach.

Williams was taken to the fire, where his clothes were removed and he was wrapped in towels and fed brandy, and there was no one in the crowd whose face didn't register the deepest concern for his well-being. He received all sorts of offers and advice but listened to none of it, and shortly demanded to be taken home. Markey escorted him, in a Jeep volunteered by one of the Club members, and there followed a kind of letdown that left everyone wondering what to do next. Some people got out spinning rods and started casting on the ocean side of the sandspit, others stretched out on or under towels and went quietly to sleep, while a stalwart few decided to concoct a punch made from all the half- to quarter-empty bottles.

Gibbon poked through the remains of the bake and picked out a few sausages, then found a cold beer and brought it to where Sam and Lennie were sitting and looking out to sea. He offered them each a sausage, which they declined, then opened his beer. There was silence for a few moments before he spoke.

"Christ, I had to laugh," he said. "He went down so slow."

14

Had the weather been a little warmer the clambake would probably have lasted all night, but as soon as the sun went down a chill set in, and the remaining celebrants began to gather up their belongings. Those with children had left a long time ago, and those in charge of the bake had buried the stones and the dried-out rockweed, so all that remained was to search the area for stray clothing and bottles, burn whatever paper or plastic goods were left, then extinguish the fires and bury the ashes. The flag was taken down and ceremoniously folded, and the people bundled themselves into their automobiles and boats, and left. The headlights went in single file in one direction, and the red and green running lights went in another, and by the time the fat, orange moon had risen the sandspit was cold and deserted.

"I don't want it to stop," Lennie said as Gibbon drove her and Sam into town. "Isn't there someplace else we could go?"

"Tomorrow's a workday for me," Gibbon replied. "But tell me where you want to go, and I'll drop you off."

Lennie turned to Sam. "Think of something," she said.

Sam laughed. "I'm trying," he said. "But all I've thought of so far is the Sink Hole, and I'm sure that's no treat for you."

"No, let's go someplace else. What about—" She stopped, as it became clear that she and Sam were both thinking about Felicity's shack. "No," she said. "I imagine Phil's probably there by now."

"You got a car?" Gibbon asked.

Lennie looked at Sam. "Can you build one?" she said. "I'll do anything not to have to go home."

"I can try," Sam replied. "But I can't promise you much. The Army taught us to repair cars, but not how to build them."

"Anyway, it's too late to start. The stores where you'd have to buy the nuts and bolts are all closed."

"I tell you what," Gibbon said. "You take me home, and you can have this car the rest of the night. I use the Wagoneer to go to work."

"You sure?" said Sam.

"Sure I'm sure. This one's no good for lugging paint and ladders and all."

"Well—" Sam looked at Lennie.

"Say thank you to the nice man," she said. "And tell him of course you'll take his car."

"I guess there's your answer," Sam said, to Gibbon. "And thank you."

"Don't mention it," Gibbon replied. "Always happy to help a friend."

They left Gibbon off at his house, which was dark and deserted-looking. As they drove away, Sam said, "All right, you name it—where do you want to go?"

"Anywhere," Lennie replied. "Anywhere and everywhere. Paris, Rome, London, San Francisco, Biarritz, Key West— did you know that Key West is three hundred and twenty miles south of Cairo, Egypt?"

"The subject never came up," Sam said. "But I'll take your word for it."

"I've never been to any of those places, but I'd like to go. I'd like to go to Tucson or Teheran or Timbuktu or Tuckahoe, and then go all the places that begin with, say, an 'M'—

Melbourne, Minneapolis, Montreal, Mexico City, Manitoba, Macedonia, Milan—"

"Macedonia isn't a city, it's a country."

"Who said anything about cities? I'm just naming places— a place can be a city or a town or a country or the inside of your hat."

"Excuse me. I didn't realize."

"Where have *you* been? Have you been to any interesting places?"

"A few. Right now, would you settle for the moors?"

"I was wondering how long it would take you to suggest that. Yes, please."

The moon was now well up in the sky, and its cold light picked out the rutted road that ran through the moors. The road branched often and in many directions, and Sam simply followed the track that seemed to lead toward the center of the island. The land rose gently and gradually in a series of small hillocks, some with ponds in the hollows and others with tangled underbrush, and the road finally crested on the top of a low hill, from which the surrounding ocean was visible in almost every direction. To the eastward it shone with the reflected light of the moon, then along the south shore it was simply a dark line; due west it was hidden behind the cluster of lights that marked the town, and to the north it could be traced by the winking green light of the sea buoy. Far to the northeast, the beam of a lighthouse flashed and was gone, then flashed again. Sam set the brake and turned out the car lights, and in a moment he felt Lennie's hand in his.

"There's an interesting phenomenon around these parts," she said. "Have you ever heard of mattress grass?"

"I can't say that I have," said Sam. The pressure from her hand was light but constant, and he felt a warmth flow from it that was almost like a transfusion.

"Its real name is corema, or something like that," she went on. "It grows close to the ground, and is very thick,

and the branches—it's a bush, really—the branches inter-
twine so they make a big spongy bed, like a mattress."

"Well, I'll be," said Sam. "I never heard of it."

"There's some right nearby. Would you like to see what I
mean?"

"I'd be fascinated."

They got out of the car, and Lennie took his hand again
and led him off the crest of the hill to a small level space,
where the footing became soft and springy and he had the
sensation of walking on pillows. She sat down, and he sat
beside her, and she said, "Do you see what I mean?" and his
next coherent memory was that he was looking down at her
face; her eyes were closed and the moon was reflected on
her teeth, and he felt like a balloon about to explode. When
next he opened his eyes she was looking up into his face and
smiling, and he dropped his head beside hers and waited for
his heartbeat to return to normal. It was a long time before
either of them spoke. Finally, Sam pulled himself into a sitting position.

"What's the name of that grass again?" he said.

"Corema," she replied.

He nodded. "I see what you mean."

"Do you approve?"

He turned around, and faced her. "What do you mean, do
I approve? Of course I approve! What kind of nutty question is that?"

"I just like to make sure," she said, in a small voice.

He stretched out again, bringing his face close to hers.
"You need have no worries on that count," he said. "I mean,
I should think that would be obvious."

"You never know. Have you ever been married?"

"No."

"It's an interesting trip. You find out a lot about people.
Or about a person."

He started to ask a question, then checked himself and

said, "I can only tell you you have nothing to feel insecure about. On the contrary."

She smiled, and reached under his shirt and caressed his back. "Those are the nicest words I've ever heard," she said.

"I can think of a lot nicer ones than that."

"I don't want to hear them if you have to think of them. I want them to be spontaneous." Her hand had by now reached his spine, and her fingers were counting his vertebrae.

"How does 'I love you' sound?"

Her fingers stopped. "Don't say that."

"Why not?"

"Because you can't mean it."

"Who says I can't? I do."

"I say you can't because you don't know me well enough. This is the first time we've ever been together, and it takes a lot more than that to constitute love. Believe me, I know. Say anything you want, but don't say that until you know what you're talking about."

"Excuse me. May I say I find you attractive?"

She smiled. "By all means."

"Seductive?"

"If you mean it in a nice way."

"I do. Adorable?"

"I think you're crowding it a little there. Better back away from that one."

"Enchanting?"

Her hand, which had been lying on his back, now tightened and pulled him toward her. "That did it," she said, and this time she kept her eyes open.

When, finally, they returned to Gibbon's Jeep, clouds had begun to reach across the moon, and fog lay like lakes on the moors. Sam turned the car around, and as they started down the hill he said, "I hope you realize I'm lost. I haven't the slightest idea of how to get out of here."

"That's all right," she replied. "I'm not going anywhere."

He drove in silence, guessing at each fork in the road and occasionally running into fog so thick he could barely see the ruts ahead. Lennie sat close to him, staring contentedly at nothing in particular. Once, when he was confronted with the choice of three different roads, he brought the car almost to a stop and she said, "Perhaps we should have brought a compass."

"A compass wouldn't do much good here," he replied. "What I need here is radar." He took the center road, and shifted gears.

"Didn't the Army teach you how to find your way?" she asked. "I thought that was part of your training."

"Yes and no," he replied. "They taught you how to read a compass, but that's no good unless you have a map."

"Were you ever in combat?"

"God, no. They'd given up the idea of fighting by the time I joined."

"Then why'd you join? I'm sorry—I don't mean to sound snoopy, but I just wondered."

"There's no secret to it," he replied. "Although I must say, by now it sounds a little silly."

"Why?"

"Well"—he paused, looking for the right words—"I may have told you, my father was in the Danish Resistance."

"You didn't. When was this?"

"World War II. The Germans occupied Denmark, and then the Danes formed a Resistance movement that finally turned into open street warfare. They drove the Germans crazy."

"So?"

"So after the war my parents came to this country—my mother's American—and every now and then my father would talk about his days in the Resistance. He didn't talk about it much, but sometimes he'd meet another Dane who'd been doing the same thing, and then they'd get into the akvavit and beer, and talk all night. I got the feeling he'd been doing something great—he and all the others had a sort of camaraderie, fighting for a cause, and they'd shared an experience they could all be proud of. Brothers under the skin, and all that sort of thing."

"I should think they would."

"Well, they did, and I guess they were right. But I somehow got the idea that Army life was all like that—that all you had to do was join up, and you'd find yourself in one big brotherhood—and to me that sounded like the cat's ass. Make lifelong friendships, be able to reminisce with your buddies—stuff like that. My father tried to tell me it wouldn't be the same, but I didn't listen. He'd done it, so there was no reason I couldn't. I overlooked two very important things."

"Such as?"

"First, he wasn't actually in the Army, and second, he and the others had a common enemy in the Germans. When I joined up there was no common enemy except the officers, and there was no feeling of brotherhood at all—everyone was out to get what he could, and screw the next man. Looking out for Number One, I believe it's called. The colonel was interviewed by some newspaper once, and he happened to be feeling bitter that day, so he spoke the truth. He said, 'I have the best officers' club in the Eastern Defense Command, I have the most luxurious NCO club, and the best-stocked PX; I have color television in all the mess halls and stereo hi-fi in the latrines; I have tennis courts for all officers and squash courts for those of field grade; in short, I have the best damn outfit in the United States Army. The only thing I don't have is any fighting men.' He was transferred two weeks later, and assigned to Thule or some place like that."

"So what did you do?"

"I put up with it, but I didn't like it. I went AWOL once, and all that did was show me that the stockade was the one place they hadn't tried to improve. I spent the rest of the time trying to figure out what was wrong, and I'm still not sure I have the answer. I just wish I could say something for sure, because it looks as though everything's in a big mess. The guys who were in Vietnam, for God's sakes, at least can share their scars—their psychic scars, and the bogey men that ride their backs—I don't even have that." He stopped, and said, "Please excuse me. I'm beginning to sound sorry for myself, and that's the last thing I want to do."

"Don't apologize," said Lennie. "I can see why."

"I'm just confused. If looking out for Number One is the most important thing, then I'll be a son of a bitch if I want to play. There's got to be something more worthwhile than that."

"I can think of a few things," Lennie said.

"Good. I wish you'd tell me."

"Sometime I might."

They had been going through a cottony patch of fog, and now the road rose slightly and they came out into the bright moonlight. Ahead they could see low hills rising like islands in the sea of fog, but nowhere was there a light or a beacon to guide them on the proper course. The moon had passed its height and started down in the west, and with that as a hint they were able to find the North Star, but those aids were only temporary, and in a moment the clouds had closed in again and the moon and stars were gone.

"You know something?" Sam said. "We could keep driving like this all night, and not get anywhere. I suggest we pull off the road, bed down in the best place we can find, and wait until morning. What do you think?"

"It's fine by me," Lennie replied. "Although I suppose I should warn you, I look like hell in the morning. Or so I've been told."

"I'll take that chance," said Sam. "And I'll be the judge, if it's all right with you."

"I think you're biased."

"Don't ever forget it."

He drove off the rutted road, and stopped in a grassy patch near some scrub oak. Then he rummaged in the back of the Jeep and found a tarpaulin, from which he shook the sand, and with Lennie's help he spread it under the branches of the scrub oak. It smelled of smoke and rockweed and sausages, but it made a satisfactory ground cover for them to lie on. Then he found a tattered blanket, which had clearly been used for clambakes and little else, and between them they managed to brush, snap, and shake out most of the sand that had become embedded in its fibers. Finally, having removed their shoes and made whatever other preparations were necessary, they crawled under the shelter of the branches and pulled the blanket over them. Lennie fitted herself to the contours of his body, and lay her head on his chest.

"Body heat is the best," she said. "That's better than any electric blanket."

"I'll buy that," Sam replied.

There was a silence, and then she said, "You want to know something?"

"What?"

"I've been told I'm a cold fish."

"What idiot told you that?"

"You guess."

"Well, he's out of his skull. You're well rid of him."

"Still, it makes a girl wonder. Especially when he runs off with some cheap little troll from the doughnut shop."

"I tell you, you're better off without him. Forget him."

"If it had been anything but the doughnut shop—but no. And what's more, he hates doughnuts. The sight of a cruller makes him ill. I bought him a jelly cruller as a present once, and you know what he did? He ground it right in my face. I'd meant it as a little joke, but boy, you'd think I'd given him a package of instant syphilis. Just add water, and stir. You never saw anyone get so mad. And he's the one who calls *me* a cold fish."

"Anyone who calls you a cold fish should have thirty days' psychiatric observation."

"I think what hurt the most was we'd come here to get away from it all. 'Let's go someplace and lead the simple life,' he said. 'Down-to-earth, grass-roots living, where people are people and you don't have to put up with phonies.' So we come and lead the simple life, and look what happens. Six months, and he's off with a cruller pusher. Talk about your looking out for Number One."

"Where is he now?"

"He's around, still leading the simple life. I see him every now and then."

"You mean you still speak to him?"

"No. I see him across the street, or going into the P.O., or something like that. I wouldn't know what to say to him if I spoke."

"You could tell him to go to hell."

"I think he may already be there. Something tells me Ms. Cruller Pusher is giving him a hard time."

"In other words, you're still in love with him."

"I am not! I hope he rots!"

"Uh-huh."

"I mean it! If I were still in love with him I wouldn't be here with you now! What kind of a person do you think I am, anyway? Do you think I—"

"O.K., O.K., I'm sorry. I didn't mean it that way."

"Then what way did you mean it?"

"I meant"—he spoke slowly, to make sure he got the right meaning—"I meant that you still think of him, and still talk about him, so you clearly haven't dropped him out of your life. There's still something holding you to him."

"Yes, and I still have the scar from where my appendix came out. That doesn't mean I love my appendix."

"I guess I have no answer for that. I'm sorry I spoke."

She had raised her head, and now she put it back on his

shoulder. "So am I," she said. "I was beginning to feel loving again, and now you've got me all tensed up."

He reached his hand around, and stroked her forehead. "There's a remedy for that," he said. "Just close your eyes, and count to ten backward."

"I said this earlier, and I'll say it again," Lennie murmured as she was drifting off to sleep. "If this is secession, we ought to do it more often."

"I say amen to that," Sam replied. "Provided we all survive."

15

Markey had left his blue Mercedes at the end of the paved road before the sandspit began, and the Jeep driver took him and Dustin Williams there, then turned around and headed back toward the clambake. Williams stood, shivering and wrapped in towels, holding his soaking clothes while Markey fumbled for the keys to the Mercedes. The only dry items on Williams were his white loafers, which he'd removed before stepping on the door, and they protruded like two white rats from beneath the towel that clothed his nether limbs.

"Hurry up with those keys," he said to Markey. "I'm freezing to death."

"All in good time," Markey replied, finally unlocking the door on the driver's side. "We've got lots of things to talk about, you and me."

"I'm not talking about anything until I'm warm," said Williams. "I'm used to the tropics, you know."

"Then you're in the wrong place," Markey replied, opening the right-hand door. "In more ways than one."

Williams got in, threw his clothes on the back seat, and began to drum on the floor with his feet. "Turn on the heater, can't you?" he said.

"The heater's no good until the engine's running," said Markey as he turned the ignition switch. "The general rule around here is that we do one thing at a time. It might help you to remember that."

"What do you mean?" said Williams.

"Just that. Don't try to rush things, or get ahead of yourself."

"I don't know what you're talking about."

Markey put the car in gear, and turned it around and headed down the road. "Well, let's get to the point," he said. "You haven't got your offshore rights yet—you're aware of that."

"What do you mean, I haven't got them? You got your money, didn't you?"

"My money, yes. But that's unofficial. I still have to get the Selectmen to agree to terms of your lease."

"When are you going to do that?"

"Our meeting will be tomorrow."

"So?"

"So I don't want you to think you're going to get these rights for nothing."

"Obviously. I'm—we're willing to pay a nominal sum. But don't think you can charge us as though we've already found the oil; this is a highly speculative business, and for all we know we may come up with nothing. The whole thing may be a bust. Paul Getty once told me he had to spend millions—literally millions—before he made his first oil strike. I don't have quite the capital Paul did, so when you come to set your rates I want you to take that into account."

"What do you think would be fair?"

"Well, considering the fact we've already paid you thirty-five thousand—"

"Forget that. I told you, that was unofficial."

"Well, I'd say five thousand a week would be about right."

Markey laughed. "Don't be insulting," he said. "I said this once before—you're not dealing with a bunch of hicks."

"All right, then, tell me what *you* think is fair."

"I'd say a minimum of twenty G's a week, plus three percent off the top of whatever you bring up."

"That's insane! This is a speculative business! I'm not going to pour money like that down the pipe, and take a chance of coming up with nothing!"

"Supposing you've already found oil—what would a fair rate be then?"

"*If* we found it, and *if* it was a productive strike, I'd say ten a week, but no more."

"All right, then, I'm going to charge you twenty. Ten because I know you've already found oil, and an additional ten for lying. Plus—"

"What the hell are you talking about? When did I ever lie to you?"

"You've been lying yourself blue in the face. I happen to know you've found the oil, and have told your crew to carry on as though nothing had happened."

"Who told you that?"

"We monitored your radio messages."

"Those messages were in code. You couldn't—"

"You admit you sent them, then."

"Uh—we have a sort of communication, but—"

"Well, your code wasn't as tight as you thought it was. Agnes Tuttle's husband took it down, and broke the code, and has the slips to prove it. And while we're talking about Agnes Tuttle, how the hell come you went to her before you came to me? Were you trying to cut a few corners, or something?"

"Not in the least. I simply thought you'd be too busy to concern yourself with—"

"Bullshit. You thought you could sweet-talk her because

she's a woman, and maybe get a little sack time to cut down the ante. Well, buster, you were batting in the wrong league when you started that game. Any man so much as lays a finger on Agnes, she'll tear his cock out at the roots and club him to death with it."

"I had no such—"

"One guy tried to get wise with her once, and he spent two weeks in the hospital with a broken arm and contusions of the groin. Agnes studied judo during the war, in case the Germans should invade. It was their good luck they never tried."

"I don't have to put up with all these accusations, you know. I happen to be a good friend of F. Lee—"

"Of course you don't have to. You can just pick up your toys and go home. But I'll tell you what I'm going to do. At the Selectmen's meeting tomorrow, I'm going to announce that oil has been found off our shores, and that you have offered twenty G's a week plus three percent off the top for the right to drill it. If the Selectmen approve—and I'll damn well see to it they do—the story will run in this week's paper, and if you don't want the rights there are sure as hell of lot of oil companies that do. So you can take your choice—agree to those terms, or watch somebody else walk off with the candy store. It's up to you."

"Your skirts aren't so clean, you know. Are you going to tell them at Selectmen's meeting how you took thirty-five G's as your share of the deal?"

Markey took a deep breath. "If that was a threat," he said, "I'll give you a chance to withdraw it right now. If you try to make an issue of it, I can't be responsible for anything that happens. But let me give you one tip: your word around here isn't worth cold snail shit compared to mine. You can make all the accusations you want, and all it'll get you will be thrown in jail, or sent off-island to a mental hospital. If you try to buck me, you're dead."

"I have my connections, you know. It isn't as though you were dealing with—"

"Go ahead. Try anything you want. Only don't say I didn't warn you."

"Do you think there's a lawyer on this island who could buck F. Lee Bailey *and* Edward Williams Bennett? Do you realize what they'd do to you?"

"O.K. You've been warned. How's your fire insurance?"

"What's that got to do with it?"

"Is your house insured for full replacement value?"

"I don't know. Why?"

"You live pretty far away from things out here, don't you?"

"Will you tell me what the hell you're getting at?"

"Homer Benbow, the Fire Chief, is an old friend of mine. We went to school together here, and played on the football team. Homer played left guard, and he was good enough so he got several offers from off-island schools, but he loves the island too much to leave it. He loves the island more'n he loves his wife and his girl friend put together, and I'm here to tell you that's some lot of loving."

"So?"

"So he's worried. I don't know how many times he's come to me and said, 'George, I'm worried stiff some night there's going to be a fire out Cratchett's Farm way, and we just don't have the water to put it out. The mains in that area are so old and so clogged up I could piss a better stream than we'd get out of the fire plugs.' That's what he's said to me, and there's nothing I can do about it."

"Why not?"

"It's not up to the Selectmen. It's up to the Water Company and the DPW and the likes of that, and to get new mains they'd have to have authorization from town meeting. What with one thing and another, the town has never voted the money."

Williams was quiet for a while. "I think I get the picture," he said at last.

"Good," said Markey. "I had a feeling you might."

There were five Selectmen. Aside from Markey, who had the longest tenure, and Agnes Tuttle, the newcomer, the Board consisted of Norris Webster, who had served often but never for more than two consecutive terms; Denton Norquist, the owner-operator of a large, ramshackle hotel on the waterfront known as the Sea Buoy Inn; and Padraic O'Toole, an attorney who had studied law while serving on a Coast Guard lightship. He was also an expert basket weaver and, when sober, an accomplished scrimshander. His clients were mostly indigent wrongdoers who had thrown themselves on the mercy of the court, and, in view of Judge Pepper's penchant for leniency, O'Toole's record of acquittals was impressive.

Sam was on hand to report the meeting for the newspaper, and there was also a scattering of townspeople, some with petitions they wanted to place before the Board, and others who had come out of curiosity, to see what would happen on this first meeting after secession. Markey rapped for order at eight o'clock and there was a rustling and creaking as everyone settled in their chairs.

"I think," Markey began, "it might be appropriate if this was to go into the record books as Selectmen's Meeting Number One, the start of a new era in town government. Are there any objections?" He looked around the table as though daring someone to object, but nobody spoke. Norris Webster had glanced at Agnes out of the corner of his eye, ready to take the opposite stand on anything she might say, but since she remained silent he had nothing to contest. He settled lower in his chair, and waited.

"All right," said Markey, to the stenographer. "So let it be recorded." He cleared his throat.

"I heard a funny one the other day," O'Toole began, but Markey rapped him silent.

"If you don't mind," Markey said, "we have some important business to take care of, so let's leave the jokes until later."

O'Toole blew his nose loudly and left his handkerchief on the table.

"The first item of business," Markey said, "is what I think you'll agree is an extraordinary piece of good news." The minor rustlings in the room stopped as he went on, "I am happy to announce that oil has been discovered close off our shores, and the town has been offered twenty thousand dollars a week, plus three percent of the take, to let a prospecting company set up a well. I hardly need point out the benefits that will accrue to the island under this arrangement."

"How do we know the oil is there?" Norris Webster demanded.

Markey hesitated, then turned to Agnes. "Perhaps you'd better explain," he said.

"My husband is the technical expert," Agnes replied, "but from what I gather from him there's a thing called a magnetometer, that can tell what's at the bottom of the ocean, and this has indicated the presence of a good deal of oil."

"Rubbish," said Webster. "The only way to tell is to go down there. And how come your husband knows so much about it? Is he in league with these prospectors? Because if he is, we've got a conflict of interest here that—"

Markey rapped sharply with his gavel. "Let her explain before you make any accusations," he said. "Go ahead, Mrs. Tuttle."

"My husband has been listening to their radio messages," she said, as calmly as she could. "They've reported finding the oil, and"—she started to mention their attempt at secrecy, but decided it was irrelevant—"from what the messages say, it can be an important strike."

"Isn't that wiretapping?" Webster asked. "Can you use information you've got by eavesdropping?"

"You don't need to tap wires to hear what's on the radio," Agnes replied. "If it's on the air, it's public property."

"I'd have to be convinced of that," said Webster. "The whole thing sounds kind of slippery to me."

"What is this going to do to our beaches?" Norquist asked. "The summer people aren't going to like it if the beaches are all fouled up with oil."

"Screw the summer people," said O'Toole, to nobody in particular.

"If these drillers are careful there should be no trouble with oil spills," Markey said. "But just to be on the safe side, I think we should put a clause in their lease whereby they are responsible for cleaning up any oil that may inadvertently be spilled."

"A fat lot of good that will do," said Webster. "I think the whole idea stinks."

"May I remind you of the amount of money this will bring the town?" Markey said. "In one year, we will have netted one million and forty thousand dollars on the lease alone, and that doesn't take into account the three percent of whatever they sell the oil for. That kind of money is not to be sneezed at. Remember, we don't have State aid any more, and we're going to have to make up for it in some other way."

"Isn't there some *other* way we could raise the money?" Agnes asked. "I'm not sure I like the idea of all those oil people tramping around the island."

"If you have a better idea I'd like to hear it," Markey said. "This is as good as an outright gift of a couple of million dollars a year—maybe three. Maybe four."

"Still, what good is the money going to do us if we turn into an oil field?" Agnes said.

"We're not turning into an oil field!" Markey replied, his face darkening. "The oil is offshore, not on the island, and the tankers will take it directly from the drilling rig. The only thing we'll see of the oil is the money it brings us!"

"Can they get tankers out there?" Agnes asked. "That's pretty shallow water."

"I don't know if they can get tankers out there or not—maybe they'll have to lay a pipeline to deeper water—all I know is there's a lot of money there that the island can damn well not afford to pass up. You seem to forget we're on our own now, and have to make our own way."

"I'm perfectly well aware of that," Agnes replied. "I just don't want us to cut our own throats for the sake of some quick money."

"We're not cutting our throats! We're making ourselves secure!"

"Security is the opiate of the masses," O'Toole said loudly. "Security, thy name is woman."

Webster, who had been looking at Agnes, now spoke up. "I agree with the Chairman," he said. "I think this is too good an opportunity to miss."

Agnes glanced at him in surprise. "You were the one who said you thought it stunk," she said.

"That was only your part of it," Webster replied. "I think we ought to take the money where and when we can. My theory is you never know where the next dollar is coming from, so you'd better grab what you can when you can."

"Your theory is public knowledge," said Agnes. "There's even talk you practice it in your sleep."

"Was that a crack?" Webster said, bridling.

"Take it any way you want," Agnes replied.

Markey tapped with his gavel. "Let's keep personalities out of this," he said.

"*I'm* not the one who brought up personalities," said Webster. "She was the—"

"All right, then, forget it," Markey cut in, with another rap of the gavel. "We'll never get anything done if we sit here and squabble all night."

"Press close bare-bosom'd night," O'Toole intoned, his eyes closed. "Press close magnetic nourishing night! / Night of south winds—"

"Can we save the poetry reading until later?" Markey asked sharply.

"Night of the large few stars! / Still nodding night!" O'Toole went on, and flinched at the crack of Markey's gavel, then concluded, "Mad naked summer night." His head sagged forward, and he slept.

"I think it's time we put this to a vote," Markey said. "We can discuss the pros and cons until we're black in the face, but we're never going to get any action until we vote. And, if I may make the suggestion, I'd like to see this vote a unanimous one. If anyone is tempted to vote against it"— and here he looked at Agnes—"I would ask that they forget their doubts and instead have confidence that everything will work out for the best. The future of the island is at stake here, and the most important single thing is to show confidence in our leadership. If we present a divided face to the world we'll be easy prey for all the jackals who'll be waiting to take advantage of us, but if we are united, then there's nothing we can't accomplish. Just remember the slogan: 'United we stand, divided we fall.' Now, then—"

"There's another slogan, too," Agnes put in. "It's 'Don't tread on me.'"

"Correct," said Markey. "We've got it on our flag. Now, then—"

"It can be read a number of different ways," Agnes observed, but Markey wasn't listening.

"All those in favor of accepting this offer from the oil company," he said, "will signify by—"

"By the way, what's the name of the company?" Agnes asked. "Does it have a name, or is it just this Dustin Williams character?"

Markey scowled. "That's an incidental detail," he said. "We'll get that when we draw up the contract. Right now, all we're voting on is the policy—do we or do we not accept their offer? All those in favor raise their right hand." He and Webster put up their hands; Agnes and Norquist kept theirs on the table, and O'Toole snored quietly into his shirtfront. Markey's lips tightened as he said, "Opposed?" and Agnes and Norquist raised their hands. Markey turned to Norquist. "What's the matter with you?" he said. "What don't you like about it?"

"I told you," Norquist replied. "I think it may scare off the summer people."

"So supposing it does—what difference does that make?" Markey's face had turned the color of mahogany.

"To me, it makes a lot of difference," Norquist said. "They're how I make my living."

"You mean you'd deny the town several million dollars, just so you can fill up that lousy fleabag? Is that what you're saying?"

"I'm saying that whatever money the town gets doesn't come to me personally. I have my own bills to pay."

"You ever hear the expression that no man is an island? You think you can put yourself ahead of everybody else around here? For Christ's sakes, where's your community spirit?"

"My community spirit is as good as my bank account, and no better. You can't spread community spirit on a cracker, and if you don't believe me just try it."

"All right. Suppose I tell you that some of the money the town makes *will* come to you—what would you say to that?"

"I'd say I'd have to see it to believe it. How is it going to come to me?"

"In lowered taxes. In improved facilities. Any one of a hundred different ways. If you're living in a prosperous community, it's only common sense that you'll be prosperous, too. Any moron ought to be able to see that."

"O.K. I'll believe it when I see it."

"Suppose I tell you that I personally will guarantee you'll benefit from it. How about that?"

"That would be different. How do you do that?"

"Never mind. Just take my word."

"Interesting."

Markey took a deep breath. "All right," he said. "Let's vote again. All those in favor—" He raised his hand, but again Webster was the only one to join him. "What's the matter?" he said, to Norquist. "Are you calling me a liar?"

"Not in the least," Norquist replied. "I just want to see proof."

"All right. You'll see it." Markey reached across and grabbed the sleeping O'Toole's right hand, and held it up. "I have his proxy," he said. "He's for it. The motion is carried, three to two." He tapped his gavel, and dropped O'Toole's hand. Then he looked from Norquist to Agnes. "Now," he said, "should we make it unanimous?"

"What's the point?" said Agnes. "You've had your way."

"It looks neater, that's all," Markey replied. "I like to think of appearances. Do I hear a motion to make it unanimous?"

"I so move," said Webster.

"I second it. The motion is carried, three to two." Markey tapped his gavel. "The decision to accept the terms is unanimous."

Later, when the meeting had adjourned, Sam went up to Markey. "May I ask you a question?" he said.

"About what?" said Markey.

"That vote on the oil."

"It was unanimous, don't forget that," Markey said. "All that preliminary chatter doesn't count."

"It was about the vote itself. The first time around, it was a tie. Can you break a tie with the vote of a man who is asleep—or as in this case, passed out?"

"You forget, we're independent," Markey replied with a

grin. "When you're independent, you can do anything you want."

16

It wasn't until Saturday that Sam had time to see Felicity and find out what she'd discovered behind the shack. He didn't think it would prove to be much of anything but he was nevertheless intrigued, mostly because his first reaction had been that it was a bear trap—and if that were the case, then his whole theory of the foot might be awry. He almost didn't want to know, because he'd become attached to the foot as a symbol of hidden goings-on among the islanders.

He went to the Sink Hole at noon, and the first person he saw was Lennie, who was coming away from the bar with a tray full of beers. Her face took on a sudden glow, and she stopped like a mechanical toy that had just wound down.

"Hi," she said. "I thought you'd forgotten me."

"I couldn't do that," he replied. "But I've been working. I had to do the story on the clambake, and then the Selectmen and the oil, and what with one thing and another I've barely had time to sleep."

"You don't have to explain."

"Yes, I do. I don't want you to think I've forgotten. My God, how *could* I forget?"

"I don't know. Some people have short memories."

"Well, I don't."

"That's nice to hear."

"I can tell you one thing, and that is sleeping on the ground isn't all it's cracked up to be. I was stiff the whole next day."

"So was I, but it was worth it."

He cleared his throat. "Is Felicity around?"

"Why?"

"I wanted to see her about that—you know—whatever it was she found."

Her face was expressionless as she said, "She's around here someplace—you can't miss her."

"Look—please don't think—" he began, but she'd gone, and was briskly setting the beers in front of some customers across the room. Sam started to follow her, then realized this was not the place to try to explain. Dear God, he thought, why do women have to make things so complicated? Is there never a simple way to be in love, or must it always be walking a high wire between adoration and rage? He looked around and saw Felicity coming out of the kitchen, and when he approached her she smiled.

"To what do I owe the honor?" she said.

"I wondered if I could take a look at that piece of iron—the thing you found behind the shack."

"Anytime. You want to go out this afternoon, or wait till tonight?"

"This afternoon would be fine."

"Should I bring some sustenance?"

"Don't bother. I really just want to see that thing."

She gave him a long stare. "Oh," she said at last. "I do believe you mean it."

"I do."

"All right. Come around at three, and I'll have the bikes."

As he went out he looked for Lennie, but she was nowhere to be seen, so he decided to relax and not try to explain anything. If he tried too hard he'd look suspicious, and probably end up worse off than he already was. To hell with it, he thought. If my conscience is clear, that's all that matters.

He met Felicity at three, and in her bicycle basket she had some sandwiches and a bottle of wine. "You never can tell when you may get hungry," she said. "I thought it best to be on the safe side."

"Probably a wise idea," he replied as he mounted the bike she gave him. "Did you ever find out who owns that shack?"

"I never tried," Felicity said. "I don't believe in looking a gift horse in the mouth."

He laughed. "Pretty soon you may own it, just by squatter's rights."

"I'm not sure how I should take that."

"Don't sweat it. It was just a remark in passing."

They pedaled out of town, and after a while their road branched off from the one that led to Cossett Point, where Sam lived. He figured that although the roads diverged he probably didn't live very far from Felicity's shack, and while this was of no particular interest at the moment he filed the fact away for future reference. He had been on the island almost two months and was still learning how to find his way around, and he automatically made notes of distances and directions when they were brought to his attention. He hoped that some night he and Lennie could go back to their patch of mattress grass on the moors, but he knew she'd have to be the one to lead the way; he could no more find his way across the moors than he could across the landscape of the moon. It occurred to him, in retrospect, that Lennie had known exactly where they were going, so their return would depend entirely on her.

When they reached the shack they dismounted and leaned their bicycles against it, then Felicity took his hand and led him around to the dunes behind. He saw the place where he'd buried the garbage, and he also saw similar freshly turned areas, and he said, "Is this where you said the dog had been digging?"

"Here and there," Felicity replied. "But he's quit since I changed the place. He just kind of digs at random now. But there's where I found the thing." She pointed to a spot in the dunes where either wind or waves had scooped out a hollow in the sand, and half buried in the hollow was a large, rusty bear trap. Sam squatted down and examined it and tried to open the jaws, but the power of the springs, plus the clotting action of the rust, kept them locked as tight as though they were welded. Between the jagged teeth he could see bits of material, which looked more like cloth than like animal hair, and when he tried to pluck them out they shredded in his fingers and turned to lint. Next he examined the chain, which was attached to one end of the trap, and he looked with particular care at the last link, fingering it to see if he could detect any signs of wear.

"What are you looking for there?" Felicity asked.

"They usually attach this to a stake," he replied. "Or something that'll keep the animal from dragging the trap away. But this must have been a new trap, because there's no wear on this link or any of the others. Whatever it was, it was a one-shot affair."

"Do you think maybe the hunter just left it and forgot it?" said Felicity, who was beginning to show signs of restlessness.

"Not likely. It's an odd kind of trap to set, since there are no bears on the island. It's got to have been set for something else, something big, and not something the hunter was likely to forget." In his mind he was measuring the distance to where he'd found the foot, and he reasoned it was perfectly possible for a dog to have carried it from here to there, either looking for a place to hide it or to take it home and gnaw on it at leisure. Sam put the trap down and stood up.

"Now what?" Felicity asked. "Would you like a little wine?"

"Not right now, thanks. I want to see if I can find where the trap was set."

"How do you expect to do that—Ouija board?"

"I have no idea. I just want to look."

"Will it disturb your thought processes if *I* have a little wine?"

"Not in the least."

They went back to the shack, where she got the wine bottle from her basket and proceeded to open it, while Sam examined the ground in front of the building. She filled a plastic glass, said, "Cheers," more or less to herself, and took a long swallow as Sam got down on his hands and knees and began to prowl around the door. "I see now why Sherlock Holmes never married," Felicity said. "Did you ever hear the report he was gay?"

"Never," said Sam, scooping some earth away from the steps.

"Well, if not gay at least anti-woman. It seems his mother was fooling around with someone—Professor Moriarty, I think—and his father caught them at it and blew her away with a shotgun, and ever after that Sherlock thought that women were ugly ugly ugly. Male chauvinist pig, is what he was."

"Was this in the original Conan Doyle?" Sam asked, looking at something he'd picked up.

"Uh—I don't think so." Felicity finished her wine and poured another glass. "I think I saw it in a movie. *The Whatsitsname Solution,* I think it was called."

"Look at this," Sam said, standing up.

"What is it?"

"It's a pad eye." He showed her a semicircle of metal with screw holes at either tip. "It could have hooked through the trap chain, and held it to the doorstep or something here."

"Is it all right to ask why?"

Sam got back on his knees and began to examine the wood around the edges of the step. "So that whatever he caught couldn't get away," he said.

"I thought you said they used pegs." Felicity held the wine glass out to him. "Care for a sip?"

"Not right now." He ran his fingers along the wood at ground level, then dug down an inch or so and repeated the process. "They did use pegs for animals," he said. "But suppose a man had been caught. A man could pull the peg out of the ground, and crawl away."

"Isn't that a kind of elaborate way to catch a man? Wouldn't it be simpler to call him on the phone? I mean, make a date, and then throw a net over him when he showed up?"

"It would depend on what you wanted him for. He might not answer the phone."

"Still, to go to the trouble of buying a trap—where do you get one of those things, anyway?"

"A sporting-goods store, I guess." Sam practically put his nose in the dirt as he peered at the step.

"Some sport. You know how Humphrey Bogart would have done it, don't you? He would have gone to see the man and had it out with him eyeball to eyeball, and then slugged him a couple for good luck and taken off with the guy's pigeon. There was a man, that Bogart. They don't make them like that any more."

"There we are!" Sam said suddenly. "That's where the pad eye went!" He fitted the pad eye against two screw holes in the wood and found that they matched.

"You know the thing I liked best about Bogart?" Felicity went on, sipping her wine. "It was that he could be tough and gentle all at the same time. That's the kind of man I could really go for—slug you one minute and treat you like a piece of spun glass the next—just thinking about him makes me go twitchy all over."

"So that's what he did," Sam said, standing up. "He put the trap and chain in front of the door and covered them over with a little sand, then he screwed the chain to the step here, so the guy couldn't get away. Then—"

"You know how he got that scar on his lip, don't you?" Felicity said. "He got it in World War I. He charged a Ger-

man machine-gun nest single-handed—rat-tat-tat-tat-tat—
and he wiped out all the Krauts except one, and that one
lunged at him with a bayonet and split his lip, just as Bogie
stuffed a grenade down his throat, and ka-POW! No more
Kraut. I read it in the Sunday paper, one of those question-
and-answer columns."

"About what?" Sam asked.

"What do you mean, about what? About Bogie's lip."

"Who said anything about Bogie's lip?"

"I did, you dum-dum! What do you think I've been talking about?"

"I haven't the faintest idea. I've been talking about whoever set the trap here."

"How do you know he set it here, if we found it all the
way out back?"

"Because this is where the pad eye was!"

"Just because the pad eye was here doesn't mean the trap
had to be. If you ask me, that's just reaching for it."

"Can you think of any other reason for the pad eye to be
here?"

"No, but if you're going to play guessing games you could
say it was to tie up the *Queen Mary*. That makes as much
sense as a bear trap."

"The bear trap is nearby, and the *Queen Mary* isn't.
There's one difference right there."

"Have some wine. It'll improve your thinking."

Sam reached for the glass she offered, and took a long
swallow. "Thank you," he said.

"Now that we're over that hurdle, would you like a glass
of your own?"

"Yes, please."

She went to her bicycle basket. "Pastrami sandwich?"

"No, thank you."

She poured a glass of wine and handed it to him, then
refilled her own. "Now," she said. "Should we make ourselves comfortable? I for one am tired of standing."

"Sit down, if you'd like. I want to look around some more."

She settled herself in the doorway to the shack and said, "Did you know it's possible to turn gay overnight?"

"No," said Sam, scanning the ground. "I never heard that."

"It's a common phenomenon. Even some holly trees do it."

He gave her a quick glance, then went around to the dunes behind, picked up the bear trap, and brought it back and laid it in front of the step.

"You probably thought I was putting you on about the holly," she said, "but it's happened. It's the female that has the berries, but every now and then a male tree will suddenly start growing berries like wild—I mean, like a mad, possessed *thing*—and there it is. Gay as a grig."

"Well, what do you know about that?" Sam put the trap directly in front of the step and then, trying to avoid Felicity's knees, reached the chain around to where the pad eye had been set in the step. "It fits," he said.

"So if a tree can do it you can be sure other things can," Felicity went on. "I read about a colony of gay sea gulls out in California, all males and all wild about each other, and the only problem was, they were frustrated because nobody was laying any eggs. All that screwing, and nothing to show for it . . . Are you listening to me?"

"I'm hanging on every word," Sam replied. "Now, the only question is why did he do it, and whom did he catch?"

"Nobody knows why they *did* it," Felicity said. "All they know is that it happened. And if you'll pardon my seeming to point the finger of suspicion, I wouldn't be surprised if you were going the same route. Was there anything wrong the last time we were out here?"

"Wrong with what?" Sam asked.

"With *me!* What do you think?"

"With you? No. Didn't you feel well?"

"I felt fine! So what's the matter with me now?"

"You'd know better than I. I'm not a doctor."

"Then, God damn it, why are you just standing there? Why aren't you making a move?"

"Well, for one thing, I'm thinking."

"Thinking? I'd say you were in a coma."

"No. I'm just trying to figure out what went on here, and why."

"Don't you feel a little relaxation might help you think?"

"It depends on what kind of relaxation you mean."

"All right." She stood up and brushed off the seat of her dress. "I know when I'm licked." She finished her wine and tossed the glass in her bicycle basket.

"Look," said Sam, "I told you when we started out that this was all I was coming for."

"Yes, but I guess I didn't really believe you. I've never drawn a blank like this before."

"It's nothing personal. It's just—"

"I know, I know. You're faithful to Lennie, and all that sort of thing."

His jaw tightened, and he said, "You girls don't keep many secrets from each other, do you?"

"She hasn't told me a thing. I was only guessing, until you confirmed it just now."

"Oh."

She half mounted her bicycle, keeping one foot on the ground. "Are you coming back, or do you want to brood some more?"

Sam looked around. "I guess I might as well come back," he said, and then, as an afterthought, "I'll bring the trap along, too. You never can tell."

"To horse, then. I still have to work tonight."

Something seemed to have changed gears inside her; she was crisp and businesslike, and Sam surmised it was to cover up her frustration, or anger. As they rode in silence toward town, he reflected that there weren't many people who could, without really trying, antagonize two women in so short a space of time as he had. I guess it's just a gift, he thought, and one that I've only recently developed. I just hope it doesn't develop any further.

The Land Office didn't open until nine o'clock Monday morning, when Charlie Ketchum came in to open the windows and air out the room. Sam appeared a few minutes later, when Ketchum was closing the windows, and in as offhand a manner as he could muster he said, "I happened to be going past, and saw your door open. There's a question maybe you could answer for me."

"Depends on what it's about," Ketchum replied, dusting off his hands. "If it's about land, most likely I can; if it's about women, my memory don't go back that far." He cackled, to indicate he'd made a joke.

"It's about land, in a way," Sam said. "There's a shack off in the Cossett Point area—actually, the road branches off the Cossett Point road—and this shack is down by the water, in the dunes really. It just occurred to me to wonder who owns it."

"Let's get a map here, and see," Ketchum said. "I think I know which one you mean, but we might's well make sure. There's a lot of shacks along that strip of beach." He spread the map out on the table, weighted down the corners, and went on, "Now, here's the Cossett Point road . . . here's one fork . . ." He traced the road with his finger.

"Not that one," Sam said, looking over his shoulder. "It's farther on down."

"Then it must be this one." Ketchum's finger ran down to the shoreline, and stopped by a small square that indicated a building.

"That's it," Sam said.

"That's Lot Number 287," Ketchum said, reaching for a ledger. "You thinking of buying it?"

"I don't know," said Sam. "That depends on a lot of things."

Ketchum leafed through the ledger and ran his finger

down a column. "That land," he said slowly, "belongs to—oh-oh."

"What?" said Sam.

"That's a piece Dennis Fenwick picked up. It's part of his estate."

Sam had a feeling of letdown. "When did he pick it up?" he asked.

"Just recently, I guess. It used to belong to George Markey, then Fenwick got it like he did so much else—by paying overdue mortgages or taxes, taking land as a hidden fee for services—you name it, he did it. He was a busy one, that Dennis." He cackled again.

"There must be a date somewhere," Sam said, with new excitement. "Where's the deed?"

"Christ only knows. All that property of Fenwick's is in a mess. But I know for sure George Markey owned it last year, so it's got to be within that time. But if you're looking for to buy it, I'd advise you to look somewhere else. It'll be years before Fenwick's property's straightened out. Maybe never."

"Thank you," said Sam. "But it may not be necessary for me to buy anything. I may have all I need right now."

"You're some lucky if you do," said Ketchum. "There's not many folk can say the same."

17

The Governor switched off the television set and looked at his aide. "This is a fine kettle of fish," he said. "Now what do we do?"

The aide shrugged. "I'd say don't panic," he said. "Just because they've struck oil doesn't mean they're another Kuwait, or Saudi Arabia. Let's see how much money it gets them, before we do anything rash."

"You just heard what the guy said. A million plus, and three percent off the top. Right away that's more than they got from us, so they can tell us to go pack it in our ear."

"Let's see how they use it," the aide said. "It's one thing to have the money under State supervision, and it's quite another thing to have it all dumped in their laps. They may go wild and blow it all before they get it."

"It doesn't sound that way," the Governor observed sourly. "It sounds as though they had every penny earmarked as to exactly where it was going. I wish to God we could keep that kind of track of the money up here. Do you realize how much we lose each year, just by evaporation?"

"I realize," the aide replied. "But I also know there's a difference between where you budget your money and where it actually goes. My uncle was in the Military Government in Germany after the war, and he said that you don't even know what corruption is until you get down to the grass roots. A certain amount is expected in high places, he said, but you don't expect it down at the local level, and that's where it's as thick as weevils. The way he phrased it was: the farther down in the grass roots you get, the closer you come to the manure."

"Your uncle sounds like an observing soul," the Governor said. "Do you think he'd like a job?"

"He might have, ten years ago. But one day he went to the Piggly Wiggly supermarket to meet a friend, and hasn't been seen since."

"That'll happen in the best of families," the Governor said. "My condolences to your aunt."

"She remarried, a girdle manufacturer. They're very happy."

"Then my congratulations. That still isn't solving our problem. How big a State Police troop do we have on that island?"

The aide opened a folder and leafed through some papers. "Is that possible?" he said, half to himself. "I guess it is. We have two troopers there, Sergeant Mancusi and Corporal Sutkin. They alternate the duty."

"*They'll* be a lot of help. I think we'd better tell them to keep a low profile until they get specific instructions otherwise." The aide scribbled a note, and the Governor went on, "Which leaves us with the National Guard. How do we get them out there without making it sound like D Day?"

"We don't," said the aide. "That's why I think we should cool it."

"Still, we ought to be ready. The more entrenched these people get in their independence, the harder it'll be to round them up."

"There's a difference between being ready and going hooting out there like Attila."

"I don't want to go hooting anywhere, but we've got to get them back. What's the best way to put troops out there?"

"Offhand, I'd say fly 'em. Either in cargo planes or, if the field isn't big enough, load 'em into choppers. Those big ones will carry a lot of men."

"What about paratroops?"

The aide opened another file folder. "You may remember, the National Guard had an experimental paratroop program," he said. "The last time they staged a jump there were eighty-seven Guardsmen involved, and a total of sixty-nine casualties. They break down as follows: fractured legs, 4; ditto ankles, 8; sprained backs, 17; slipped disks, 8; broken jaw, 1—apparently one man got tangled in his parachute shrouds and landed face first—mild concussions, 18; severe ditto, 3; mild hysteria, 3; acute ditto, 3; desertions, 4." He closed the folder and said, "Of course, the 101st and 82nd Airborne Divisions have better records than that, but they're Federal troops, and you'd need an act of Congress to get them. No Federal law has been broken here, so far."

The Governor leaned back in his chair and closed his eyes. "Let's just have the Guard ready," he said. "Tell the General I want a quiet alert, if such a thing is possible. Nothing official as yet, but I want them ready to move on short notice. And tell the Air Guard to be ready to move the troops when I give the word."

"They're going to want to know more than that," the aide said. "They're going to want to know how many troops they'll have to carry, and where. They've got to scrounge up the fuel, and make sure the planes are in working order—there's a million small details like that."

"Tell them I'll let them know when the time comes. Right now, I just want to be sure we can make the move if we have to. It would be a hell of a thing if I gave the order to go, and then found everyone was on vacation and the planes were all torn down for overhaul."

"I'll tell them," the aide said. "But I can't guarantee how much secrecy you'll have. People are bound to put two and two together."

"Well, let's get Fred in here. He may have some ideas." The Governor pushed an intercom switch and said, "Ask Mr. Dampeer to step in, would you?" The intercom made an acknowledging squawk, and he sat back.

"One more thing," said the aide. "Do the troops get real bullets or rubber ones?"

"Real ones," the Governor replied. "If they're going to run into resistance, they're going to have to defend themselves."

"I'd be awfully careful about that," the aide said. "A frightened shoe clerk with real bullets is a menace to the whole community."

"But supposing the natives attack? They've got to have some sort of protection."

"They'll have helmets and riot sticks and shields, not to mention tear gas and all the rest of it. That's what they've been trained to use. I needn't remind you what can happen if they have real bullets: one nervous trigger finger, and the whole world comes apart."

"Yeah. All right, then, make them rubber, but don't advertise it. Let people think they're real."

There was a knock at the door, and the press secretary put his head in. "You wanted me?" he said.

"Come in, Fred," the Governor said. "We have a little plan here, and we're going to need your cooperation. Sit down." The press secretary took a chair, and the Governor went on, "We're going to have the National Guard on a provisional standby, but we don't want the word to get around. If we move against the island we want to do it as quickly and cleanly as possible, and that's going to depend on its being a surprise. Do you follow?"

"I follow," said the press secretary.

"Now, inevitably, the press is going to get wind of this, and I want you to have some story ready that will make the whole thing seem run of the mill, and not even worth following up. Pretend it happens every day. Is that clear?"

"It's clear, all right. How I do it is something else again."

"That's what you're being paid for, to handle the press."

"Any success I may have in handling the press comes from the fact that they believe me, and if I try to feed them some wild-eyed story it's going to shoot my credibility all to hell."

"That's your worry, Fred. All I want is the result—I want you to convince them this is an everyday occurrence."

"I can do it if you'll let me say one thing."

"What's that?"

"If I can say that we have islands seceding from the State every day, then I can convince them that the National Guard is on a daily alert. Otherwise, they're going to hoot me out of the hall."

"That isn't funny, Fred."

"You're damned right it isn't funny. Nobody is more aware of that than I."

The Governor stared at him for what seemed like a long time. "Perhaps you'd like to be doing something else?" he said. "Like farming, or digging clams?"

"At least that would be honest work." The press secretary got ready to rise.

"If I may suggest something," the aide put in, "I think we may get this ironed out fairly easily. Fred, if anyone asks you why the Guard is on alert you say it's part of their training. Say their training covers all aspects of duty, and that being on standby alert is one of them. That is the literal truth, and nobody can deny it."

The press secretary paused, then sat back again. "Suppose they ask me point-blank if this has anything to do with the island," he said. "What do I say then?"

"Say you have seen no orders relating this to the island. Again, the literal truth, because there will be no such orders. They will simply be told to stand by."

The press secretary thought for a moment, then sighed. "All right," he said. "But if we all get out of this with whole skins I'll be surprised."

"Fred," the Governor said gently, "did anyone ever tell you there's such a thing as being too honest?"

"Not that I can remember," said the press secretary.

"Then you might bear in mind the definition of an ambassador, as being an honest man sent to lie abroad for the commonwealth. It'll ease the pain in your scruples."

"Thank you. I'll try to remember that."

When the press secretary had left, the Governor looked at his aide. "Do you think Fred is running for something?" he said.

"No," said the aide. "What would he run for?"

"I don't know, but all this carping about honesty worries me. It sounds as though he's trying to establish a base of some sort. Whenever a man gets over-honest, you'd better start looking for the reason."

"Well, I'll see what I can find out. I don't think it's too serious."

"I hope not. I'd hate to have anything happen to him."

The Conservation Board met a week after the secession vote, and when Dr. Amberson called the meeting to order it was clear there were several important matters on his mind. He mentally called the roll; Corning and Markey and Webster were all present, and only Dr. Pardle was missing. "Anybody know where Lucius is?" Dr. Amberson asked.

"No," said Markey. "But it's small loss."

"I think he said he was going off-island to some seminar," Corning said. "It sounded like he's been hooked on acupuncture."

Markey laughed. "He'll come back looking like a Chinaman."

Sam, who was sitting as far back in the room as he could in the hope they'd forget he was there, made a note to check on Dr. Pardle's whereabouts. He had no idea what it might lead to, but he had started collecting all sorts of random information, just in case.

"I'm sorry Lucius isn't here," Dr. Amberson said, "because I'd like all members to have a say. But I think in the circumstances we'd better not wait for his return."

"*If* he returns," Markey said, and laughed again.

"Our first item of business is a tricky one," Dr. Amberson said. "It appears that this oil company—I have their name here someplace—the A.B.C. Oil Products Affiliates, whatever that may mean, wants to put up three oil-storage tanks on the south shore, with a pipeline leading out to the drilling site. Their reason—"

"It'll never last," Webster put in. "One good winter storm'll tie that pipeline up in a bowknot."

"They claim they can make it strong enough," Dr. Amberson said. "They'll sink concrete pilings into the ocean bed and sling it from them, so there'll be a certain amount of give in the line. They say it's necessary because they can't get tankers out to the drilling site, so they've got to bring oil ashore and then transfer it to tankers in the harbor."

"Why are they coming to us?" Corning asked. "What have we got to do with it?"

"The land they want for the storage tanks is Conservation land," Dr. Amberson replied. "It's part of a tract deeded to us as a wildlife sanctuary."

"What the hell, let 'em have it," Markey said. "If we charge 'em enough it'll be worth it. The wildlife won't know the difference anyway."

"I'm not sure we're legally allowed to," Dr. Amberson said. "The clauses in the deed are pretty specific."

Markey waved a hand in dismissal. "Change the clauses," he said. "Who the hell cares?"

"Let's make sure we get enough money for it, though," Webster said. "Let's assume there's going to be a legal wrangle, so let's have the A.B.C. company agree to pay us X amount of dollars, plus any legal fees that may accrue. Then it'll be worthwhile."

"Well, there's one other objection," Dr. Amberson said. "I don't think we should let them have it."

"Why not?" Markey asked.

"This is Conservation land. If Conservation is going to mean anything at all it should be kept the way it is—it should be conserved. We're not in the business of selling real estate; we're here to protect the land, and I don't think we should lose sight of that fact."

"Oh, bullshit," Markey said. "Be practical."

"I've an idea," Corning said. "I happen to own a big chunk of land adjacent to that tract, and I'd be happy to sell it if they come up with the right price. I agree about the Conservation land, and I think it should be preserved, but my land is just as good as far as they're concerned, and very little farther away from the drilling site. They'd just have to angle their pipeline a little differently."

"You're all heart, aren't you?" Markey said. "What's the matter with giving them what they ask for?"

"We've just been into that! It's not supposed to be sold!"

"Then we can lease it to them. Let them do what they want with it—for a price—and then when they're through it can go back to being a wildlife sanctuary. That way we're not stepping on anyone's toes, and we're turning a tidy buck in the bargain."

"As Norris just pointed out, there'll probably be a legal wrangle if we let them have the Conservation land. I can guarantee there'll be no wrangle at all with my land, provided they meet my price."

"Speaking of legal wrangles," Dr. Amberson said, "are you sure your title to that land is free and clear? I mean, have you checked it out with Charlie Ketchum?"

"I'm sure it's clear," Corning replied. "I haven't checked it out with Charlie because I don't see the point."

"Just to be on the safe side." Dr. Amberson pulled a telephone toward him and dialed a number.

"Will Charlie be in this late?" Corning asked.

"He usually stays late the nights we have meetings. Do you know the lot numbers of your property?"

"No, but Charlie can look them up. He has all the papers there."

Dr. Amberson spoke into the telephone, and after a few sentences hung up. "He'll call back," he said. "It'll take him a couple of minutes to look it up."

"It's a waste of time, anyway," Corning said. "I know it's clear."

"Well, we might as well be sure." Dr. Amberson turned to Markey and said, "While we're waiting, I have a non-Conservation question you might be able to straighten me out on."

"Glad to," Markey replied. "What is it?"

"I just got my electricity bill, and the so-called surcharge has doubled. How does that happen?"

"Oh, that. Yeah. We had to raise the rates."

"Why?"

"Well, with secession and all, we don't have the mainland to fall back on. We have to charge more."

"I don't get it. What are you doing now that you didn't do before?"

"I told you. We're on our own."

"So you figure you can charge more, and get away with it?"

"That's a kind of snotty way to put it."

"But the truth?"

"Look at it whatever way you want. The rates have gone up now, and they're likely to go up again. It's a simple fact of life. You want to be independent, you're going to have to pay for it."

The telephone rang, and Dr. Amberson, still looking at Markey, picked it up. "Yes," he said. He was quiet for several moments, then said, "Thank you, Charlie," and hung up. He turned to Corning. "That land is all part of Dennis Fenwick's estate," he said.

"It can't be!" Corning shouted, his eyes bulging. "That land is mine! I paid good money for it!"

"That's something you'll have to take up with Charlie," Dr. Amberson said. "He says Dennis had the deeds drawn up shortly before he died."

"That's impossible!" Corning was gasping as though he'd been drenched with ice water. "It can't *be!*"

"Well, let's say there's some question about it," Dr. Amberson said. "So for the moment I think we'd better not offer it to the oil company. That leaves us back pretty much where we started."

"I say let 'em have the Conservation land," Markey said. "I know all the namby-pamby arguments against it, but this is for the long-range good of the island. This'll make us so rich we won't have to worry about bird sanctuaries or anything else."

"We've still got the legal hurdles to get over. We can't just sell—or lease—the land right off the bat. The whole structure of the Conservation Board demands that things be done legally and without leaving any loopholes."

Markey examined the tip of the pencil with which he'd been doodling during the discussion. "Well, that brings up another point," he said. "I wasn't going to mention it now, but since it's come up we might as well get it over with."

"What's that?" Dr. Amberson said.

"Let me put it this way: With our new setup, being an independent government and all, the first thing we're going to have to do is streamline things, in the interest of maximum efficiency. I mean, the more different committees and whatnots we have, the more it's going to clutter up the town business, and at this particular point in time the last thing we need is clutter. We've got to be able to make decisions fast, and act on them just as fast, or we'll be up the proverbial creek wearing barbed-wire jockstraps."

"So?" said Dr. Amberson quietly.

"So when the Selectmen meet I'm going to move we make a study of which committees can be done away with immediately, which can be streamlined or incorporated into others, and which have to stand pretty much as they are. I have my own ideas, but I'd also like to hear what the other Selectmen think."

"And?" said Dr. Amberson.

"And it's my opinion—this is unofficial, mind you, until the Selectmen decide—it's my opinion that the duties of the Conservation Board can be taken over by the Selectmen. I mean, Norris and I know what the problems are, and since we're Selectmen we can look after conservation matters without having to change our hats. Lucius Pardle isn't going to be missed by anyone, and that leaves only you and Emil here to be streamlined out. It may be a shock at first, but I think you'll agree it makes sense."

"You have my resignation as of this minute," Dr. Amberson said, without emotion.

"Let's not be hasty," Markey replied. "I told you this was unofficial. Until the Selectmen act, you're still Chairman of this Board."

"As I see it, the Selectmen have acted," Dr. Amberson said, standing up. "In the interest of efficiency and streamlining, I will save them the trouble of having to do it again. Would you like my chair, or will you run the rest of the meeting from where you sit?"

"God damn it, Carl, I wish you'd be a little more graceful about this," Markey said. "There's nothing personal here—it's just for the good of the island."

"Then for the good of the island I will leave it in your hands," Dr. Amberson said. He took the papers and pamphlets from his briefcase and put them on the table, then tucked his empty briefcase under his arm, and left.

When the door had closed behind him, Markey looked at Corning and said, "What about it, Emil? Is there anything you'd like to say?"

Corning, who seemed to be in shock, started to speak, then shrugged and shook his head. "I guess not," he said. "I can't see what good it would do."

"Well, then, let's wind up the meeting. Norris and I will make our report to the Selectmen on Thursday." Then, for the first time, Markey saw Sam in the back of the room. "You!" he said. "What are you doing here?"

"I'm from the paper," Sam replied. "I was here last meeting."

"This was an executive session. You shouldn't have been here."

"Nobody said anything about that to me. Dr. Amberson let me in."

"Well, Dr. Amberson is no longer Chairman. I am the Chairman, and I say it was an executive session."

"Whatever you say," Sam replied.

"Now, get out."

"Yes, sir." Sam rose and made his way to the door. When he got into the corridor, Markey came out the door and took him by the arm.

"What's this I hear about you snooping around my shack?" he asked.

"I wasn't snooping," Sam said quickly. "I was just—interested. Anyway, I'm told it's no longer yours."

"Don't believe everything you hear. And stay away from that shack in the future. Understand?"

"Yes, sir."

"And if you print one word of this meeting, you'll regret it."

"What am I to—"

"Never mind. I'll talk to Lester Turpin. Now, get lost."

"Yes, sir. Good night."

Markey went back into the room, and Sam wandered outside and breathed deeply of the night air. He went down to the docks and looked at the stars until he stopped trembling, and then he turned and slowly made his way to the Sink Hole.

18

It was Saturday afternoon, and the troops who were assembling in the National Guard armory had for the most part planned something else for the weekend. They had the confused, disheveled look of people who had dressed during a fire, and many of them waited their turn at the armory's one pay telephone to relay last-minute thoughts and instructions to friends or relatives at home. Officers with clipboards periodically called out names, and the troops gathered in loose clusters and exchanged rumors and speculation. Their packs and heavy equipment had been left at the entrance to be loaded aboard the baggage van, so all they had to carry were their helmets, their canteens, and their M-14 rifles.

"What gripes my ass," said a short, stocky private with buck teeth, "is the load they shovel on them recruiting commercials. 'Be like the Minutemen—join the Guard and protect your freedom!' 'Mr. Employer, do your patriotic duty and let your men join the Guard!' Shit, you'd think we was about to repel an invasion, or something."

"Spelvin, for all you know we may be doing just that," another one said. "You may be dead by sundown."

"God damn it, McGinty, don't talk like that!" Spelvin said, turning red. "What the fuck kind of way is that to talk?"

McGinty shrugged. "I just thought it'd make you feel more patriotic," he said.

"I'd feel more patriotic if I had something in this canteen," a third man said. He unscrewed the top of his canteen and sniffed. "Man, I can still smell them juleps from last summer."

"Ol' Sniffer Butler," McGinty said. "Whyn't you carry a girl's bicycle seat around, instead of that empty canteen?"

"Someday I may have to fill it," Butler replied. "I got to be ready for all emergencies, like it says in the Guardsman's Manual."

"You take my advice and you'll fill it with water right now. You may be just one hell of a long way from your next julep."

"You know what I heard?" Spelvin said. "I heard they were sending us to take over the fishing fleet."

"Now, why the Christ would they do that?" McGinty said. "What do we know about fishing?"

"Don't ask me," said Spelvin. "That's just what I heard."

"Does anyone have any rum?" Butler asked. "I'd sooner have rum in this thing than water."

A whistle shattered the air; someone shouted, "Fall in!"
and the Guardsmen rearranged themselves into platoons,
shuffling into line and dressing automatically to the right
for the proper interval. Sergeants called the roll in their
units, then reported to the lieutenants, who in turn reported to the captain and then ordered their troops to stand
at ease. There was total silence as the captain looked from
one end of the line to the other, then drew in his breath to
speak. It was as though everyone else had stopped breathing.

"Men," the captain said, "in a few minutes we will be
boarding a convoy. Our destination will remain secret until
such time as it may be divulged; until then, all I can say is
that we are on a training maneuver. If any of the media
should approach you—and I doubt that they will, since all
preparations have been kept secret—but if they should, you
should tell them that this is routine training and nothing
more. I trust that is clear." He looked at the lieutenants,
said, "You may commence boarding," and turned away.

The lieutenants about-faced and snapped out commands;
the troops did a left face and then, slowly getting out of
step, they filed out of the armory and into the olive-drab
trucks that were lined up the length of the block. Floodlights went on, flashbulbs popped, and television cameras
whirred as a mass of reporters and photographers closed in
on the troops, shouting questions and thrusting microphones
into their faces. Frantic lieutenants tried to keep the reporters away, but it wasn't until a detachment of police with
nightsticks appeared that a path was cleared. Finally the
last Guardsman climbed into the rearmost truck; the tailgate
was slammed shut, and the convoy started off into the gathering dusk, leading a line of press cars that followed along
like wolves.

Omar Tuttle came into the house from his workshop and
went to the kitchen, where Agnes was preparing the traditional Saturday-night baked-bean supper. The kitchen

smelled of steam and beans and pork and brown bread, and Tuttle began to salivate just thinking of what lay ahead. In one hand he held a sheaf of notes, and he looked through them for a moment before speaking.

"I think something's going on," he said at last.

"What's that?" said Agnes, opening the oven to peer inside.

"I'm not sure, but I think the boys in the Statehouse are about to make a move."

"How can you tell?" Agnes closed the oven door and looked at him.

"First, I picked up this message on the police frequency." He referred to one slip of paper. "It's for Ed Mancusi, and it tells him and Ralph Sutkin to stand by and await further orders."

"That could be anything."

"Yes, but then there's one to the tower at Gorking Air Base, telling them to expect six troop-carrying helicopters later on tonight."

"Oh," said Agnes.

"Then, again on the police frequency, there's instructions to clear the roads for a troop convoy headed south for Gorking. Convoy to leave the Guard armory at 1830 tonight."

"Maybe I'd better tell the King," Agnes said, going to the telephone. "Have you been listening to the news as well?"

"No," Tuttle replied. "I've been too busy with this other stuff."

Agnes turned on the television, then picked up the telephone and dialed Markey's number. After two rings a voice answered, and she said, "Hello, Ella. Agnes. Is George there? . . . Do you know when he'll be back? . . . Oh . . . No, I haven't, but Omar has several . . . Oh-ho. When did you hear that? . . . I see. Well, ask George to give me a ring when he gets back, will you? Thanks. 'Bye." She hung up, and said, "There was a radio report earlier this afternoon that the National Guard were being alerted for secret maneuvers. The King has gone out to the airport to check on things there."

"Secret maneuvers could mean anything," Tuttle said, watching a man on the television screen use a stick deodorant. "We may be a little early to get it on this news. Leave it on, and I'll go back to the shop and see what I can pick up."

"What about supper?" Agnes said. "It'll be ready in five minutes."

"Call me when it's on," Tuttle replied. "For all we know, this may be more important." Then he remembered the plans he and Corning had made the day they went fishing, and he said, "Oh—will you call Emil and give him the news? I think he might like to be alerted."

"What's he got to do with it?" Agnes asked.

"As I remember it, it's pretty involved, but he ought to know anyway."

He went out, and Agnes dialed Corning's number. Corning answered, and she said, "Emil? Agnes Tuttle. Omar says he thinks you'd like to know it looks as though the State is going to try something."

"In what way?" Corning asked. His tone was lethargic, almost bored.

"From what we can gather, they may be going to send troops in by helicopter. That's only a guess, but it's the way it looks."

Corning thought about this, then said, "They didn't mention any ships?"

"Not that we heard."

"I had plans for repelling a seaborne invasion, but now— my God, Agnes, I don't know. Maybe it would be better if they took us back."

"What do you mean by *that?*" Agnes's tone was one of shock and disbelief.

"The way George Markey's carrying on, we're going to have a dictator that'll be worse than any State or Federal government we ever dreamed of. It's the real out of the frying pan and into the fire."

"Don't let him get you down, Emil; that's only temporary. As soon as we're established, we can get rid of George like an old shoe. He won't last a week."

"You think not?"

"I know not. We can have a special election and throw him out on his head. What we need most now is to be united."

"I guess you're right. Well, if you get wind of a seaborne invasion, let me know. Otherwise, I'll just do what I can."

"All right, Emil, and don't worry. Things will work out."

"I hope you're right, Agnes. I sure as hell hope you're right."

She hung up and glanced at the television, where a couple in bed were offending each other with their early-morning breaths, then she went to the back door and called, "Supper's on!" Tuttle appeared, and she said, "Or perhaps I should say, 'Chow down,' if we're going to be military."

"We may be more military than we want," Tuttle replied. "They've just alerted the ambulance at Gorking to prepare for casualties."

Sam was at the Sink Hole, trying to talk to Lennie through the cacophony of the Saturday-night blast, when Felicity came up and touched his arm. "You're wanted on the phone!" she shouted.

Sam thanked her and rose, and made his way to the telephone by the rest rooms, where the receiver was hanging down the wall like a snared grouse. He covered one ear and shouted, "Yes?" then put a hand over the mouthpiece to cut down the feedback of room noise.

"Lester Turpin here," came a faint voice. "Can you hear me?"

"Barely," Sam replied.

"I want you to go out to the airport and see what's happening. Give me a call from there, and I'll explain. O.K.?"

"O.K.," Sam said, and hung up. He returned to his table and looked for Lennie but couldn't find her, so he finished his beer and left some money under the empty stein, and made his way through the crowd and out into the night.

When he got to the airport, he found a group of men gathered around the television set in the Prop Wash Lounge. He recognized Crazy Louie Gonzales and Gimpy Dalton and the Mouse, and there were one or two others whose faces looked familiar, but for the rest he didn't know if they were pilots or mechanics or simply people who had drifted in to have a beer while they watched television. Gonzales saw him and beckoned him over.

"Did you hear the news?" Gonzales said.

"I've heard some," Sam replied. "What's the latest?"

"George Markey was just here, and he's put us on an all-night alert. He says we've got to be ready to go up at a moment's notice."

"And do what?" Sam asked.

"That depends, but we've got to be ready for anything. Have some coffee—it's on the house." Gonzales was in a state of barely controlled excitement that made his eyes glitter.

The television showed a commercial on diaper rash, then one on unpleasant household odors, and then the announcer came on with the ten o'clock news. The first film clip was of the Guardsmen getting into their trucks at the armory, and there followed one of the long line of headlights going down the highway, and then the announcer said, "WFIJ has just learned that the convoy's destination is Gorking Air Base, where the Guardsmen will be transferred to helicopters and taken offshore to stamp out the secession movement on the island of—" The rest of his sentence was lost in the shouts and hoots and catcalls of the men around the set, and Sam turned and hurried to the telephone booth. He called Turpin, who picked up after the first ring.

"Yes, I heard," Turpin said before Sam could complete a sentence. "You stay there and cover whatever goes on at the airport. I'll take the police and Selectmen, and Grace will stay here and be a clearinghouse for all messages. Check in with her every now and then."

"Right," said Sam, who was beginning to catch the feeling of excitement. "I'll get back to her in an hour."

"Every two hours ought to do. It may be a long night."

It was midnight when the troop convoy went through the gates of Gorking Air Base, and when the last truck cleared the barrier the MP's closed the entrance to all traffic, blocking the pack of press and television cars that had been trailing the convoy. Private Spelvin, who was in the rear of one of the trucks, peered out and saw the tower beacon and the runway lights and the darkened hangars, and his eyes widened in amazement.

"Son of a bitch, it's an airport," he said. "They're gonna take us out of the country."

"They can't take me," McGinty said, with satisfaction. "My passport's expired."

"Well, they're gonna take us somewhere," Spelvin said. "They didn't bring us all this way to look at the airplanes."

"You heard what the captain said," Butler put in. "It's a training maneuver."

"Training for what?" said McGinty. "How to make your ass go to sleep?"

"Sooner or later we're bound to find out." Butler unscrewed the top of his canteen and sniffed at the neck. "I wish to hell I'd put some Bourbon in here," he said. "I could sure use a shot right about now."

"I could use something more than that," Spelvin said. "Riding in a car always makes me horny."

"That's because you're sitting on your prostrate gland," McGinty said. "You sit on that too long, and it'll make even dogs look good."

"Speak for yourself," said Spelvin. "I'm more selective."

"For all the good it does you." McGinty yawned, folded his arms across his chest, and closed his eyes, just as the truck jolted to a stop and there came the rattle and clang of tailgates being lowered. "God damn," he said. "Wouldn't you know it."

Someone undid the tailgate of their truck and shouted, "Everybody out! Fall in along the roadway!" and the Guardsmen climbed stiffly down and began to form into a double line. Men with flashlights appeared in the darkness, and the lieutenants shouted orders, and the Guardsmen filed into a large, empty barracks building, which suddenly blazed with light. Squinting against the glare, they could see rows of double-decker bunks, skeletal and bare of any bedding, and that was all.

"Fall out!" a lieutenant shouted, and the men drifted slightly apart. "You will stay here until further notice," the lieutenant went on. "You may go anywhere you want in this building—there's a latrine down at the far end—but you are not to leave the building until so ordered. Is that clear?"

"Hey, Lieutenant, how long are we going to be here?" a man asked.

"I don't know," the lieutenant replied, "but if I were you I'd try to get some sleep."

"On what?" said someone else. "We don't even have our packs to lie on!"

"Your packs are in the baggage van," the lieutenant said. "They'll be along shortly."

At the gate, the sentry went to the cab of the large truck that had just drawn up out of the night. "Whaddaya got there?" he asked.

"National Guard gear," the driver replied. "Where's it go?"

"Hold it." The sentry went to a telephone by the gate, spoke into it briefly, then came back. "Duty officer says put it by hangar Number Three," he said, pointing across the field. He went back into the sentry box and raised the barrier.

"Is there someone over there to take it?" the driver asked as he went slowly through the gate.

"If there isn't, just leave it there," the sentry replied. "Someone'll be along later."

In the pale light of 5 A.M., a sergeant put his head inside the barracks, flicked on the lights, and blew his whistle. "Reveille!" he shouted. "Rise and shine! Let go of your cock and grab a sock! Everybody up!" There were groans and yawns and curses as the Guardsmen, who had slept wherever they could find space to lie down, gradually brought themselves into standing positions. Some went into the latrine, others groped through their pockets for cigarettes, which they lighted between spasms of coughing, and still others stared out the windows while they scratched themselves awake.

"Christ, what a night," Spelvin said. "I'd sooner of slept on a picket fence."

"I did," McGinty replied. "And I'm here to tell you it was no bargain."

The sergeant put his head back in the door. "Fall in outside in ten minutes!" he bellowed.

"Hey, Sarge, what about breakfast?" someone asked. "We gotta eat, don't we?"

"Combat conditions," the sergeant replied. "You'll eat later."

"*Com*bat?" said Butler, aghast. "Is he crazy?"

"We'll soon find out," McGinty said. "Someone sure as hell is."

The troops formed up ten minutes later, and saw on the field six large, potbellied helicopters, with the vanes on their rotors sagging toward the ground. When the roll had been called and the reports made, the captain stepped forward, cleared his throat, and said, "Men, our mission today is to capture and secure that island which, as you have all heard, has seceded from the State. We do not anticipate much resistance; we feel sure that your presence at the critical centers of control will be enough to deter any firebrands who may hanker for a fight, and by moving at this hour of a Sunday morning we feel we will have the element of surprise on our side. Your officers have been briefed on your various objectives, and you are to follow their orders without question. To bring the possibility of casualties to a minimum, you have been issued rubber bullets so that, in the unlikely event you have to fire toward a group of civilians, there will be no fatal injuries. Rubber bullets may bruise, but they do not kill. Finally, I want you to know that I shall be in the lead helicopter, and I shall not ask one of you to do anything I would not do myself." He paused, and looked around, then concluded, "Good luck, and happy landing." He stepped back; the lieutenants shouted, orders that were echoed by the sergeants, and the troops began to move toward the helicopters.

As they shuffled forward, Spelvin reached into his bandolier, brought out a clip, and examined the bullets. The tips gleamed with a coppery sheen. "Hey, Mac," he said to McGinty, "do you have rubber bullets? I sure as hell don't."

McGinty examined his ammunition and shook his head. "Same old stuff we always had," he said. "I had this clip last time we were on the practice range."

"Hey, Sarge," Spelvin said more loudly, to the sergeant, "what's this about rubber bullets? We got regular ammo here."

"Shut up and don't ask questions," the sergeant replied. "You'll get your rubber bullets later."

"Along with our packs, I suppose," said Spelvin. "Whatever became of them?"

"Quiet in the ranks!" a lieutenant shouted. "This isn't a Girl Scout picnic!"

The scene in the Prop Wash Lounge was something like that in the barracks: men were sleeping on the floor, in chairs, on the lunch counter, and on the bar, while a few stayed awake and drank coffee as they listened to an all-night radio program. The television would not start until six, and the last news broadcast had been a recap of all the earlier ones, with no action forecast until the coming of daylight on Sunday.

The telephone rang, and Gonzales rose from his chair and picked it up. "Yeah?" he said. "Yeah, Omar, this is Louie . . . They have? When? . . . Thanks, Omar." He hung up and shouted, "Scramble, you bastards, scramble! They're coming!"

"Who says so?" the Mouse asked, finishing his coffee in one gulp.

"Omar Tuttle heard the choppers request clearance from the Gorking tower—they're cleared and they're on their way! Six of them!" He hit Sam between the shoulder blades and said, "Come on, kid, we're off!"

Sam, who was only half awake, followed Gonzales automatically as the pilots raced for their planes, and it wasn't until he was strapped in his seat and Gonzales had started the engine that Sam realized he hadn't intended to fly. His idea had been to do the story from the ground, where he could get an overall view of the action, but it was too late for that because Gonzales's plane was already rolling, and he couldn't think of a plausible excuse to get out. So he tightened his seat belt, said a silent prayer, and scanned the skies to the north as the plane seemed to leap into the air. The pink of the morning light was beginning to fade, and the lower clouds were backlighted, making them look like dark cotton with luminous edges; higher up, the sky was pale blue and the air was clear. Below them, Sam could see the other planes taking off, streaking across the ground and then fanning out into a wide formation. Two planes, he noticed, were attached by a long, looping line between their wing tips, and he was glad that Gonzales's plane was not similarly rigged. Things are going to be hairy enough, he thought, without adding any extra hazards.

Gonzales climbed in a slow spiral to four thousand feet, where he could see the whole area spread out below him like a map. To the east the water glinted in reflected sunlight; beneath him the other planes were climbing in a loose arc, and to the north he could see the low line of haze that marked the mainland. Suddenly he said, "There they are!" and pointed. Far below, a line of six dots emerged from the haze, looking like dragonflies with oddly fluttering wings. Gonzales spoke into his microphone and received scattered acknowledgments, then he headed his plane toward the dots and eased back on the throttle.

"What are you going to do?" Sam asked. His mouth had gone dry, and his gums felt gritty.

Gonzales grinned. "Just watch," he said, unnecessarily. "And hold on to your hat." He spoke once more into his microphone, then eased the control stick forward and pointed the nose at a spot in front of the lead helicopter.

Sam felt his stomach go hollow as the plane dropped, then as it gathered speed he was pressed into the back of his seat, and he instinctively braced himself by grasping the instrument panel in front of him. The engine noise rose to a snarl and then a roar; the lead helicopter was plainly visible but still below them and some distance away, and then suddenly Sam saw the boggle-eyed face of the pilot as they flashed by, and he felt pressure on his seat and all he could see was sky.

When Gonzales leveled off they were once again above the helicopters, which had now broken formation and were trying to avoid the small planes that buzzed at them from all angles. Sam saw the action in a series of flashes, as though on an old-fashioned movie projector: one second he'd see the underside of a small plane, then a quick flash of a careening helicopter, then the tail of an airplane, then blue sky, then a head-on view of a helicopter, then the moor roads directly below. Once he saw a helicopter with something enmeshed in its rotor blades, flailing the air like a monstrous whip, and then he saw a long strand of rope dropping earthward, trailing, of all things, what looked like a child's balloon. He pointed at it and said, "What's that?" and Gonzales grinned.

"Our own brand of flak," he replied. "Clothesline." He dove beneath a helicopter, then pulled up in an Immelmann turn above it.

"Why the balloon?" Sam asked, when he could speak.

"Keeps the line straight out," Gonzales replied. "So's not to drop in a coil."

The National Guard captain saw the clotheslines, too, and with some difficulty made his way forward to the pilot's seat. The pilot was sweating, trying to look out in all directions at once, and taking what evasive action he could as the small planes darted about him. A long streamer of white drifted toward the windshield and the pilot started to avoid it, then let it come. It hit the windshield, tore, and vanished. "Sons of bitches," the pilot said.

"What was that?" the captain asked.

"Toilet paper," the pilot replied. "The bastards are dropping bumwad along with the clotheslines, and I can't tell which is which until I'm almost on it." He yanked the control column to one side as a blue-and-white monoplane hurtled past, then reversed the controls to avoid a length of line that was trailing a red balloon. The helicopter bucked and yawed like a bronco, and from the troops in the rear came a chorus of shouts and curses. The sour smell of vomit wafted forward.

"What do you think?" the captain said. "Can we make it through?"

"Captain, I honest to Christ don't know," the pilot replied. "If we throw a blade, or get the rotors fouled up, we'll drop like a stone."

The captain was quiet for a moment, while he considered the alternatives. He'd always been taught that a good officer knows when to cut his losses and to recognize an impossible situation when he sees one, and he balanced the embarrassment of failure against the possible loss of life if he should press on. After all, it wasn't as though it were a real war, he thought. It was a simple domestic squabble that could probably be settled by some other means and without danger to life and—

"There goes one now," the pilot said, pointing out the window. "I think it's Charlie."

"What? Where?" the captain said, trying to see out.

"Guy's got his tail rotor fouled. He's beginning to spin, but he's still got some control. If he gets down quick enough, he'll be all right."

"All right," the captain said. "That does it. Pass the word for a one-eighty turn. Do you think that man needs help?"

"There's nothing we can do," the pilot replied. "He either crashes or he doesn't." He spoke into his microphone, dove to avoid an oncoming Beechcraft Bonanza, then pulled the helicopter into a sharp turn and headed north. There was further talk on his radio, and he looked back at the captain. "Charlie's all right," he said. "He just put it down in the underbrush."

"Any casualties?" the captain asked.

"Only to his pride," the pilot said, and with one finger flicked the sweat from his forehead.

The downed helicopter rested in a patch of scrub oak, its tail rotor clotted with clothesline that had formed a large, fibrous mass around the hub. The main rotor blades sagged limply about it, like ribs on a broken umbrella, and the engine exhaust ports exuded a faint, dying breath of heat. The door opened and a pale, shaken sergeant put his head out, looked around, then clambered awkwardly through the scrub oak to firm ground. He was followed by the pilot and then, one by one, those Guardsmen who still had strength enough to move. The last three out were Privates Spelvin, McGinty, and Butler, and of the three Butler seemed to be in the worst shape. He was green, and had beads of sweat beneath his eyes and the stunned look of a man who has been given up for dead and then revived.

"I need a drink," he croaked. "Doesn't anybody even have some gin?"

"What you need is a walk," the sergeant said. "Spelvin— McGinty—you go with Butler into the town, and get help."

"What kind of help?" Spelvin asked.

"What kind do you think? We'll need transportation, we'll need a repair crew, we'll need food—"

"Aren't we supposed to be invading these people?" Spelvin said. "Do you think they're likely to help us?"

"The invasion's been called off," the pilot said. "The other choppers have gone back."

"Oh," said Spelvin. "O.K., then—transportation, repair crew, and food—is that all?"

"That'll do for now," the sergeant said.

"Come on, you guys." Spelvin led the way as they tramped through the underbrush, and they finally came to a rutted road. They followed this for about a mile until it joined a paved road, on which they turned in what they assumed was the direction of the town. They had walked for about ten minutes when they heard the sounds of an approaching car, and looking back, they saw a paint-spattered Wagoneer, which slowed down as they held out their thumbs. The sign on the side read: "Arthur Gibbon—House & General Painting."

"Which way is the town?" Spelvin asked when the car had stopped.

"The way I'm going," Gibbon replied. "Hop in." He wore a shirt and jacket and tie, all appearing too small for him, and it was clear he was on his way to church. "You fellers from around here?" he said as he started up.

"No," McGinty replied. "We're from the mainland."

"I thought you looked unfamiliar. We don't see many guns like that, either."

McGinty looked at his M-14. "No," he said. "These are sort of special."

"You don't know where a man could get a drink, do you?" Butler said. "I'm like to die if I don't get something soon."

"Bars don't open till one o'clock Sunday," Gibbon replied. "If I had any on me I'd let you have it, but I don't."

"What about food?" Spelvin asked. "And transportation, and mechanics?"

Gibbon laughed. "You don't want much, do you?" he said. "You won't find nothing open before noon Sundays. If I was you, I'd go home and take a nap."

"I wish to God I could," said Butler.

"Just out of curiosity," Spelvin said, "have you heard anything about an invasion of the island?"

"Invasion?" said Gibbon. "Who by?"

"The State—the National Guard."

Gibbon shook his head. "I quit listening to the news when we seceded," he said. "That was such a lot of damn foolishness I figured there was nothing they could say would interest me. If I feel like a little home entertainment, I play my Victrola. Is that what you guys are doing? Are you going to fight the invaders?"

"Not exactly," McGinty said. "I guess we're what you'd call observers."

Gibbon laughed, and shook his head again. "It sure takes all kinds," he said.

The Governor and his aide and the press secretary stared stonily at the television set, watching an interview with George Markey. It had been taped on Sunday afternoon, and rerun at intervals since then, both on the local station and on the network, until by a conservative estimate it had been seen by most of the eastern seaboard. Markey was flushed with the first warm glow of victory, and his usual bombast was replaced by an easy, almost benign confidence.

"It was simple," he told the interviewer. "It was the classic example of good old Yankee know-how—the David and Goliath story all over again. They came out here with their troops and their helicopters and their napalm, and—"

"Jesus *Christ!*" the Governor exploded. "Who said anything about napalm?"

"Nobody," the aide replied. "He made it up."

"—they were put to rout by Yankee ingenuity," Markey went on. "When you don't have a military budget, and don't have napalm and machine guns and tanks, you have to think of some new angle, and that's just what the boys did. A few lengths of nylon clothesline, and some dime-store helium balloons, and the Goliaths were licked. We hope they've learned their lesson, and will leave us alone."

"I understand you even took some prisoners," the interviewer said.

"That is correct. We brought down one helicopter full of troops, and while they are free to return to the mainland any time they want, I'm told that most of them want to stay here. Perhaps prisoners is too strong a word—guests, or visitors, would be more correct. We always welcome visitors, provided they don't try to force their will upon us." He smiled, and added, "And can pay their way. Freeloaders are no more welcome here than anywhere else."

"What do you see as the future of the island?" the interviewer asked.

"I see it as unlimited. We have seceded from the State and have proved that we are not to be trifled with; our future is our own, and we intend to make the most of it. With our oil reserves, there is nothing we cannot do."

"And the Federal Government?" the interviewer said. "What is your position as regards them?"

Markey paused only briefly, then said, "I believe the Federal Government should take a lesson from what has happened today. We are a free and independent entity, of, by, and on our own, and any attempt by the Federal Government to interfere will be met by the same treatment as was met by the State today. That goes for Federal taxes, Federal projects, and the whole Federal shooting match. We can take care of our own, and we don't need help or interference from anyone."

"In other words, you consider yourselves a separate country."

"That is correct. And you may quote me."

The interviewer thanked Markey and then turned to the camera, and the Governor switched the set off.

"Cocky bastard, isn't he?" the aide said.

The Governor didn't reply, but looked instead at his press secretary. "Fred," he said at last, "to say that you have let me down would be to plumb the depths of understatement."

"There was nothing I could do," the press secretary said. "I gave them the story you told me to, and they didn't believe me—for which I can't say I blame them. And I can't keep them from getting the news on their own."

"You could have given them a story that would have taken their minds off the real one."

"Such as?"

"It doesn't matter. It's too late now. You should have acted while there still was time."

"Offhand, the only story I can think of would have been that you'd been arrested, and had hanged yourself in your cell. That would have had a certain appeal, now that I think of it."

The Governor stared at him. "You once expressed an admiration for the life of a clam digger."

"I said it was honest. Don't you admire honesty?"

"Don't crowd me, Fred. All I can say is, don't crowd me."

"Then, without crowding you, may I ask when you'd like

to hold a press conference? The media have been on the horn ever since that Markey interview was first run."

"I'm going to let you handle that. If they want to know where I am, tell them you have no idea."

"And where will you be?"

"In Washington. And I'll want a tape of that interview to take with me. Do you think you can arrange that?"

"I think I can. Compared to some of my other assignments, that will be a piece of cake."

"And you'd better familiarize yourself with the tide tables, too. You may be digging clams sooner than you think."

19

The day had started badly for Muriel Baxter. It was Tuesday, June 1, three weeks after secession and the first day of school after the Memorial Day weekend, and already she sensed a loosening of the stays, so to speak, that had held her life together. The mood of the town was one of euphoria, and the Memorial Day speeches at the cemetery had sounded the clarion call of every cliché in the lexicon of patriotism, but beneath the surface ran a black river of doubt—at least as far as Miss Baxter was concerned—and the feeling that all the trumpeting was a prelude to disaster. The signs were small, but they were everywhere: the Memorial Day tourists, for instance, were more numerous than ever before, but they seemed to have come as they might to the zoo, to watch the animals being fed, and perhaps catch a few of them in the process of mating. They were leering rather than festive, and there were others, not exactly tourists but certainly newcomers, who had made themselves so much at home that they left a trail of garbage and debris wherever they went, and gave obscene replies to anyone who had the temerity to object.

But the worst group were the workmen from the oil-drilling company, who had begun to filter in shortly after secession and who apparently now considered the island their own. They drove with complete disregard for the traffic laws; they all but wrecked the Sink Hole one night when the owner declined to advance them credit on an $87.50 bar bill; they intimidated Chief Maddox's hapless police force, chaining one officer with his own handcuffs to the wheel of his cruiser; and they took the position that they could have any woman they wanted.

It was one of this group that Miss Baxter encountered on Tuesday morning when she left her house on the way to school. He was standing in Apple Lane, looking around in numbed stupefaction as though he had just been dropped there from another planet, and when he saw her coming up the path he observed her as he might a particularly interesting bug.

"Hey," he said, raising a hand. "Wait a minute."

Miss Baxter, who had started to go around him, slowed. "What do you want?" she said. She could smell the stale liquor on his breath and see the brown cigar-butt smears around his lips.

"I wanna talk to you," he said, coming toward her.

"Sorry," she said, moving out and away, "I'm busy right now."

"Yer goddam well not too busy for me," he said. "Come here." He lunged at her but she jumped away, and before he could regain his balance she was hurrying down Apple Lane toward the corner. "Snotty goddam bitch," he muttered, and watched her out of sight.

She found herself short of breath as she walked the familiar route to school. It was the first time she'd been so rudely accosted, and she wondered if there could be any connection between this man and whoever it was that had been in her house a few weeks earlier. The fact that *that* man, or person, had used cologne proved nothing one way or the other about this one; he could have drenched himself in cologne before he started out last night, and by now it would have all worn off or been absorbed by the other, ranker odors he exuded. It was highly unlikely that there was any connection, but in Miss Baxter's mind it was part of the general pattern, and as such it was deeply disturbing. She resolved to ask her landlord for permission to change the locks on the house, just as a precaution.

The first day of school after any holiday, no matter how brief, was always a trial, and this one was no exception. The students, if such they could be called, were restless and slow to settle down, and their restlessness was compounded by the knowledge that there were only three more weeks of school anyway, so the whole business of learning and reciting was pointless. In another month it would all be forgotten, and with luck they'd never be asked about it again. Ralph Lutchens, the boy whose father had castigated Miss Baxter in front of the class, was particularly intractable. He feigned indifference to everything she said, and would answer her only after she had called his name at least twice. He was fourteen but large for his age, and his hands were too big for the rest of him. He used them like semaphores, to send messages to friends across the room. Finally, Miss Baxter decided to call him to order.

"Ralph," she said, "may I ask you something?" He grinned at a neighbor and said nothing, and she said, "Ralph!" Slowly, he rolled his eyes toward her.

"Yeah," he said.

"I'd just like to know if there's anything that interests you," said Miss Baxter. "Anything at all."

"Yeah," said Ralph, and his grin widened. "Pussy." Several students giggled, and one laughed outright.

"That's not what I meant," Miss Baxter said, feeling her

face go hot. "What I meant was, if I knew your interests, then perhaps I could find a book you'd like to read. You're bored by Mark Twain, you're bored by Conan Doyle, and you're bored by J. D. Salinger. Can you think of any kind of book you might like? That's in the school library, that is," she added hastily.

"All that library stuff is a crock of shit," Ralph replied. "If I was you I'd forget it."

"Ralph, you will not use that kind of language in here," Miss Baxter said. "I want you to apologize."

"To who?"

"To me."

"Don't make me laugh."

"Ralph, do you want me to take you to the principal?"

Ralph shrugged. "Suit yourself. It's nothing to me."

She started to rise, then realized that if she took him to the principal, chaos would take over in the classroom. She also remembered the way his father had shaken her, and decided she was not equal to another bout with Mr. Lutchens. She sat back in her chair, and said, "We'll go into this later."

"Anytime," said Ralph cheerfully. "Just remember what my daddy said."

Miss Baxter turned to another student, a girl in jeans who was loudly chewing bubble gum. "Mary, is it absolutely necessary that you make all that noise?" she said.

"Yes," said Mary, blowing a large, pink bubble and cracking it.

"You will please take the gum out of your mouth until the end of class."

Mary made a gulping gesture, as though swallowing. "I can't," she said smugly. "I swallowed it."

Miss Baxter stared at her, trying to spot the wad of gum in the girl's cheek, but Mary stared back unblinking, and after a while Miss Baxter gave up. She looked at another girl and and said, "Doris, can you tell me what you found most interesting in 'The Wreck of the Hesperus'?"

"Nothing," said Doris. "It was a drag."

"Did you read it all the way through?"

"More or less."

"What was there in the ending that was particularly ironic, in contrast to the opening verses?"

Doris gaped. "Come again?"

"What did you find in the end of the poem that contrasted with the beginning?"

"Beats me," said Doris.

"Do you remember the description of the captain's daughter? 'Her bosom was white as the hawthorn buds that ope in the month of May'?"

"Yeah. Does that mean she had tits?"

There was scattered laughter, and out of the corner of her eye Miss Baxter saw Mary resume chewing her gum. "Mary Maloney," she said sharply. "Come up here."

Mary hesitated, then rose and approached Miss Baxter's desk.

"Take that gum out of your mouth."

Mary clenched her teeth. "I told you. I swallowed it."

"You were just chewing it. Open your mouth."

This time, Mary did swallow it. Then she opened her mouth wide. "You see?" she said.

"Do you have any more?"

"Why?"

"I said do you have any more?"

"Yes."

"Put another piece in your mouth, and chew it." Mary paused, then obeyed. "Now swallow it," Miss Baxter said. Mary did. "Do you have any more?" Miss Baxter asked, and Mary burst into tears.

"You're a mean old bitch and I'm going to tell my father!" she said. "You can't do this to me, it's bad for my health!"

"You were the one who thought of it," Miss Baxter replied.

"I know my constitutional rights!" Mary's face turned

red, and was gnarled in a grimace of outrage. "You wait and
see what happens to you!"

"Go back to your seat and be quiet," Miss Baxter said.
"And blow your nose." Then she turned to the class.
"Would anybody care to discuss 'The Wreck of the Hes-
perus'?" she said, and was answered by total silence.

The rest of the school day followed pretty much the same
pattern, and by three o'clock Miss Baxter found that she was
jumping at small noises and had a tendency to shout when a
spoken word would have sufficed. She decided that what
she needed was a long walk, so instead of driving her battered red Volkswagen to the supermarket she put a basket
over her arm and set out on foot. As she made her way to
the shopping center she noticed more newcomers, who were
visible everywhere, and once or twice she thought she recognized the drunk who had accosted her that morning.
Then she reasoned that he must long ago have gone home to
sleep it off, and she told herself that the oil workers probably all looked something alike. She knew this wasn't true,
but she didn't want to believe that the man was purposely
following her.

The supermarket had not been restocked since the holiday, and Miss Baxter was unable to find many of the things
she wanted. Her shopping list was a meager one, but she
needed certain items like soap and paper towels and bread
and coffee, plus the canned or frozen foods that made up
the rest of her diet, and it was staples such as these that
seemed suddenly in short supply. When she got to the
check-out counter she found that although her purchases
were fewer than usual, the total on the cash register was almost three dollars more than she usually paid. She looked at
the check-out girl in amazement.

"How did it get that high?" she asked.

"Secession," the girl replied, opening a brown-paper bag
and dropping Miss Baxter's goods inside. She tore the tape
off the register, put it in the bag, and said, "Everything's

gonna cost more now, they say, because we're a separate country. It's like we were buying the food from France."

"That doesn't make sense," Miss Baxter said as she counted out the money.

"I don't see it myself," said the girl, "but that's what the manager told us to say. He's the one should know."

As she left the supermarket, Miss Baxter was aware that a man was looking at her, and when she glanced at him he smiled. She nodded and went on her way, and it was several minutes before she could identify him: he was the one who, the day of the television interviews, had hurried after her with a release and then had promised to bring her a copy, which he never did. She tried to remember his name, and concluded she'd never known it; he was simply a man who had appeared with a slip of paper, then vanished. Men seem to be popping up everywhere these days, she thought; it's a pity they can't be a little more attractive.

Edgar Morris watched her leave, and felt the same urge he had every time he saw her. He was supposed to go to the Lions Club meeting that night, and he knew that if he missed it Hosmer Curtin, the undertaker who was also Club Tail Twister, would fine him for his absence, but Hosmer had fined him so many times, and for such a variety of minor offenses—such as going to the men's room before dessert—that the punishment no longer carried any sting. He felt it would be worth one more nick from the Tail Twister to try his luck with Miss Baxter. After all, he had nothing to lose beyond a twenty-five-cent fine, and practically everything to gain.

Miss Baxter threw the remains of her veal pie in the garbage, spooned instant coffee into a cup and added boiling water, then closed the neck of the plastic garbage bag and secured it with a piece of wire tape. She accumulated garbage at such a slow rate that by the time the bag was full the earlier deposits had begun to reek, and she wanted it out of the house as quickly as possible. She lifted the bag from the wastebasket, and took it out the back door to the covered metal container.

The man who'd accosted her that morning was standing there, his face lighted by the glow from the kitchen window. She screamed, and hurled the garbage bag at him, but he ducked it and caught her before she was able to get back in the house. She screamed again, and he clapped one hand over her mouth.

"Shut up and you won't get hurt," he said in a low voice. "Nobody's gonna hurt you if you keep quiet." She tried to struggle but it was as though she were encased in concrete, and after a few moments she gave up. "That's more like it," he said. "Now, let's us go inside and have a little talk." He steered her in the back door, and through the kitchen to the living room, where he stopped. At least, she thought, he didn't go straight to the bedroom; the longer we stay out of there, the better my chances are. She turned her eyes toward him, and he smiled. "No need to get in a sweat," he said. "It isn't like I was going to kill you, or anything." She noticed that he no longer stank as he had that morning; he was cleaner, and comparatively sober, which meant he was in better control and therefore more dangerous. She had nothing to fear from a staggering drunk, but a man who'd just had a few drinks was something else again. As calmly as she could, she tried to say something, but his hand muffled the words. She repeated it, and he raised his hand slightly, ready to clap it back if she should scream.

"Thank you," she said. "It was getting hard to breathe."

"You can breathe all you want if you don't scream," he replied. "If you scream, I don't promise nothing."

"What do you want?" she asked. She'd heard that a direct, unexpected remark or question would sometimes throw a man off balance, and she needed time to think what to do next.

He laughed. "That's easy," he said. "Ask me something hard."

"Tell me first what you want."

"Christ, don't you know?"

"It's only fair to warn you I'm diseased." *That* ought to give him something to think about.

He laughed louder. "Like hell you are."

"How do you—what makes you think so?"

"That's not the way you say it. You say, 'I got a dose,' or 'I picked up a nail,' but you're not the type. I bet you never—"

"Little do you know, buster. I'm the—"

He'd been holding her from behind, and now he spun her around and, pinning her arms with one of his, reached the other hand under her dress and made a swooping grab at her underwear. He got the elastic on her panties and pulled, and she raised one knee to fend him off, just as there came a knock at the front door, and she shrieked, "Come in! Whoever you are, *come in!*" The man shoved her backward and she fell over a chair, then the front door opened and Edgar Morris stood there, holding a bouquet of yellow daffodils.

"Hey, what's going on here?" Morris said. The man rushed at him, hit him a blow on the side of the head that sent him and the flowers flying in all directions, and then disappeared into the night. Miss Baxter was the first to recover, and she picked herself up, trying to readjust her underwear as quickly as possible.

"Are you hurt?" she asked.

Morris touched the side of his head, and waggled his jaw. "I don't think so," he replied, and struggled into a sitting position. "I guess you'd more call it surprised." Miss Baxter came over and helped him to his feet, and as she did she caught the smell of his cologne. It was familiar, but she couldn't prove anything by that alone.

"I'm terribly sorry," she said. "Here—let me pick up your flowers."

"They're for you," Morris said. "Although I guess this is a

funny way to give them. I hope I didn't interrupt anything."

"Only imminent rape," replied Miss Baxter, who was beginning to have the feeling she was losing her mind. "He caught me when I took the garbage out, and—well, you saw the rest. Or most of it. To say you were welcome is an understatement."

"Glad to do it," said Morris. "Do you want to call the police?"

Miss Baxter stood with the fragmented bouquet in her hands, and said, "My God! Of course! I must be crazy!" She looked for a place to put the flowers, and Morris took them from her.

"Here," he said. "While you call, I'll put them in something." He shook his head to clear the ringing in his ears, and went into the kitchen while Miss Baxter picked up the telephone.

Her hands were shaking as she dialed the number, and when the duty officer answered she could barely speak. "I want to report a rape," she said. "I mean—almost rape. Attempted rape." She took a deep breath, and tried to compose herself.

"Who's calling?" the officer asked.

"Muriel Baxter. I live at 15 Apple Lane." She found that by speaking slowly she became calmer. "A man grabbed me outside the back door, then took me in the house and started to rape me, then got away."

"Did he rape you, or didn't he?" the officer asked.

"No. Someone else came in, and he ran."

"Who came in?"

"Uh—" Miss Baxter realized she didn't know Morris's name, and said, "He's in the kitchen now. Fixing some flowers."

There was a short silence, then the officer said, "Who is he?"

"The man who came in. He brought the flowers."

"What's his *name?* Look, ma'am, this is just for the record —it don't mean a thing to me."

"Just a minute." Miss Baxter put her hand over the mouthpiece and called, "What's your name?"

Morris appeared in the kitchen door. "Me?" he said.

"Yes. The police want to know."

"It's none of their business."

Miss Baxter started to relay the message, then said, "I think it might be better if we told them."

"Edgar Morris."

Into the phone, she said, "He says it's Edgar Morris."

"Oh," the officer said. "And what was the name of the man who tried to rape you?"

"I haven't the faintest idea. I think he was one of those construction workers."

"Can you give me a description of him?"

"Well—he was tall—or medium tall—and sort of heavy—"

"Color of hair? Color of eyes?"

"Sort of neutral, I guess. The hair, I mean. Brownish. The eyes were blue. I remember the eyes." The back of her neck went cold and she shivered.

"Beard?"

"No."

"What was he wearing?"

"Regular clothes. Nothing special. A jacket—no. A sweater? I don't remember. It was dark."

"All right, Miss Baxter, I'll make a note."

"Aren't you going to send an officer? For all I know he may still be lurking around."

"Well, I'm a little shorthanded right now. There's only one man in the cruiser, and I got to save him in case of an emergency."

"You don't consider rape an emergency?"

"Attempted rape? No, not if the man's got away."

"Suppose I had been raped. Would that have been an emergency?"

"That's another kettle of fish. As it stands—well, if he's caught raping someone else, we'll let you know."

"Thank you very much."

"Don't mention it. Have a nice day."

Miss Baxter hung up, feeling more than ever that she was losing her mind. Morris handed her the daffodils, which he'd put in a long-necked vase, and she thanked him and set them on the card table. Again she caught a whiff of his cologne, and she hesitated and then said, "Were you ever in this house before?"

Morris looked straight at her, and saw she knew the answer and that his only hope was to level with her. "Yes," he said. "I came back that day to tell you they had no extra release forms, but you weren't here. I—just looked through the house, in case you might have been napping somewhere." He realized that didn't sound right, but didn't know how to emend it so changed the subject. "What did the police say?" he asked.

"They said they'd make a note. The officer on duty said they were shorthanded so could only answer emergency calls, and since this man had left the house it was no longer an emergency."

"That's the police for you," Morris said. "Always ready to harass a citizen, but when you really need them, where are they? Shorthanded. It makes you wonder."

"That's right," Miss Baxter said, and then she remembered something. "Weren't you the one who spoke up for anarchy at town meeting?" she asked.

"Uh—yes," he replied, hoping not to get into an argument. "There are times when it seems to make sense. Other times . . . well . . ." He let the sentence trail off.

Miss Baxter felt her sensation of unreality grow with every word that was spoken. "Now, what can I do for you?" she said briskly. "What brought you here at this hour of the night?"

"I was supposed to go to a Lions meeting," Morris began,

then stopped and said, "I guess that's got nothing to do with it."

"You couldn't prove it by me," said Miss Baxter. "At this point, I'll believe anything."

"Well, the Lions have a dinner every so often." Morris was glad for a conversational gambit. "They discuss Lionism and they sing songs, and they—"

"What kind of songs?" Miss Baxter asked. "Sit down, won't you? There's no point standing."

Morris took the chair she indicated, and as she sat on the couch he said, "Oh, songs like 'There's Something About a Lion,' and 'My Wild Irish Rose,' and 'Hail, Hail, the Lions Are Here,' and songs like that. You know, old-time favorites."

"Are the Lions a singing society, then? Like the Whiffenpoofs?"

"Oh, no. Lionism is devoted to good works, especially as it concerns eyesight. They collect old eyeglasses—you don't by any chance have a pair of glasses you're through with, do you?"

"As it happens, I don't. But I'll remember you in case I should."

"Most people's eyes change over the years, and the Lions collect their old glasses and distribute them to the needy. Proper eye care is so expensive these days—do you know what a corneal transplant will set you back? Just for one eye?"

"I have no idea. How much?"

"I forget the exact figure, but it's a bundle. So with so many people who can't afford eye care, the Lions sort of take over and help where they can. It's a very worthy group."

"I can see that. Would you care for a drink? I'm afraid all I can offer you is a little wine."

"Yes, please. That would be fine." Morris found his mouth was getting dry from talking, but he desperately wanted to

keep the conversation going. He knew that sooner or later
he was going to make a move, but fear of rejection and what
that might lead to made him put off the moment as long as
he could. He felt he was literally talking to save his neck, and
he didn't know how long he could keep it up.

She returned with two glasses of Chablis, handed him
one, then resumed her place on the couch. "So you came
here to see if I had any old eyeglasses," she said.

"No, not exactly." Morris took a gulp of his wine, and
said, "I don't usually bring flowers when I go to pick up
glasses." He laughed, touched his lips to his wineglass, then
added, "I don't usually bring flowers to anybody."

"Then I feel specially honored," said Miss Baxter. "Not
only do you save me from being raped, but you break a
long-standing pattern and bring me daffodils. What can I
possibly do for you?"

Morris swallowed. "This and that," he said.

"You still haven't told me why you came here."

By now his palms were sweating, and he wiped them on
his trouser legs. "I wanted to talk to you," he said.

"About what?"

He knew as well as he knew anything that if he said,
"About going to bed with me," she'd throw him out of the
house, but he couldn't think of any other way to say it. He
could think of a lot of coarser ways, but they'd be even
worse, and he was flatly unable to put words to what he had
in mind. "I don't suppose you've ever seen any of my wood-
carving," he said.

"I don't know," she replied. "What do they look like?"

"All sorts of things. I find pieces of driftwood that remind
me of things, and then I carve them out and give them a
finish. Birds, whales, dolphins, horses—whatever. The summer people buy them like hot cakes."

"I think I may have seen some. They're quite handsome."

"Thank you."

"And you'd like me to buy one?"

"Oh, no no no! That's not it at all! I'd like you to pose for one." There it is, he thought. Now I've done it.

Miss Baxter stared at him. "*Pose* for one?" she said. "How does one pose for a piece of driftwood?"

"Well—it's hard to explain." He started to gesture with his hands, then set the wineglass down and went on, "I see things in the wood when I carve, and I find these days the thing I see most is you. No matter what the shape of the wood is, I seem to see you in it somewhere, so I thought— well, it came to me that—I mean, if I could *really* see you, then I might . . ." He stopped, wringing his hands and cracking the knuckles. His body was quivering as though an electric current were pulsing through it.

To Miss Baxter he looked like a deadly earnest, tortured student, fumbling through a recitation he'd learned by heart but couldn't quite remember. She'd had occasional students like that, long ago, and her heart had always bled for them. She was suddenly awash with compassion, and, by now in such a haze of unreality that she might have been some other person, she rose from the couch and came across and took his hand.

"Come on," she said. "I guess there has to be a first time for everything."

20

There were more than the usual number of townspeople at the Selectmen's meeting on June 3. Before calling for order Markey looked around the room, and was not particularly pleased to see Dr. Amberson and his wife among the specta- tors, as well as Emil Corning, Edgar Morris, and Lester and Grace Turpin. Sam was, as usual, covering the meeting for the paper, so that meant the Turpins were present for some other reason, and it made him uneasy. Even Daisy, the maid who helped around the Markey house, was there, and to Markey this seemed to hint at a plot of some sort, a packing of the house to give voice to a grievance. He couldn't imagine what it was all about, but it seemed more than a little ominous.

Of the Selectmen in attendance, he could count only on Norris Webster for support. Agnes Tuttle and Denton Norquist had been against him the last time and were therefore unreliable, and Padraic O'Toole's vote on any given issue would depend on how much he'd had to drink. Now that he thought of it, Markey realized he'd never get a really unanimous vote on anything, because Webster was bound to vote against Agnes no matter what it was about. This gave him two votes that canceled each other out, plus one, O'Toole's, that would be as erratic as a squirrel, and with a large audience present he didn't dare repeat the stratagem of casting O'Toole's vote for him. He'd simply have to play it by ear, and see what the people had in mind.

He rapped the meeting to order and said, "Before we go on to the unfinished business, I'd like to make a report—call it a State of the Island report if you like. Our lease of the oil land off Gander Rip has so far netted the Town treasury forty thousand dollars in hard cash. As soon as the oil starts to flow that will, of course, be increased by an as yet undetermined amount, but we can safely anticipate anywhere from one million to two million dollars in the first year. On the theory that money breeds more money, I have instructed the Chamber of Commerce to throw away their old budget and to spend as much as they like in advertising the island, not only emphasizing its obvious summer advantages but also stressing its possibilities as a winter resort as well. We may not have skiing here, or the traditional winter sports, but I like to think that with a little ingenuity we can come up with ideas that will bring tourists here all year round. We can have ice-fishing carnivals, for instance, and iceboat regattas; we can re-equip the movie theater and have a film festival that will lure people from all over the world; and we can have a gambling casino that will make Las Vegas and Monte Carlo look like pikers. I am having a prospectus drawn up that will be sent to the various national and international gaming interests, inviting them to bid for the license to operate such a casino.

"Some of you are already aware of the steps that have been taken to streamline the Town government, and there will be more of this streamlining as time goes by. Our first move will be to consolidate those agencies and functions that used to be State-controlled into the Town's domain, and to this end State Troopers Mancusi and Sutkin have been assigned to the force of Chief Luther Maddox. Also, Judge Cyrus Pepper, who was appointed by the State, has been reappointed by me to carry on his duties in the local court, so there will be no break in the orderly business of dispensing justice. All police and judicial matters will be under Town control, and responsible to the Town government."

He looked around the room, as though daring anyone to challenge him, then said, "We will now proceed with unfinished business."

Padraic O'Toole put up his hand. "I have a question," he said.

"What?" said Markey.

"The lunchroom on the ferry is a goddam outrage," said O'Toole. "I had a tuna-salad sandwich last summer that looked like a dog's breakfast, and what's more the bread was stale."

"That's not a question, that's a statement," Markey told him.

"You're goddam right."

"You said you had a question."

"When am I going to get a decent tuna-salad sandwich?"

"I'll have someone look into it." Markey turned away from O'Toole and nodded to Dr. Amberson, who had raised his hand. Dr. Amberson stood up.

"This is not a question so much as a proposal," he said. "Since the Town government is being, as you put it—ah—streamlined, some offices will take on less importance than before, while others will take on immeasurably more. I think that is a safe assumption, is it not?"

"Go ahead," Markey said warily.

"Would you agree to what I have just said?" Dr. Amberson asked.

"I didn't challenge you. I said go ahead." Markey sensed a trap, and was figuratively walking on tiptoe.

"Since, then, we agree that the importance of various offices will change, I hereby propose that the Town hold a special election, with the duties of each office spelled out in detail, so that the voters can know exactly what it is they're electing people to."

"I second the motion," said Jeanette Amberson.

"I agree," Corning put in, as Markey rapped his gavel for silence.

"You don't change Town laws as easily as that," Markey said. "You can't just have an election any time you want, or there'd be no—"

"I'm sorry, but I disagree," Agnes Tuttle said. "Any time—"

"The Chair has the floor!" Markey said, glaring at Agnes. "You'll speak when you're recognized, if you don't mind."

"Hear, hear," said Webster, and Agnes subsided, glowering. She glanced at Corning, whose eyebrows barely flickered as he returned her look.

"As I was saying," Markey went on, "if you have an election every time you turn around you'll never get anything done. This whole new structure is being set up in the interest of efficiency, and to—"

"Make the trains run on time," Agnes muttered, but O'Toole was the only one who heard her.

"Who said anything about trains?" he asked loudly.

"Mussolini," Agnes replied, as Markey pounded the table with his gavel.

"There will be order in this room!" Markey said, his face beginning to turn red.

"I ordered a tuna-salad sandwich, and what did I get?" O'Toole said. "Slop."

Markey turned back to Dr. Amberson. "Any proposal must be submitted in writing," he said. "It must have the proper number of signatures, and it must be cleared by the Board of Selectmen before being acted upon. We cannot take up our time with every idea that happens to pop into someone's head." He tapped his gavel, and Dr. Amberson sat down.

"May I say a word?" Agnes asked.

"Go ahead," Markey replied. "But be brief."

"According to the Town bylaws, any time a sufficient number of voters want to call a special election it can be done. There is no limit to the number of elections that can be held."

"We just had a special election a few weeks ago," Markey replied. "How many do you want?"

"As many as the voters think necessary. Provided they get the signatures, there's nothing to stop them."

"It still has to be certified by the Selectmen. If they think they can get it through, good luck to them."

"Ha!" said Webster. "Fat chance of that!"

Corning was the next one to raise his hand. "I have a question," he said, and when Markey nodded he went on, "You said a few days ago that the oil company was not going to touch the island, but was going to pipe their oil to tankers offshore. Now it turns out that—"

"I said I hoped that would be the case," Markey interrupted. "I can't predict down to the last detail everything the oil company is going to do. So long as the money keeps coming in, I don't think we should be too fussy about how they make it. In the long run it's the money that counts, and don't let anyone tell you different."

"Hear, hear!" Webster said, more loudly than before.

Lester Turpin had his hand up, and it was a moment before Markey noticed him. When he finally was recognized, Turpin rose and said, "Mr. Chairman, this is a personal question, but I hope you won't take my asking it as anything but journalistic curiosity, with nothing personal intended."

"What is it?" Markey asked.

"In the event there is a special election," Turpin said, "will you run for your present office on the Board of Selectmen, or will there be some other title more in keeping with your—ah—expanded duties and responsibilities?"

It was hard for Agnes to keep from smiling as Markey pondered his reply. But when he spoke, all traces of smile vanished from her face.

"My case is a somewhat special one," Markey said slowly. "If I were to run for any new office I would have to resign from those I now hold, and that would leave a void in the Town's leadership. During the period of campaigning, through the election itself and the counting of the ballots, then the selection of a new Chairman—all that time the Town would be leaderless, in a state inviting anarchy. Therefore, *if* a special election were called for, and *if* the Selectmen approved such an election, I would have to remove myself from the race and simply continue in my present position."

"In other words," Turpin said, "you will continue as head of the Town government, no matter who else is elected to what?"

"That is correct," Markey said, and tapped his gavel to close the subject. "Now, if we're through with the questions, perhaps we can get on with the Selectmen's business. There has—"

"I have one more question," Edgar Morris said, rising.

"All right, but make it brief," Markey said.

"It'll be brief, all right. Last night I had a guest in my house, and when I came to turn on the lights there wasn't a light would work. The house, the street, and that whole part of town were without electricity, and—"

"Do you usually entertain your guests in the dark?" Markey asked, and laughed loudly.

"My point is," Morris went on, coloring, "if we're being made to pay double and triple what we used to for light, I think it's only fair we should *have* some light when we need it. Otherwise, what is all this extra money going for?"

"That's not a matter for the Selectmen," Markey replied. "You'll have to take that up with the electric company."

"That's what I am doing. I called them, and they said I'd have to talk to you. This is the first chance I've had."

"We can't take up the Selectmen's time with your social problems," Markey said. "Write me a letter." He tapped his gavel and went on, "We will now proceed with the business of the meeting. Any petitions, suggestions, or questions should be submitted in writing, and they will be considered at the appropriate time." He glanced once at Daisy, his maid, who had sat quietly listening, and he wondered briefly why she had come. It crossed his mind that Ella might have sent her but he couldn't imagine what for, so he put her out of his thoughts and settled down to the business of reorganizing the Town government.

A small group of the spectators gathered on the sidewalk after the meeting. They included Sam, the Turpins, the Ambersons, Emil Corning, and Edgar Morris, and they spoke in tones of muted outrage, as though afraid of being overheard.

"I think you ought to write an editorial," Dr. Amberson said to Turpin. "This son of a bitch is taking over the town without one person lifting a finger to stop him."

"I think it's too soon for an editorial," Turpin replied.

"We ought to find out what he's going to do before we attack him."

"If you ask me, it's too late," Grace Turpin said. "He's got all the power he needs, and he isn't going to give it up."

"I've been afraid of this all along," Corning said. "I told Agnes, but she said not to worry. She said we could get rid of him when the time came."

The door to the building opened and the Selectmen came out, and the members of the group stopped talking. As Markey came past them he said, "Well, what have we got here—a rump parliament?" He laughed and added, "Get enough horses' asses together, and you'll have a rump parliament!" His car drew up to the curb and he got in, and repeated the remark to Ella as he drove off into the night.

Agnes had dropped back as the other Selectmen went by, and she now joined the group. "It might be a good idea if you didn't stand around like this," she said. "He's already got you all tagged as enemies."

"So what can he do?" Morris asked. "He can't throw us in jail."

"Don't be so sure of that," Agnes replied.

"I happen to know he can't, because the police are shorthanded," Morris said. "Any time they should be making an arrest they're shorthanded."

"In your case they might make an exception," Agnes said. "At any rate, I think it would be smarter to meet at someone's house."

"What are our chances of getting rid of him now?" Corning asked. "You thought there'd be no trouble the last time we talked."

"I think all we can do is wait," Agnes said. "Sooner or later he's bound to do something stupid."

"Christ, I don't see how we *can* wait," Corning said. "He digs himself in stronger every day. He's technically head of the Town government, and what he says goes."

"Not if he's outvoted," Agnes replied.

"Fat chance of that," Corning said. "You know how he handles that problem."

"If you ask me, we ought to revolt," Morris put in. "Start a counterrevolution, and wipe the whole slate clean. It's times like this when a little anarchy is the only answer."

"There's no such thing as a little anarchy," Turpin said. "That's like being a little dead."

"Well, we've got to do something," Corning said. "But I agree with Agnes—we shouldn't stand around gabbing about it in the street."

"I'd suggest we meet at my house," Agnes said, "but in the circumstances I don't know if that would be very smart."

"Why not?" said Morris. "It's the least likely place, and therefore the safest."

"So how do I report this?" Sam asked.

"Report it like any other meeting," Turpin told him. "Give the facts as they happened, and let the reader draw his own conclusions."

"Only leave our names out of it," Dr. Amberson put in. "Just say he was responding to questions from the floor."

"My God, listen to us," Grace Turpin said. "We call our-selves free citizens, liberated from government oppression, and already we're talking like the conspirators in the Gun-powder Plot."

"Hear, hear," Morris said, then looked at his watch. "Oops, I'm late," he said. "I've got to be going."

"I didn't know anarchists carried watches," Corning said. "I thought you wanted to be free from all restrictions."

Morris smiled. "That all depends. Some restrictions are more agreeable than others."

"He must have a girl," Grace observed after Morris had left. "It's the first time he hasn't reeked of that god-awful cologne."

"How do you figure that?" her husband asked.

"We've been into that, remember? It's only the loners or the men whose wives are off-island that use that kind of stuff. The fact that he's quit must mean he's got a girl, and she's told him he can relax." As an afterthought, she added, "Or, more likely, she's begged him to."

"You and your intuition," Turpin said. "You ought to start an advice-to-the-lovelorn column."

"No, thanks," said Grace. "I have enough on my mind as it is."

"You and all the rest of us," Dr. Amberson remarked. "If you ask me, we've got some pretty heavy thinking to do."

"Thinking, hell," said Corning. "We've got to act. Either that, or we're all dead as mackerel."

Sam arrived at the Sink Hole about an hour before closing time. He found Lennie, who'd been waiting on a table of oil workers and was on the rim of hysteria, and he said, "How would you like to go somewhere after you're through?"

"I'm going nowhere except to bed," she replied. "If I don't I'm going to kill somebody."

"That sounds fine with me," said Sam. "I like a bed as well as the next man."

Lennie shook her head. "Anyway, Phil wants to talk to you," she said.

"I didn't come to talk to Phil, I came to talk to you. Whatever she has to say can wait."

"I don't think so. You'd better talk to her."

"If I do, then you'll get teed off and it'll take me all tomorrow to calm you down."

"Hey, miss!" a man shouted. "Knock off the chatter and bring those drinks! You think we got all night?"

"Will you do me a favor?" Lennie said. "Will you talk to Phil and see what's on her mind? Otherwise we're all going to go crazy! Now, good night!" She hurried away, and Sam looked around until he found Felicity. She was standing at the service bar, waiting for an order to be filled, and as he approached her he saw that she was pale and her eyes had a strange, staring look.

"Hi, there," he said, and she jumped. "I hear you want to talk to me."

"God, yes," she said. "Can you get out to the shack?"

"I suppose so. I'm busy in the morning, but I can get out there around noon. What's it all about?"

"I mean right now—tonight!"

"Why? What's the rush?"

"I can't tell you here. Have you got wheels?"

"Yes, I rented a bike. But why tonight?"

"I said I can't tell you here! Go out behind the shack, near where the trap was, and you'll see that I mean!"

"Just give me a hint, will you? I'm damned if I want to—"

"You'll find out! Now, *go!*" Felicity took her loaded tray from the bartender and made her way to a table, and Sam shrugged, bought a beer, and finished it quickly. Then he went out, checked the flashlight on his bicycle, and started the long ride out of town.

The road was dark, and few cars passed him, and Sam had the sensation of riding into the mouth of a black, yawning cave. The sky was overcast, blotting out the stars, and once he'd left the lights of town behind he had nothing but the faint glow of his flashlight to guide him. He came to the fork where the Cossett Point road branched off, and for a moment he was tempted to keep on to the right and go home. Whatever it was would surely wait until morning, he thought, but the urgency in Felicity's voice made him think again, and he took the left fork and headed for the beach. He could hear the slow rhythm of the surf and smell the salt in the air, which for some reason increased his sense of isolation. He seemed to be the only living thing in a dark world of wind and water.

The shack appeared as a black patch against the dim lines of breakers beyond, and when he reached it he dismounted and leaned his bike against the wall by the front door. Then, playing his flashlight in all directions, and wishing he'd been able to put in new batteries, he went back toward the spot in the dunes where the trap had been. At first he saw nothing unusual, but then there was an area where there seemed to have been recent digging, and he crouched down and examined the earth. Something protruded from the churned-up soil, and thinking it a piece of driftwood he reached down to pluck it out, but it wouldn't come loose, and it wasn't until he brought the fading beam of his light directly onto it that he saw it was a brown, shriveled hand. He let go quickly, and wiped his own hand on his trousers, then found a piece of wood and began cautiously to scrape away the earth. There were bits of rotted cloth, and bones with fragments of flesh clinging to them, and the top of a skull that had been split open like a melon. One gold molar gleamed among the otherwise white teeth in the gaping mouth, and a faint stubble of beard showed in the parchment-like skin that adhered to the maxillary bone. On a hunch, Sam scraped the earth away from the area of the feet; he uncovered one rotted shoe with the foot still in it, and the other shoe and foot were missing. The leg ended in a splintered break at the bottom of the tibia, and that was all. By now his flashlight gave out only a dim blur of orange, and he switched it off and stood up. His heart was pounding as he tried to decide what to do next. A glance at his watch showed him he didn't have time to get back to the Sink Hole before it closed, and the only man at the police station would be the night duty officer, who by now would be getting ready for his relief and would pay no attention to anything that might keep him late. The only thing to do, Sam reasoned, was to wait until tomorrow, and in the meantime try to decide just how and to whom to make his report. For reasons he found hard to explain, he did not want to tell Chief Luther Maddox.

He rode home in total darkness, nagged by the irrational but persistent feeling he was being followed.

21

The next morning, before going anywhere else, Sam went to the newspaper office and told Turpin of his find. Turpin pursed his lips and looked thoughtful.

"They sometimes find Indian remains," he said. "You sure that isn't what this is?"

"This is fresh," Sam replied. "A year old at the most—and besides, it can't be an Indian because he has a gold tooth."

"I'd report it to Ed Mancusi," Grace Turpin said. "If you report it to Luther Maddox it'll be the same as telling George Markey, and since it used to be his shack he might have had something to do with it."

"Oh, don't be silly," Turpin told her. "You're imagining things. Besides, the State Troopers are under local jurisdiction now."

"They're supposed to be," said Grace. "But I'll bet a fig they're still taking orders from the mainland. If you tell Ed Mancusi he'll give it a good checking out before he passes the word on to the Chief."

"All right," said Turpin. "But I still don't see it as a story."

"A man who got caught in a bear trap and then killed isn't a story?" Sam said. "I can tell you I'd want to read about it."

"There's probably some very simple explanation," Turpin said. "But go ahead if you want—tell Mancusi, and see what he says."

Sam found Mancusi in his home, wearing civilian clothes and listening to the police radio that was set up in the back room. Mancusi greeted him cheerfully, and said, "What can I do for you?"

"First, what's your jurisdiction?" Sam replied. "Are you State, or local, or what?"

"Well, put it this way: the locals have told me I'm under their jurisdiction, but the State is still paying me. Why?"

Sam filled him in on the story, and concluded, "I'd like to find out who this guy was, and who set the bear trap for him, and why. From what little I know of Maddox, I don't look for too much cooperation from him."

"Well, well, well," said Mancusi quietly. "Let's ride out there and have a look." He opened a cupboard and took out a camera and assorted boxes, jars, and tubes, all of which he packed in a black leather carrying case. Then he called his partner, Ralph Sutkin, and told him where he was going, and showed Sam out the back door to the garage. "I think we'd better take a civilan car," he said. "The cruiser attracts too much attention."

When they reached the shack Mancusi drove on past, and parked the car at the end of the road by the beach. Then they walked back, and Sam led him to the spot. For him it was like revisiting a dream, although the bones looked different in the daylight, and considerably more human. Looking at the hand at which he'd tugged, Sam found it hard to believe he had ever mistaken it for driftwood. He watched with interest as Mancusi photographed the scene and then squatted down and probed for clues in the dirt. Mancusi picked up little bits of rotted clothing and put them in an envelope; he removed the shoe and examined it but found nothing of any interest; he examined the break where the other foot had been; and he dug down into the general disintegration in search of a wallet or other identification. Finally he took an impression of the teeth, using wax which he softened by kneading between his hands, and then he stood up.

"Doc Wiesel can do a better dental impression than that," he said. "But I'll keep this one as a standby. For the rest, I guess it's a job for Hosmer Curtin."

"By the way," said Sam, "I saved the trap. Would that be of any interest to you?"

"I should say it would. Just hang on to it for the time being."

"So what do we do now?"

"Now I'm going to dust the shack for fingerprints. I don't expect to find much, but you never can tell."

"I can tell you right now what you'll find," Sam said. "You'll find some of mine, and you'll find some of that waitress, Felicity whatever, who works at the Sink Hole."

"I know her well," said Mancusi, with a smile. "And if I'm not mistaken, there'll be more than just her fingerprints around the place."

"Could be," said Sam. "I'm not an expert at these things."

"You do all right," said Mancusi.

As they drove back to town, Mancusi said, "I think your best move is to report this to the Chief. Just tell him what you found, and let him take it from there."

"Should I tell him I've told you?"

"Not unless he asks. I'm going to see if Doc Wiesel can make up a dental chart from this impression, and I'm going to check with the Missing Persons Bureau on the mainland. Nobody's been reported missing here, so this has to be an off-islander. If I can do all this without Maddox getting in my hair, so much the better. I'll let you know what I find out."

Mancusi let Sam out three blocks from the police station, and as he walked the last distance Sam thought back on that night in April when he'd come in with the foot, and Maddox had warned him not to rock the boat. I'm sure as hell rocking the boat right now, he thought; I may even be making it capsize. He wondered what the consequences would be, and for a moment he was tempted to forget the whole thing —Turpin certainly wouldn't mind dropping the story—and to string along with those who looked only on the bright side of things. It was a comforting way to live, but he knew he wouldn't be able to sleep at night if he didn't follow the story through. He told himself he was morally committed to it, but in total honesty he knew it was simple curiosity; the fact that it was morally correct was secondary. And the fact that it might be dangerous was all but irrelevant. To him, danger was something that gave a warning long in advance; he hadn't experienced the kind that can strike before it has really been recognized.

The Chief was in his usual seat at the front desk. He looked at Sam coldly, and said, "Now what?"

Sam adopted an air of total nonchalance. He picked at a piece of loose paint on a chair and said, "You remember the foot I brought in a while back."

Maddox said nothing, but his eyes began to glint like those of a wolf. "So?" he said at last.

"So I believe you told me it was a bear's foot."

"That's right."

"Then I think I've made quite a discovery: I've found the body of a man whose left foot was that of a bear. That's pretty unusual around here, isn't it?"

"In Christ's name what are you talking about?"

"I told you. I found a body with one foot missing."

"Where?"

"Behind a shack, out in the Cossett Point area."

Maddox, who had half risen, settled back. "That don't prove nothing. There's an old Indian burial ground out that way."

"Did the Indians have gold teeth?"

"Don't look at me. I'm no dentist."

"Well, I just thought you'd like to know." Sam turned and started to leave.

"Wait a minute," Maddox said. "Was this in a house, or on the beach, or what?"

"It had been buried, but then it looks as though a dog had started to dig it up. The wind and weather did the rest."

Maddox made a note. "If this is a joke, your ass is in one big sling," he said.

"It's not," said Sam. "Go see for yourself." At the door he stopped and looked back. "And unless you've thrown that foot away, I think you'll find it matches," he said.

"That was a bear's foot," Maddox said, and picked up the telephone.

"That's what I said," Sam replied. "I've made a real discovery."

Late that afternoon, Mancusi called the paper and asked for Sam. "I have news for you," he said when Sam came on the phone. "Missing Persons has a Roscoe Jessett, forty-seven, a shoe salesman from Sippewissitt, who went on a road trip a year ago October and never returned. It is not definitely known that he came here, but it also isn't known that he didn't. He'd come here a few times before and had done a certain amount of business, mostly in ladies' shoes. It looks like he's your man."

"What about the teeth?" Sam asked. "Did they match?"

"They can't be absolutely sure, but they think so. Doc Wiesel is going to make another impression, and that'll nail it down. There are no discrepancies, but they just want to double-check. Something about his insurance."

"Has Maddox gone to look at the body?"

"I have no idea. He doesn't tell me any more than I tell him, and that's just the way I like it."

Sam thanked Mancusi, then hung up and went into Turpin's office. He told Turpin all he'd found out, and concluded, "I don't see how we can *not* print it. It's not only legitimate news, but by running the story we may help find out who did it."

"I don't see how you figure that," Turpin said.

"There may be people who have something to contribute. If the story appears in print, it may encourage them to talk."

"If I've said this once, I've said it a thousand times," Turpin replied. "This is not an investigative newspaper."

"If you don't mind my saying so, it's not a newspaper at all," Grace put in, from her desk outside the door. "It's a broadside for advertisers, which also carries a cooking column and a lot of garbage about the waterfront."

"There's no need to be bitter," her husband replied. "If I'd wanted Woodward and Bernstein, I'd have hired Woodward and Bernstein."

"At our space rates, we couldn't hire white mice," Grace said, coming into the office. "I don't see what you have against running a little legitimate news on those few occasions when it comes up and hits us in the face. I'm surprised you even deigned to admit the island had seceded."

"What's making you so prickly?" Turpin asked. "Don't you like your work here?"

"I love it, but I don't see why we should hide from the news. I'm as fond of yellow warblers as the next person, and a good sunset will positively wipe me out, but I don't see why the paper should be all made up of that."

"It isn't! We run the court calendar every week, and the—"

"I know, and the Selectmen and the DAR and the Girl Scout notes. You don't need to tell me what we run; I'm just telling you what we *don't* run—we don't run news if it might offend someone, and that, to my way of thinking, is plain chicken. If we'd taken a good, strong stand against secession the island might not be in the trouble it's in now, which, believe me, is plenty."

"That's absurd and you know it. Nothing was going to stop these people from seceding."

"Probably not. But at least you might have given them something to think about, which would have been a step in the right direction."

Turpin took a deep breath, let it out slowly, then turned to Sam. "All right," he said. "Write what you've got, but for

God's sake don't make it libelous. Use 'alleged' and 'reported' wherever you can."

"Yes," Grace put in. " 'An alleged corpse, in what was reported to be an advanced state of decomposition, was allegedly found in an apparently shallow grave.' You get the
picture—say as little as you can, in as many words as possible."

"You know your trouble?" Turpin told her. "You've been
cooking too much. I think I'll take you out for dinner tonight and get you smashed."

"You're on," said Grace. "It may be our last chance before
the Gestapo arrives."

The telephone in the Markey house began ringing at eight-
thirty the next morning. The first caller was Miranda Corning, who opened the conversation by saying, "Ella, dear,
how perfectly ghastly! I'm *so* sorry."

"Sorry for what?" Ella replied. "What's ghastly?"

"Oh, you haven't read the paper?"

"No, ours comes with the mail. What's this all about?"

"Well . . . no matter, then. I'll talk to you later. 'Bye,
now."

The next caller was Jeanette Amberson, who said, "Really, what a terrible thing to have happen!"

"I don't know what you're talking about," Ella said. "Will
you please let me in on the secret?"

"It's no secret now, I guess." Jeanette suddenly became
evasive. "Although you know how newspapers like to blow
things up. There's probably some very simple explanation."

"About *what?*" Ella screamed. "Will nobody tell me *anything?*"

"From what I gather, it's a fairly complicated story,"
Jeanette said. "Oops—there goes the doorbell. I'll talk to you
later."

Markey had already had his breakfast and left the house,
and Ella was still in her dressing gown. She went into the

kitchen, where Daisy was cleaning up the breakfast dishes, and said, "Daisy, have you by any chance seen the paper today?"

"No, ma'am," Daisy replied. "I been working on my distributor since sunrise. Looks like someone put gum on the points."

"Would you mind running down to the paper store and getting me a copy? There seems to be something important in it, but nobody will tell me what it is."

Daisy dried her hands and took off her apron. "Something told me this was going to be a busy day," she said. "Here it's barely nine o'clock, and already the schedule's shot to hell."

When she came back with the neatly folded paper, Daisy handed it to Ella without comment. "Did you see anything world-shaking in it?" Ella asked.

"No, ma'am, I didn't look," Daisy replied. "I can keep my mind on just so many things at once."

Ella took the newspaper into the library, sat down at her desk, and unfolded the paper with care, almost as though opening a fragile Christmas present. Her eyes skimmed over page 1 but found nothing unusual, then she turned inside to page 2, and she was beginning to think the whole thing was a practical joke when, halfway down page 3, she saw the headline: "Body Found Near Cossett Point," and with a feeling of numbness spreading over her she read:

A gruesome discovery was made last Thursday when the body of a man, believed by authorities to be that of Roscoe Jessett, 47, of Sippewissitt, was found in a shallow grave behind a shack in the Cossett Point area. One foot was missing, and authorities speculated that it had been severed when the deceased allegedly stepped on a bear trap, which had previously been discovered nearby. The severed foot had been found two months ago and turned in to Police Chief Luther Maddox, with inconclusive results. According to the State Missing Persons Bureau, Mr. Jessett, a shoe salesman for the Slip-on-E-Z Company, allegedly left home a year ago October on a selling trip, and failed to return. The shack behind which the discovery was made is the property of the estate of the late Dennis Fenwick, having been allegedly acquired in a land transfer from George Markey, the previous owner.

Ella read the item again, and then went into the downstairs bathroom and was sick. When the nausea passed she rinsed her face, rearranged her hair, and went into the kitchen. Not trusting herself to hold a cup, she said, "Daisy, would you bring me some coffee in the library?"

"Yes, ma'am," said Daisy. "Did you find what you were looking for?"

"Yes," Ella said, and returned to her desk.

The phone rang, and she answered it mechanically. It turned out to be Dolores Webster, and Ella said, "Dear, can I call you back later? I'm all tied up right now," and hung up. Daisy brought her coffee, and she sat staring out the window, while the coffee got cold and she relived the afternoon she had hoped she'd never think of again. She heard Jessett's cry as the trap smashed his foot, and she recalled her panicky flight home and her pleading with Markey for help, and she found she could remember every word that had been spoken. Though she'd wanted to forget it, the words had sunk into the back of her mind and were now emerging as a unit, like a petrified plant from a peat bog. The front door opened, and Markey came in.

"I suppose you saw the goddam paper," he said.

"I saw it," she replied.

"I'm going to sue those bastards blind, and I'm going to get that smart-assed reporter, whatever his name is. You mark my words, I'm going to have him strung up by the—"

"You mark my words," Ella cut in. "You are a liar and a murderer, and I don't know which I loathe you for the most. You—"

"Now, wait a minute," he said. "Your skirts aren't so—"

"*You* wait a minute!" Ella shouted, standing up. "You told me you'd taken care of him—you told me you'd taken him to a doctor, and then had him sent off-island. Your exact words were 'You don't have to worry, he'll be taken care of.' You said you'd arranged for an ambulance plane, and that you'd let bygones be bygones provided he never came back to the island. Is that right, or isn't it?"

"Something like that, I guess. But what do you expect me to do—you expect me to kiss this son of a bitch who's been taking you out to my shack—to *my* shack, mind you—and—"

"He didn't take me out—I took him out! He wanted me to go off-island with him, but I wouldn't! I knew people would talk, so I—"

"If you knew people would talk, then why'd you take your own car? Any goddam fool knows you can't do anything around here in your own car without the whole island knowing about it. If you'd *wanted* people to know what you were doing, you couldn't have picked a better way."

"Maybe I did," said Ella. "Maybe I wanted them to know, but didn't have the guts to be brazen about it."

"Well, then, don't come whining to me because your lover boy got his head split open. He got what he was asking for, and no less."

"Suppose I'd stepped on the trap—what would you have done then?"

"You'd have got the same thing. Times like that, a man can't be choosy."

"Well," said Ella, "I guess it's nice to know where one stands."

"And about time, too."

"Are you home for lunch?"

"No. I'm going down to the police station."

"To give yourself up?" Ella's voice assumed a false note of hope, and he glared at her.

"No," he said. "To swear out a warrant against that reporter."

He left, and Ella went into the kitchen. Daisy was making

herself elaborately busy, and after watching her for a moment Ella said, "I imagine you heard what was said."

"I wasn't listening," Daisy replied, scrubbing the sink. After a moment she added, "But the mister's voice does carry, don't it?"

"It does indeed," said Ella. "From here to eternity."

When he got to the police station, Markey found only the desk sergeant on duty. "Where's the Chief?" he asked.

"Out back, sitting in the cruiser," the sergeant replied. "He said he wanted to be alone."

Markey went around to the rear, and found Maddox sitting glumly behind the wheel of the cruiser. "Do you mind if I join you?" he asked.

"Hop right in," Maddox replied, opening the right-hand door. "The more the merrier."

"Are you out here for any particular reason?" Markey asked, getting into the car.

"Privacy," the Chief replied. "I'm trying to figure out how I can run down that Jensen bastard, and I need to be alone."

"You mean the reporter? The one they call Sam?"

"That's the one. He's too goddam nosy for his own good. I told him a long time ago to mind his own business, but he wouldn't listen. He's just about made himself a candidate for a traffic accident."

"Better than that, you can arrest him," Markey said. "Then shoot him when he tries to escape."

"That would be fine, but I got no grounds to arrest him."

"Yes, you do. I'm going to swear out a warrant."

Maddox's eyes widened. "For what?"

"Trespass. I warned him to keep away and he didn't, so I'm going to have him arrested."

"Hot damn," said Maddox. "You been to the judge?"

"I'm going there now. I just thought I'd tell you, so you can have a cell ready."

"How are you going to hold a guy on a trespassing charge? The paper will probably go bail for him."

"This'll be more than just a trespassing charge. This might even be accessory to a murder."

The Chief grinned. "Now you're talking! You get me the warrant, and I'll have him in here so fast he won't know what hit him."

"By the way, the story in the paper said that foot had been brought to you. Who brought it?"

"Jensen did, but that was a lotta crap. That was a bear's foot he was trying to plant on me. Probably just a red herring."

"Fine. Obstruction of justice—that's another charge."

"Keep going," the Chief said. "We'll have this bastard trussed up like a Christmas turkey."

It was Saturday, and Judge Pepper was not in his chambers. Markey went to the judge's home and rang the bell, and the door was opened by Matilda Pepper.

"Is the judge in?" Markey asked.

"He's resting right now," Matilda said. "Can you come back later?"

"I'm afraid not. This is important."

"Well . . . just a minute. Come in." Matilda disappeared upstairs and Markey went into the living room, and after about five minutes the judge came down, looking as though he'd just awakened.

"Sorry to keep you waiting," he said. "I've been a little off my feed."

"Think nothing of it," Markey said jovially. "I don't mind a little wait now and then; it gives me time to think."

"What can I do for you?" Judge Pepper asked, easing himself into a chair.

"I'm here to swear out a warrant for the arrest of one Samuel Jensen," Markey said. "He is, if you want my opinion, a danger to the community, and should be locked up."

"What are the charges? Do you have the written information?"

"I don't need to write it down; I have it all in my head. The charges are, first, trespassing, in that having been warned to stay clear of a certain property he proceeded to trespass upon it, and to dig without permission on the premises. Second, obstruction of justice, in that he gave false evidence to the Chief of Police, in an attempt to distract him from the true clues to a crime. Third, again obstruction of justice, in that he found an instrument used in the commission of a crime, and did remove it from the premises and hide it, thereby preventing the police from the performance of their lawful duty. Fourth—"

"What was this instrument?" the judge asked.

"A bear trap. Fourth, since the crime in question was that of murder, the defendant in his obstruction of justice was in fact acting as an accomplice to the person or persons who committed the crime, and is therefore guilty of conspiracy."

"Who did commit the crime?" said Judge Pepper.

"Person or persons unknown. For all we know, it was the defendant Jensen."

Judge Pepper thought for a moment, then said, "You talk a good legal line, but I'm afraid there isn't much substance to your charges. Aside from the trespassing the rest is supposition, and—"

"Supposition, my ass!" Markey exploded. "He did it! He did everything I said!"

"But your reading of the facts is supposition. There isn't—"

"That's for a jury to decide. I'm giving you a list of reasons this man should be locked up until his case can come before a jury, and I'm not going to sit here and listen to a lot of argle-bargle about suppositions. He did it, and that's all there is to it! Now, let's have no more nonsense, should we? You just make out a warrant, and let the jury decide on the man's guilt. After all, that's the American way, and we don't want to change that, do we?"

Judge Pepper sighed, and rose from his chair. "All right," he said, "but the prosecutor had better have some pretty strong evidence."

"Don't worry," said Markey. "He will."

Sam was on his way to the Sink Hole that evening when the police cruiser cut in front of his bicycle and stopped, making him turn sharply into the gutter to avoid hitting it. The doors opened and two officers jumped out and ran toward him, one of them with a drawn gun.

"Hey!" said Sam. "What's all this about?"

"Get off your bike," said the cop with the gun.

"What for? What have I done?"

"You'll find out. Get off your bike!"

"Not until you tell me what—" Sam began, but the other cop wrestled him off his bicycle and punched him in the back of the head with a blow that jarred his vision, and the next thing he knew he was pinned over the hood of the cruiser, being frisked. "God damn it!" he shouted. "You can't do—" Another blow made his teeth snap together and his mouth taste of old pennies, and he was quiet. He was aware that a few people had stopped to watch, but in the darkness he couldn't tell who they were, and they stood by like a silent Greek chorus while he was handcuffed and bundled into the cruiser, and the door slammed behind him. The cops got in the front seat and the cruiser started off, and Sam noticed with interest that there were no inside handles on the rear doors. These people take no chances, he thought. When they arrest someone, they want him to stay arrested.

When they got to the police station, Maddox was sitting behind the desk. His eyes glinted as Sam was brought in, and he rose and came forward as though to greet him.

"Here he is, Chief," the cop with the gun said. "All trussed up like you ordered."

"Is it all right to ask what this is all about?" Sam asked.

"You'll find out," the Chief replied, glancing at a slip of paper.

"What am I being arrested for?"

"You can add resisting arrest to the charges," the cop with the gun put in. "We had to fight him to get him over the hood."

"That's a goddam lie!" Sam shouted. "You started slugging me before I could—"

"Shut up," the Chief commanded. "You'll get your chance to talk."

"I still don't know what I'm here for. I think you owe me that."

"I don't owe you nothing." The Chief put the paper down and said, "All right, lock him up."

"I demand a lawyer!" Sam said, his voice rising, as the cop with the gun prodded him forward.

"You'll get one," the Chief replied. "All in good time."

"Aren't I allowed a phone call? You can't just lock me up like this!"

"You think we can't?" The Chief grinned. "Just watch."

"What about a phone call?" Sam asked as the cop hustled him toward the cell. "Aren't I allowed to make one phone call?"

"To who?" the Chief asked.

"To Lester Turpin. I want him to—"

"He ain't no lawyer. He's a goddam newspaperman."

"I don't care. If I get one call, I want it to be—"

"You know your trouble?" the Chief said. "You still think you're on the mainland. You're going by mainland rules, and you forget we seceded. Out here, we do things our own way."

22

Next morning, the officer on duty came to Sam's cell and unlocked it. "You got a visitor," he said, turning away. "Follow me." As he trailed the officer into the adjoining room, Sam reflected that it would have been the simplest thing in the world for him to have bolted out the door and been a half block away before the officer missed him. But that would have been about as far as he'd have got, because he could have been picked up in a matter of minutes by the radio cruiser. Still, he made it a point to remember that security in the jail was, to say the least, loose.

He'd had the faint hope that Lennie might have come to see him, and he was therefore doubly disappointed when he entered the room and saw Padraic O'Toole. O'Toole was washed and shaved, but his shirt was rumpled and his eyes red and watery, and he exuded the fumes of last night's Bourbon. He held out his hand, and Sam shook it without enthusiasm.

"What brings you here?" Sam asked.

"I'm your attorney," O'Toole replied. "Appointed by the court. You're in big trouble."

"I am now," said Sam. "What are the charges?"

"Well, you're not accused of rape or sodomy, and you're not accused of any parking violation, but you're accused of about every offense between those two extremes. My advice to you is to plead guilty, and throw yourself on the mercy of the court. As you may know, this is one of the most merciful courts this side of the Bide-a-Wee Home, and you'll do better to admit your guilt than you will to fight."

"Who preferred these charges?" Sam asked. "What did I do, and when?"

"That's immaterial. The warrant has been sworn out, and it can only go poorly for you if you protract the business of the court. You'll be found guilty anyway, so make the best of it."

"I repeat, who is my accuser? I won't plead to anything until I know who's accusing me of what."

"Your accuser is First Selectman George Markey. He swore out the warrant and accused you of, among other things, criminal trespass and the obstruction of justice, not to mention being an accomplice to a murder. That's just for openers; there are several little frills along the way."

"I'm not guilty of that, and he knows it."

"Not even of trespass? Didn't he tell you to stay away from his property, and didn't you then go back and dig up a stiff in the back yard?"

"It's not his property any more. He can't accuse me of trespass if he doesn't own it."

"A trifling technicality. He's already contesting Fenwick's seizure. Take my advice, my boy, and plead guilty."

"I'll be goddamned if I will. Will you tell Lester Turpin where I am?"

"Why?"

"I'd like him to know. I have the feeling I'm at the bottom of a well, and will be forgotten if someone isn't notified."

"You need have no fear of that. You may wish you *were* forgotten."

"Will you do as I ask? Will you tell Turpin?"

"I'll do what I can, but don't expect too much." O'Toole went to the door and called the officer. "You can take this man back to his cell," he said.

"What about bail?" Sam asked. "Can't I get out until the trial?"

"You're in without bail," O'Toole replied. "You're considered a dangerous person."

The officer beckoned him to follow, and again Sam saw

how easy it would be to escape, but he decided not to try it
until nighttime, when he might have a better chance of getting away. How he'd ever get off the island was another
matter, but that was something to be worried about later.

Late that afternoon Lester Turpin came by, ostensibly to
give him some corn muffins Grace had made, and when the
officer left them alone Turpin said, in a low voice, "I had a
caller today. You know Daisy, the Markeys' maid?"

"No," said Sam. "Why?"

"She overheard a very interesting conversation between
Markey and his wife. I told her to tell Maddox about it, but
she seemed afraid to. Has she been in?"

"I wouldn't know her if I saw her, but I don't think anyone's been in. After all, it's Sunday. Did O'Toole tell you I
was here?"

"No. Whatsername—that girl you took to the clambake—"

"Lennie."

"That's right. Someone saw you being arrested and told
her, and she called me. I told the group at Agnes's, and—"

"What group at Agnes's?"

Turpin glanced at the door, and lowered his voice to a
whisper. "I can't tell you now. Some of us had got together,
to discuss the future." Then, raising his voice to normal, he
said, "Grace says she buttered the muffins while they were
hot, so that butter's all melted, but if you want more here's
an extra stick." He produced a foil-wrapped quarter pound
of butter, and called to the officer, "Melgrim, you want to
check this butter to make sure there's no file in it?"

"I'll take your word for it," the officer replied, leafing
through a magazine.

"All right, then," Turpin said to Sam. "Enjoy the muffins,
and if you want some marmalade or anything like that, I'm
sure Officer Bostwick would be happy to fetch it for you."

"In a pig's ass," the officer said, without looking up from
his magazine, and Turpin laughed and went out. Sam hesitated, and when the officer didn't look at him he turned and

went back to his cell by himself. It's almost as though they wanted me to escape, he thought as he pulled the cell door closed and heard the click of the lock. Or at least as though they wanted me to try.

He was immensely cheered when, at eight o'clock that evening, the night desk officer turned out to be Ed Mancusi. Mancusi was wearing his State Trooper's uniform, but his own badge had been replaced by one of the town's Special Police badges, the kind issued to temporary duty officers at dances, fraternal conventions, and large funerals. Mancusi took the keys the other officer gave him, read the logbook and signed himself in, then said good night to the departing officer and settled behind the desk. He was quiet for what seemed like a long time, and then he came back to Sam's cell.

"They really hooked you, didn't they?" he said.

"It looks that way," said Sam.

"There's a note in the Order Book saying you're to be considered extremely dangerous, and are not to be allowed to escape."

"That's funny, because I get the impression they're giving me every chance."

"That's right. Then they can shoot you."

"Oh." Sam thought a moment, then said, "Where's Maddox, by the way? I haven't seen him all day."

"He spends most Sundays getting laid; he's very devout that way. But today I get the picture he's off doing what he can to scrape up more evidence against you."

"Like what, for God's sake?"

"Like that bear trap. He took that from your place, and is going to say you hid it to cover up the evidence. He's trying to connect you with the murder."

"He can't! I wasn't even here! I was the other side of the world!"

"You'll have to prove that." Mancusi studied the bars on

Sam's cell, and after a few moments he said, "The more I think about it, the more I think you'd better get out of here."

"Sure—and be shot as I go down the street. Good idea."

"That's no problem. Right now, at any rate. But something tells me they're going to do a number on you, and they're going to do it quick and thorough. You'd best get the hell away while you still can."

"Is it all right to ask how?"

"I'll let you know in a little while. You once borrowed Art Gibbon's Jeep, didn't you?"

"Uh—yes. The night of the clambake. Why?"

"Just checking my memory. Let me make a couple of calls."

Sam could hear Mancusi talking on the telephone but couldn't hear what he said, and after a while Mancusi came back. "It is now," he said, glancing at the clock over the desk, "exactly 8:14. In forty minutes, at 8:54, you will go out back, as though to the toilet, and Gibbon will be there with his Jeep. You will get in, and get your ass out of here as fast as you can."

"Where to?"

"That'll be for you and Gibbon to decide. I don't want to know."

"Won't Maddox have your neck?"

Mancusi smiled. "It won't be mine. Did that clown Bostwick let you out of your cell during his watch?"

"Yes, when Lester Turpin came—and remind me to tell you about that."

"Later. Did he lock you back in your cell, or let you do it yourself?"

"He let me do it."

"Good." Still smiling, Mancusi unlocked the cell, tore off the back of a cardboard match folder, and wadded it into the hole where the lock tongue went. "You jammed the lock like this, and when I relieved Bostwick everything looked hunky-dory. Then, later on in my watch, I thought I heard someone fiddling with the cruiser out front, and when I went out to look you slipped out the back way and disappeared. By the time I came back, all I could do was sound the alarm. I'll give you, say, a half hour's head start before I do that. How does that sound?"

"Everything considered, it sounds just fine."

"And I'll tell Ralph Sutkin if he sees Gibbon's Jeep anywhere, to mistake it for a cow. We'll all probably be rung in on the search."

"You're sure Maddox isn't going to hang this on you?"

"Look, pal, whatever he may decide to do to me is nothing compared to what he's sure to do to you if you stay here. In his book, you've got top priority."

"All right. I just don't want anyone else to get in trouble."

"Everyone's in trouble, so it's just a matter of degree."

At 8:50, Sam heard Mancusi stand up from the desk and go out front, and a minute or so later he heard the sounds of a Jeep backing into the lot behind the station. He opened the cell door and raced down the hall and outside, and in the darkness he was just able to make out the shape of Gibbon's car. He jumped in and slammed the door; Gibbon started off without lights, and didn't turn them on until they reached the street. Then, driving slowly so as not to attract attention, he zigzagged through the back lanes and streets that led to the fields behind the town.

"Where are we going?" Sam asked as they passed a dark cemetery. He'd thought for a moment Gibbon was going to hide him among the graves.

"That's a good question," Gibbon replied. "I don't know."

"Won't it be better if you just leave me off somewhere, and let me make out on my own? There's no point getting you any more involved than you already are."

"Christ, I couldn't do that. They'd nail you the minute the sun comes up."

"But you're sticking your neck out for no reason! It doesn't make sense!"

"To me it does, so let's hear no more about it. My only problem is I got to think like a cop thinks, and that ain't easy. If I was a cop, where would I look for you?"

"You'd go to my place, then the newspaper, then I guess the Sink Hole, and then, maybe as a long shot, the Waterfront Club. Beyond that"—he shrugged—"I'm still a stranger here."

"Like hell you are. I guess the best thing's to take you to my place. We can think better if we have a beer."

Sam had a sudden flash of déjà vu, and couldn't identify the reason until he remembered his father's telling him about having to go underground during the Resistance, and spending his days one jump ahead of the Gestapo. It was a thin comparison but a valid one, and he felt about Gibbon the way his father must have felt about *his* associates. He told himself he would die for Gibbon if it became necessary, but one corner of his mind admitted he was glad the emotion didn't have to be put to the test. The bond was nevertheless startling in its intensity, all the more so for the suddenness with which it had appeared.

Remembering his father's stories, Sam said, "There's one rule about being a fugitive, and that is you can never sleep twice in the same place. You've always got to keep moving."

Gibbon glanced at him out of the corner of his eye. "You been a fugitive often?" he asked.

"No, but I've been told by those who know," said Sam.

Gibbon considered this, then said, "I think our best move'll be to get you off-island. They'll be watching the airport and the ferries, but I think Emil Corning can figure out a way. He's got a lot of boats they'll never suspect, and maybe tomorrow night you can get away. You know how to read a compass?"

"Yes," said Sam, "but is Corning likely to want to throw away a boat, just like that?"

"We'll see. We'll never know till we ask."

When they got to Gibbon's house they went inside without turning on the lights, and Gibbon guided Sam to a chair where he could sit without being seen through the front window. Then he snapped on a light, went to the refrigerator, and came back with two beers. "Emergency rations," he said, handing one to Sam. "For use by fugitives only." He sat down at the telephone and dialed a number, and after a few rings he hung up. "Emil must be out," he said. "I'll try him again in a bit."

They had been at Gibbon's for about a half hour when they heard the police siren outside. They both stiffened, holding their breaths while they waited to see if it would slow down, but it continued at its hysterical pitch, and after a moment they saw the flashing blue lights go past the window. Gibbon let out his breath.

"They sure like to advertise their coming," he said, and reached for the telephone. This time Corning answered, and Gibbon spoke in a low voice for a few minutes, then hung up and looked at Sam. "He's got a boat," he said. "He'll have it ready and gassed up in an hour, and we'll get you on your way before midnight."

"What's there in it for him?" Sam asked. "For all he knows, he'll never get his boat back."

"Christ, you don't know much, do you?" Gibbon replied. "You think everyone around here does nothing except for money?"

"Well . . . more or less. Except you."

"You got a lot to learn. You figure you can run the boat if you have one more beer?"

"Sure. Why not?"

"I just wondered. It's a long way across." Gibbon rose and headed for the kitchen, just as there came a hammering on the front door. "Get under the bed!" he said, and as Sam hurtled into the adjoining room the knocking was repeated. "Wait just a goddam minute, can't you?" Gibbon shouted, and then Sam crawled under the bed and tried not to breathe as he heard the front door being opened. He heard voices but couldn't catch the words, and as his eyes became accustomed to the darkness beneath the bed he saw he was surrounded by empty beer cans, old shoes, a pair of paint-spattered dungarees, and other indistinguishable bits of clothing. It looks as though it's almost time for spring cleaning, he thought, then realized that it might make good camouflage for him in case someone looked under the bed. He was trying to arrange himself under the dungarees when the front door slammed, and he heard Gibbon's footsteps approaching.

"You can come out now," came Gibbon's voice from the doorway.

Sam crawled out from under the bed, stood up, and began to brush himself off. "What did you tell them?" he asked.

"I said I'd seen a car go past here hell-bent a little while back," Gibbon replied. "I didn't tell 'em it was the police cruiser. Then I asked 'em if they'd like to step in and have a beer, and they said normally they would but tonight was something special."

"What's special about it?"

"The Chief is some pissed off about you getting away. They say he wants you back dead or alive and he's not so fussy about the alive part."

"He sounds like a bad loser."

"You could put it that way. He ain't used to losing."

"You think they'll wait around?"

"No. They like to set up a hue and cry, just to prove they're busy."

A half hour later, Gibbon and Sam left the darkened house and got into the Jeep. There were no signs of the police, and Gibbon theorized they were checking various places where Sam was known. "They won't go to the docks till the first ferry tomorrow," he said. "We got lots of time."

It was a winding road, with no streetlights or houses, and

it wasn't until they rounded a sharp S-turn that they saw the police cruiser, parked diagonally across the road and leaving room for only one car at a time to get by. Its blue lights blinked like sparks, and in the glare of its headlights two officers watched the road.

"*Jesus!*" Gibbon said as he stamped on the brakes. He tugged at the shift levers and put the Jeep in four-wheel drive, then turned off the road and sent the car crashing and bumping and grinding through the underbrush. Behind him the officers shouted; a shot rang out, and Gibbon switched off his lights and headed across country into the moors. There came the glare of lights as the cruiser swung around and tried to follow, then the lights went dim and all that could be heard was the frantic blowing of police whistles.

For several minutes the Jeep careered along until finally a rutted road appeared, and Gibbon followed this as best he could in the dim light of the stars. Then, far ahead, he could see headlights approaching, and he stopped, backed, and headed once more into the underbrush. He hit a large clump of scrub oak, the Jeep slowed and stopped, and the wheels began to spin. He tried to back, but the wheels spun and the tires shrieked and the smell of burning rubber filled the air, and Gibbon finally turned off the engine and said, "You better run for it."

"What'll you do?" Sam asked as he opened his door.

Gibbon gave a cackling laugh. "I'll ask 'em for a lift," he said. "They got nothing on me."

Running and stumbling, Sam clawed his way through the thickets, not caring where he went so long as he put as much distance between himself and the Jeep as possible. His first thought was to get on a hill, or a rise in the ground, so as to see where to go next, but in the dim recesses of his mind he recalled the rule against silhouetting yourself atop a ridge, so he stayed in the hollows and used, when he could see it, the North Star as his guide. This had the one advantage of preventing him from going in a circle, but beyond that it was of little use. He remembered the clump of scrub oak where he and Lennie had spent the night, and he thought that if he could find that he'd be safe at least for a while, but that was halfway across the island, and a compass and sextant wouldn't have helped him find it from where he was.

Once or twice he heard shouts in the distance, and thought he saw faint pinpoints of light, then darkness and silence settled in, and he reasoned that nobody would be fool enough to try to find him on the moors at night. What they would do, which made a great deal more sense, would be to wait until daylight, and then set up a skirmish line like beaters at a hunt, and methodically comb the area until they found him. And if that were the case, he was simply wasting his strength by running away from them now. Running from nonexistent pursuit was one of the classic signs of panic, and panic would undo him faster than anything else.

With that decided, he got down on his hands and knees, burrowed under a bush, and went to sleep.

There had been a meeting at the Tuttle home earlier that evening, attended by the Ambersons, Emil Corning, Lester and Grace Turpin, and, appearing for the first time together, Edgar Morris and Muriel Baxter. In order to make it look like a social evening, Agnes had set up two bridge tables and laid out cards, a backgammon set, and a cribbage board, but no surface trappings could disguise the fact that the purpose of the meeting was deadly serious. Agnes had at first drawn the living-room curtains, but then, realizing this would create attention and possibly suspicion, she had opened them again, but she kept glancing at the windows as though expecting to see some eavesdropper lurking outside.

When she had made drinks for the guests she said, "Let's sit at the tables, and at least look as though we're playing. The less this seems like a meeting, the happier I'll be."

"Where's Omar?" Corning asked, taking a seat next to Jeanette Amberson.

"Out in his radio shop," Agnes replied. "He said he'd keep an ear out for any police messages."

"Good," said Corning. His feud with Dr. Amberson, which had started at town meeting and had almost brought them to blows, had been forgotten in their common purpose, and he found that Jeanette Amberson was a person he had unaccountably overlooked in the past. "The last thing we want in here is the police," he said.

"I feel exactly like Anne Frank," Grace Turpin put in, "and I can't tell you how I hate it. I expect every minute to hear the pounding of the Storm Troopers on the door."

"I think," said Corning slowly, "the first thing we have to do is admit we made a mistake. Or most of us did." He looked at Grace and her husband and said, "The Turpins, as I remember, were in the minority."

"It's obvious secession was a mistake," Agnes said. "We agreed on that last night. The question is, what are we going to do about it now?"

Corning looked around the room. "Anyone have any new ideas?"

"Revolt," said Morris quietly. "Take to the streets. Enough of us have guns so we won't have to worry about the police."

"Edgar, don't talk like that," Muriel Baxter said. "Next thing, you'll be wanting a guillotine."

"Not a bad idea," said Morris, and her lips tightened.

"I'd prefer it if we tried a less—uh—strenuous approach," Dr. Amberson said. "I think maybe our first move should be to find out how many people agree with us. See how many people agree with us, before we move."

"Good idea," said Lester Turpin. "I could run a questionnaire in the paper. Call it 'Thoughts upon Having Seceded,' or something like that. Word the questions so people could say what they thought without coming right out in the open."

"They wouldn't have to use their names," Grace said.

"Let them say what they think, and say it anonymously. You'll get a lot more honest reactions that way."

"Maybe yes, maybe no," Turpin replied. "Remember the questionnaire we ran about sex education."

"In retrospect, that whole idea was a ghastly mistake," Grace said.

"This is all very well, but a questionnaire takes time," Corning said. "They've already put that young Sam Whatsis in jail, and we don't know who may be next. I think we've got to move while we still can."

"When you say we ought to move, how do you propose to do it?" Turpin asked.

"I still like the questionnaire idea," said Dr. Amberson. "If we move without enough support, we're all dead."

"The only answer is to take to the streets," said Morris. "Once we start things rolling they'll snowball until nothing can stop us."

"Are you *trying* to get yourself killed?" Muriel Baxter asked. "Because if you are, you've certainly picked the right way."

"Nothing was ever accomplished without a little bloodshed," Morris replied. "What I really like is the guillotine, and so far nobody's come up with a better idea."

"I think we're working at cross-purposes here," Agnes said. "I think we ought to do this legally from start to finish, or we won't have a leg to stand on."

"Oh, please," said Morris, half to himself. "Spare me any more legalistics."

"It's legalities," said Muriel Baxter.

"Well, whatever it is, spare me."

"I could get a majority among the Selectmen," Agnes said, as though Morris hadn't spoken. "I know Denton Norquist will vote with me, and if I can get Paddy O'Toole to stay sober long enough—"

"That's the biggest 'if' there is," Corning cut in. "That's

like saying if frogs had wings they wouldn't be bumping their butts on the ground all day."

"So what do you suggest?" said Agnes.

"I suggest," said Corning, "that we don't actually take to the streets, but that we isolate those people who might give us trouble. George Markey, Norris Webster, Luther Maddox —they're the hard core, and they're—" He stopped, as the back door opened and Omar Tuttle came into the room. Tuttle was wide-eyed with excitement, and his voice cracked as he spoke.

"Sam Jensen escaped!" he said. "They're out to kill him— the cops have orders to shoot him on sight!"

There was a silence, then Corning said, "So now it starts."

"Where did he go?" said Agnes. "Does anyone know?"

"I presume he's headed for the moors," Dr. Amberson replied. "I know that's what I'd do in his place."

"We've got to help him," Agnes cried. "We can't let them just shoot him!"

"Shoot them first," said Morris. "That's the only thing'll stop 'em."

"By God, *I'll* shoot them!" Lester Turpin said, standing up. "Does anyone here have a gun?"

"Lester Turpin, you sit down this instant!" Grace said. "Are you out of your mind?"

Turpin paused, then slowly sat. "I guess so," he said. "It must have been an instinctive reaction."

"It's a fine time to go instinctive," Grace told him. "All these years you've been the man of reason, the champion of the consensus, and now suddenly you fly off the handle and almost let your instincts get you killed. What kind of a kook did I marry, anyway?"

"It's too late to worry about that," Turpin replied quietly.

"Indeed it is, but I don't intend to have you shot out from under me in the prime of your life. Next time think a little before you get on your white charger."

"Sorry," said Turpin. "I got carried away."

"This isn't doing anything to help Sam," Agnes said. "We can sit here and talk all night, and it won't do him a lick of good."

"I agree," said Dr. Amberson. "Supposing he has gone to the moors, I don't imagine he can stay there too long without being caught. I think what he may try to do is creep back into town, either tonight or tomorrow night, and hide out in somebody's house. Since he knows we're on his side I imagine it will be one of ours—probably the Turpins' first. I suggest we all go to our homes and stay there, and keep in touch in case we should hear anything. How does that sound?"

"I guess it's the best we can do," Corning said. "It leaves a lot of questions unsolved, but until someone comes up with an answer to at least one of them, I can't think of anything else. But for Christ's sake let's someone think of something fast."

"I'm sure someone will," Agnes said as they all prepared to leave. "This has been like every meeting I've ever been to: everyone talks around in circles and then adjourns, hoping someone will come up with an idea the next day."

"Let's just hope the next day isn't too late," said Corning, and with that they filed out quietly into the night.

Somewhere across the town a dog barked, but otherwise the only sound was of their slowly receding footsteps as they went their separate ways.

23

Normally, the Monday-morning ferry in early June brought only a handful of passengers from the mainland, plus the building, hardware, and food supplies that kept the island going. The passengers were either those with their own cars or those with an allergy to flying, and they clustered at the lunch counter and drank scalding black water from plastic cups, into which they morosely dunked small, stale cheese crackers with peanut-butter filling. When the weather was bad, a trip on the ferry ranked as pleasure along with duty on a Roman trireme.

On Monday, June 7, however, the steamship people were astounded by the number of tourists who came swarming down to the dock to take passage to the island. They came in chartered buses and they came prepared for a good time; they carried guitar cases and cooler chests and golf bags; some had airline flight bags filled with bottles, while others had knapsacks bulging with what looked like cans of beer; and their costumes wore the unmistakable stamp of people who didn't care how barbaric they looked so long as they were comfortable. The men wore shorts and floral sports shirts open to the navel, the more hirsute among them doing away with the shirt entirely, and the women wore everything from crotch-splitting shorts to dirndl skirts to sequined brassieres to platform-soled shoes to bare feet. Most men wore either porous golf caps or imitation yachting caps with yellow braid on the visors, while the women's headdress consisted of bandanas, floppy garden hats, and white sailor caps with anchors embroidered on the front. Dark glasses and cameras were the rule, and some individualists sported T-shirts with comical mottoes like "I Got Scrod Last Night— What Did You Have?" By every indication, these were people who intended to enjoy themselves or die trying.

When the tourists disembarked at the island, the dock workers and porters and cab drivers were open-mouthed and incredulous. "Christamighty, it's August already!" one cabby said, to which another replied, "Just close your eyes and take their money—it can't last forever."

"Hey, Ezra, where's the Chamber of Commerce?" one tourist shouted at the first driver.

"My name ain't Ezra, and it'll cost you five bucks to get there," the man replied. "I ain't the Information Bureau."

"Well, screw you," said the tourist, walking away.

"They talk just like August, too," the second driver observed. "I better take a look at that calendar again."

The tourists fanned out into the town, some picking up maps at the Information Bureau and others asking questions of anyone who would answer them. Some wandered aimlessly about, while some seemed to know where they were going, and within a half hour they had covered the town and, in some cases, hired taxis to take them to addresses away from the center. Two tourists, a man and a woman, went to the Tuttle residence; the woman asked Agnes about the best place to shop for maternity wear, while the man drifted out back to Omar's radio shop. One pair even called on Father O'Malley, asking for advice about getting married on the island, and three men visited the Markey home, asking to see the Chairman of the Selectmen. Ella Markey told them her husband was off on business but would be home for lunch if they wanted to come back, but they said thanks, they thought they'd wait. Since they were all wearing Masonic pins, Ella went to look for Daisy to get them refreshments, but Daisy had vanished.

The largest group of tourists, six in all, converged on the police station. Officer Bostwick was on duty, and when one of the tourists asked to see the Chief, Bostwick didn't look up from his magazine as he replied, "He's out on business."

"Call him in," the tourist said. One other tourist got behind Bostwick's chair, while a third came in alongside. Bostwick looked up angrily.

"I told you he's out on business!" he said. "There's a manhunt on—now, get the fuck outa here!"

Bostwick felt something cold at the base of his skull, and the tourist behind him said, "Freeze, buster, unless you want your brains blown out."

"Now call the Chief," said the first tourist. "Tell him the

man they're after has been caught, and all cars should return here. Get every other car, and give them the same message."

The other tourists put down their guitar case, flight bag, and portable radio, produced two M-16's, six tear-gas canisters, and the components for a radio transmitter. Bostwick watched them in a daze as he tried to raise the Chief on the police radio, and when the Chief finally came through it was all Bostwick could do to talk. The words formed in his mouth, but they wouldn't come out. He finally managed to stammer the message, and there was a click as the Chief's radio went off.

The first tourist looked at the men who were setting up the radio. "How're you doing?" he asked.

"We'll have it in a minute, Lieutenant," one of them said. "We still got five minutes to H hour."

"Well, get the reports as soon as you can." The lieutenant reached down and took Bostwick's gun from its holster, then turned to the other two. "You take the M-16's and stand by the door," he said. "I'll keep this turkey covered, and you disarm the others as they enter. Stand inside the door, so they won't see you till they're all the way in."

The two men said, "Yes, sir," and posted themselves by the door. One brought the tear-gas canisters within reach, then stood motionless while he waited.

The lieutenant looked at his watch, then said to the radiomen, "All right. Let's get the reports."

One by one, the various stations reported in: the electric company, the telephone exchange, the town office building, Omar Tuttle's radio shop, the Fire Department, the shipyard, and the airport had all been secured, and the general reaction had first been surprise, then in most cases relief. There had been no resistance whatever. The only station where there was nothing to report was Markey's home; he was out, and his wife didn't know where.

"I gather he's the big tamale in this whole deal," the lieu-

tenant said, when he got the report. "That State Trooper—
uh—Mancusi says he's open to charges of corruption, brib-
ery, and I guess even murder. But that's not our worry;
that's up to the State Attorney General."

"What about that oil rig?" one of the men asked. "We
gonna have to take that over, too?"

"That's the Coast Guard's baby," the lieutenant replied.
"We just worry about dry land."

"I tell you, I had some worry about dry land this morning," the man said. "I thought I was never going to see it
again."

"My old man was at Iwo Jima," another man said. "He
said that piece of land made the water look like being in the
sack with Betty Grable."

"Who the hell's Betty Grable?" said the first.

"Search me. But my old man had a lot of pictures of her—
that was before he met my mother, of course."

"Shut up," the lieutenant said quietly. "Here comes the
Chief. And, by God, he's got Markey with him."

At the Tuttles' house, the coming of H hour took on the
appearance of a social rather than a military operation.
When the supposed lady tourist asked Agnes about maternity clothes, Agnes glanced at the woman's midsection and
said, "For you?"

"Ah—yes," the woman replied, suddenly aware she'd neglected the padding necessary to fortify her story. "It's a
long way off, but I thought I might be able to buy something here with a—you know—nautical motif. Those shops
on the mainland have no imagination."

"I hardly know what to tell you," Agnes said. "The summer shops aren't open yet, and as for the winter ones—well,
a lot of the girls here make do with oilskins. They're nice
and loose."

"I was thinking of a seashore design," the woman said,

with a quick glance at her watch. "You know, shells and fish, and whatnot."

"Do you want them in the print, or are you going to hang them on the dress?" Agnes asked. "You can make a nice arrangement of scallop shells, if that sort of thing appeals to you." As an afterthought, she added, "Or a fishnet—wrap yourself in a fishnet, and nobody will ever guess what you've been up to. Do I gather that's your husband with you?"

"Yes," the woman replied. "He's a radio ham. He wanted to have a chat with your husband."

"How did he know where to come? There's no sign on the shop."

The woman smiled. "Word gets around."

"I guess it does." Agnes paused, then said, "May I offer you something while you wait? Coffee? Tea? A bloody mary?"

"Coffee would be fine, if it's all made."

"It won't take a second. I'll be right back." Agnes started to leave the room, and the woman followed her.

"Tell me about the Board of Selectmen," she said as Agnes went to the stove. "How do they operate?"

"My, you have been asking questions, haven't you?" Agnes replied.

"Not really. It just came out in the conversation." The woman looked at her watch again, then reached in her bag and produced a pistol. "I'm sorry about this, Mrs. Tuttle," she said. "But if you'll just back away from the stove . . ."

Agnes turned, and saw the pistol pointed at her, and gasped. "What do you want?" she said. "Is this a"—instinctively, she raised her hands—"are you—"

"We're the Army," the woman replied, patting Agnes's sides to check for a weapon. "All right, now, let's go back into the living room."

"But what—why—" Still with her hands up, Agnes preceded the woman out of the room.

"You can put your hands down," the woman said. "This is

just a precaution." As they came into the living room the back door opened and Tuttle appeared, also with his hands up, followed by a man with a gun and a walkie-talkie radio.

"O.K., Sarge," the man said. "No sweat."

"Is it all right to ask what this is all about?" Agnes said.

"We're here to put down a revolt," the female sergeant said. "Or cancel the secession, or whatever you want to call it. The National Guard couldn't hack it, so they called in the pros. Please sit down, both of you. We might as well be comfortable."

"If that's what you're here for, you can put away your guns," Agnes said. "Just last night there was a group here, trying to figure out a way to rescind the whole idea."

"Oh?" said the sergeant. "Very interesting. How many people feel the same way?"

"I don't know, but I suspect a lot."

There was a metallic squawk on the walkie-talkie, and the man holding it pressed the talk button and said, "Tuttle house and radio secured. No problems." There followed the crackling of other reports, and then a voice said, "Stand by for further instructions. Out."

"I can tell you one person who's going to give you trouble," Agnes said, "and that's George Markey. He and the Chief of Police are the real bad guys."

"We knew about Markey, but not about the Chief," the sergeant said. "Thank you for the tip. The State cop tells us Markey's ripe for a murder charge."

"I'm not surprised," Agnes said, then a thought struck her, and she added, "Oh, my God—Sam!"

"Sam who?" said the sergeant.

"Sam Jensen. He's hiding on the moors." She gave the sergeant the details of Sam's story, and concluded, "If the police get to him before we do, they'll kill him!"

"We're trying to round the police up now," the sergeant said. "Keep them from doing anything stupid until the dust settles."

"Is it all right if I make some phone calls?" Agnes asked. "I think the others ought to know what's happened."

The sergeant looked at the radio operator, who shrugged. "Our orders are to hold you incommunicado," the sergeant said. "I guess that means no phone calls."

"But this is important! A man's life could depend on it!"

The sergeant turned to the radio operator and said, "See if you can raise the lieutenant. Tell him the story, and see what he says."

The radioman pushed the talk button, blew into the set, and called a code name. A garbled reply came back, and the operator tried to relay his message, but he was cut off by a blast of static. He shook the set, and pounded it with the heel of his hand, but it gave out only a sullen crackling sound. "Goddam set's crapped out," the operator said. "I told the sombitch it was no good, but he said it'd do for now. Stupid fuckin' idiot—"

"Mind your goddam language," the sergeant cut in. "You're not at home." Then, to Agnes, "Excuse us, Mrs. Tuttle. This is the first job of this kind we've ever done, and it's kind of unsettling."

"Think nothing of it," Agnes replied. "Would you like sugar or cream in your coffee?"

"Sugar, please," the sergeant said. "Two lumps."

As Agnes rose and headed for the kitchen, she said, "Incidentally, I assume you're not really interested in maternity clothes?"

"That's right," the sergeant replied, smiling, and with her knuckles touched the wooden arm of the chair.

When Sam woke up he lay still for a while, looking at the bushes over his head and listening for any sounds of nearby people. But all he heard was the far-off croak of a pheasant, and he carefully rose on his hands and knees and looked about, trying to remain as well concealed as possible. It was still early morning, and the sun had not yet burned off the patches of fog that lay in the hollows, and he reasoned that his chances of remaining hidden were good until an organized search was started. Then all he could hope for would be to avoid capture until nighttime, when, if he could make his way to the boatyard, Corning's boat might still be ready.

Running in a crouch, he went down into a hollow, where the grass was lime green and the earth was moist. But there was no water, so he moved on, running between clumps of underbrush and trying to keep as low as possible. He came to a pond and, lying in the reeds at the edge, put his head in the water and then cupped his hands and drank. It tasted brackish but it was cold, and it gave him a temporary lift just to have something inside him. He wondered what he might possibly find to eat; there were no berries this time of year, and even in the unlikely event he caught a rabbit or field mouse he had no way of cooking it, and he had no desire as yet to eat any fish or animal raw. He was a long way from starvation, but he didn't want to get so hungry that it made him do something foolish.

He wiped his face and beard with his shirttail and then moved on, and as he came to the top of a rise he saw a dirt road and, cruising slowly along it, a blue-and-white police car. It stopped in a cloud of dust and two officers leaped out, and almost simultaneously Sam heard the crack of a pistol and the thud of a bullet at his feet. As he turned and ran there was another shot, and a whining snarl as the bullet ricocheted off a rock. He ran as fast as he could, crashing through the smaller underbrush and skirting the rest, and all the time trying to keep to the low ground. Once or twice he glanced back but could see no signs of pursuit, and then he heard the wheep-wheep-wheep of the siren and realized the police were trying to follow him in their car. Why, the dumb bastards, he thought, and circled back to where he'd seen a heavy growth of alder and scrub oak. Carefully, so as not to leave a trail, he made his way into the center of the copse, and lay down until his heart slowed and his breathing returned to normal. So much for moving around in the day-time, he told himself. From now on, I don't go anywhere until it's dark.

But when darkness came, he seemed little better off than before. He left his hiding place and climbed a low hill, and was startled to see automobile headlights crisscrossing the moors in all directions, effectively cutting him off from any hope of getting to the shipyard. It occurred to him that his one chance for survival was to make his way to the ocean, where they wouldn't be looking and where he could swim until he was out of the area of pursuit, and might possibly, with any kind of luck, run into someone who would hide him. Otherwise, he knew he was doomed. He headed to-ward the shore, crouching down every now and then when a beam of light came near him, and after about an hour of al-ternately running and hiding, he heard the sound of the surf and could smell the salt in the air.

He had been unaware of the wind during the day, but as he neared the shore he realized it had picked up consid-erably, and the surf had increased to where each wave made a hollow boom as it broke, followed by the churning sound of water racing up the beach. When he came through the dune grass onto the sand he could see the white lines of breakers towering out of the darkness, and he could feel the sting of spray on his face. The waves were breaking before they hit the beach, their tops tumbling over and hurtling forward into the final explosion as the full force of the water crashed onto the sand. His mind became numbed with ter-ror at the idea of trying to swim, but he saw no alternative except to go back and probably be shot. Perhaps, he thought, if he could get out beyond the first line of breakers he'd be all right; he could tread water and let the current carry him along until he was far enough away to come ashore. Insanely, his mind fixed onto the phrase "between the devil and the deep blue sea," and he repeated it over and over to himself as he stripped down to his shorts, folded his clothes and put them and his shoes in the dune grass, then walked into the water.

The minute he felt the waist-high backwash he knew he'd made a mistake. He was pulled off his feet and down under the crest of the next wave, and he had just time to take a deep breath before he was drawn under and turned and tumbled about until he literally had no idea which end was up. He was in a black world of swirling, churning water; once his shoulder scraped sand, and then his knees, and then he was turning again and his lungs began to ache. Suddenly his head came out of the water; he opened his mouth and took a deep, gasping breath, and then more water pounded down on him and he went under. The next time he was able to breathe he realized he was beyond the surf line; the waves still came rushing past him but they didn't break, and by facing into them he could tell when to duck and when it was safe to breathe. But he knew he couldn't keep it up long; his arms felt as though they were made of cement and cramps were beginning to shoot through his legs, and any attempt to drift was out of the question. Better to go back and take his chances with the police than to face inevitable drowning.

Slowly, timing his strokes between passing waves, he headed toward the breaker line, but the backwash from each wave made it impossible to get a foothold on the sand. Finally, with no real choice, he let a wave take him, boil him around, and then hurl him up the beach like a piece of driftwood. When he felt the beginning of the backwash he dug his hands and feet into the sand; the water swirled around him and tugged at him like a giant octopus, but it finally subsided and he scrambled as far up the sand as he could before the next wave broke. This time the backwash was negligible, and when it passed he stood up, staggered about a dozen steps, and collapsed. As he lost consciousness he felt that he was still under water, and his whole world was spinning into a bottomless void.

It was bright daylight when he awoke, and he heard a familiar voice talking to him. He struggled into a sitting position and saw Gibbon standing over him, grinning.

"You don't care where you sleep, do you?" Gibbon said.

"How'd you get here?" Sam asked, rising painfully to his feet. He was stiff and sore and cold, and would have fallen if Gibbon hadn't put out a hand to steady him. "Where are the cops?" he said. "Did they see you come?"

"No need to worry about the cops," Gibbon replied, and gave him an outline of what had happened since his escape. "You been safe since yesterday noon, but you didn't know it. Where are your clothes?"

"I left them around here someplace," Sam replied, looking at the beach grass. "I had an idea I could swim to safety."

"Only a gah-damn fool would try that," Gibbon said.

"So I found out." Sam spotted a shoe in the grass a few yards away, and said, "There they are." He began to dress, and went on, "What about Markey? Did they lock him up?"

"They sure as hell did," said Gibbon. "On a number of counts." He cackled, and continued, "When the Coast Guard took over that oil rig old Williams come steaming into town, and he was so mad he told about the bribe money he'd given Markey for the lease. It didn't do *him* no good, because the Selectmen didn't have the right to sign the lease anyway, but it added one more count to the bill against old George. It don't look like George will see daylight for some little spell."

"What about his wife?"

"Don't know. There's some would like her to run for Selectman, but I don't think the island's ready to have two women on the Board. We got to have a new election anyway, so we'll see."

"You going to vote?" Sam asked, tying his shoes.

"You never can tell. I might, just this once."

"All right," said Sam, running his fingers through his hair. "The first thing I want is some chow. I feel I haven't eaten for a week, and if I don't get something soon I'm going to start gnawing my belt."

"I figured you might be hungry," Gibbon replied as they left the beach. "I brought a little something in the Jeep, just in case."

"I can tell you one thing," Sam said. "If you want to run for anything, I'll vote for you. I'll dummy up votes for you. If I have to, I'll kill for you."

"Don't get carried away," said Gibbon. "That won't be necessary."

They got in the Jeep, and Gibbon produced a bag of sandwiches and beer, and as he started up he said, "The cops've got your bike. You want me to take you there?"

"Please," said Sam, his mouth full. "As though you hadn't already done enough."

"I done nothing nobody else wouldn't do," Gibbon replied.

"Oh, no. And my name is Anwar Sadat."

"Never heard of him."

Gibbon left him off at the police station, where a soldier was casually standing guard at the door.

"I want to reclaim some personal property," Sam said, and the soldier nodded for him to go inside, where Officer Bostwick was sitting glumly at the desk. It was easy to believe that Bostwick had taken the full force of the Chief's rage at Sam's escape. Pretending concern, Sam said to Bostwick, "I understand you were looking for me. Was it anything important?"

"Very funny," Bostwick replied. "Get lost."

"Not until I get my bike back."

"I don't know nothing about your bike."

"I had it when I was arrested. You're responsible for it."

"Look out back."

Sam went around behind the station, and there found his bicycle leaning against the side of the building. He mounted it and, recalling that this was her day off, rode in the direction of Lennie's rooming house. He was astounded at the number of people who greeted him along the way; it seemed as though every third person either waved or nodded or spoke, and he was completely baffled by his sudden popularity. From having been a hunted fugitive the day before he was now a celebrity, but he couldn't think of anything he'd done to deserve it. He decided not to inquire too deeply into the reason, but to relax and enjoy it while it lasted.

When he reached Lennie's he knocked on the door, and she answered it with her hair in curlers. "Oh, my God, it's *you!*" she cried, and threw her arms around his neck and kissed him. Then she remembered her curlers, and clapped her hands to her head and said, "Wait a minute!" She vanished, and reappeared shortly with a scarf over her head, and kissed him again. "I thought they'd killed you and I was nearly going out of my mind because there was nothing I could do and to keep myself busy I did all the housework I could think of but it still didn't do any good." The words tumbled out in a breathless gasp, and then she took a deep breath and, more calmly, said, "Come in, won't you?"

"Thank you," Sam replied as he stepped inside. "I'm not really dressed for calling myself, but it's a long way to my place and I need to wash up and things like that." He looked around her room, where she had set up an ironing board on which she was pressing a long skirt. "Do you think I could use the shower?"

"You can use anything you want. Ask for it, and it's yours. The shower is down the hall on the right."

She produced a bath towel and soap, which he took where she indicated, and when he returned he had the towel around his waist and was carrying his clothes. "Just one more favor," he said, running one hand along his throat. "May I borrow your razor?"

"It's over on the washbasin, there. I'm afraid it's pretty dull."

"No matter. It isn't as though this were going to be a full shave, or anything." As he let the water run he looked at his clothes and said, "Those really ought to be burned, but I imagine there'd be talk if I were to go home wearing your clothes."

"Whatever you like," she replied. "I told you, it's yours."

When the water was hot he took a bar of soap and the razor and carefully trimmed his beard while Lennie went back to pressing her skirt.

"My, this is a domestic little scene," she said after a few moments. "I feel as though we'd been married for years, and that's something I promised I wouldn't let myself think about."

"Why not?" The razor scratched his throat like an angry cat.

"Because I didn't want to become attached. Here today, gone tomorrow, and all that sort of thing. I've been to that fire."

"It doesn't always have to be like that."

"No, but it's the way to bet. You'll pull out of here one of these days, and then I'll have to start all over again."

"What makes you think that?"

"It figures. Looking out for Number One, and all that."

"I'm the one who's against that kind of thing, remember?"

"Could be, but still, there's nothing keeping you here."

"Yes, there is."

"Like what?"

"Like a number of things. Like friends—when you get in trouble you find out who your friends are, and it can surprise the hell out of you."

"I imagine so. I wouldn't know."

"Then let's put it this way: Suppose I were to pull out and leave. I'm not saying I will, and I'm not saying I won't. Would you come with me?"

She put down the iron, and stared at him. "You don't mean that."

"I most certainly do."

There was a short silence, and then suddenly she was crying.

"Oh, my God," he said. "*Now* what have I done wrong?"

"You haven't done anything," she replied, wiping her eyes. "It's just that I feel so sorry for you."

"For *me?* Why should you be sorry for me?"

"I don't want to be a pain in the ass to live with but I'm afraid I will be, and I love you so much I don't want to do anything to make you unhappy and that's why it makes me sad to think what I might do. That's all." She sniffled once, loudly, and then began to laugh. "You see what I mean?"

"I'll take my chances," he said. "I have no fear at all."